"Is it customary for the o̶ only me?"

"Do you deny what we sha̶ ̶

"I seek not to have the ent̶ ̶ ̶ ̶ ̶ ̶ ̶ ̶ ̶ ̶ ̶ ̶ ̶ ̶ ̶ ̶ ̶ ̶ shame.

"What shame? You are widowed, a mother, not an untried virgin."

Her skin colored, and Gaelan felt the tip of her dagger through his garments. He arched a brow, admiring how she secreted the dig with her sleeve and her courage to do it.

"The state of my virtue has little to do with your enslaving my people, does it now, PenDragon?" she condescended. "And I make no invitation to *you.*" Repugnance dripped from her words. "Learn your manners, sirrah, and cease showing your lack of breeding."

His lips curved and she blinked, frowning softly. "Now who is hurling insults?" She made a sound of frustration and Gaelan would have sworn she fought the urge to stomp her foot.

His smile widened and Siobhàn was struck hard how boyish he looked just then. Codswallop. There was not a shred of youthful innocence in this man. She slipped the knife into its sheath and stepped back, suddenly aware of the eyes upon them. "Spare me any more humiliation, PenDragon. Begging for my people is all you will ever gain from me. Ever."

He bent, gazing directly into her turbulent green eyes. "One day soon, my village princess, I will have you begging me for more than the fate of your people."

Her expression told him he was fool to hold such high regard for his prowess.

"Shall I prove it? Here and now?"

If he thought to conquer her body as well as her people, she would set him a'right and quickly. "By the gods, you are an arrogant man," she hissed.

"'Tis a failing." He shrugged without remorse. "It comes with never having been defeated."

She tipped her delicate chin, her eyes glacial. "Then prepare for your first, sir knight. For you will find, as my husband did, that battling on the field cannot compare to a war with me."

Books by Amy J. Fetzer

MY TIMESWEPT HEART
THUNDER IN THE HEART
LION HEART
TIMESWEPT ROGUE
DANGEROUS WATERS
REBEL HEART
THE IRISH PRINCESS

Published by Zebra Books

THE IRISH PRINCESS

Amy J. Fetzer

Zebra Books
Kensington Publishing Corp.

http://www.zebrabooks.com

ZEBRA BOOKS are published by

Kensington Publishing Corp.
850 Third Avenue
New York, NY 10022

Zebra and the Z logo Reg. U.S. Pat. & TM Off.

First Printing: June, 1999
10 9 8 7 6 5 4 3 2 1

Printed in the United States of America

For my fellow writers and friends of the Low Country

Brenda Rollins, for her great Southern girl jokes and
explaining "pluff mud."
Nancy Michaels, for selling my books, constantly.
Carolyn Davidson, who's so laid-back you'd think she was
born in the south.
Ginni Farmer, for being as neurotic about her writings as I
am about mine.
Joyce Austin, for your enthusiasm and insisting it's okay to
call people 'sugah.'
And to Charlotte Hughes, for her unconquerable sense of
humor
and the strength she didn't know she had.
You've given new meaning to the words *Southern
hospitality*
and have made returning to the home of my heart sheer joy.

Thanks y'all.

LOVE IS A DRAGON

Fear the wrath
marvel the splendor
So damned fierce
yet, oh so tender
Mystique lures the curious:
reputation keeps at bay.
The menace makes them flee
while the beauty makes them stay.
Behold! The enchanted creatures
of which you have heard stories,
enduring spellbound knights
disregarding tainted quarry.
Fire rides in its breath
while ice dwells in its heart.
Feeble minds think twice
while forked tongues dart.
It has the long sharp talons—
they rip the tender hide
the animalistic howls
last throughout the night.
Love is a Dragon
your heart a maiden fair
To be sacrificed at dawn
or rescued from the lair.
And you, the shining knight
must be prepared to duel;
though love is a grand and gentle creature
its fury can be cruel.

—*B. Edward Hancock*

Chapter One

Donegal, Ireland
1169

Gaelan swore his bones were turning brittle.

Only Ireland could be this cold in spring, he griped, and would avow on his finest sword, the last tree he passed looked painfully familiar. 'Twas bloody humiliating, a knight of his caliber, hopelessly lost and walking in circles. He shook his head sadly and could almost hear Sir Raymond's jests. "Mayhaps m'lord should pack a sack of crumbs to mark his trail," he mimicked bitterly to the dense mist. "Or mayhaps a ribbon tether?"

Ah, the disgrace of it would surely kill him.

Compounding his misery, the hem of his fur mantle snagged on a branch of Blackthorn, dragging him back a step. The gnarled talons refused to release him and with a curse, he wrenched it free, the angry clank of armor echoing hollow in the forest, making him feel more isolated and lost as he adjusted the pelt about his exposed neck and shoulders again. A ghostly gray mist hovered in the forest air, cloaking him up to his thighs. Icy wind moaned like the bale of a bereaved old woman, skating along the cobbled and mossy earth, knifing through his chain mail and driving the chill deeper. A few feet behind him, Grayfalk stopped, the destrier dipping his big head and prodding the velvety ground for a nibble to ease his hunger. Gaelan dug in his sack of provisions and offered the weary beast a fistful of grain, then proffered a portion of drying cheese for himself.

"Make well us of it, my lad," he murmured with a glance to the thick brambled forest as he swiped the back of his gloved hand across his mouth. " 'Tis all you'll have if this barren land is any indication of what precedes us." His dark gaze scanned the shadowed trees, undefinable sounds dancing around him like dandelion fur, untraceable, making his senses jump. "Fairy folk," he muttered around the food. Aye, let us not dismiss the magic. Fodder for fools. But whilst his vassals were inclined to believe the local tales, embellishing them enough to terrify the young pages and squires, Gaelan was not. He'd no time to lend credence to fables when he'd a future to render into his hands.

. . . as soon as he discovered where in all of Christendom he was.

Giving the loyal beast a pat, he trudged on, his chain mail slapping his thighs, the leather straps of his breastplate creaking like weary bones. Above him, the sun desperately groped through the low-lying fog, the wind suddenly heavy as wood smoke.

And much warmer.

Gaelan's forehead wrinkled at the abrupt change and he paused, squinting between the misshapen branches. He sucked cheese from his teeth and swore he heard bells. A tiny tinkling. His head whipped back and forth, his ears pricked to the faint sound, his hand not far from the hilt of his sword.

Then beyond a thinning in the copse, he saw a woman dart

into view, running, her skirts hiked nearly to her knees, mist swirling about her bare calves and clinging to her like fitted garments. A basket looped her arm. She must be freezing, he thought, his gaze following her. She tossed a glance to whence she'd come, her deep red tresses briefly shielding her face and in the faint morning light, specks of gold glittered from her hair. The bells. The sight of her enchanted him, held him by the throat and kept him there, unmindful of the cold—or that this could be his source back to his encampment.

By God, she was a tall one.

Then he heard the rumble of footsteps, rapid, closing in. His gauntleted hand slipped beneath his mount's pelts, closing around his crossbow as his gaze snapped to his far left. He counted five men running at full speed for the lass.

"A lady in distress, Grayfalk." He slid a glance at the horse. "What say you we lend aid, hmm?" Grayfalk snorted and Gaelan swung up onto the saddle. "Make haste, lad. She's in need."

With a prick of spurs, Grayfalk lurched, and Gaelan maneuvered his mount around the trees, following sound, following her. Ducking beneath low branches, he knew if he could get ahead of the brigands, he could catch her first. As if a great hand divided the trees, he was suddenly free of the dense thicket. Grayfalk sensed his master's urgency, tearing across Irish soil.

Siobhàn O'Rourke thanked the Goddess for her long legs and fought the laughter bubbling in her throat. They imagined themselves so clever. Yet she'd heard the village boys in the underbrush, failing miserably to hide their presence whilst they waited for the chance to startle her. This time, 'twas she who startled them. Eager for some lively sport, she pressed on, vowing to outdistance the lads. Covering several more yards, she stumbled, bruising her toes. Wincing, she hopped on one foot, soothing the ache. They'll catch me now, she thought, then stilled, lowering her foot to the cold ground, frowning at the sky before turning toward a thunderous sound.

"Jager me," she whispered, suddenly breathless. A man, nay, a *giant* astride a massive warhorse charged across the land. Steam shot from the horse's nostrils in sharp gusts, leather sacks and weapons slapping the beast's bellowing sides as its hooves ripped the ground black. 'Twas consonant to a dream; Finn MacCoul come to avenge every wrong of her people. A warrior lord from the mist. A gold-brown fur flowed from his shoulders and only his huge chest and arms gleamed with polished armor. He wore no coat of arms or helm, his dark hair over long and catching the wind, yet as he neared, Siobhàn knew an English knight when she saw one. They'd taken the lives of so many of her countrymen already. Then she realized he was racing straight for her.

Siobhàn darted out of his path, but he swerved, bending low over the horse's broad neck. She turned and ran. But the lads were in the clearing and she waved frantically, calling out. The forewarning lost precious time. He was upon her, the horse's breath warming the back of her head, and Siobhàn prayed if she met her death, that it not be trampled beneath English hooves.

Gaelan's arm snaked out, snatching her off the ground. She screamed, flailing wildly, losing her basket as he tucked her to his side, then wheeled Grayfalk about. The sharp turn sent the animal rearing back on his hind legs, pawing the air, and even as Gaelan's efforts commanded the beast to settle, he adjusted the woman across his lap.

"You are safe, lass," he said, not sparing her a glance and urging Grayfalk toward the brigands.

"From what, pray tell? I was not in danger!" Siobhàn shoved her hair from her face and tried slipping from his lap, but his arm clamped down on her waist, chasing the breath from her lungs and making her dizzy. "Do you seek to crush me to death? Release me this instant!'' She pounded his arm, tried prying his fingers.

The giant ignored her, freeing his battle-ax from its bindings. Clods of dirt kicked up as he rode hard, arm raised, and Siobhàn's eyes widened as he swung back to strike. Her gaze flew to the boys caught motionless with fear.

''Nay! Oh, nay!'' She latched onto his arm, yanking hard.

''Leave off, woman!'' He shook her free as if she were no more than a kitten.

''Nay, nay! Cease!'' She drew her knee up and drove it into his stomach, trying to unseat him. He caught her tighter, her breasts bruising against his armor. ''Escape, lads! Flee!'' she shouted, her voice muffled against his cold metal chest.

Her efforts cost him and the boys scattered like feathers on an unexpected breeze.

Gaelan yanked back on the reins, his breathing labored. He looked to the cloudy heavens, praying for an attack of patience, taking his time to secure his ax and remove his gauntlets, then finally bringing his gaze to the interfering wench. He found a woman full grown and lush, older than he expected. She had the most intriguing eyes, like a stone he saw once at court. Green, yet flecked with yellow and blue. And they were on fire with anger.

''You, sir, are a pea-headed . . . imbecile!''

The warrior eyed her. ''Me thinks you should be rewarding me, lass''—he inclined his head ever so slightly toward the boys vanishing into the forest—''instead of cursing like a shrew.''

His dark gaze bore down on her, yet his deep voice was deceptively soft, caressing. Siobhàn ignored it. ''A reward, is it now?'' The arrogance of the man. ''For hacking at children?''

His brow tightened, his gaze flicking to the tree line now shrouded in mist.

''Aye, boys.'' She gave his shoulder a shove, attempting to slide from the saddle again.

Suddenly, he imprisoned her, her body flush to his. The iron hardness of his thighs flexed beneath her bottom, the band of his arm about her waist unyielding, yet gentle. This close she couldn't help notice his face, carved and hewned with a lifetime of war, square along his jaw, high upon his cheeks and framed in flowing ribbons of dark hair. Unduly handsome, if she had to admit. Which she did not. He bore a scar across his left brow, a thin break in the dark wings hovering over eyes the hue of freshly tilled earth. Gazing into them, Siobhàn felt her heart skip. 'Twas as if the man could reach into her soul and cradle it in his palm if he desired.

Codswallop.

Yet his face neared, the scent of leather and man surrounding her.

She jerked her head back. "Do not dare further, sir knight."

He winced at the pricking in his side and lowered his gaze to the blade tucked neatly beneath his breastplate. His gaze returned to hers and he arched a dark brow. "What plan you with that, lass?"

She scoffed. 'Twas not clear enough?

"And after I've stolen you from harm?" He tisked softly.

"Hah. I was never in peril, English, and me pet is protection enough."

"I saw no pet." Yet as he spoke, out of the corner of his sight a furry white creature leapt from the treeline, stalking them. Grayfalk sidestepped, threatening to bolt.

The jostling pressed their bodies more tightly and Siobhàn felt more than his hard thighs beneath her as he controlled the mount. A swift, nearly violent ache shot through her, quickening her heart, yet she refused to break her gaze from the Englishman's. He stared back through unreadable dark eyes, only the lines bracketing his mouth growing a wee bit deeper. 'Twere not real, she thought, those feelings.

The dog hopped, the horse shifted and the knight cursed.

"Culhainn, be still," she said in Gaelic and her rescuer

frowned, confused. Good. Her English was, at best, disjointed.
"I pray your detainment was worth a fortnight of my herbs?"

Gaelan's eyes flared as the red-eared beast barked in
response. What folly this?

"This giant"—she said with a thorough study of the
knight— "might have slaughtered the lads, as well as me."
She spared a quick glance over her shoulder, her tone chiding.
"How like you that on your noble conscience?"

Again the animal responded, but this time with a bow of his
great head, an infantile whimper.

"And ashamed you should be," she said in English, yet the
woman did not take her gaze from his face.

Gaelan could feel it, moving over his features, probing and
intent, though he'd little trouble feeling everything about this
woman. Her hills and curves were burning into his body. His
groin thickened as she shifted on his lap and he let her wiggle,
enjoying it. A lovely piece she was, generously shaped, her
face holding the blush of excitement and as comely as any one
he'd seen. Her garments were stained with dirt and berry nectar,
frayed at the hem and sleeves, and idly he wondered from
which village she'd come and if she could lead him out of the
forest. But most, he wondered what that ripe wet mouth would
feel like beneath his own.

"Would you stab me for a kiss, lass?"

"Aye." She pricked his side to demonstrate.

His lips quirked, his face nearing, and heedless of her threat,
Gaelan let his hand slide up her back to cup her head. "Such
sass and spice," he whispered, his gaze flicking between her
mouth and her eyes.

Culhainn growled, low and deadly.

"Do you not fear death?"

He shrugged ever so slightly, his intent clear, and Siobhàn
swallowed. He was going to kiss her. Or at least attempt it.
Perhaps a kiss would suffice him and gain her freedom, she
considered briefly. Nay. Would she let him do more, she'd find

herself flat on her back and likely ripped clean in half by this giant. She dug the blade a wee bit deeper.

He didn't flinch, his fingers moving luxuriously in her hair and tipping her head. Bells chimed from the end of a dozen thin braids, singing to him.

"Slay me"—he breathed against her lips—"*after* I drink of you."

His mouth slanted over hers, the hot jolt making her flinch. He tasted of wine, and where she expected brutality, she received a slow rolling deliberation that was already difficult to fight. Siobhàn's temper fizzled like a tallow flame snuffed out. Yet with her bloodlines, a defiant flicker refused to die and she shoved uselessly at his chest, her hand splayed over cold armor as his lips twisted insistently over hers, begging a response.

He held her prisoner, yet she did not struggle.

He took, but she did not give.

His mouth soothed and nurtured, catching her lower lip and pulling softly before his velvety tongue lushly outlined its shape. A soft, helpless shudder spilled from her lips and he drank it.

'Twas so distant from anything she'd experienced before, so unlike Tigheran's harsh grindings that offered more of a taste of blood than desire. 'Twas a magic he gave and the brewing heat ignited in her belly, curling about her waist and sliding warmly downward to settle between her thighs. Ah Goddess, 'tis unfair. You offer me this—and make him my enemy!

Yet without the scrutiny of her people, away from the rules of society and her place in it, Siobhàn sorted the harm from the exquisite indulgence and dared to explore him. A wildness in her urged, for aside from the man and his misguided heroics, his touch, his mouth made her feel like a woman again. Selfishly, she wished it to persevere and with the dirk still at his ribs, her free hand moved hesitantly up his enormous chest, touching his cheek. He rumbled with satisfaction and his kiss grew harder, deeper, his desire breathing life into her. 'Twas savage and greedy, this kiss, yet mysteriously fragile. And the threads of her restraint broke.

She wrapped both arms around his neck, fingers pushing deep into his hair, and he moaned his pleasure, his embracing arm tightening, bringing her off his lap and higher against his chest. His hand rode down over her waist, her thigh, sliding around to cup and knead her buttocks, and the blaze in Siobhàn raged along her blood, grew heavy between her thighs. Her body quickened with her heartbeat, and clutching the dirk in her fist behind his head, her unencumbered hand sought the feel of his skin.

Please, she thought frantically. *One touch is all.*

Gaelan's greediness was unstoppable and he enfolded her breast, waiting for the slap, the shriek, yet knew even before he caught her whimper of excitement that she would give him more. And like a thief, he took, his thumb brushing heavily over her nipple, feeling her arch into the pressure, the tender bud peaking sweetly for him through the layers of cloth. That she allowed him such liberties gave Gaelan reason to believe she was familiar to a man's exploring. So be it. For he was wanting to explore her, thoroughly.

He tasted the line of her mouth and she opened wide for him, her tongue plunging between his lips and dueling his for victory. He groaned at the sheer torture of her closeness, his hand busy after the hem of her skirt as her delicate fingers feathered over the shell of his ear, driving a shiver down to the very core of him before gliding over his bare throat to taunt him further. When her fingertips met armor, by God, he wanted to rip it off to give her better access. He wanted to take her to the ground and push his throbbing body deep inside her and assuage this fire she created. When her incredibly warm hand found an opening, pushing beneath his hauberk and mail to stroke his shoulders, Gaelan frantically searched for a way to have her. Now. In the saddle.

The horse stirred restlessly beneath them, scenting their

desire. The wolf remained in the clearing, its head tilted, ice blue eyes watching. Morning mist faded, swept away by the heat of their passion. His hand touched the bare skin of her calf and she flinched.

Suddenly he tore his mouth from hers, their breathing matched, harsh and quick as he gazed into her unusual eyes. A flush of embarrassment spread across her lovely face.

"I need more of you, lass." His coarse fingers slid higher, seeking tender skin, her thigh. "Now." A touch of alarm skated across her features and Gaelan smiled tightly, his body prepared for a fulfillment he would not receive. Forcing women was not his way.

Still holding her close, he suddenly twisted a look at the forest, scowling, all tenderness vanishing from his features.

"M'lord?" Siobhàn glanced about for Culhainn, but the craven beast had vanished.

He turned his dark gaze on her, even as he secured his ax and unsheathed his sword. "Who are you, lass, that brigands make duty in chasing you?"

"Me? I am inconsequential." She waved loftily, then stretched her neck to look around him. "Think not 'tis *you* they seek, invader?" Her gaze moved past his shoulder to the land beyond and her eyes flared. "Sweet Goddess."

" 'Twill be safer behind me," he said and without preamble, grasped her about the waist and shifted to deposit her on the horse's rump. Siobhàn blinked, clinging for balance as he neatly spun the steed about. His destrier pranced as nearly a dozen men in assorted tartans, their faces wrapped in soiled rags, rode murderously toward them. From three directions.

Yet he did not ride.

"Flee!" She jerked impatiently on his hauberk. " 'Tis impossible odds!"

"I never bend to a challenge," he tossed calmly over his shoulder as he pulled on his gauntlets.

"Ahh! Words of an English fool," she muttered, bracing herself for the impact of the first thrust.

A piercing Irish war cry shattered the air, riders advancing.

Yet her rescuer simply grinned at his opponent, the other man's arm raised high to lop off the knight's head. They passed so close legs brushed, and with a sickening sound, the Englishman drove his sword into his attacker's chest, then just as swiftly shook the dead man off like a piece of discarded mutton. Then he charged, striking a numbing blow to the next challenger, unseating him without harm. Yet as he controlled the horse's motion with only the pressure of his thighs, she knew he was ill-matched for the remaining warriors. Her presence thwarted his very survival and as he struck out again and again, she used the distraction to slide to the ground, rolling away from the dangerous jumble of hooves. Siobhàn scooted back on her bottom, her dirk tight in her grasp. She watched. Watched this warrior demolish man after man, decapitate a horse with a single stroke of his broadsword, but when one opponent signaled and three gathered for attack, she knew she would watch him die.

English or nay, he did not deserve such slaughter. And Siobhàn was powerless but for one defense. On her knees her arms down at her sides, the dirk in her hand, she concentrated, calling upon the elements to do her bidding. The thick, blue white mist rose swiftly, moving over the land, rising, and she prayed it was enough to shield the giant.

Suddenly the woods erupted with silver knights and archers, startling her. Arrows whizzed through the air, striking horse flesh and human, screams of pain and the clash of metal nauseated her and she bowed her head, covering her ears—unaware of the knight charging toward her.

Gaelan spurred his mount across the body-littered green, yet as his vassal lifted an arm, he knew he would not reach her in time. "Nay!" Regret and rage sliced through him as Sir Owen clubbed her to the ground. Gaelan rode, a specter of an avenging knight trampling the fallen and sending the remaining bandits scattering pell-mell into the fog. Around him, blood flowed from gaping wounds, steaming the air as he skidded to a halt and slid from Grayfalk's back. With a dark growl, he dragged Sir Owen from his mount and drove a fist into his unprotected jaw.

Owen staggered, genuinely puzzled.

"Could you not see 'twas a woman!"

The knight swiped his lip with the back of his hand, inspecting it. "She's Irish. And armed."

Gaelan's fist connected again, and this time Owen hit the cold ground. "Are you so hungry for blood you murder the *innocent?*" His roar carried to the trees, startling a flock of birds.

"Nay, my lord, but we are here to fight—"

"Women?" His gaze glowed with fury. "I am aware of my duty, knight. 'Twill do you well to find your tongue and hold it!" Gaelan's voice lowered to a sinister hiss. "Afore I cut it from your head!"

Around them, men murmured at the threat.

Gaelan made no attempt to curb his temper and ordered him off.

"Raymond! Mark! Andrew! Give chase!" Gaelan barked, kneeling where she lay sprawled on the ground. His men obeyed, archers already heading to the dead to retrieve their arrows as Gaelan's hands moved roughly over her body, searching for broken bones.

Grabbing up his helm, Owen climbed to his feet, glancing over his shoulder as he collected his weapons, the sight of his lord lifting the woman in his arms striking him hard. She lay limp and helpless, and in the excitement, he'd likely killed her. He regretted it and knew with Gaelan's temper, he would pay for his carelessness. 'Twas only a matter of when.

Gaelan strode to his horse, swinging up onto its back and cradling the woman on his lap. "Do not perish now, lass."

Biting the tip of his gauntlet, Gaelan removed the glove and brushed his fingers over her head, probing gently. He cursed foully when his fingers came away stained with blood and his gaze lifted to Owen's. The younger man paled at the rage borne there.

His dark gaze snapped to the vassals gaping at him and Gaelan knew his manner confused them. He did not perceive it well himself, for he'd never reacted like this to so simple an injury. Annoyed that his troops would find him weakened for a female, his temper simmered, his gaze thin and pricking on each man. He questioned them mercilessly and discovered he was only a day's ride from camp.

"Your reluctance to leave your warm pallets and come search has cost us days of travel and two brave men. Care for the dead. The wounded ride." His gaze fastened on a knight adjusting his weapons. "Sir Owen?"

Owen turned his head and without expression, addressed Gaelan. "My lord?"

Gaelan flicked a hand toward the forest. "Lead the way."

With his sleeve pressed to her temple, Gaelan held her close, whispering for her to rouse, praying that she'd waken and be whole again. He wished he knew her name. Suddenly he felt the exhaustion of traveling in circles for two nights and he cursed his arrogance for not hiring a villager to guide them across this godforsaken land, then cursed his gallant act on behalf of the king. If not for that one moment of unpaid service to his liege, his presence here would not have wounded this fair Irish lass.

Chapter Two

A motley collection of men roamed through the encampment, tending duties, changing the watch. Several souls braved the cold to hover over large cook fires, stirring and ladling food into wood bowls for a line of hungry soldiers and bowmen. Youths with scarcely a hair on their chests sat cross-legged on the damp earth, repairing bridles or boots. A woman or two sauntered through the throngs of rough men, gaining a friendly pat on the backside, a coin and an appointment for after nightfall or garments to launder. No one stood idle.

The rumble of hooves brought heads up as the small brigade rode into the center of the clearing, young squires and pages racing to take mounts for care and feeding. The ring of hammers on dented armor or the grind of wet stones honing a fresh edge to a blade lent its usual peace to Gaelan as he slowed his mount. The smell of roasting meat punctured the air between the odors of unwashed bodies, burning peat and the cool, bracing scent of coming night. Eventide in Ireland, Gaelan thought, somehow

washed away the dreariness and soil of the day with her
approaching mist.

He glanced about, noting the curious looks directed at the
bit of baggage in his arms. His returning scowl sent all but the
fearless back to their duties as he swung his leg over the neck
of his mount. He hit the ground with a jolt. The lass didn't
stir, yet as he crossed the yard to his pavilion, he heard shocked
gasps, the slide of several broadswords leaving their scabbards.
He paused and turned, his gaze lowering to the white wolf, its
teeth bared, its body crouched low for attack. On him.

He was wondering where the beast had gone. Gaelan glanced
at his men, terror and boldness in nearly fifty faces. Several
devout souls crossed themselves. His own hounds barked
wildly, challenging the threat to their territory, and were quickly
restrained. He continued on to the tent, yet the deepening growl
made him turn back again. His gaze went to a man poised with
a loaded crossbow.

"Be takin' me but one shot, m'lord."

"Nay," he said softly and slowly bent to one knee, the lass
cradled in his arms.

"My lord?"

" 'Tis the woman's protector." A murmur of surprise rose
softly from the gathered crowd. Gaelan tucked his hand beneath
his armpit and removed his glove, then extended his unprotected
fingers to the beast.

The hair on the animal's spine rose in silent warning.

Nearly a dozen more swords left their homes.

"My lord? Dare not," someone warned.

"I've meat, mayhaps a bribe?" Reese, a strapping young
man who'd one day be a great knight, stepped forward. Yet as
he did, the animal spun around, growling and snapping, lips
pulled back to bare savagely sharp fangs for the stunned crowd.

"Culhainn!"

Still facing Reese, the wolf twisted its majestic head toward
Gaelan, ice blue eyes challenging.

" 'Tis Culhainn, eh?'' A powerful creature, Gaelan thought, snow-white fur tipped with gray and fanning out on end around its broad neck like a royal collar. The red ears were startling, offering an almost mystical attribute to an already strange animal. Intelligence glittered from cerulean eyes. For so loyal a pet, he would have expected the huge wiry-faced wolfhounds he'd seen since arriving, not this canine warrior, and Gaelan chanced that the top of this animal's head reached his thigh. A stout claim, for he'd yet to meet another soul to match his own size.

Gaelan offered his hand to the hungry beast again. The growling lessened as Culhainn pawed forward and Gaelan allowed the wolf to scent him. The animal sniffed, drawing closer, and when the wolf tilted his head, pale blue eyes gazing calmly into dark brown, Gaelan knew Culhainn picked his mistress's scent from his garments, his skin. The wolf settled back on its haunches and did the unexpected; he wagged his tail. And whimpered.

Gaelan's lips twitched. "Mighty puppy," he murmured, encouraging him closer, his fingers singing into the thick coat behind its ears. He didn't proceed further, not trusting his new friend against attack with his people so close, and rose slowly, his arms full of the woman. "Disband. Prudently," he ordered with a warning glance. He looked down at Culhainn. "Stay put, beast, and there will be food for that empty belly instead of English fingers."

Culhainn barked once and Gaelan arched a brow, a scoff escaping his lips before he ducked into the tent and immediately strode to his pallet. He laid her gently in the soft center, then covered her with a fur. He brushed his knuckles across the smoothness of her cheek, his thumb over her lips, then stepped back. He'd no time to waste with wenching, he thought, busying himself with removing his scabbard and dropping it upon a chest. Plowing his fingers through his hair, he wondered what to do with her. He scoffed ruefully. Oh aye, he knew what he would like to do with her and it entailed a bit of loveplay beneath those furs, but surely someone would miss the lass, a father or mayhaps, a husband. A few coins paid would suffice for the injury his man had inflicted, but Gaelan did not want to think who'd he pay it to. A husband most likely. She was too comely to go unnoticed and old enough to be wed a few years. The thought sat like spoiled beef in his belly and the possessiveness he felt toward one he scarcely knew agitated the bloody hell out of him. His booming voice proved it when he called for his page, ordering water and cloths and a bit of broth.

"M'lord?" came a timid call moments later.

"Come forth, boy."

" 'Tis a wish that I could, sir."

With his hands on his hips, he stared at the moth-eaten ceiling and shook his head. "Culhainn, allow him passage. 'Tis for your mistress he comes." The wolf must have stepped aside, for the boy burst through the flap, glancing nervously back over his shoulder and nearly colliding with Gaelan. He lifted his gaze to his master. "Over there," he barked and the boy made haste to lay the items down, his fear carrying him swiftly out of the tent.

Children. An annoyance, Gaelan thought, for he knew he'd no patience for their incessant questions and clumsiness. It was difficult enough to train men for battle without worrying over the welfare of helpless babes.

A peal of soft laughter sounded close, and Gaelan glanced to the open tent flap, his lips tugging in a reluctant smile. The boy, Jace, knelt a safe distance before the wolf as the animal raised its plump paw, stroking the air. Jace scrambled back on his rump, but Culhainn, brave soul, didn't move. Gaelan returned his gaze to his guest, wondering what name fit *her*. He supposed he should see to her injury, he thought, and knelt beside the well-stuffed pallet, pushing back the fur to examine her wound. It was hardly a scrape and he knew the power of

Owen's blow and hitting the ground sent her into the void of unconsciousness. He shook her gently, then sighed when he received no response, and turned to the bowl and rags on the small stool. He soaked a cloth and tipped her head to clean the wound, guilt gentling his touch.

He studied her dispassionately, resoaking the rag, wringing it out and swiping her face clean, then her throat. Clothing often told of one's life and her kirtle was of no significance, a heavy dull brown, modestly cut. But that the side laces were strained told him her body was lusher than he first thought. Or felt. The cap of her sleeves were stitched tight, fanning wide at her wrist, her undershift a coarse linen, heavy and serviceable, puffing out around the bodice and through the slits in the length of the sleeves. A bluish-red stained her fingertips, her lips bearing a tinge of a berry sampling. A smile ghosted across his lips and even as he wondered where she found fruit in this weather, he wanted to taste those delectable lips till . . .

Was there no peace with her near? He shot to his feet, throwing the rag in the bowl. This insufferable pounding through his being disturbed, yet he recognized that it drove deeper, contrary to anything he'd experienced before. He chose not to examine it. It would lead him nowhere. Yet without pause, he took her hand, and turning the palm up, bent deeply to bring it to his lips. He frowned. Her skin was warm, too warm, and he touched her forehead, brushing back the wild curtain of hair, his hand lingering when it should not.

A thin vapor hovered over her skin like a barrier, warning him not to touch when he'd already tasted. It was unnatural for her skin to be hot enough to create steam, and Gaelan bent over her, loosening her laces, her breasts expanding with the freedom. Briefly he closed his eyes, summoning the tatters of his knightly attributes before gathering her into his arms. He worked the fabric over her head, drawing the feminine layers along. His forearm brushed the side of her naked breast. Gaelan grit his teeth. God's blood, her skin was soft and hot, and his imagination brewed images of tasting that skin, this woman, until he thought he'd rent apart.

Duty served, he threw a fur over her nakedness and lurched to the opposite side of the tent. Damn me, but he ought to be knighted again for that. And the shadowed glimpse of her body, lush and full and itching for a man to love scorched along in his brain, again. And again. He slammed his eyes shut. But the vision taunted, exploding with the cool drape of deep red hair and tinkling bells framing her breasts and hips as she sat up in his bed, beckoning him, aching for him as he suddenly was for her. Gaelan plowed his fingers into his hair and sought a needed distraction.

Fortunately, Jace entered with a trencher of roasted meat and cheese, and Gaelan didn't realize how hungry he was till he scented it. Quickly, he loosed the armor breastplate himself, handing it to Jace, amusement lighting his dark features as the lad staggered under its weight. Gaelan stripped off his mail and hauberk, the leather jerkin and his worn linen shirt, then bid the boy to his duty of cleaning it and bringing his armor to Reese for polishing before dismissing him. He reached for a pitcher of water.

He prayed it was cold.

Off in a corner, beyond the frayed rug, Gaelan sluiced water over his head, soaping his chest and hair, then rinsing himself. With a chilling growl, he shook his head like a dog, sending water in a fine spray into the air, then took up a scrap of linen and rubbed himself dry.

The muddy haze lifted sharply and Siobhàn blinked, realizing water dripped down her face. She was about to brush it aside when she heard movement. Keeping her eyes sealed to mere slits, she glanced to her right. Her breath caught. *Jager me.* Arm muscles as big as her thighs jumped and flexed as he rubbed the cloth over his deeply sculpted chest. Water glistened on his skin, skin she never thought to see so bronzed by the sun, the dampness molding his braies to his buttocks, his hips and the prominent bulge between broad thighs. Siobhàn wet her lips and admired his physique, a swift, hot ache pulsing through her loins.

Long of limb, he was by far the biggest man she'd ever clapped eyes on. By the Goddess, 'twas no wonder he could cleave a horse's head from its neck. And what would he do to her? She'd considered the possibilities when she'd roused once along the journey, but the pain in her head and her inability to overpower him had sent her diving blissfully toward oblivion again. With the hard jolting ride here, she'd welcomed it. Now she need only pretend that condition till he departed. Relying on his good graces to release her was not a risk she chose to take.

Oblivious to her scrutiny, he plucked a chunk of mutton from the trencher, shoving it into his mouth as he strode to the chest and rummaged a bit, slipping a lawn shirt over his head. He moved to a table, grasping an urn of wine, splashing a healthy draught into a dented goblet. He drained it without ceasing, then filled it again before taking a seat near a small brazier and stretching out his long legs.

Ah Goddess, you were too generous with this Englishman, she thought, wincing at the dull throb in her head. She was glad his back was to her and indulged in a thorough look of such a fine specimen of masculinity. The linen—definitely not Irish, she judged—stretched tight over his shoulders, his damp hair wetting the fabric. But as she watched him eat, a strange pleasure rolled through her body and in the same instant, she realized she was naked.

A blush, hot and vivid, raced up from her bare knees and her gaze narrowed on his back. Dare you much, my lord knight. The absolute insolence of the man, taking off her garments for a head injury. Who was he jesting? Curse him, she thought, wishing he'd leave so she could go too. He was a fool if he thought lack of clothing would keep her malleable, and though her meager garments told him he'd gain little by ransoming her, Siobhàn was not willing to gamble on it. Her gaze slid about the tent, searching for an escape route and touching on a scarred stool, a table tilting to one side, the battered chest. His accommodations were well used and not fine to start, and she deduced she was a prisoner of the lowest of English knights. Although she'd encountered only two in her life, naught she saw claimed otherwise. An array of weapons and armor lay on racks and trunks near the tent's far wall, yet she noticed there were no personal items in view. As if no one truly dwelled here. Except a warrior. Did he not have a favored mantle clasp or a book, mayhaps? Even as she considered that he likely could not read, she felt a tinge of pity for so lonely an existence. That was *if* she could pity an English invader. Which she did not.

Siobhàn forced her emotions aside and closed her eyes, biding her time till she could be free of this camp and this Englishman.

Gaelan kept his back to the woman and considered feeding her a bit of broth, then dismissed the notion. He had few honorable qualities remaining and if he moved too close to her, he'd break them, draw back the fur and have himself a decent look at her. It was not the looking that disturbed him, but the desperate need to touch and *be* touched by her that did. Shaking his head, he warned himself to dismiss the idea. He'd no time to let his prick rule him. And he was not one to dwell on his desires. The brazier warmed his cool skin, the pavilion walls shielding Ireland's chill. The wine dulled his desire. Yet against his better judgment, he looked back over his shoulder, the flickering candlelight dancing across her face. God's blood, she was beautiful. And in repose, she was far removed from the spirited lass digging a dirk in his side. He looked at the very spot, the scratch already healing. It was a scar he'd enjoy remembering.

"Gaelan? Call the beast off. Damn me, he's huge."

"Nay, Raymond, I come anon."

Selfishly, he didn't want Raymond to see her and he rose, donning a jerkin and grabbing his mantle. Tossing the fur over his shoulders, he paused beside her, staring, then gave into his impulse and bent to brush his lips across hers. His forehead wrinkled. Her skin was still warm to the touch.

"Wake, sweetling."

She didn't.

Reluctantly, he left the tent, taking the half-eaten trencher and setting it before Culhainn. The wolf devoured it before he'd taken a step.

Raymond gazed down at the wolf. "You say he is hers?"

"Aye. As well as one could possess an animal."

"A woman commanding a magnificent creature." Raymond shook his tawny head, amazed.

Gaelan scoffed. "You know not *this* female." He allowed himself a small smile as he settled to a stout stool, edging it close to the fire. Around them, his vassals moved a distance away, allowing them privacy just beyond his pavilion. "How go we for armament and provisions?" he asked, his expression fading to a scowl of concentration.

"We are amply supplied. The earl paid his debt to you."

Gaelan cast Raymond a side glance, arching a brow.

"Aye, fortunes shine again," the vassal said, highly amused, and from a spot near his foot, lifted a flagon of wine, affirming their replenished stores. Gaelan dismissed his offer of wine and Raymond sloshed a greedy portion into a wooden cup. "He sent a courier with the gold owed my lord."

Gaelan smirked at the use of *my lord,* for Raymond and he had come into their own together as squires, fostered to Gaelan's father, before his sire knew who he was. Though Raymond's lineage bid he earn his spurs and be knighted, Gaelan was no more than the bastard of a camp follower. In sooth, if not for a benevolent knight making him a squire, Gaelan would be laboring *for* Raymond, though neither man worked harder for the profit they possessed now.

"Excellent work." He gave his shoulder a familiar jostle. "My thanks."

Raymond blinked. "I did naught to hasten him, I swear." He crossed his heart to prove it. "Me thinks he feared your wrath, Gaelan."

"I cared not for his self-absorbed demands," Gaelan muttered in disgust. "The man has not lifted a sword in his king's defense, yet struts as if the cocksure noble had foiled the Irish kings all by himself, then bleating over the Henry's favor to DeLacy. I swear by all that is holy, I am well rid of Pembroke, for neither man cares for the destruction they wreak."

Raymond arched a brow. "Neither do you, or have you suddenly changed?"

Gaelan's gaze slanted to Raymond, but DeClare was unaffected by the savage glance. "I care for the lives lost, aye, but the cause—?" He scoffed, scooping a fistful of stones and transferring them from hand to hand in a slow pour. "Nay. I have long since given way to the workings of any sovereign's mind. Henry hired my sword, 'tis all."

"And the debt nearly four summers old he chooses now to repay? How feels that?"

Gaelan stared off at the cook fires now warming tired bodies. The sounds of people seeking a spot to spend the night and a comfortable position to do it, poked the night air. Exhausted himself, Gaelan wanted to find his bed. A tired man fought poorly. A man with a hard cock and nowhere to ease it never slept either, he thought with a glance at his tent.

"Gaelan?"

He turned his gaze back to Raymond, disliking the merriment born there at his expense.

" 'Tis a magnificent price for keeping his head on his royal shoulders."

Gaelan's own shoulders moved restlessly and he flipped a stone into the blaze. That Henry chose now to reward him for killing an assassin troubled Gaelan. No matter the power, he would not be the sport of another man's whims. Which was why he had complete authority necessary to take his payment. "No more than afore, old friend." He sighed, pitching the remaining stones aside and dusting his palms. "My sword, as well as yours and theirs"—he gestured to the sleeping camp—"fights for the man who can pay the highest fee."

Raymond scoffed darkly and leaned close, his voice low. "Do not think you can lie to me, Gaelan. Beneath the next siege lies the opportunity you've sought all your life."

Gaelan's eyes flared. "And that be?"

Raymond grinned hugely, a natural state for the knight. "A worthy purpose. A home and land for a lifetime."

Tension tripped through Gaelan. "I am a Cornish bastard. Knight or nay, that remains unchanged."

Raymond took the bait of an age-old disagreement. "But *whose* by-blow—"

"Speak not a word of it, Raymond DeClare," came in a dark voice. "Claim all you wish of your infamous name, but leave me to my own."

Raymond's lips thinned. Gaelan refused to use his blood lines for bettering his life. He seemed satisfied with warring for other men's causes, but Raymond knew otherwise. At present, though, he kept that thought to himself. One did not poke at a wounded beast and live.

"And be forewarned, do not fill your head with notions of prize and respect with this siege." Gaelan sneered more to himself. "With stone and mortar? Let Henry have it for some fat lord he owes favor." He shrugged. "I take my payment in coin. I can ask for no more."

That was untrue and the root of their constant disagreement. Raymond stood, the motion knocking over the stool. "Your blind quarrelsome cross-grained self often astounds even one as common as I, m'lord." Raymond bowed deeply and Gaelan smirked, a smile fighting with his scowl. The second son of a baron and Pembroke's nephew, Raymond was as common as the king.

"Get your Norman hide to bed, whelp. Your prattle exhausts me."

Raymond left him, the flagon of wine tucked to his chest. Gaelan gazed at the fire, dismissing the spark of need Raymond's words ignited. A purpose? A home? A life of permanence? It was a notion Gaelan never allowed himself to consider. Well, mayhaps *once* in the past two days, he amended. He wanted and needed no more than a filling meal and a battle worthy of his skills. He'd no lands, no family awaiting his return, therefore where he slept was inconsequential. He could gain naught but coin for his services—therefore he'd never aspired further. His lot was a life without gentleness, he insisted silently, without caring beyond survival. Were he to die, none would mourn, and Raymond would fill his boots and lead. 'Twas as he'd expected, no more.

Then why, a ghostly voice asked, was the road traveled increasingly unsatisfying of late?

Land for a lifetime. 'Twas within reach.

Cold, tired and still hungry, Gaelan exhaled slowly, folding his arms over his chest and closing his eyes. For the flicker of a moment, he imagined himself a sedentary man, his life simple, without threat of an opponent's sword in his gullet. Would he grow restless for battle? Would he be as unsuitable for confinement as he was for a family? Regardless, the image of the red-haired woman flooded his mind and he fed the vision. She was beside him, living and loving. Love? He scoffed, his eyes still shut. What tenderness was found in an army's garrison beyond the friendship of a comrade and the easing of his needs between a pair of willing thighs?

He shifted his shoulders, muscles suddenly tight. He would not know much of hearth and home even if the opportunity presented itself. His last occasion was years prior at court and he'd found he'd no taste for the pomp of noble life. Nor did he fit in there. Opening his eyes, he stared at the heavens, pinpoints of light blinking on a river of black. For certain he did not belong here. But 'twas his due, his reward for deflecting an attack on Henry's life by an Irish overlord.

Siobhàn opened her eyes cautiously, then threw back the pelts, reaching for her clothes piled on the ground. She'd heard enough. *Henry hired my sword, is all.* Is *all!* He was a mercenary, following no ideal, no cause, laboring, nay, *slaying* for tainted coin and naught else! Ahh, she should have known. Fitting her kirtle down around her hips, she yanked at the laces, then looked around the pavilion for her weapon. She did not believe for an instant a war-maker like him would care anything for a single blade when she was certain he had many to join his English arrows. Not devious enough to search his possessions, or the lack, she scrounged the threadbare rug for any weapon. Surprise brightened her face when she spied her dirk stuck in the wood table. Wrenching it free, she carefully pushed it down between her laced breasts and looked for a means of discreet escape. Guards would be posted about the perimeter, she thought. As a precaution, she threw the furs over the pallet, making proper indentations.

She snapped her fingers twice and Culhainn pushed through the flap, moving on silent paws to her side. "Shh," she hushed when he whimpered, stroking him behind his ears. She could not walk out in plain sight. There were still too many people milling about. She stood still, arms straight, palms out, her senses attuned to the land as she commanded the mist to rise and cloak her escape. When the bluish vapor snaked through the entrance, she quickly searched the tent folds for a rip or a seam and found a stake improperly secured. Dropping to the ground, Siobhàn pried it loose, praying the entire pavilion did not fall upon her, then rolled beyond the confines. She snapped her fingers again and when the wolf appeared to her right, she motioned to the forest. Culhainn leapt into the thicket, yet before she followed, she briefly peered around the edge of the tent. She spotted the mercenary resting before a dying fire, the mist cradling him. He appeared asleep. Good. She wanted naught but to flee from a man who'd no purpose beyond slaughtering her good folk for worthless coin from a greedy king. 'Twas too much like Tigheran, her husband.

Half asleep, Gaelan jolted. For several seconds, he struggled for balance on the stool, then climbed to his feet, heading to his pavilion. He ducked inside, the scent of her lingering in the air as he lit a taper and moved to the pallet. He'd heard her stir earlier and bent to check her fever, tossing back the coverlet and stilled. His gaze narrowed.

He bellowed for the watch. Rapid footsteps, the jingle of swords and weapons colored the night. Gaelan ducked from the tent, folding his arms over his chest and glaring down at the seven men. The torchlight illuminated his face like a portrait of Lucifer.

"Which of you will regale us with the tale of a woman and a wolf escaping unnoticed by trained *warriors?*" The last shook the air, scattering animals and children.

"Gaelan, nay!"

He met Raymond's bleary-eyed gaze. "Oh aye. And from the look of it, 'twas whilst you and I sat chatting!"

Raymond stepped closer, peering at his leader. "Hence, not only has she foiled *you,* but two brigades of knights, archers, footmen, squires, cooks—"

Gaelan put up his hand, the failure bruising his pride enough.

"Extraordinary woman, I'd gather." Raymond rocked back on his heels, hands clasped behind his back.

Gaelan dismissed the guards with the flick of his hand and looked at his grinning friend. Gaelan's lips twitched. His shoulders shook. Then he burst, his deep chuckle rumbling in the night.

"By God, the lass is bloody fearless." He was impressed, even as regret sluiced through him. Though he'd no intention of holding her against her will, he'd entertained the notion of taking her as his mistress for a time, but alas . . . he shrugged, his smile lingering as he stared at the darkened woods. Then his eyes narrowed suddenly, his pleasure suspended. "Pray she does not alert anyone of our presence, DeClare. Or the Irish will be prepared for a battle they cannot win."

Though it would matter little if she did. For he did not earn his spurs by his father's name or royal favor. Sir Gaelan PenDragon had never been defeated. And in a short time, every clansman for leagues would seek his head when he laid siege to Donegal Keep.

And its princess.

Chapter Three

Siobhàn was certain the village boys told every soul who'd listen of her *capture*. Explaining her overlong absence was a dilemma she debated with every step homeward. Briefly she considered a visit to the village to assure the boys she fared well, but she did not want them to be punished for the unfortunate end of a silly game. Yet neither did she wish to alarm her people of the English. There were few men able-bodied enough left at Donegal to fight, and delivering them into panic would serve no purpose now. And English soldiers on Irish soil was common of late. Just not so close to Donegal.

She paused just beyond the torchlight and gazed up at the stone walls of Donegal Castle, wondering over her reception and experiencing a familiar mix of pride and love for the place she'd called home these years past. It was said the Druids laid the first stones of Donegal and Siobhàn liked to believe it was the reason it still stood tall after so many years.

Bracing herself, she moved to the west postern door and pried it open, peeking around the wood. The leather hinge creaked, drawing the attention of a dozen folk lingering nearby. Surprised gasps and sudden shouts littered the air and Siobhàn groaned, cursing the Englishman's part in this. She had so hoped to enter unnoticed. She stepped fully inside, moving steadily across the outer ward, then the inner bailey toward the keep as her people crowded about, tossing questions and offering thanks to God for her safe return. The chatter confirmed her suspicions; the lads had been too scared to speak of the incident, likely fearing their pursuit of her the cause.

"Aye, I am fine. Oh nay, Davis," she said when the old man threw his only cloak across her shoulders. "You need the warmth more than I."

He shrugged, ever silent, for a Norseman had cut out his tongue years before.

"I will launder it." And she would weave him another, she thought, moving up the wide stone steps. Her heart lifted as she strode through the wide doors of the great hall, her gaze seeking the startled faces for her son.

Voices, excited and relieved, pattered throughout the hall and Rhiannon rose from her place at the hearth, catching Connal's hand and moving toward the entrance.

When Siobhàn appeared at the doorway, Connal bolted from his aunt's grasp, crying out for his mother. Siobhàn's face brightened and she stooped, opening her arms. He leapt into them.

"Ahh, my little prince, I have missed you." She closed her eyes, savoring the warmth of his embrace. It felt like weeks, instead of hours since she'd held him last.

"Where were you, Mama?"

"I lost my way." A lie, to be certain, but she would not worry her son any longer. Over his head, she met her sister's gaze, and Rhiannon bit the inside of her mouth to keep from smiling outright. Siobhàn lowered Connal to the floor, sweeping the cloak from her back and handing it to a passing maid. The maid hugged her too, praising God for her safe return, and Siobhan's heart gladdened with the affection. She strode quickly across the hall, dodging children and servants.

"Siobhàn, 'tis been dark for hours," Rhiannon said, embracing her sister. "I was worrying."

"You?" A tapered brow lifted as she leaned back to meet her sister's gaze. "I do not believe that."

Rhiannon inspected her with a critical eye. "Your basket?"

Siobhàn shrugged, accepting a goblet of watered wine from Bridgett. She drank deeply, then glanced at the keep, noticing chores undone. "Rhiannon, could you not for a few hours—?"

"The basket, sister." Rhiannon grasped her hand, sensing peril and pain and . . . pleasure?

Siobhàn recognized the gloss in her sister's eyes and jerked back from her touch. Oftimes, she wished Rhiannon was not a seer. That she could delve her feelings without benefit of speech made for little privacy.

"Do not question me. Nay." She held up a finger in warning. "Take heart that I am safe and you have left this keep in shambles." She did not want to remember the Englishman. Not the way his kiss felt, the sight of him unclad and wet, nor her disappointment upon discovering his profession. She'd had enough of war in her life and she would not tolerate another instance. Fair face and brave or not.

Turning away from her sister's intense gaze, Siobhàn clapped her hands loudly and the noise in the hall lowered, servants of various sizes, ages and shapes frozen in their duties. "I beg your forgiveness, my friends. I did not mean to worry you."

Smiles wreathed the crowd.

"Sean said fairies took you," a young girl said.

A youth of three and ten looked at the girl, offended. "I did not. 'Twas Shamus who spoke such lies." Sean gestured to the older boy.

Shamus glared at the younger servant. *"He* said the O'Niell took ye, holed you up in his castle, he did."

"He is too honorable for so despicable an act, and as you see, 'tis untrue," Siobhàn said dismissingly, then turned her gaze to a stout man of nearly fifty, bent and slow-moving. "Davis? Change the rushes in the morn; 'tis foul in here." He nodded and trotted off. She addressed another. "Bridgett? Is there water warming, for I need a bath."

"Aye, my princess. Meghan will tend you."

"The day is almost over, my friends, and from here I view a dozen chores left unattended." People scattered to their duties. "And Connal," she said, lowering her gaze to the child. She smoothed her hand over his red-brown hair, his plump cheek, then tipped his head to look him in the eye. "Have you tended your studies today?"

Connal's gaze briefly swept to his aunt's. Rhiannon chose to look elsewhere. "Nay."

"And why not?"

Connal stole another glance at his aunt. "I was playin'."

"And what activity was so important that you allowed your aunt to take you from your studies?"

Connal blinked, pleased his aunt would gain the blame. "She made a bubble from a bladder and we kicked it about the yard." His lower lip curled down. "Till Dermott broke it."

Siobhàn lifted her gaze to her sister, folding her arms over her middle. "Did he learn anything today?"

"Aye, that bladders pop. Now come, eat something." Rhiannon moved close to her sister and flung her arm around her shoulder, directing her to the long table. Behind her back, she waved discreetly to Connal, and the child scurried off toward his bed.

"Do not think to fool me with your cheating, Rhi," Siobhàn said, glancing over her shoulder to see Connal disappear around the wall leading up the narrow staircase. Her gaze shifted to her sister, who was calling for a trencher and wine. "He broke a promise."

"Nay," Rhiannon said, dropping beside her. "I did." Her green eyes pleaded with her older sister. "Do not punish him. 'Tis only that he looked so unhappy whilst you were gone."

"Think you that he has too much studies?" Siobhàn shook her head. "Tell me true, Rhi, for oftimes I think learning from books is useless."

Rhiannon's face warmed with affection and she covered Siobhàn's hand. "Mayhaps a few moments at a time and nay hours? 'Tis so new to him, this sitting still."

Siobhàn laughed softly. "Aye, aye," she said, accepting the trencher and wine from Bridgett. She sampled the mutton, aware of Bridgett standing close and awaiting approval. Siobhàn nodded. "A fine hand with the spice, friend." As Bridgett bobbed and departed, Siobhàn turned her attention back to her sister. "Now shall we discuss the state of this castle in so short a time?"

"Only if you reveal where you hid for half the night."

"I will not." She jerked her hand out of her sister's reach. "I need not touch you to know the why of it comes from a man."

Revealing that English knights slept so close to Donegal would not scare Rhiannon, but her people were a matter unto themselves. How capable could they be, she thought, when with the exception of fifty or so, their largest and strongest were lost on Irish soil like lambs in the mist.

Siobhàn cast a quick look around for eavesdroppers. "Do not speak of it, please. Culhainn was at my side, and what man can get past him?"

'Twas true enough, Rhiannon thought, but didn't believe Siobhàn. Yet if she chose to keep her moments away from the keep private, Rhiannon would respect her wishes. Her gaze scanned her garments, stopping on the bloodstain at her shoulder.

"You're hurt." Rhiannon pushed Siobhàn's hair off her neck to examine her wound.

"Nay, nay, oh leave off!" she hissed, pulling her hair back. " 'Twas an accident and naught else. Leave it at that."

Rhiannon's brows rose sharply.

Siobhàn leaned closer. "Forgive me, Rhi. I am weary and in need of a bath. Mix a potion for this ache in me head?"

Rhiannon rose and moved to her cabinet by the hearth, withdrew a key and unlocked it, spreading the doors wide. Siobhàn watched as her sister mixed and stirred herbs into a cup, added wine, then heated it with a hearth iron. Steam rose from the wood cup as she crossed the hall. Siobhàn drained the potion quickly, thanking her.

"Now, sister, about the chores—'

"I think I hear Bridgett calling." Rhiannon scooted back and with a laugh, Siobhàn waved her off and focused on her meal. She ate quickly, then headed to her chamber for a bath, pausing at Connal's bedside. She knelt and tucked the coverlet beneath his soft chin and his eyes drifted open.

"Mama? You're angry with me?"

"Oh nay, poppet." She brushed her lips across his forehead. "I love you too much." A soft bahhing came from beneath the covers and Siobhàn eyed her son. He giggled and she drew back the bunting. A tiny lamb peeped its nose at her, round dark eyes begging to let it sleep with its master. "Connal," she scolded. "Did you think to trick me?"

"Can Dermott stay?"

"Aye." She tucked them both in and Connal smiled, utterly pleased with this day. "But you both must bathe in the morrow." The boy gasped and his mother sent him a warning glance. The lamb reeked of the stables. "Swear to me or I take him now."

Connal lowered his gaze and muttered, "I swear." Siobhàn

kissed him again and made to leave. "But not with yer stinkin' weeds!"

Siobhàn blinked at her son, her mouth open at his defiance. She snapped it shut. "Then 'tis with lye and a grooming brush, laddie, since you dare take a tone with me." She stepped out and closed the door, smiling at his attempt at cursing.

Siobhàn walked to her chamber, thanking Meghan as the woman passed with empty buckets; then slipping inside, she closed the door and was at once thankful she afforded a chamber to herself. The demands on her constant, she valued the sparse moments of privacy. Tigheran had always insisted she care for him, refusing to allow a servant to tend his smallest need. Life with him had left her exhausted, unhappy and, she admitted, terrified. Unease worked into her bones, stirring painful memories, and she cast them off with her clothes, not wasting a moment to slip into the hot, scented water. She would scrub later, she thought, resting her head gingerly on the rim. For now all she desired was the heat of the water soothing away the ache in her bones.

Steam curled in the cool air. The blaze in the hearth roared and crackled, flames eating freshly placed peat and wood. Siobhàn sank deeper into the bath, hot water sliding over her skin like a lover's caress. Her senses more intense with fatigue, she fought the masculine image taking shape in her mind, drawing on her disgust at discovering his profession, his self-serving cause.

Yet it came, clear and strong, powerful as he was big. She saw his body glistening with water, his ropey muscles twisting as he dried himself, the desire in his eyes when he wanted more than a kiss of reward. No man had looked upon her such as he had, no man had kissed her with such gentle command and dark hunger. She shifted in the bath, a feeble attempt to ease the heat stirring through her body, yet warm water and silken herbs rushed over her sensitive skin, intensifying the sensations she wanted to crush.

Siobhàn swallowed back a moan of despair.

Do not taunt me like this, Englishman, she thought. You are my enemy and here to war. And I will not betray my people. Especially not for my own desires.

Chapter Four

Surrounded by six warriors and her sister, Siobhàn's brow knitted, her gaze shifting between the two feuding villagers.

Someone was lying, she thought, yet could not tell which.

Around them the servants and slaves moved in their duties, but she had to solve this problem before she could get on with her own chores. "Munn, you say the milch cows are yours?"

"Aye."

Siobhàn put up her hand, silencing young Liam before he could speak.

"Was it not part of the stipend paid to her each year as your wife?"

Caught, Munn's craggy features tightened, flushing with embarrassment. "Aye, m'lady."

"Then you have no claim. They are hers. She can do as she wishes." She dismissed him and motioned his wife, Kathleen, forward, beckoning her closer than the rest, and the young woman knelt at her feet. Siobhàn leaned forward. "This is a battle over you, is it not?"

Kathleen turned her head, glancing at her husband of three years and then at Liam, then back to her princess. "I fear to confess, but aye, my lady, 'tis so."

Siobhàn need not ask as to who held the girl's heart and leaned back, waving Kathleen to a spot near her side, then looked between the two men.

"Munn, have you been cohabiting with your wife?"

"Aye, my lady." 'Twas a tired response, and Siobhàn wondered if the girl had been unfaithful to her husband. Though he was far older and bent, infidelity was unacceptable. "Have you shared yourselves?" She looked between husband and wife.

"Aye, we have," they said as one, and a tortured look came over Liam's face.

Then they have had relations enough to beget a child, one she was certain Kathleen wanted, if the talk was correct. Siobhàn studied the group. Kathleen had the right to be married to whomever she chose. 'Twas brehon law. She saw no way to decide without leaving one hurt and alone. But an unhappy marriage was a life of misery, she knew, and best served in solitude.

"You may divorce, if you choose."

Munn did not protest.

"I choose," Kathleen said quickly and Liam beamed a bright smile.

"You must then offer recompense to Munn. Two milch cows from your life with him." Wed three years, she'd likely have as many cows or sheep from *coibche,* her bride price, and could part with the ones he had provided, her due for each year she spent as his wife.

Siobhàn glanced at Munn. He nodded, sending a disgusted glance to his wife. Siobhàn rose, dismissing the group of onlookers, then pinned Liam with a hard stare. "Do not shame her. Wed this day, pay her father one cow in *coibche,* and you must earn one each year after for her. They are hers by brehon right."

"I will, my princess," Liam said, smiling.

"Do, or I will rule differently and not in your favor."

His look turned solemn and Siobhàn focused on Kathleen. "If you do not bring forth a child, you know he can do the same to you?"

Kathleen flushed, obviously stunned the gossip had reached Siobhàn's ears, and looked nervously between her princess and her future husband.

"I will never," Liam whispered. "Child or nay." He clutched her to him and kissed her.

"Ahh! Get out of my keep!" Siobhàn waved irritatedly, yet smothered a smile. They were so much in love it hurt to look at them. She addressed her clansman and retainer. "Is there any more this day, Brody? Please say 'tis not so," she pleaded soulfully, her expression pitiful.

"Nay, none, my princess." He grinned. "You may go play with the bread dough again."

Siobhàn smiled, perking up then and left the dais, moving through the people crowding the hall. Snatching her apron, she tied it over her drab woolen kirtle as she left the hall, crossing the yard to the cookhouse. She scarcely had her hands deep in the heavy folds of dough when someone called out.

"The bread will have to rise without my help," she muttered, and cook smiled.

Driscoll, her clansman and captain of what remained of her guards, appeared in the doorway.

"How many this time?" she said tiredly.

"Seven, m'lady."

Siobhàn tried not to show her anger. Raiding livestock was a way of life, but not often on Donegal lands. "Was anyone hurt?" When he nodded, she jerked off her apron, leaving the cookhouse and crossing the bailey. Her palfrey was saddled, a boy holding the leads.

"Mama, may I come with you?"

She spun about, smiling as Connal raced to her side, his lamb trotting after him. She stroked his sweaty hair back, rubbing a smudge of dirt from his nose. "Nay."

His little forehead wrinkled. "You never let me leave."

" 'Tis dangerous for you, sweetling." She wanted to soothe him, remind him that he would be a great king one day, but her dreams of late warned her of the future and its drastic changes. Besides, little boys needed time to chase butterflies, keep frogs in a bucket and get into mischief, something Connal did rather well of late. "There are people who are hurt, my son, and I cannot worry over you and tend to them." He nodded, looking too grown up for his age, and she eyed him. "Should you not be about your lessons?"

His expression drooped miserably and he nodded, tromping back toward the keep. Her heart nearly twisted at the sight and she sighed, turning to her guardsman and climbing onto the small thin saddle astride, adjusting her garment about her legs.

"You should be well used to me ridin' like this by now, Driscoll," she said at his sour look.

"I long for the day to arrive," he muttered, shaking his head and following her. Five more men gathered about them as they rode through the gates toward the herders in the hills.

An hour later Siobhàn slipped from the mount and raced to the burning shack. Driscoll lurched, pulling her back from the flames. "Nay, lass, nay. There's naught to be done now." He cursed under his breath, looking away from the bodies strewn just inside the door. "They were not so when I spotted them."

" 'Tis unholy, that," she whispered, taking a step closer, bile rising in her throat. "They're gutted like pigs." She paled with fury, looking at him. "This serves no purpose, Driscoll. Take the stock, aye, but to murder? Death will not tend more sheep, milk more cows. They have destroyed their livelihood." She flung a hand at the smoking hut. "And to do so in the light of day?" Raids came in the dark, and it took weeks to discover the culprits and repay the deed. But this, she thought, staring at the blood-soaked ground. This left no witnesses and could not have garnered more than a half dozen sheep and cows.

And four lives.

"Outlaws do not need a reason, I'm thinking."

She tossed her hair back over her shoulder. "And I bid you keep that opinion to yourself." His features tightened at the censure, yet she met his gaze head on. "We cannot afford panic and outlaws or nay, a rival clan could have easily done this. Those wishing me to swear to Henry. Speculation will breed fear and we cannot afford its price." 'Twas a reminder that there were too few trained men left to control a riot. "And I am thinking we need to protect them better. Aye, I know we've few men to aid them," she said when he opened his mouth to protest. "But suggest to all in this area that they move closer to the castle. We cannot help if they be dead afore word reaches us. You decide what is necessary for other safeguards." With brisk strides, she moved to her horse, swinging up and riding off without escort.

Driscoll motioned two men to follow, then raked his fingers through his snarled hair. Stubborn female, he thought, watching her ride like a man. And though he did not like it or her plan, she was his princess and he would obey. The past years widowed and ruling as Connal's regent, she'd proven herself wiser than her dead husband, even without the power of the ancients in her blood.

His gaze shifted about the land, searching for signs of the attack. If the culprits were wayward brigands raping the countryside, Driscoll vowed to find them and gut them as they had this little family. And if this was, as she suspected, clansmen wanting her to swear to the king, then God save them, for he knew she would not. Ever.

Siobhàn rode ahead for privacy, to shed tears for the family who'd come with her after her father had died, after she'd wed

Tigheran. For the little girl who'd played with Connal only a sentnight past and had pretty freckles across her nose. She swiped at her face, and not for the first time considered Lochlann O'Niell's recent offer of marriage and protection. But his alliance was bending toward the English king, she felt, and her dead husband's half brother said he'd swear to it to save his people, his lands. Siobhàn did not know what she would do if forced between life and death, yet an oath to the English king, in her heart, was betraying centuries of Celtic heritage. But so far Lochlann's lands were untouched, his people hail and hearty, whilst hers suffered.

And then there was Ian and his constant suit to consider. The Maguire was handsome, fair and strong, and she'd known him since she was a girl, had loved him once, yet the telling factor was not her happiness, but her people's—and Ian had thrice times the men she did. Lochlann had equal the amount of strength in numbers, and together they would strike a formidable blow on the raiders, if necessary. But their lands were nearer to the battlefields, and an English alliance would prove necessary.

In Donegal, it was not. 'Twas of no strategic value except that the shore bordered the land and none had yet to master the shale cliffs to attack. The king's emissaries had not approached her—that was a troubling thought to add to the pile—yet she saw no reason to submit to England's demands when the armies had not found their way here. Clan Rourke and her brethren were untouched but for the recent raiding, a peaceful remote place, prosperous in fishing and farming and herding. And a bit of magic.

She glanced back at the curl of smoke in the cloudy sky, wishing for her cousin Fionna's conjurings to protect them from more heartache. Mist will not help us this time, she thought, looking to the west and offering a prayer to keep the Englishmen beyond Ulster.

* * *

Gaelan frowned at the dark patch in the sky as he reached for his hauberk, slipping it over his head. Around him the camp broke, pavilions falling in soft billows to be rolled and stored, fires extinguished and pages griping about the early hour.

Raymond moved to his side. "What make you of that?" he asked, his gaze on the smoke twisting in the sky.

"Send a man to see. I will not have the king's prize in ashes afore I take it."

Raymond's lips quirked. "Hungry for it, are you?"

Gaelan slanted him a glance as he strapped padded leather about his thighs. "Are you not eager for a siege?"

"Nay."

His brow arched.

Raymond shrugged as if that explained his feelings. "Have you considered instead of accepting the coin of Donegal's worth, taking it for yourself, making a home?"

Gaelan was tired of this conversation. "To be beholding to Henry? My knights, my archers, sent off when he beckons? I think not, Raymond."

"What cost is it? You have legions." He gestured to the field, unable to see the ground for the human blanket covering it. "They would follow you regardless of the purse, and most would find honor in serving Henry's cause, even if you do not."

Gaelan stood motionless as Reese fastened the iron greave around his legs. "They are free to do as they please."

Raymond scoffed. "Nay, they are too loyal."

His head jerked up, his brow high. "Such a thing does not exist."

"You have not dealt with many Irish on our journey here, have you?"

He straightened, a reluctant smile curving his stony countenance. "One or two."

"This is not Dublin, Gaelan. There is no court and politics here. Look at this place. We have traveled for miles without seeing a village. And the woman . . . where did she come from, if not nearby?"

"Mayhaps she was a ghost, a fairy," he said bitterly. He did not have the time to think on her. She was gone and he had tasks to tend. Tasks toward his future. He wanted the coin so he could disband and live out his years in comfort. And to do it, he would tear down every last scrap of Donegal, force its princess and her people to submit and give the lot over to Henry.

He had to. He did not belong in an Irish castle.

Then where? a voice whispered. *A land without a lord is land free for the taking, and Henry bids you keep it.*

A bastard did not often gain such an opportunity, Gaelan knew, and as Raymond was quick to needle. Yet Gaelan was wise enough to know his limits, and his worth.

Reese cleared his throat and Gaelan looked down, taking the helm and tucking it under his arm. He strode to Grayfalk and mounted, positioning the blue-plumed helm on his head.

Raymond eyed him, then swung up onto his destrier. "You will not have to fight the Irish."

"They will not win."

Raymond scoffed behind the face guard. "Nay, they will all drop dead at the sight of you."

He grinned. "So be it."

Siobhàn found her home in an uproar, people rushing about, yet accomplishing naught, men ordering weapons a'ready, ladders lining the wood and stone walls in defense.

When she rode into the inner ward, Brody came to her as she slid from the saddle.

"The English are here."

"They have been for years, Brody." She checked the mount's hoof and plucked a stone free.

"Not the PenDragon."

Her head jerked up, her eyes narrowing. "Nay."

He nodded.

"How far?" She sent the horse to a stable boy and walked briskly toward the hall.

"Beyond the Finn River. A messenger just returned." He gestured to a young man in the center of the hall, breathless and sweaty, gripping a wooden cup of wine and draining it as fast as he could.

"Gather some restraint, Egan," she said, patting his shoulder. "Taste the wine afore you swill it."

He choked and sputtered, his eyes widening, and at the sight of her, he leapt to his feet. "I saw his pennant and the English king's. The PenDragon with a battalion headed this way."

"Are you falling to tales, Egan?"

He gulped for a breath. " 'Tis no tale, princess. He thirsts for battle. He has no heart, no honor, and kills for the highest bidder."

A mercenary.

A horrible weakness raced through her blood and she felt the color leave her face. Snatching Egan's wine, she ignored the horrifying stories floating around her and drained the remnants of his drink.

Nay. He was only one knight of many. Had she not heard him mention a DeClare in his midsts? Surely a relative of Pembroke did not serve a Cornish bastard? She set the cup down, smiling a weak apology, then glanced about. Her folk were staring at her, nervous and afraid and looking to her for guidance.

"Bring everyone from the villages inside. Send two men to scout, Brody, yet wait for Driscoll to return. He will know how best to handle that and can read their direction." They could be headed to Maguire land or O'Niell's. Yet the responsibility lay on her shoulders, and she knew beyond doubt, if she sent word to Ian and Lochlann to send warriors, it would not matter. The PenDragon had nearly a thousand. They were mere hundreds with more women, old folk and children than men. The border clans would keep to themselves, protecting their own or submitting. Even if, collectively, the clans came to their aid, it was suicide. Donegal Castle would not survive a siege.

There would be no contest but for how much Irish blood would spill. And if the PenDragon wished it, the soil would run red with it by nightfall.

Chapter Five

Gaelan swung, driving his sword downward across the man's body, the blade sailing deep into his shoulder and chest. The impact splattered blood over his armor, and with a growl, he followed through, severing his opponent's arm, then wheeled about to take on another bandit.

What did these fools think to accomplish with an ambush? he thought again, driving a man back with his boot, dispatching another; then as the living fled, he and his troops gave chase. But as if he fought ghosts, the bandits vanished. Gaelan reined up, his mount skipping to a halt as he studied the thicket. Not a branch moved, no trail left to follow. He turned Grayfalk back toward the clearing.

Twice attacked in as many days, Gaelan could see no purpose and would swear they were the same men who'd attacked him in the copse with the woman. Such foolhardy tenacity was abominable, for this time they knew they were sadly unmatched for battle. Were all Irish willing to die so readily?

He looked around at his men and was well pleased the cost

was in injury and not lives. Sir Raymond leaned over his mount's neck, trying to catch his breath, waving Gaelan off when he started for him. Sheathing his sword, he dismounted, striding to the nearest body and jerking the oiled rag from the ambusher's face. Disgust raged at the sight of the soft chin and beardless face of a boy. There were no excuses for sending the unseasoned into battle. With a curse foul enough to rot trees, he severed a portion of the tartan wrapping the youth. Staring down at the lad, he stuffed it inside his bloody breastplate before turning back to his mount. His intention for clemency to the Irish obliterated, he dug his spurs into Grayfalk's side and rode toward Donegal, prepared to take his due, at any cost.

"Silence," Siobhàn shouted over the din, and the talk ceased. She looked around the hall filled with her clansmen, to the faces she'd known for years, to the warriors prepared to die for the wood and stone castle. And they *would* die. The Pen-Dragon was close enough to see their torches. "The burden of keeping peace will be mine, Driscoll." Clearly the folk held the same opinion as he, that she could not do it, and she wondered if they'd oppose the method were Tigheran here, then knew they would not have dared.

"Siobhàn," Rhiannon warned and her sister speared her with a glance. "You cannot sacrifice yourself."

Siobhàn's brows rose, her look aghast. " 'Tis not my intention. We will not offer resistance and they will have no reason to slaughter us."

" 'Tis a dishonor not to fight!"

She rounded on Driscoll. "And 'tis a crime to survive?" She stepped closer to him. "Would you have me bury your wife, your children?" She lashed her hand toward the dark-haired lad bravely smothering his fear beside his older sister. "How will you all stand against English swords and Welsh bowmen? We are Irish, not idiots!"

Her temper high, her expression begged them to understand her motives. Survival, warmth and food would help her people. The PenDragon's reputation preceded him. He pillaged and burned. He slaughtered all who opposed to justify his coin. He was a landless knight with naught but a valiant name to call his own. Siobhàn doubted the king of Camelot would claim such a destructive man as an heir.

"Send for the O'Niell," came from several servants and freemen.

"Aye, the English will be no match for his warriors and ours."

"'Tis too late. O'Niell nor the Maguire would arrive in time." She suspected that was the PenDragon's intent, though she'd not call for more souls to perish when she could resolve this without bloodshed. She spun about, striding toward the doors. "Bridgett, you and Rhiannon see to the preparations. This eventide, we feast instead of mourn."

Grumbles of disagreement came from behind her as she swept out the heavy doors and into the yard. She possessed no guilt over her decision. Not a drop of Irish blood was worth the English king's claim, she thought, as several women rushed to her, halting her flight.

"Our thanks, princess, praise be," a woman crooned, hefting her child as she hugged her. "They will not admit, but 'tis for the best."

"I am frightened," Kathleen whispered, her eyes teary. "He wishes to die so easily." Her gaze shifted to Liam, tapping a club into his fist.

"The way of war and men," Siobhàn groused, then eyed the group, twisting to catch each woman's gaze. "I trust you will help convince the others to be civil?"

They nodded collectively. "He will take us prisoner, make us his slaves, won't he?"

Siobhàn lifted a child, inspecting a cut she'd tended days before. "I do not know, Alanna." Satisfied, she met the woman's gaze. "He is a warlord, not a man of the land. I will not lie and tell you he has not come to war on us, for he has. But I will do my best to see none suffer." With a kiss to the babe's brow, she handed him back to his mother.

"And who will protect you, m'lady?"

No one, she thought, yet smiled and smoothed a strand of brown hair from the young woman's cheek. Their concern moved her deeply and Siobhàn was further convinced she'd made the right decision.

"I will not need protection, for mercenary or nay, he is a knight, a nobleman. I am still the princess of Donegal and he is on Irish soil." Codswallop. Naught will matter to this warrior, she thought as she moved through the group toward the ladder leading to the parapet. Yet English knights were sworn to protect the weak, and she prayed that the PenDragon, regardless of his foul reputation, possessed a shred of honor.

Or she would find herself laying beneath him this night. Irish law or not.

Moments later a blue-white mist enveloped the stone and wood keep, the vapor shifting across the land, only delaying the inevitable.

Gaelan slowed his mount, the fog heavy, yet in the distance, Donegal loomed. It was massive, covering a larger amount of land than he'd expected. Turrets and a tower hovered above the fog, the outer curtain skirting a small mountain. A stone wall topped with wood. Easily besieged, he thought, and easily burned. He rode hard through the mist, and swore this land wept for its people.

On the parapet, Siobhàn leaned back against the battlement, unable to stare at the landscape another moment. The guards watched her with covert glances. Culhainn moved to her side, nudging her palm, and her fingertips whispered over his luxurious coat. "You think me a fool too?" she said to the beast, and he tipped his big head back and licked her hand. "Your loyalty astounds, Culhainn, when you will have to share your place with his hounds." The dog whimpered, then suddenly spun about, growling as Rhiannon approached.

"Good beastie," Rhiannon said, rewarding him with a slice of meat, and the animal settled in a plop at his mistress's feet to feast. "Keep him with you," she said. "None will pass close enough to do harm."

Before Siobhàn could assure her sister that she would be careful, Culhainn leapt to his feet, lunging at the wall and barking. She jerked around as the rumble of hooves shook the earth.

"Jager me," she whispered. Her heart pounded, her tranquil calm evaporating at the vision unfolding in the mist. Torches, spitting red fire and protected from the wind with black metal hoods, lit the twilight, glowing like phantom eyes from a skull. Silver flashes of armor sparkled with each trod, the jingle of spurs and weapons, the crash and creak of carts peppered the air. God save us, she did not think so many would be mounted.

A man raised his arm and the army halted, the banners snapping in the breeze; a rearing black dragon clawed its deep blue background, his head looking over its back, the bend sinister of a bastard slashing meanly across the grand hazard. Held higher above it and in the forefront was the king's banner proclaiming this mercenary the English monarch's voice . . . and iron hand. Her gaze scanned the invaders, searching for the familiar, for the giant in the ranks, when a single mounted knight nudged his horse forward, the huge black destrier prancing elegantly.

The PenDragon.

Each story that spread across Ireland came to her, unfolding into reality as he tossed a fur mantle over his right shoulder.

Blood stained the silver and black armor in a hideous drip. She glanced at her sister and recognized her horror.

"We are done for, Siobhàn. He has killed already this day and has the taste for more."

"By my soul, he will not find it here," she hissed, fingering the dagger at her waist.

PenDragon tipped his head, and though Siobhàn remained a few feet back, aware he could not see from his position unless she fairly leaned over the mortar wall, she swore he met her gaze. A chill curled up her spine.

"Donegal keep," he called into the stillness. "I am Gaelan PenDragon, servant of his majesty King Henry. Do you yield?"

"Unmask, sir knight, so I might see my foe."

Frowning, Gaclan's hand stilled on its way to unfasten his helm, the voice bearing an odd tinge familiar to his ears.

"A woman, Gaelan?" Sir Raymond said from just behind him.

"I cannot believe 'tis the princess, but who knows with the Irish and their strange ways." He yanked, pulling the helm off and tucking it beneath his arm at his side.

Siobhàn instantly lurched back from the wall.

Rhiannon gripped her arm. " 'Tis he?" she fairly shrieked.

"Aye. He cannot know I am here, not yet. We must get him inside afore we meet."

Her sister smirked. "You have already met. And right thoroughly, I imagine."

Siobhàn jerked from her grasp, irritation flaring in her eyes. "Mind your tongue, Rhiannon. If he knows 'tis me, we will have no power to bargain. None. I stuck him with my blade, I escaped his capture." And I let him kiss me as if I were naught but a bush woman bedding her way across the county.

Rhiannon frowned. "What plan you then?"

"Make him wait, offer comforts he has not known."

"Ahh, weaken him."

"Yours is the face that weakens men." She looked at the

army prepared to destroy her home, her life, her kinfolk. "Open the gates," she said to the tower guards, then motioned to Rhiannon. "Bid him welcome."

Her eyes widened. "I cannot."

She gave her a push. " 'Tis no time to be mush-hearted, Rhi. He will certainly not be."

Siobhàn fled down the battlements, running into the keep, grabbing Driscoll and delivering her plan. With Culhainn at her heels, she headed above stairs and slipped into her son's room. He flew into her arms, his tiny hands lost in her hair. The bells chimed, soothing her, and for long moments she held him, then helped him undress for bed.

"Will he kill us all, Mama?"

"Oh nay, my poppet, nay," she cooed, kneeling beside his bed and tucking in the coverlet. "I would not let him hurt you, I swear." Oh, she would die for this innocent child, she thought. So willingly.

Pressing her lips to his forehead, she stood, then went to her chambers. She dropped to her knees, lighting a candle, sprinkling herbs around her. Culhainn watched her from the far side of the chamber. Softly she chanted words as ancient as the stones beneath her home, calling on her ancestors to give her strength to endure his wrath.

Gaelan unsheathed his sword as the gates opened, men and women spilling out like rats, calling greetings and gesturing them inside. He rode forward, suddenly surrounded by at least fifty people.

He frowned at Raymond.

DeClare shrugged. "Irish hospitality."

He was not stupid enough to fall into a trap and barked a command, motioning them back, and only a few scattered. "Does a soul in our ranks speak the tongue?"

"I speak yours."

Gaelan looked down as a tall, thick-chested man neared, his torso wrapped in the dark green and blue tartan, his legs covered in furs. His hair was overlong, his features hidden in a heavy beard.

"I am Driscoll, her highness's personal guard." He tipped a bow.

"Bring her to me."

"She is . . . indisposed, sir."

Gaelan smirked to himself. Indisposed. Likely cowering under her bed.

"She bids you enter and rest yourselves. There is food for your knights. Come, come." Driscoll turned away, expecting him to follow, and Gaelan nudged his mount forward, giving orders for the brigades to secure the exits. He did not want her highness fleeing into the night. And since he knew naught of the royal family, he could not demand a hostage sent out, when it could be a commoner they cared little about. He needed the princess in his power to succeed. He brought ten knights and their squires inside with him. The gates remained open, several of his archers lining the way and as he entered the inner ward, Gaelan scowled at the meager fortress, ill-placed buildings, the wood and mortar he could penetrate with a battering ram.

"What think you of this, Gaelan?" Raymond asked.

"Me thinks we are being served up for a pagan sacrifice." He dismounted, handing his leads to Reese and ordering Sir Niles and the other knights to remain there and report his suspicions. Gaelan and Raymond mounted the steps, Sir Owen, Mark and Andrew directly behind them.

"At least they have not dropped dead at the sight of you."

Gaelan arched a brow in his direction, smirking, then strode into the hall, people scattering like rabbits. The conversation fell like breaking glass. He'd grown accustomed to such a response and was loathe to admit how much it rankled him lately. He approached her man Driscoll, taking note of several other warriors with battle-axes and spears flanking a large pair of chairs.

"Bring your princess to me at once."

Driscoll folded his arms over his chest, widening his stance. "You would ignore her hospitality?"

"She would ignore the king's man?"

"This is Ireland, sir, not England. And here the princess rules."

"Not anymore."

The guard unfolded his arms, pulling at his short sword in open threat.

"Driscoll!"

Gaelan's gaze snapped to the staircase, a shapely figure stepping from the hollow where it curved into the wall and disappeared to lead above. She met his gaze, her own assessing and judging in one glance as she came to him, her pale blue gown regal, her carriage straight. Her hair was golden red, unbound, uncovered, and flowing to her full hips.

"Your princess is lovely, Gaelan." Raymond kept his voice low and his guard high.

Gaelan glanced at him, his lip curling. "She is Henry's to do with as he will, DeClare. Ask for her. He might give her to you."

Raymond scowled. "I take no woman who does not come of her own will."

"Ahh, a conscience. And who was accusing me of having none only days ago?"

Tartan-clad warriors surrounding her, she stopped yards from him, her gaze sweeping his bloody armor before meeting his gaze.

"You are the princess of Donegal?"

"Nay, I am Rhiannon in-Murrough. Her sister."

Gaelan was surprised she spoke English. "Her highness does not greet me herself?" Did she not care for the welfare of her people?

"She abides her own will, my lord," she said cryptically, her gaze slipping to Driscoll before coming back to him. She waved to the tables, to the seats above the salt. "Come, dine, my lords." She clapped and servants moved, offering food and wine.

Fuming quietly, Gaelan debated with demanding the princess appear against brawling with women and so few soldiers. Damn the insolence of the haughty bitch, he thought, then reluctantly took his seat as lively music filled the air. Brightly clad dancers spun to the center of the stone floor and he glanced at Raymond, who was thoroughly intrigued and devouring food as if he'd not eaten this day, but Gaelan had no time for such frivolity. He wanted this matter done. That they did not resist told him they were prepared to acquiesce, but the welcome was false at best. He glanced down the table at the knights enjoying themselves, and it amazed him that men who were so ready for battle an hour ago, were enjoying the delights of Donegal's harvest and charming its women.

He stood and drained his goblet of surprisingly good ale, waving off the servant and setting down the cup. The noise lessened and he scanned the crowd. "Continue," he said, then swung his gaze to Raymond. "If you can pull yourself away from the lass, DeClare, remind the men to repay Donegal's courtesy in kind."

Raymond yanked a girl onto his lap, grinning at her. "If you insist."

"Do not be so taken, friend. Have you not noticed there are few men here?"

Raymond scowled sourly at his superior. "I have. As I have noticed her highness has still not given you an audience."

Gaelan looked at the sister, a frown marring his brow as she moved toward him.

"Is there aught I can do for you, sir knight?"

There was something odd about the woman, he thought, and

when she touched his arm, her eyes seemed to shift like a ripple of water.

"Summon me when your *princess*," he said with disgust, "can find the . . . mettle to face me."

Rhiannon inhaled at the blatant insult, obviously wanting to say something, yet thinking better of it.

"Or," he said with a glance at the Irish warriors, "I come for her myself." Gaelan brushed past, his armor clanking in the stillness as he strode out the doors.

Rhiannon looked at the dark-haired knight, her expression perplexed.

"I suggest you do what e're is necessary to get your sister down here. Do not make him search, lass; you will not like the result of his temper."

Rhiannon nodded, fleeing to the stairs, catching Driscoll and Brody's gaze and sending them a worried look. Siobhàn's plan would not work, she thought, climbing the staircase. He was prepared to force submission, then give their lives over to the king, without regret, without a shred of conscience. 'Twas times such as this, Rhiannon thought, when she wished she could not feel another soul's thoughts and emotions. For in the Pen-Dragon, she felt only emptiness, dark pain and a spark of longing he tried to hide, even from himself.

Gaelan handed Reese the stained armor, bid him clean it, then find his way to the hall and partake of the feasting. The lad nearly tripped over his own too large feet in his haste to be done and gone. Gaelan curried Grayfalk, then stripped down to his braies and washed, slipping a loose lawn shirt over his head, his belt about his waist. He was just securing the fastenings when an infant lamb trotted in to the stable on wobbly legs, looking at him before scampering pell-mell into the corner.

Sweet Jesu, I scare even animals, he thought, disgusted. Was Raymond the only one to match him?

A moment later, a cloaked figure darted inside, calling softly for the lamb.

"You've named your livestock?"

Siobhàn spun about, her hood falling back as the air left her lungs. Why was he not in the hall?

His brows shot up. "You!" Gaelan half smiled, moving toward her.

She darted out of his reach, deciding escape was better than capturing her son's pet. But he was fast for such a large man, catching her about the waist and slamming her against his bulk.

Instantly, Siobhàn shoved at his chest, kicked his shin.

He squeezed. "Cease. I will not harm you."

"Hah." Oh sweet Mary mother, let none see me like this. "You are the PenDragon."

His expression turned sour with irritation. "Why does everyone mutter my name like a prayer to Satan?"

"It bodes ill for those you destroy and conquer." She wiggled, groaning at the effort, then sagged miserably and met his gaze through a curtain of hair. "Well." She hung against him like a limp rag. "You have proven yours is the greater strength. Do you wish to crush my ribs too?"

Smiling, he eased his hold a bit, noticing her hair was damp and curling. "Nay. I would keep you this time." With the backs of his knuckles, he brushed her hair off her shoulder, his gaze scanning her beautiful features, remembering her fire, the heat of her mouth. "You escaped."

"Was I captive?" She arched a tapered brow. "I did not know. Not after your man clubbed me."

His expression softened. "He was punished."

" 'Twas an accident!" She could only imagine what form of castigation he'd inflict.

Surprise slapped him. Another woman would be demanding Owen's head, or at least coin for her trouble. "You live here?"

"Aye."

He grinned hugely. He would take this wild creature as his

mistress, he thought easily. "You were a long way from home, girl."

She scoffed, shoving uselessly at his big chest. "I am no girl, m'lord."

"I know." He ducked his head.

She slapped a hand over his mouth, her sharp eyes warning. "You would shame me?"

He peeled her hand off. "Nay, sweetling—" He lifted her, carrying her to a more secluded spot. "I would pleasure you." Falling back against the wall, Gaelan released her legs and instantly pressed her to him, letting her feel her command over his body. Only this woman made him hunger to join with her so deeply, he could not think clearly. And this night was one in which he needed all his faculties. But right now, he wanted only to feel.

"Unhand me this instant."

Her tone was so imperious, he had to smile. "For a kiss." He leaned.

She shoved. "Is everything a bargain with you, mercenary?"

"With you, I fear, it must be."

He ducked, covering her mouth with his, and though she flattened her hands on his chest, she did not push, still as glass in his arms. He felt her battling her own response and nurtured her lips, his pulling softly at her lower lip before he ran his tongue over the lush outline. Once, twice, he dipped his tongue between and for an instant, hers chased his. Her shudder tumbled into his mouth, her lips worrying his, her fingertips digging into his chest with a restrained power he wanted to release all over him.

He drew back a fraction, meeting her gaze. "Give to me, lass."

"Nay." But oh, when he looked at her like that, like he wanted to devour her, Siobhàn's knees went soft as goose down. And her will turned to water.

His lips curved at her rebellion, a look of dark sensuality in his eyes as his hand slid down to the base of her spine, pressing her to his thickening groin. Her eyes fluttered closed, a sweet invitation she was unaware of offering.

Then he kissed her, his mouth molding warmly over hers, his hands driving up her slender back and sending the bells to tinkling. The sound spun through his heavy heart. And when her arms wrapped around his neck, arching her lush body to his, Gaelan felt his dead soul fracture. His kiss intensified and her tiny fingers slid softly into his hair, stroking delicately, and he moaned his pleasure.

The rich sound rumbled against her breasts, spiraling heat and energy through her blood. She felt his strength surround her, hard muscle and man, magnificent power restrained in a gentle touch she'd never expected from the PenDragon. Passion, sultry and burning, broke inside her, and though she knew he was the wrong man, the worst man to find it in, his touch left her powerless and when she was hungry for more, she knew she could never have it. The denial of it drove suppressed desire to the surface and her hands clawed down his chest, and dove beneath his shirt, molding the contours of his skin, stroking his nipple, and his pleasure came in a tighter embrace, his thickening groin . . . his tongue wildly stroking her mouth and making her come apart inside her clothes.

No man had ever done this to her, made her feel this desired, this sensual. And he was her enemy. He was here to conquer, to hold her people in bondage to the English king, to make her his leman, if he chose. She could not bear that.

She tore her mouth away, her breathing harsh on his lips as she met his gaze.

"Gaelan," Raymond called, his voice near.

Siobhàn shoved out of his arms, and this time he let her go. She ran, brushing past the knight and heading toward the tunnels.

Raymond glanced at the empty doorway, then to Gaelan. "The creature from the forest?"

Gaelan smiled, straightening uncomfortably. "Still with plenty of fire."

"And speed, I see," Raymond said, chuckling. He eyed his friend, not bothering to disguise his awareness of their tryst, but gentleman enough not to mention it.

Gaelan turned toward his garments laid across the stall and donned them carefully.

"You are coming inside?"

"Aye." He reached for his sword, strapping it on. "I have wasted enough time—"

"Not from what I saw," Raymond snickered from behind.

Gaelan stilled, smiling to himself, then turned, positioning the sword. "If the lady princess is not awaiting, we return to camp and lay siege."

Chapter Six

The impertinent woman was not waiting.

His sorely tested patience snapped, and he brushed people aside, heading for the doors. "Come. We burn her out."

Loud gasps vibrated with cries for mercy.

Raymond whispered a soft warning.

He ignored them, striding to the doors, his men at arms at his heels.

Someone called his name. Gaelan paused, looked, meeting Raymond's gaze, and the man nodded ahead.

Gaelan swung around. She stood hidden in the darkness of the staircase, Driscoll and his warriors flanking the landing.

Gaelan's gaze thinned as he moved closer.

"You wished to see me?"

"I wish to see more than shadows."

She moved forward, gliding into the light on a rustle of cloth.

Gaelan staggered, his eyes flaring as he stared down at his village lass.

Had he not held the deceiving little wench in his arms only

a half hour past, he might not have recognized her. Gone was the worn dress with frayed sleeves, replaced with a deep vivid green gown trimmed in gold, black and silver threads creating the neverending knots he'd seen so often with the Irish, edging the scooping neckline and along her long draping sleeves. The shade made her green eyes darker, more intense, as she stared back, still on the last step, meeting his level.

And he could do no more than look.

Her wild curling hair was tamed, full and spiraling down her back to beyond her knees, deep red and as before, braided in spots, the little bells entwined. Yet this time, ahh save me from this woman's beauty, he thought, this time banding her forehead was a circlet of silver, the design of the Celts carved into the smooth, polished metal.

This was no village girl, he thought. This was the princess of Donegal.

And his prize.

"You have lied." His voice was low and biting.

Siobhàn's eyes flared. "And you, PenDragon, never once asked my name."

She shifted past him and his gaze followed, sweeping over the length of fabric falling from her shoulders and trailing the floor. Beneath the drape of her hair, he could see the pattern of knots, thistles and winged creatures, and when she grasped her skirts to step onto the dais, he noticed the splits in her sleeves and silver bands circling her upper arms. Magnificent, he had to admit, as she turned to him and with an elegant wave, gestured to the space beside her, her expression void of emotion, of the light he'd fed on in the barn.

Gaelan met with her, gazing down, absorbing her noble stature, taking in the details his anger fogged; the leather and silver girdle slung low on her hips, a jewel-handled dagger and a fistful of amulets and charms dangling from its chains; the thin strips of silver hanging from her lobes, the delicate bones of her face and shoulders, her proud young body ripely displayed in the fitted gown.

"Introduce me to her," Gaelan said into the sudden silence, and her man Driscoll stepped close.

Driscoll met her gaze briefly and the princess nodded.

"Before you stands a descendant of first high king Brian Boru, the eldest daughter of Prince MacMurrough, granddaughter of the high king of Ulster, wife and widow of King Tigheran O'Rourke, Siobhàn ban-Murrough O'Rourke ... princess of Donegal."

At the last, Gaelan's eyes flared, and as he took her hand and brought it to his lips, beyond her, he caught the horrified look on Raymond's face.

"Your highness. Your servant, Gaelan PenDragon."

His lips never met their target as she pulled free. "You serve only yourself, English."

His gaze sharpened.

Siobhàn returned his stare with malevolence, then stepped back so as not to crane her neck to look at him and lose what little ground she had. She hated that she was weakened by the sight of him, his clean shaven face, his shiny dark hair, overlong and brushing his shoulders. His black surcoat gleamed of conquered wealth in its silver and jewel trim, the blue dragon emblazoned across his chest reminding her of the kind of man she must battle. He was furious with her. She could see it smoldering in his dark, fathomless eyes, but Siobhàn could not fall prey to her emotions. Her people's lives would be decided in the next few moments.

Around them, folk listened and watched as she moved to a high-backed chair, carved and dark, and she swept the cape aside, offering him the seat beside her before she sat. Gaelan remained standing, inclining his head to Raymond, and the knight rushed near.

"Gaelan, she is—"

"I know. The contracts."

Raymond reluctantly handed them over.

Gaelan slapped the documents on the small table before the chairs.

Siobhàn didn't spare the curled parchment a glance. She knew they were terms of surrender and there would be bargaining before she relinquished her folk to him. "Why have you come?"

"To conquer for Henry."

She scoffed. " 'Tis simple thievery."

His spine stiffened at that. "A land without a lord is land free for the taking."

She leapt to her feet, anger hissing in her words. "I am the authority here, PenDragon. And the lands belong to us." She gestured to her people. " 'Twas entrusted to my care by my father, and his father afore, and Donegal is *ciobche* to me from my husband."

"Women do not own land."

A soft snicker of laughter rose in the hall, and the knights and squires frowned at the Irish folk smirking at them as if they were too stupid to walk upright.

"Aye, we do. 'Tis Ireland you stand on, sir, abiding by brehon law. I suggest you learn it well, or you have come for naught."

Dark outrage crept up his features from his throat. "By the church of God, the pope and Henry's alliance with the king of Leinster, you are under English rule!"

"Nay, Leinster is. This is Donegal. Would you not expect me to follow English law, were I in your country?"

Crafty little thing, he thought. "Aye. And in England you would know that your lord rules all."

She glared back, defiance in every fiber. "Must I tell you again where you have landed, English*man?*"

Simmering with the urge to shake her, he advanced. Instantly her men flanked her, javelins crossing before her chest. "You hide behind your people."

With the back of her hands, Siobhàn spread the spears and stepped closer, inches from him. "We have repelled Vikings and survived centuries without the aid or alliance of the English. We need naught of your kind now."

"You have no choice."

She delivered a haughty glare. "I have given *you* the choice, PenDragon. You may have entered this keep without resistance, but you do not have the *tuath* as your prize."

"I could destroy you all and take it."

The soft warning sent a chill over her skin. "Aye. And what will that give your king in victory? Rubble? Bodies to burn as you have done afore?" she said with disgust. "Land is naught without the hands to till it. The souls to live upon it. Donegal is naught but soil, sea and trees without her people."

He stepped closer, his voice low, yet deep enough for all to hear. "And without you, princess?"

Imaginations racing, her folk protested, cries of mercy and pity blending with English commands for calm ripped through the crowd.

She searched his gaze. How could he not see she was merely a guiding voice here? "I am naught without them, PenDragon."

"You wish them to live?"

She looked at him as if he'd grown wings. " 'Tis my entire quest."

"Then swear oath and fealty through me to the king."

"*Never.*"

A cheer rose in the hall.

He merely arched a brow, refusing to acknowledge the crowd.

"I will never swear oath to a man with no purpose but to take and slaughter for a self-serving king."

"Guard your tongue, woman!"

"In my own house?"

Her disdain was unmistakable, pushing him to the end of his patience. "Speak with me in private. Now."

She frowned, confusion rippling across her beautiful face

before she nodded. He followed her off the dais toward a partition, yet when he touched her shoulder, she instantly spun about, her dagger at his ribs, her clansmen lurching forward.

Commands to be still, and the sound of swords scraping against scabbards scarred the silence. Siobhàn's gaze slipped over the crowd, fear and anger on their faces, the camaraderie of rage from the knights restraining them. She swung her gaze to his.

"Order them back, lady, or they will die this night."

"Once again you have proven your strength will crush the weak, PenDragon."

His features yanked taut and for an instant he felt like the bully in the yard. "Do not fight me, village princess. I will win."

She tilted her head, her stubbornness softening. "And what will you win but the hatred of an entire race, sir?"

"I do not care."

Her expression tightened. "Then 'tis true, you have no soul."

He gritted his teeth. "How long will you abide this test of wills? To the point of battle?" He waved at the knights and squires, weapons trained on her folk. "Would you slay me in my sleep then? For I am here, princess, in possession. You have already submitted. I have Donegal."

Foolish man. "I have submitted to naught but your invasion of my home without bloodshed. And you, *mercenary,* know only of war, taking heedlessly what we value most dearly. Conquering Donegal is not *belonging* to Donegal."

Something moved in his eyes then, and Siobhàn wished she could decipher it.

"My lady?"

Siobhàn turned, discreetly sheathing her blade at her waist. Driscoll and Brody appeared ready to murder the man and she moved toward them, leaving Gaelan to stare after her. "I am well able to handle him, Driscoll."

"The bastard means to burn us out—"

She hushed him. "I will not allow it. I will give him my head before I will allow a single stick to be burned."

Driscoll's features twisted with shame. She would give her life for them without consequence, but it was his duty to see that did not happen. "Forgive me, princess. I know that, yet the PenDragon is not a man to compromise."

"He must," she said with complete finality. "But I need you to keep calm, please. More is at risk than our pride," she added, laying her hand on his arm. "My thanks for your vigilance, Driscoll." She smiled softly up at the brawny Irishman. "I take comfort in your presence." His harsh look eased and he patted her hand. She looked beyond him to the rest. "Please," she called, and faces turned to her. "Eat, drink sweet wine. Dance." She clapped twice and the music rose on brittle air. "PenDragon and I have much to discuss." She met Rhiannon's gaze, encouraging her to calm the folk, and her sister moved through the crowd, pouring wine for the knights. Maids carried platters of roasted mutton, still-steaming bread and the first of the harvested vegetables to the tables as she turned back to Gaelan.

She could not interpret the look on his face . . . then decided 'twas wisest not to speculate.

But Gaelan realized he jeopardized more than his future with his temper and though he'd come here with clear intent, her presence and position suddenly made him cautious. "There is plenty of time to discuss the contracts, lady," he said for all to hear. "I am not going anywhere."

His sudden change of temperament aroused her suspicions and she eyed him warily. "Neither am I." She moved back to the dais, ordering the table replaced before taking her seat and pouring wine into two goblets. After a moment, he joined her in the opposite chair.

"Shall we deal with the matter of your falsehood?"

Holding the pitcher, she reared back. "I gave no lie to who I am."

He leaned. "You could have told me in the barn."

She glanced to the side to see if anyone heard. "When you were mauling me?"

"I remember differently."

"Of course you do." She shrugged, setting the container down. "You are a man." She handed him the goblet and he took a huge sip. "Had you known who I was in the field, and with your intent, you would have kidnapped me and held me for ransom."

"Aye."

"And none would have been paid."

He arched a brow.

"Unless your desire was payment in cows."

His lips quirked at that. "You were wise to open the gates, Siobhàn."

She stilled, the cup halfway to her lips at the sound of her name on his lips. "I avoided a slaughter."

He agreed. "You bent to a greater will."

She set the goblet down with a snap, her eyes flaring with swift anger. "Bending, molding, crushing under your feet, 'tis all you know, PenDragon. And coin from your sovereign is all you desire!"

With a velvety look over her body, he said, "I desire you."

She inhaled, a tingling skating over her skin. "I pity you." She stood abruptly, furious with his high-handed manner. "Had you a tender life and home, mayhaps you could understand why I will not bend." She leaned closer, pinning him with her green gaze. "And why I will never swear fealty to a barren horse of a man, English or nay!"

Gaelan watched her go, her fiery temper stirring him, and her words this night striking him hard. For she was right. He knew not of home and hearth and the value these folk set upon it. He'd been alone since he lost his brother on the battlefield and wanted no one's pity for it. But he was in possession of Donegal and if she thought her defiance would alter that, she'd discover differently. His intention to take the keep in exchange for coin had not changed. Henry's desire was that Gaelan take it for himself, install his army here and lord over the sea border, remaining the king's guardian on the Irish shore. King Henry wanted this area pulled into the government he was establishing in Dublin, Meath and Waterford, and Gaelan realized that until today, these people were untouched by the outside. And for reasons he chose not to name, he was loathe to make this place a battleground. But if she forced him, he would. He knew no other way.

He turned his head when Raymond moved near, sliding onto the bench. "She took my breath away, Gaelan, I swear. *That*"—he nodded to Siobhàn—"is why men go to war."

Aye, Gaelan thought, slumping into the chair. "She minces no words, eh?"

Raymond watched Gaelan watch the princess and hid a grin. "What will you do? She has openly refused your claim."

" 'Tis Henry's claim and I will force it." He had to. Without it he would not have the compliance of her people.

" 'Tis not as you expected, nor I. Even Henry cannot know of the small forces here."

Gaelan spared him a glance. "Do not ease your vigil, DeClare. We have not seen many warriors, yet that does not mean they do not exist."

Raymond agreed.

"We must contend with the neighboring lords, the princes," he said with a smirk. "They were too numerous in Meath and could control only their kingdoms." He returned his gaze to Siobhàn. "But what if they gather to war for her?"

"Hold her hostage," Raymond said simply. "They will not war with the threat to kill her."

"Mayhaps, but what of the ambush? She could have sent the brigands." When Raymond opened his mouth to protest, Gaelan added, "See beyond the beauty, man, and do not discount the woman, nor the treachery of her people. We will live longer."

From his position he watched her move about the room, ignoring him and focusing on his knights. They showed her due respect, leaping to their feet and greeting her. Her smile was open, unrestrained for them. She has yet to smile for me, he thought, irritated with the thought. A maid lumbered with a heavy platter to the table and she lurched to help her, sampling the meat before ordering it sliced. Yet he heard her praise the servant on the seasoning, then looked about for the cook. His gaze darted to the wafer-thin woman near a door, then back to Siobhàn, and saw her wave and nod. She moved off, stopping to introduce herself to Reese and bless the big lad, he blushed ten shades to red as he kissed her hand. She treated him equally, offering a seat and a dinner companion, a pretty young fair-haired girl who smiled as shyly as Reese.

Gaelan sipped his wine, wondering who was the woman enchanting his knights with her smile. He'd expected to find a haughty princess, too frightened to greet him. And he found a woman more villager than noble. Was this all for his benefit? he wondered, and as she neared the end of the table, the bells in her hair chimed like the "fairy talk" the pages spoke about. All Gaelan knew was that they lured him like a sorceress's spell and he wanted to put his hands in her hair and make them sing. His doubt of her honesty burned to ashes when she stuffed a cloth in her girdle like an apron, walking about for a second, then snatching it off when she realized her blunder.

As if feeling his gaze on her, she tipped her head. Her smile melted from her face, pure distaste in her eyes. It hit him like a slap, stinging his pride. She dipped a curtsey lacking in respect and turned, coming face-to-face with Owen. Gaelan straightened in his chair, aware of Owen's disdain for the Irish. Owen bowed his head and spoke and Gaelan wished he could hear. Yet he knew the man had asked her forgiveness when he started to kneel and she caught him, shaking her head. Owen smiled for the first time since he'd struck her down, and Gaelan knew she'd absolved him.

Strange woman, he thought as knights and squires suddenly lurched back as if a hand stroked through the crowd. Gaelan frowned, rising to his feet to see the problem. The huge animal Culhainn lumbered toward her. She spoke to the beast as if he understood and it responded with a bark. Siobhàn turned, searching the crowd, and he watched her gaze grow wide and land somewhere near his feet. He looked down.

A small russet-haired boy stared up at him with something akin to awe. He yawned hugely, knuckling his eyes, then stared some more.

"Are you the bloody English fool?"

Beside him, Raymond sputtered with quiet laughter and Gaelan glared, then looked back at the boy, uncomfortable with his intense study.

"Have you rocks in there?" the child said, squeezing his calve above his boot. " 'Tis lumpy." The lad tipped his head to the side. "You've come to kill me, haven't you?"

Gaelan's feature yanked taut and he was about to bend to him when Siobhàn rushed forward, scooping the child up and holding him protectively away from him.

"Princess, I would not harm the child." It stung that she thought he would.

"He is a big one, aye?" the boy said.

"Aye," she whispered as she lovingly stroked the child's hair. "You should be abed."

"Culhainn woke me."

A sick feeling worked through Gaelan's chest. "Who is this child?"

Her chin tipped. "Connal O'Rourke. My son."

His gaze shifted between the two, finding the resemblance. O'Rourke's child. And a prince.

"Did you find Dermott?" Connal asked.

"Ahh, the lamb," Gaelan said with detectable amusement,

and Siobhàn's skin flushed, her cool green eyes hot with embarrassment, yet she did not turn them on him.

"He is in the barn, poppet. Let him sleep there this night, aye?" Connal nodded, disappointed, and Siobhàn set him down, whispering for him to get something to eat, but it was off to bed in a moment. He scampered toward the table of sweet comfits, dodging knights and warriors without thought.

Gaelan's chest tightened at the loving expression on her face as she watched her child. The son of a camp follower and a titled lord, he'd never known such affection. His sire discovered his existence when he was nearly a man and made him a squire with his younger half brother. 'Twas an opportunity he would have traded to be adored by his mother, to have known family and shared affections that bonded beyond the ties of men in battle. Suddenly he missed the precious years with his brother and loathed the ones spent wandering alone.

Are you through wandering, or will you take the purse and leave? a voice pestered. He scowled to himself, cursing the moment of melancholy. He did not belong here any more than at court.

"I will send a man to fetch the lamb," came more harshly than he intended.

Her gaze swung to him, amiability gone. "That won't be necessary. I will find the animal."

He took a step closer and fie the lass, she did not flinch a fraction, but glared up at him. He could not resist goading that insurmountable pride. "I can expect you in the barn later, or shall I attend your chambers?"

She inhaled sharply, her hand itching to slap his handsome face. Rather than give him the satisfaction and debase herself further, she turned away, taking only a few steps before he caught her elbow. She wrenched free. "Is it customary for the overlord to insult his victims, or only me?"

"Do you deny what we shared in the field and in the dark?"

"I seek not to have the entire keep learn of my shame."

She needed their every confidence, she thought, and could not allow them to see her weakness for the knight, or they would believe she was giving them over to serve herself. Which she would not.

"What shame? You are widowed, a mother, not an untried virgin."

Her skin colored and Gaelan felt the tip of her dagger through his garments. He arched a brow, admiring how she secreted the dig with her sleeve and her courage to do it.

"The state of my virtue has little to do with your enslaving my people, does it now, PenDragon?" she condescended. "And I make no invitation to *you.*" Repugnance dripped from her words. "Learn your manners, sirrah, and cease showing your lack of breeding."

His lips curved and she blinked, frowning softly. "Now who is hurling insults?" She made a sound of frustration and Gaelan would have sworn she fought the urge to stomp her foot.

His smile widened and Siobhàn was struck hard how boyish he looked just then. Codswallop. There was not a shred of youthful innocence in this man. She slipped the knife into its sheath and stepped back, suddenly aware of the eyes upon them. "Spare me any more humiliation, PenDragon. Begging for my people is all you will ever gain from me. Ever."

He bent, gazing directly into her turbulent green eyes. "One day soon, my village princess, I will have you begging me for more than the fate of your people."

His thinly veiled threat smarted and her expression told him he was fool to hold such high regard for his prowess.

"Shall I prove it? Here and now?"

"Do you wish to keep your tongue in your head?"

Standing inches apart, his head bent, he spoke for her ears alone, his voice a silken growl as he whispered, "I wish to put it in your mouth, lass. To use it to pleasure your ripe little body in ways you have never imagined. I would hear your pleas for succor."

She reared back, resisting the urge to rub the gooseflesh skipping down her throat. If he thought to conquer her body as well as her people, she would set him a'right and quickly. "By the gods, you are an arrogant man," she hissed, yet images exploded in her mind, of this man tasting her body, making her feel more woman than she had ever felt afore his coming.

" 'Tis a failing." He shrugged without remorse. "It comes with never having been defeated."

She tipped her delicate chin, her eyes glacial. "Then prepare for your first, sir knight. For you will find, as my husband did, that battling on the field cannot compare to a war with me."

Her words slammed him in the chest, not for the challenge, but to remind him how delicate the situation had become. She held the will of her people, and mayhaps a neighboring chieftain or two, as well as the border villages. And short of slaughtering half of them for control, Gaelan knew he had to seek swift domination of the Celtic beauty as soon as possible.

Before she learned 'twas he who killed her husband.

Chapter Seven

Attention abruptly shifted to the shouts and clang of metal to metal beyond the open doors. Music droned to a sick halt, chatter faded. Scowling, Gaelan instantly drew his sword, and around them the knights followed, driving her folk back as a cry of pain rent the air, distant, hollow. Male. With only a glance warning her against rebellion, he caught her arm, pulling her toward the darkness beyond the doors. A soldier burst into the dim light, breathing heavily, blood on his hands, and her people's cries punctured the air.

Siobhàn twisted, warning them sharply to be calm as the soldier and Gaelan spoke briefly.

His gaze flicked to her. "You have a guest, it seems." He leaned near. "Uninvited, I hope, for your sake."

"I hailed no one, PenDragon."

"We shall see," he said, ushering her through the doors into the torchlit yard. Beyond the light, bowmen atop the inner curtain pointed arrows into the yard, indistinguishable figures shifting in the darkness, moving closer.

Irish warriors. Clad in gold and green tartans and fur leggings, they were stripped of their weapons and held back at swordpoint near the inner gatehouse.

Sir Owen and the guards prodded several men on and Siobhàn recognized them as a single fellow stumbled forward, his nose bloodied, his cheek scraped down to the bone. A few feet from her, he dropped to his knees, then tipped his head back.

"Lochlann," she whispered, starting for him, but Gaelan's grip held her back. She leveled him a venomous look. "Let me go to him!" She tried twisting out of his grasp, but he refused. "What harm can he do now?" She gestured to the archers.

"Do not make demands in this, princess. He attacked my patrol on the edge of this castle." Gaelan scoffed. "By rights he should be dead."

"By your rights we all should be littering the ground beneath your feet, PenDragon, but we are not."

He bent, his lips near her ear. "It can still happen," he said and she stilled, wondering what atrocity he'd inflict on them for a purse full of gold. It infuriated her that their lives and homes could be tallied on royal parchment and delivered to such a man at the whim of a foreign king.

"Is this how you treat those who have already sworn fealty to your king?" Lochlann interrupted, struggling to his feet.

Siobhàn gasped, horrified. "Lochlann, nay!"

Lochlann's gaze swept from the PenDragon to hers, a flush of regret in his face. "You have not, I see." He smirked to himself, half admiring her. "I expected as much from you."

Her gaze thinned. "And I more of you, O'Niell."

His skin flushed with anger. "My people still live on their own lands."

"And so do mine." His betrayal stung. She'd have expected such acquiescence from Tigheran, for the last time she'd seen her husband he was off to Dublin to swear allegiance. But not of Lochlann. Though oftimes hotheaded, he was so unlike his half brother; more handsome, younger, with rich, dark brown hair and blue eyes that danced with his emotions. And he respected her position as a leader.

"You have proof of this alliance?" Gaelan demanded.

"With my mount."

Gaelan ordered the horse searched and Sir Mark stepped into the light with a roll of parchment. Gaelan released Siobhàn and sheathed his sword. He glanced at the parchment, then met his gaze. "Why did you not make yourself known to me, O'Niell?"

Lochlann's spine stiffened, his pride already in ruins. "I could match you in a battle, PenDragon; she could not. She is my half-brother's wife and I swore to defend her, as did many clans." His tone warned him of coming trouble.

"You could be hung for this attack, you know."

"Irish blood is thicker than paper." Lochlann nodded to the parchment proclaiming him lord of his own on Henry's behalf. "O'Donnel and the Maguire would do the same. We'd see no harm come to her and her folk."

"Admirable," Gaelan sneered. "But the choice lies with the princess." He looked down at her. "When she swears, the threat will die."

Her expression wreaked of pure denial, though she kept her gaze on O'Niell.

"Henry awarded me my own lands." Lochlann's lips twisted with humorous irony. "Do the same, Siobhàn."

She jerked from Gaelan, coming to face the O'Niell, her hands on her trim hips. She got out two words in Gaelic before Gaelan ordered her to speak English. She sent him a heated look, yet obeyed. She had naught to hide. "See to your own holdings and I will tend to mine, O'Niell." Both understood her implication. His lands and people were sparse compared to hers. She risked the enslavement of more lives.

"Come to Coleraine with me. There, I can protect you from him."

"You cannot protect your own people from rival clans, Loch-

lann.'' She made a sour face. ''And now you have made a deal
with the English devil.''

Fury pulled his features. ''This bastard''—he snapped a
hated glance at Gaelan, who watched them with bland interest—''will return to England and you will have your *tuath.*''

''Nay, some soft lord will have it. *England* will have it!
Swearing to him or to this king will be a lie, can you not see
that? They have done naught to earn this right, this trust. There
is no enemy to protect from, but them!'' She pointed to the
archers and knights.

Lochlann frowned. ''But you let him in without a fight—I
thought—''

She advanced to stop inches before him. ''I spared lives. I
suffer the price of this, not them.''

His gaze swept her, hurried, anxious. ''Has he touched you?''

''You cross the line, O'Niell,'' PenDragon growled behind
her, his patience at an end.

''Nay.'' But Siobhàn feared it would not be long before the
lusty knight took what he plainly desired.

Lochlann's shoulders drooped with relief as he said, ''I worry
you take on too much when there is no hope.'' He brushed a
strand of hair off her temple, fingering it lightly.

She caught his hand, cupping it to her cheek, and behind her,
Gaelan stiffened. ''We have lived on hope afore, Lochlann.''

''England is strong and determined, lass. They will—''

A little shriek bit the air and Siobhàn stepped back as Connal
came running headlong into Lochlann. Gaelan warned his men
not to fire as Lochlann caught the boy, thick bare arms lifting
him high above his head and shaking him like a piglet.

''You are here! We are saved!''

Gaelan's features tightened as Lochlann hugged the child,
then set him to the ground.

Connal glared up at Gaelan. ''Go now. Or Uncle Lochlann
will kill you.''

''Connal!'' Siobhàn gasped. ''Hold your tongue, child!''

Connal pouted up at her and she cuddled him close as Gaelan neared, staring at the boy, who slipped behind his uncle, then to Siobhàn before bringing his gaze to the O'Niell. The Irishman's hostility was unmistakable, but that the O'Niell had his hand in Siobhan's, the boy tucked to his side angered him more than his arrival with forty armed men. They looked too much the family for his liking.

"Come to me, princess." Galean held out his hand.

She took a step, but Lochlann caught her back. "You dare touch her with hands stained by innocent blood!" Lochlann said, hatred in his blue eyes. Siobhàn hissed something in Gaelic and he glared back, his lips clamped tight.

"What I do with her is no concern of yours." He let his gaze linger over her curves before meeting her gaze. "She is my prisoner."

Siobhàn's gaze thinned before she pulled Connal forward and sent him inside to his aunt. She looked at Lochlann. "Go home."

"I will not leave you to this beast! I came for you!"

She turned her back on Gaelan. "Why do you think I am so helpless?" she asked. "You know I will not leave, yet you insult him and he will take it out on us."

"Enough!" Gaelan moved between them, forcing her behind. He focused on the O'Niell. "You and your men may leave, unassisted and with your mounts." He folded his arms over his chest. "Yet weaponless."

When Lochlann looked to revolt, Siobhàn moved beside the Englishman, unable to help her dear friend. "Do as he bids, O'Niell; 'tis generous and you threaten O'Rourke *tuath*."

Something flickered in Lochlann's gaze then, making her frown, for the blaze of his hatred fell on her, briefly, then cleared. He nodded, and sweeping his cloak over his shoulders, he and his men were escorted out. She dragged her gaze from the gate and looked up at the PenDragon.

The suppressed fury in his eyes drove the breath from her lungs.

He leaned close to whisper, "Get inside." He did not give her the chance to gainsay him, pulling her none too gently back into the keep. Every pair of eyes followed their trek through the hall and into the barren solar filled with dust and a desk. The instant they found privacy, she wrenched free and rounded on him.

"Nay!" He advanced, making her step back. "Dare you undermine my authority! I am lord here, not you!"

"I would spare them bloodshed."

"He is sworn to Henry. He raises a sword to me and he raises it to the king!" His expression darkened like passing clouds. "Lochlann O'Niell is a fool to enter here with so many more to keep him out. My men have orders to kill anyone who ventures too close. Count yourself lucky 'twas not his head presented to you!" He backed her up against the desk, slapping his hands on either side of her hips, hemming her in. "Interfere again, woman, and I will separate you from that child and all your people until you learn to behave!"

Her gaze remained locked with his. "I am not a child, sir; do not treat me as one."

"I will until you see reason and swear oath!"

"We have traveled this road afore, PenDragon. I could swear this night, but 'twould be meaningless. You leave soon and another will come and do the same. And I will fight."

And another would take her to his bed, make her his whore, defiling her, breaking her spirit before he enslaved her people. The very idea sent him into a silent rage and he stepped back, clenching his fists. "Do not hold account to rumor or assumption, princess." He arched a dark brow, speculation in his gaze. "This could change as quickly as it has today."

She looked confused for an instant. How much more could they expect? "If you seek to kill me to eliminate the obstructions, then do so." As she said it she knew he wouldn't. She was a plaything still and he was not done with her.

"Do not tempt me." Yet the thought of hurting her to gain her compliance sickened him, just as the thought of her touching the O'Niell had twisted his gut into knots. Jealousy—it could be only that—spirited through him and even as the words left his tongue, he regretted asking. "Do you wish to wed the O'Niell?"

She blinked, then frowned. " 'Twould not change matters atween you and I; I would still rule Donegal."

"You rule no more!" That she would not give him an answer angered him further. "As Henry's liege, I can give you to him."

Siobhàn straightened. "I am not a gift to be handed over, PenDragon, simply because I am female. Nor do I wish a marriage again. With anyone."

He stood inches from her. "You have no choice."

"You just asked me to make one," she scoffed, flicking her hair back over her shoulder. "Brehon law, Englishman. I have the right to deny any suit. The death of Tigheran by the hand of one of your own"—his features yanked taut then—"left me a wee bit vulnerable. Not stupid."

The reminder set his temper on edge and he gripped her upper arms, dragging her up against his hard frame. "You are a foolish woman, Siobhàn O'Rourke." She flattened her palms over his chest, her heart skipping at the unmerciful look in his eyes. "Do you not realize that there will be more behind me? Ambitious, cruel men. Petty Irish kings whom Henry has granted armies! Pembroke and DeLacy argue now over earldoms of Ireland. And only the wrath of Henry himself will stop them!"

"Then I will—"

A cry sounded from behind and Connal bolted, driving his head into the back of Gaelan's knee, buckling his leg. He released Siobhàn, straightening as the child wedged himself between them.

"Do not hurt my mama!" he shouted, staring up at him, his round eyes filled with fat tears.

"Oh, my brave lad," Siobhàn cooed, gathering him in her arms. Connal grabbed her dagger, viciously swiping the air before Gaelan's chest, and she caught the hilt. "What think you to do, son?"

"Kill him afore he kills us." Still Connal tried to reach the knight, grunting with his effort, and Gaelan watched, transfixed by the courage in one so small.

Siobhàn wrestled the dagger free of his little hand, her gaze flicking to PenDragon's. She was surprised to see regret in his dark eyes. He stared as she stroked her son's head, pressing it to her chest. "There, there, my prince. Shhh," she hushed, touching kisses over his soft hair, rocking him. "Your father would have been proud, but the knight will not kill us."

"But Uncle Lochlann said—" The boy yawned, his anger dying with his fatigue.

"I'm saying he will not." Her head tipped ever so slightly, her gaze never leaving Gaelan's. "Will you?"

Gaelan swallowed thickly. He prayed circumstances never forced him to break such a vow and said, "Nay, I will not."

Connal's eyes flashed open, his bravery gone as he wrapped his arms tightly around his mother's neck. "You swear?"

Gaelan could only nod and Siobhàn dipped to sweep her train over her arm, then rushed from the room.

Guilt spirited through Gaelan as he stood outside the chamber door, watching her tuck her son into bed. She looked angelic in her regal garments, crouched on the floor, stroking his hair off his forehead, adjusting the bedclothes. He was envious of the gentle touch, having experienced naught in the past that was not the practiced maneuver of a well-paid whore. And even then, they trembled with fear to the point that, too often, he could not assuage his needs and found relief in the icy waters of the nearest river.

But all he could think now was that she was left in this position, assuring a small boy he would not die and fighting for her home, because of him, not the king's edict. He'd taken her husband from her, Connal's father, when a child needed his sire most. And for this singular moment, it did not matter that Tigheran tried to assassinate Henry, but that he'd died at the end of Gaelan's sword. He'd torn her world apart years ago and now he was here to do it again. A fortnight prior he would not have cared a wit. A sennight prior he would have rammed his way inside, imprisoned her people, and burned the keep to the ground. The thought of doing so now twisted like a fist in his chest. But she was pushing him to drastic measures and if he did not have her acquiescence, he could not tell the king he had control. Nor could he leave.

"You must stay abed, love."

Connal yawned adorably and snuggled into the covers. "I miss Dermott."

"Dermott stinks and will not be allowed beneath those clean bedclothes until he's bathed."

"But he cries."

"As do you."

His chin jutted. "I do not." The boy's gaze drifted past to meet Gaelan's, and Siobhàn twisted.

"I wish to speak with you," Gaelan said.

Siobhàn considered shooing him out, but as irritated as he looked now, she doubted he'd comply. She turned back to Connal, kissed him, then stood and blew out the candle. The odor of smoking tallow burned the air as she crossed to Gaelan, looking back to wink at her son, then seal the door.

She walked briskly toward her own chambers. "Do you not have weapons to sharpen, mercenary? The O'Niell is gone, the feasting is done, your garrisons surround us, what more do you wish?''

"To be abed myself.'' This day was more of a strain than a battle.

She paused on her chamber's threshold, frowning back at him. "Then go, PenDragon. I'm sure my barns will offer more comfort than you are accustomed too.''

His lips quirked in a predatory smile. "Oh-ho, nay, princess.'' He advanced, making her back step into her chamber. "If you think I mean to let you out of my sight, you are mistaken.''

"You cannot think to sleep here!'' Beyond the gossip that would spread, having him so close led her erotic thoughts down paths they'd no right to venture. And what if he should want to share her bed—how was she to resist?

"I do. For you have proven yourself a deceitful lass.'' He unstrapped his sword belt, laying the weapon on a table.

The sight of it, its hilt spotted with blood, reminded Siobhàn of his caliber, despite his handsome face, and to anger him further would cost her much in negotiation. She'd already stretched her will to the point of shattering and tried for civility.

" 'Tis unnecessary. I would not flee without my son. Nor would I risk our lives and leave my folk to suffer your retribution. I swear.''

He eyed her. Her word meant naught to him. "Fine. Then I will return to my tents.'' Her shoulders sagged with relief and he moved to the door, bellowing for Sir Mark and Andrew. They appeared in moments. "We return to camp.'' The knights frowned at him, yet nodded. "We take the child, Connal, with us.''

"Nay.'' Siobhàn rushed to him, gripping his arm. "He is but a babe still!''

Gaelan stared down at her, his expression void of the turmoil he was feeling. The last thing he needed was a screaming child in his camp, but he needed more than her assurances. "He will be treated fairly."

Siobhàn did not believe him. "Please." Her fingers flexed on his forearm. "You frighten him."

Her glossy eyes nearly undid him, and he steeled himself against their effect and remained silent.

"Have you no heart?" she whispered, her beautiful eyes robbing him of his breath.

"Nay."

She thrust away. "Very well. Remain in my chambers," she gritted, then snapped her fingers. Culhainn appeared at the doorway, growling at Gaelan, then sauntering across the room to his mistress. She stroked his white coat and spoke in Gaelic to the animal. "Keep a vigil atween us, and should he move during the night, eat him."

Gaelan frowned, waving off the knights with an order to guard the child's door.

Siobhàn turned her back on the loathsome man, discarding her cape and removing her circlet, rubbing her head, then unclasping her jewels and placing them in a small chest. "What is the king paying you? Mayhaps—?" She tipped the chest to show the wealth inside, her look inquiring.

" 'Tis ten times that worth," Gaelan scoffed, dropping to a wood bench and the task of unwinding his leather cross garters and removing his boots. "I have hundreds of men to pay and house." He looked up, eyeing her from head to foot. "And I have found more than I need right here, for now."

Despite the heat of his look, her chin lifted. "There is naught for you in Donegal, PenDragon."

"And you know my thoughts, my wants?"

She arched a tapered brow. Pillage and plunder came to mind.

"I have more than thoughts of bedding you, Siobhàn."

His plain talk did little to unnerve her this day. "And they are?"

"You will know soon enough." Though he did not know himself, not yet, his mind clouded with the moments of delight he'd found in her arms. He'd time to consider the avenues, for the price of Donegal was higher than he ever afforded. "Your attempts at deterring me will not succeed. Give up."

"Never."

He pried off the boots, stretching out his legs to wiggle his toes. "I am losing my generous spirit."

"You have none. One must have a soul first."

Looking up, he set the boots neatly aside, then stood, pulling his surcoat off over his head and flinging it aside as he advanced. "Well, this heartless, soulless bastard could climb into that bed and share it with you now."

Her gaze remained fixed with his and not the incredibly carved chest peeking through the linen shirt. "You would force yourself on me?"

"I would not have to use force."

The moments below in the hall, his threats to use his tongue and make her beg him to take her beneath him, collided through her mind, warming her skin, stirring her body. "I fear with you there is a faded line atween force and seduction, sir." He was an expert warlord, aware of his enemies' weakest points and battering them till they broke. She admitted it wouldn't take overlong for hers to be burned away in his arms.

Gaelan stepped closer and she did not move. He admired that in her, for she was the only woman, the only person save Raymond, who stood before him without fear. She met his gaze, a storm of emotion in her eyes, and Gaelan's shoulders shifted restlessly. "I will not hurt you, Siobhàn. Can you not see that?"

"Nay, I cannot," she said. "You may not have beaten me, PenDragon, but you seek to rob me of my heritage at the cost of my home and my people."

"I have no intention of packing the lot of you up and sending you away."

" 'Tis preferred to slavery." She jerked off her earbobs and flung them carelessly into the chest, then kicked off her slippers.

His hands on his hips, he assessed her thoroughly. "Have you always been this stubborn?"

"A fault I fear, for never having lost a battle."

His lips worked back a smile. "Save your strength for the morrow, woman. You will need it. Now get to bed!"

Flinching, she moved away, struggling with the laces of her gown, and Gaelan caught her shoulders, turning her about.

She faced him, shoving to no avail. "I need not your help."

"You will ruin it." He pushed her around and held her firmly in warning, then opened the row of cord leading down her spine. She was bare beneath, no shift. That she'd lacked the bit of cloth all evening sent imagines blossoming through his tired brain and he brushed the fabric off her shoulders, his sword-roughened hands lingering over the curves. She turned sharply, clutching the garment to her breast. Trapped in her gaze, he let the back of his hands graze the tips of her breasts covered in green wool. Her indrawn breath filled the large chamber.

"A war with you is most intriguing, Siobhàn."

Her knees softened every time he said her name, husky, as if he wasn't certain he had the right. "I want peace."

He met her gaze. "And what will you forfeit?"

"What will you offer?"

His expression hardened with irritation and he turned away, grabbing a blanket from a stack atop a chest and throwing it before the fire. "You have no right to bargain, Irish." He added a log to the blaze, taking up the iron, stirring warmth into the cold, damp chamber.

"I should sit on a pillow whilst you plow through our villages, leaving a marker to point the way for your damned king?"

He looked up. She was on the far side of the bed, her back to him as she lowered the gown, revealing the slender dip of her spine, a shadowy glimpse of her breast, before she slid beneath the bedclothes.

"I do as I must." Gaelan yanked his shirt off, dropping to the floor and wondering why he simply did not live up to the ogre she claimed him to be and climb into that soft bed with her.

"So shall I." She snapped her fingers and Culhainn dropped to the space between Gaelan and the fire—and Siobhàn and her bed. He eyed the dog, leaning out, but it growled, massive jaws snapping, its pale blue eyes glacial with warning.

His gaze flicked to her. The smug little wench sat like a prim sprite in the center of her grand bed, her hair flowing over one shoulder, the covers at her chin and he knew the delights the bulky fabric concealed. 'Twas the source of his trouble, for once tasted, Siobhàn O'Rourke was a woman no man could ignore. Not and sleep well, he groused, adjusting his position on the stone floor.

"Go to sleep, princess." A pillow hit him in the head. He glanced up, a faint smile softening his scowl as he stuffed it under his head. She flopped onto the down, her body vanishing under the thick bedclothes. Thank the Gods, for if he saw but an inch of skin, he would be on the bed, his body inside hers without thought to the consequences. Bless me for my honor, he thought.

He'd scarcely closed his eyes when a ruckus beyond the door alerted him. He was there, sword in hand, before Siobhàn sat up.

"Reese!"

"Sir, she wants in," came from the other side of the door.

"Siobhàn? Are you a'right?" a female voice chimed in.

The sister, he recognized. "She is fine!"

"I'm to believe you, war maker?"

"Get to your bed, woman, afore I lock you in irons!"

"I will do harm to your squire," she threatened.

''Open the door,'' Siobhàn hissed. ''She will wake the entire keep!''

Gaelan glanced at her, saw her rebellion and gave in, too tired to argue. He jerked the heavy portal open and glared at her sister, Reese blocking her way and wearing only his trunks. Rhiannon grabbed the lad by the hair, and though she was nigh a hand shorter, flung him aside and stepped into the room. Gaelan blocked her path.

''What have you done with her?''

He stepped back a fraction so she could see. ''She is alive and well and nay, I sleep on the floor.'' He looked at Siobhàn. ''Tonight.'' Her color heightened, yet her gaze thinned with angry warning.

''Rhiannon, find your bed,'' Siobhàn pleaded, praying none of the keep knew he was here.

''The people will demand recompense, sister.'' Her gaze shifted to the Englishman. ''You cannot remain in here, knight. Brehon law. She chooses who shares her chamber.''

He looked at the princess. ''Recompense from who?''

''You.''

''And what is this fee?'' Gaelan asked.

''An honor-price to me and my family—''

He groaned.

''—and to the chieftains of the *tuath*, the kingdom.''

''What!''

''If you were to bed her—''

''Rhiannon,'' Siobhàn warned, then looked at Gaelan. ''I forfeit my reputation with you in here. You pay the price.''

''Can you?'' Rhiannon asked.

He swung his gaze to her. ''The question is—will I? And nay, I will not.'' Grabbing Rhiannon's arm, he bellowed for Sir Andrew, escorting her out with more force than necessary. ''See that she remains with the child.'' He propelled her into the knight's arms, then glared at Reese. ''Clothe yourself,'' he growled. ''We are not in camp!'' He slammed the door.

The bedclothes tucked across her breasts, Siobhàn folded her arms and stared. "Are the English not compensated when you cause an accident? An unintentional death? Or like the injury Sir Owen inflicted on me?"

"Aye."

"Then why do you disregard our laws?"

"Because 'tis the cost of war and the king rules here now!" He raked his fingers through his hair, his head pounding.

"You have much to learn, sir." She tilted her head, considering him. "You chose who you fight for, mercenary. Surely there were other battles the king needed your army for? Why did you come here with no plan to remain?"

Only Gaelan's gaze shifted to clash with hers. *Because*, he thought, *I killed your husband and by right of court battle, what is his, is mine.* Yet the words would not come, and it surprised him, this trickle of discomfort running through his chest. But he knew the source, for when she discovered the truth, she'd hate him as purely as she loved her people.

And the thought wounded him down to his blackened soul.

Chapter Eight

Gaelan stirred on the cold floor, still tired. Every time he moved last night, her accursed wolf-dog growled, stealing needed slumber. Rubbing his hand over his face, he stretched, keeping eyes closed, his groin aching with the dull throb of unspent desire for the woman lying naked in the bed a few feet from him. Throwing back the blanket, he sat up, looking around, the sky barely lit with daybreak.

Culhainn was gone.

And so was Siobhàn.

Leaping to his feet, he bolted to the door, jerking it open. Reese turned, his posture straight, his face freshly scrubbed.

"Good morrow, sir." He held out fresh clothes.

"Where is she?"

Reese peered around his master. "Not with you?"

"Would I be asking if she was?" Gaelan glanced back into the room, then ordered, "Find her."

Snatching the clothes, he dressed quickly, strapping on his sword as he strode first to Connal's room, finding it neat but empty, then to the squints, a small portion carved out of the wall of the upper floor wall, enabling him to view the hall. Servants moved in their duties, popping in and out of doorways banking one wall. He'd yet to know where they all led. Where the bloody hell was she? And how did she leave the chamber without disturbing him? Or Reese?

He started for the staircase and heard footsteps.

A loaf of bread tucked under his arm, Raymond greeted him with a black look. "Well, you've made matters—"

"Where is she?" he interrupted.

Raymond's scowl deepened. "The princess? Heading to the kitchens last I saw."

Gaelan braced his shoulder against the cold stone wall, raking his fingers through his hair and rubbing the back of his neck. He frowned at the chamber door again.

Raymond shoved a mug of honeyed wine in his fist. "Damn you, Gaelan, the place is in an uproar about you sleeping in her chamber." He'd settled no less than four scuffles between soldiers and Irish this morn alone. It seemed when it came to defending their princess, the fact that there were nearly a thousand foot soldiers about made little difference.

"She will tell them the right of it." Gaelan watched the activity below, impatient for confirmation.

"You mean, you didn't bed her?"

The mug halfway to his lips, he reared back. "Sweet Jesu, even you?" With Henry's conquest on tenuous thread, the king would have his head if he planted a bastard in the princess when he'd no intention of remaining in Ireland.

Raymond propped his foot on a bench and tore off a chunk of his bread, offering a portion to Gaelan. "You have been known to bed the prettiest wenches after siege."

Aye, he thought, munching on the crust. Before he'd thought little of it if a willing girl gave him a look, but Siobhàn had not, not in the forest nor the stables, and he found he wanted her to admit to her desire, if but once. He wanted her to smile at him, touch him, for being touched by the woman was more pleasure than kissing her ripe mouth. He straightened, shrugging off his fantasies. He'd kissed a peasant then, not a princess.

"Shall we seek out her highness and settle the terms?" Gaelan said. "The sooner the king's work is done, the swifter we are onto the next siege."

Raymond forced a smile and nodded. But Gaelan didn't move, his gaze on the hall below.

Ordering a swine slaughtered for the evening meal, Siobhàn left the cook house, crossing the yard and through the narrow corridor leading back into the hall. She caught a man as he passed. "Sprinkle this on the rushes," she said, pressing a sack into Davis's hand. "And get those flea-bitten hounds out of here." She gestured to the dogs snapping at servants as they passed.

He looked at her, a spark of fear in his old eyes.

"If PenDragon has an upset, then he can clean up after them." Davis snickered and nodded, shuffling off. "Meghan, open the shutters, please. Crowley, the hearth needs a good sweeping, if you don't mind. The men will be about and hungry soon, my friends. We must prepare."

"I don't see why we must feed them."

"We must keep the peace for a bit, Moira," she said to the elder woman with a touch to her arm. "And if a bit of bread and ale will suffice"—she shrugged—"so be it." She rushed to a servant trying to move a table, pulling her away from the chore. "Nay, Jana. Have you no sense?" She nodded to her pregnant belly.

Jana swiped the back of her hand across her brow and exhaled tiredly. "I did not want the PenDragon thinkin' I am not working my share."

Siobhàn hid her irritation. Did he not see what havoc he wreaked with just his presence? "Worry not, friend. What does a wandering knight know of overseeing a keep? Now"—she wrapped her arm about her waist, guiding her from the chore—"I want you lifting no more than a loaf of bread, and in an hour's time I expect to see you resting in the weaving house." She looked at a young man, one of Gaelan's pages. "You there, help move this to the wall." He appeared as if he'd disobey and her gaze narrowed.

"Do it," came a quiet command, and Siobhàn looked up. PenDragon stood at the upper portal, Sir Raymond at his side. Resplendent in a brown leather tunic, he nodded cordially, a strange look on his handsome face. She dipped her head in acknowledgment, remembering how he looked lying on her floor, his features soft in slumber, his beautiful body long and powerful. Then she recalled how much she'd wanted to touch him and she broke eye contact.

The page obeyed, and Siobhàn turned to Meghan, asking her to watch over Jana.

"Mama!" Connal rushed to her from the buttery, smiling happily. She scooped him up in her arms and gave him a noisy kiss. He giggled, then cupped her face, suddenly looking too serious for one so young.

"I feared he would hurt you."

Her love for him doubled in that instant, for his imagination must have tormented him last night. "You needn't, my prince. I can take care of myself."

He pouted a bit. "I am not a prince anymore, aye? *He* comes and takes that."

Siobhàn's heart sank to her stomach and, ignoring the knight's gaze following her like a beam of light, she carried her son to the hearth, setting him in his favorite chair. Kneeling, she gave him a bowl of bread soaked in sweetened milk as she spoke in low tones. "You are a prince of Erin. 'Tis in your blood and will never change here." She tapped his narrow chest. "You cannot allow it, for Ireland's history will be lost to the invaders lest we forget." He nodded solemnly, spooning soft bread into his mouth. "I've work to tend. Behave for Moira, and you may search for Dermott. I trust you will bathe him this morn?" He made a face, then finally agreed as she motioned to Moira. The older woman's sour mood lifted the instant she looked down at Connal. "Moira has chores too, son, so do not think to connive her into games." Connal grinned up at the woman, catching her wink. "You bend to her, not she to you." Siobhàn stood, tipping her head to whisper, "He's to stay away from the English." Kissing her son, Siobhàn left the hall, the morning sun shining through the short corridor beckoning her.

Gaelan watched her go, envious of these humble Irish folk, for their princess gave her love and caring freely, her smiles lighting the dim hall. Gaelan recognized that he had to gain control over her somehow and quickly. Although not a drop of blood was shed, he had lost authority by entering without battle. Without the sworn fealty of the princess, Donegal was not in the king's true possession.

And he wondered which of them would sacrifice the most for this scrap of land.

The sight of his men littering the ward and yard startled Siobhàn, her step faltering. They were fierce in their armor and mail, doing little except watching, prepared to kill at the slightest inclination. Archers lined the parapet, sporting long Welsh bows. Squires cared for knightly accouterment in small groups whilst pages scurried to carry water and meal for mounts, bring food and drink for their masters. We will have our larder stripped in a day, she thought, and how will we survive this winter? The inner ward gates were wide open, which was a regular event for the castle, but the sight of his legions camped in the outer bailey and beyond the curtain wall left her stunned.

Last night, in the dark, the army did not look so numerous. His knights moved from archer to soldier, relaying orders, a few leaving the keep, and she could scarcely tell one from another.

Lochlann was a fool to even attempt an attack on his patrols, she thought, and realized how fortunate he was to be taken alive. And released in the same condition. PenDragon's warning that more would come vibrated in her brain and she wondered at the validity of withholding her oath. Mayhaps if she swore oath they would leave Donegal alone? As they had O'Niell's land? Her heart twisted in her chest. She could not. The English did not believe women owned land or were capable of ruling, and if King Henry possessed her word of bond, he would give it to one of his favored lords. Nay, she thought, continuing across the yard, Culhainn at her heels. Her oath was part of her soul and that she never gave lightly.

Silver-clad knights tipped courtly bows once they recognized her and she had to smile. 'Twas not often she dressed as she had last eve, her simple clothing favored for work. She acknowledged the knights, her intent on the garden behind the kitchens, yet before she reached it, several women blocked her path, the most formidable her sister.

"Well?"

"Good morn to you too, sister."

Rhiannon reached out and touched her shoulder.

"Rhi, please." She ducked away, irritated that her sister felt she could delve into her emotions without permission.

Rhiannon's brows shot up. "He did not touch you." The women surrounding them sighed, relieved for her.

Siobhàn flushed with embarrassment. Apparently there were no secrets in her house. "Evidently he retains a bit of knightly honor still. Culhainn would have eaten off a limb or two anyway," she said with a quirk of her lips, glancing at the women, her friends. "I thank you for your concern." She gave her assurances that the PenDragon said he would not send them all away and Siobhàn would hold him to that. Though she'd no idea how.

"So another is to come and take over this keep in Henry's name?"

"Aye, I believe so."

The women returned to their duties, yet Rhiannon remained, her look suspicious. "He fascinates you, doesn't he?"

"He does not." She brushed past. "He is an unmannerly ox with a pretty face, is all. His fair Raymond is of sweeter temperament."

"Raymond has already bedded a dairy maid, I've heard."

"If she does not come to me with charges, then she was willing." She shrugged. "I do not lend to gossip. And neither should you." She pushed through the gates, closing them after her, her eyes warning her sister to leave her in peace.

She didn't. "What will you do, Siobhàn? Surely you cannot keep such a monstrous man at bay?"

"I will go about my day as usual, Rhiannon. We all must."

Rhiannon threw her hands up in frustration. "How can you be so calm?"

"I am far from calm!" Siobhàn leaned over the gate, her fingers wrapped in the iron bars. "I fear for our kin every moment, but if they witness it, they will surely do something to bring down his wrath on their heads." Her fingers flexed, her worry showing in her white-knuckled grip. "I swore to them I would accept any price from the Englishman."

"Your bravery is misplaced, Siobhàn."

Her brows knitted tighter.

"You will be the last person he would harm."

She was taken aback. "What makes you believe that?" Then her eyes flew wide, her voice a secretive whisper. "Oh, tell me you did not touch his thoughts, Rhi. 'Tis his privacy you invade."

Her features took on her defiance. "He invades our home.

We have a right to know what comes. Do you not want to know what I discovered?''

"Nay! Nay," she added more softly. "Gaelan PenDragon, be he mercenary or pauper, deserves to keep his own counsel."

"He bears a dark secret that—"

"Nay!" Siobhàn shoved away from the gate and walked the path. When Rhiannon called out, she waved overhead, refusing to hear anything secreted in the man's soul.

For naught could be as heinous as the thoughts she disguised.

She was gone.

Gaelan cursed and swung into the saddle. "You did not think she could be sending a message or meeting a conspirator!"

"I assumed you had the woman well in hand, sir, after last evening."

Gaelan's features tightened. That even his own men thought he'd brutalized the princess spiked his already elevated anger.

"She has an escort, sir."

"Aye, hers!" Gaelan ordered the portcullis sealed, the postern guarded, and Raymond and five men to join him. In moments they were riding in her direction. The language barrier kept him from discovering her disappearance until now, and he cursed himself for trusting her even the slightest. Did she not know that her son would be hostage if she did not return, that her people would suffer if she brought an army?

He was but a few miles from the keep when he spotted a village, riding hard into the center road and raising his hand. The patrol jangled to a halt and villagers froze, their children scurrying under carts and wagons. He did not bother conveying his point and dismounted, he and his men moving from house to bakery to smithy, searching. He was about to continue on to the next village when he found her. Or rather Driscoll. He stood before a squat thatched hut, his weapons a'ready.

"Step aside."

He didn't. "She is merely tending a wound, English." The Celt crossed his arms over his chest, his spear in one hand, his short sword in the other, yet held so casually, Gaelan decided he meant no threat. "She would never abandon us, not for an instant."

Gaelan scoffed and pushed past. "Siobhàn!" He could not tell if it was relief or anger spiriting through him when he saw her, unharmed, kneeling beside a small child, wrapping his thin drawn chest in cloth. The odor of sickness and herbs filled the tiny thatched cottage.

"Sweet Mary mother, PenDragon. Hush. You're scaring them," she said, not stopping in her duties.

" 'Tis what I do best."

"One gains more with gentle tones and smiles, Englishman." She glanced back over her shoulder. "Did you not find that upon your arrival?"

Covering the boy with a coarse, threadbare blanket, she spoke to the mother, motioning her close. Gaelan stepped farther inside, listening, though he didn't understand her words. He glanced at Raymond and the knight shrugged. After a fashion, he realized she was showing the mother how to tend the wound herself. The woman hugged her, offering her a crust of bread, and Siobhàn took it, biting off a piece and bidding her good day. Without meeting his gaze, she brushed past and stepped out, mounting her small horse astride and heading out of the village.

"Siobhàn!"

"Aye, mercenary," she said tiredly, reining up, then looking at him.

"You will not leave the castle yard alone."

"I did not. Driscoll has been my protector since before my husband died." She glanced at the Celt, and an exchange Gaelan could not decipher passed between them. "And before the English landed, I'd no cause to need an escort." She wheeled the mount around and sped off, Driscoll behind her, smiling.

Gaelan raked his hands through his hair and cursed.

Raymond eyed him. "You were scared for her."

Ridiculous, he thought. "There are outlaws in these woods, DeClare. And she has many allies."

"You think she left to alert them?"

"She is not to be trusted." He moved to his horse, swinging up. "I want regular patrols made in the area. They are to protect these people from attack."

"Would the outlaws attack their own?"

Gaelan made a nasty sound of discontent. "There are brigands and thieves in every country. Who knows? But I do not want any clans rallying, either."

Gaelan caught up with her in moments, though she didn't spare him a glance, her attention on the land. They rode south of the keep, toward the shore, and he admitted he could not be more curious. She dismounted where the land faded to sand, then trotted down to the water to a group of men laboring to pull a net into a boat. They greeted her with high abandon, one old fellow swinging her around as he hugged her. Smiling, she pinched his big nose and they walked to the others. Gaelan remained back, watching, Driscoll at her side, both conversing easily with the fishermen, ignoring the knights and soldiers as if they were naught but a gaggle of seagulls.

Gaelan examined the coast line, its access and defense, noticing the large boulders and the ruins of a stone building half underwater yards from the shore. Impenetrable, he thought, impatient to be gone. "Why do you check the nets?" he said when she returned to her horse. "What know you of fishing?"

Gripping the saddle, she tipped her face to the sun, a little smile on her lovely lips. Gaelan wanted to kiss them daft. "There are many more mouths to feed, PenDragon. We need food and must portion off a goodly amount for the winter." She looked at him, shielding her eyes. "Unless, of course, you intend to be gone, say . . . on the morrow?"

Cheeky female, he thought. "My hunters will provide enough game."

She scoffed. "You think we have bounty galore, sir?"

"Aye, 'tis a cold, barren place this," he said with a look at the shore.

"And England is not?"

Scowling softly, he met her gaze. "I have not seen much of it."

'Twas her turn to look discomforted. "Did you not live there, have family there?"

"I am alone and I live in yon pavilion, princess, and travel."

She shook her head sadly, mounting her horse and reining around to climb the steep hill. Gaelan felt more pity than disgust in that single look and wanted neither. Yet as he followed her throughout the day, listening to her chat with Driscoll, smile and laugh—ahh God, she had a glorious laugh—he did not like being on the edge of her life, the hated bastard who'd taken away her freedom.

"Where now, my lady?" Driscoll said, uncorking a skin of wine and offering it to her.

She declined with a sweet smile and gestured. "The herders, in the hills."

"I do not think so," came from behind.

She twisted in the saddle, leather creaking. "But I—"

"Nay."

"Why then?"

Gaelan's lips tightened. Unused to being questioned had little to do with his rising temper, for all his mind's eyes could see was her set upon by raiders, her body bludgeoned into the ground, for they were too few to defend adequately. "I do not explain myself to you, woman. Return to the castle at once!"

His roar did little to ruffle her. "I've duties to tend, unless you would care to count sheep and see how many we can spare for the next sennight of meals?"

"I will see that game is provided," he reminded.

"You cannot go about killing a free man's livestock, sir. Most of mine roam until needed. How would you know which is held in tenant and which is not?"

"I suppose I will ask the creature afore I take its head."

Raymond coughed suspiciously.

"To the stronghold, princess." He nodded ahead. She didn't move, irritating him further.

Her brow knitting softly, Siobhàn studied him for a moment. He'd been in a mood all day, the sunshine and warm breeze doing little to soothe it. "What think you, Driscoll?" she said in Gaelic and saw the knight's annoyance rise.

"Me thinks he is afeared for you, lassie."

"Codswallop," she muttered.

"Siobhàn!" he bellowed.

She winced, delivering a sour look. "Must you always shout?"

"With disobedient females who do not believe what I say, aye!"

Hating that he spoke to her like she needed a spanking, she hissed, "Very well, mercenary," then kicked her mount into speed, two of his soldiers joining them. Yet she'd recognized the oddness of PenDragon's look, as if he suspected her of something devious, and it lay in the hills.

Raymond glanced at Gaelan, neither of them following, yet Gaelan's gaze never left her, his scowl softening to a gentle smile with every thump of hooves.

"Enchanting female," Raymond murmured. "I've never seen a woman take your temper with so little thought of the consequences."

"She is a rebellious, stubborn female who does not know her place."

Raymond's smile resisted his smothering. "Then I pray for the king's sake he delivers a strong man to marry her and help her find it, for the princess has no intention of recognizing you as her master. Mayhaps you should write the missive today?''

''There is time.'' He watched her until she vanished from sight.

''When will you discuss the surrender with her, Gaelan. We need be off. DeCourcy wanted us—''

Gaelan snapped a look at him. ''I do not give a fig what DeCourcy wants. And I will find a solution when one presents itself!''

''Then send word to Henry to select a lord husband—''

''She will refuse him.''

''She cannot.''

''Aye, by her laws, she can and she will. And that, my friend, is only one fix we are in. O'Rourke swore his oath with Donegal lands, a goodly portion belonging to his wife and her family in bride price, and his death muddies the water. Aside from needing an English overlord here, Henry wants Donegal's fealty on parchment, quickly, and he does not care if it is in blood. These people''—he waved to the land—''don't have the influence he needs to curry the church's favor. That lies in Meath, Dublin, and Waterford, and he knows it. 'Tis occupation he seeks, and though his liege man might hold the fief in his stead''—he tipped his head to stare at the castle in the distance—''she is in possession.''

''Then someone needs to tell Henry he can't go sending off his lords to marry Irish royalty to gain the land into his control.''

''Would you like to sign the missive?''

''I like my head right where it is, thank you.'' Raymond was quiet for a moment then said, very softly, ''There is another solution.''

Gaelan spared him a mild glance, catching his intent. ''We are here to secure and protect the king's assets, DeClare. Naught more.''

''If you want more?''

For a moment, Gaelan didn't respond except for a tightening around his mouth. "Do not mention this again, DeClare. I know where I stand in this life, and 'tis not beside a princess." He spurred the horse and, sadly, Raymond followed.

Chapter Nine

Gaelan tossed the reins to Reese, asking after Siobhàn.

The lad nodded toward the chapel. "She returned over an hour ago, looking rather well, considering."

Gaelan's brows drew down as he studied the boy and his smug expression. "You expected me to beat her?"

Reese looked away, then met his gaze.

"Have I ever once struck you?"

"Nay, sir."

"Then why would you believe I would beat a woman in my care?"

"I have seen you in battle."

"Where I was fighting for my life, boy. There is a difference when confronting anger. I have learned to control that rage, separate it. And my oath as a knight bids me protect women such as the princess, no matter her country of birth."

"But she disobeyed."

"Nay, I did not forbid her. I assumed she would not leave. The fault is mine."

"Aye, sir."

" 'Tis clear you have a great deal to learn of being a knight."
Reese's posture stiffened, his lips pressed tight. "Aye, sir."
"Be about it, then."

Reese pulled the great stallion along, frowning back at his
master.

Gaelan glanced at the chapel, resisting the urge to seek her,
though he knew she was avoiding him, and crossed the field
to the inner ward, familiarizing himself with the grounds. The
castle was in a sad state of disrepair and he must inform the
future lord aforehand, for the cost would certainly deter a man
seeking wealth and fortune in Donegal. His lips quirked without
humor as he paused at the inner gate, looking about. The fellow,
he thought, would be well and duly shocked. 'Twas a thriving
place, but it lacked the pomp of court, the extravagance of
English castles, the excessive amount of servants. Gaelan had
always thought that a waste and made the titled soft, expecting
more than they deserved. Although it was that greed, he thought
with a smattering of truth, that usually drove the men who
employed him to fight their battles.

In the distance, he heard the smithy's hammer, smelled the
aroma of roasting pig. Around him hearty souls rushed past,
giving him a wide berth, as if he was not there, yet their
eyes told their feelings, their distrust and hatred. His shoulders
moved restlessly against feeling aught but his duty. He'd
delayed long enough. He'd rarely been inside a castle, more
often beyond the curtain wall and ramming her doors open.
And this would have been an easy assault, he thought. Though
the wall tower was manned, only his men lined the wood
parapet walk and were scattered over the outer ward field. The
inner ward held only a handful of soldiers, for it had been
Gaelan's experience that people scared for their future accomplished little work.

He squinted toward the north tower, then noticed a woman
standing a few feet away, patiently waiting for him to notice

her, a lumpy cloth in her hands. He acknowledged her with a nod. "Mistress."

"Hungry, m'lord?"

"Aye," he said with feeling, eyeing her bundle.

Her smile was tremulous, her eyes crinkling despite her obvious fear as she stepped closer and unwrapped the cloth. She lifted out a steaming meat pie, dropping it into his hand, then dipped a curtsey and dashed off toward the kitchen. Gaelan smiled, tossing the hot pie from hand to hand, yet he was too hungry and the smell too inciting to wait. He devoured it where he stood. A young girl ventured close, carrying a bucket. She dipped the ladle deep, offering him sweet milk. Gaelan drank, swiping the back of his hand across his mouth and thanking her, eyeing her as he handed back the ladle. She remained so, staring up at him, letting him look his fill of her pale bosom nearly spilling from her bodice. Then she glanced past him, her eyes rounding before she took off. Gaelan turned and found Siobhàn walking toward him.

His heart slammed into the wall of his chest. Sweet lord, she was beautiful, he thought, enjoying her sultry approach. She'd discarded the coarse work clothes for a simple gown of deep blue, delicately trimmed in silver and clinging to her lush body, yet the same girdle of leather and silver cradled her hips.

His gaze lingered over her curves and he saw her lips press tight with annoyance. He kept looking to spite it.

"Are you satisfied enough till supper, sir?"

She'd sent the cook with the pie. The simple gesture was like an arrow through his breast, bleeding him with a painful need he'd never experienced before. He'd had women do things for him, most who were sharing his bed, and he paying for the privilege, but never an act out of simple kindness. And especially not from a woman whose home he'd seized.

"I am. My thanks, Siobhàn." How could just looking at her send his heart thundering up to his throat?

"You are welcome, sir."

He sighed deeply. "Can you not call me Gaelan?"

" 'Tis best not to grow familiar."

He leaned closer. "I have held you in my arms, touched your body, kissed your mouth, Siobhàn. I would say we are already familiar."

With each word shame swept her features, and Siobhàn lowered her gaze. "Please. That was another . . . time." Another woman.

" 'Twas but yestereve you put your soft little hands under my shirt and played—"

"Cease," she hissed, bright spots of color bursting on her cheeks as she glanced left and right to see who was listening.

"Is it because I am a bastard?"

She was taken back. "Of course not. 'Tis the English who attach such a title. There are no bastards in Ireland, sir."

He frowned.

"A child does not pay for the fault of his sire. A woman can have a child for any man she chooses and the child born without the protection of vows is still seen to by all, his comfort assured in livestock even before he greets the world."

His brows rose. "Who pays for this assurance?"

"The father to the mother and her family."

"And if he refuses? Or does not acknowledge?"

"There is a penalty for ignoring one's responsibilities on both sides. A father not acknowledging his child shames himself in cowardice and shames the woman."

He looked thoughtful, glancing around at the folk.

"Your king calls us lewd, uncultured. We are not barbarians, PenDragon. We do not drink the blood of our dead, kill children too weak to survive, hold rituals on the hillside. Though . . ." He looked at her. "I admit we're a superstitious lot."

He smiled, a slow pull of his lips that lit his dark eyes and robbed her of her next breath. There was something different about him just then, a brightness in his eyes she'd never seen before, as if something was reaching inside and stirring him.

"Do not forget the magic."

She eyed him. "You do not believe it exists, I can tell."

"Nay, I do not."

Her lips quivered in a tiny smile and his heart thumped with anticipation of seeing it in full bloom. " 'Tis well that you will not be in Ireland long, then."

"I will remain as long as it takes to gain your oath, Siobhàn."

Her lips thinned and he recognized the spark of anger in her strange green eyes. "We cannot fight you, you know this. Why must you insist on my oath to Henry?"

"I may be Cornish born and a mercenary, Siobhàn, but I am knighted by Henry. 'Tis my duty to gain it."

She scoffed. "You are the worst kind of man to me, Pen-Dragon." His heart did a painful drop at her words. "A man who lives by spilling the blood of others, for others. You take land and lives for no justice of your own."

His features yanked taut, his brows drawing down. The look was menacing, almost terrifying, and for an instant she thought he would strike her.

"In my soul, I cannot swear to a man with no purpose but gold. In my *soul.*" She struck her chest, once and hard, her voice waving with the strength of her emotion. "Do you understand this?"

He didn't, by God. "You would see your people enslaved rather than become serfs to some lord."

"Nay, I would see them live as they have. 'Tis I who will suffer the price, PenDragon. Me alone, and they know this. Imprison me, beat me, do as you wish. My people belong to your king by strength." She flicked a hand to encompass the army trespassing her home. "I belong to Donegal."

To belong somewhere, Gaelan thought enviously. To call a plot of land home so fiercely was beyond him and he was desperately trying to understand. But still, he had a task to accomplish and his duty was to King Henry first. "You have yet to sign terms, princess."

"You have yet to present any that are just and fair."

Damn me, but he wanted to shake her and clenched his fist against the urge. "Your folk will not bend unless you do, then I cannot have them as vassals nor can they be trusted to follow the lord's orders."

"I see you are still in a bit of a fix, then." She would not make this easy for him.

Gaelan fumed, his temper foaming near the edge of boiling. "By God in heaven, woman, you force me when I do not want to hurt you!"

She tipped her head. "Only last night you said you would not. Are *you* not to be trusted?"

Gaelan raked his fingers through his hair and swore foully.

Siobhàn inhaled, retreating a step, and he straightened, gazing down at her for a long moment. She winced when he barked a command for his soldiers.

They surrounded her.

Driscoll rushed forward, his sword drawn. "Nay, Pen-Dragon!"

"Lock the princess in the tower."

Siobhàn's eyes widened. "Nay, I've work to do!"

"It will go undone then." He flicked a hand and the soldiers grabbed her arms.

Her people revolted, racing to her, and she shouted in Gaelic. They stilled, their gazes shifting between her and her captor. She looked at him, jerking her arms free.

"*You* do it, PenDragon."

Gaelan didn't touch her, yet nodded ahead. Siobhàn walked and people stepped back to let her pass as she entered the hall. She paused, her gaze scanning them briefly in warning not to take up arms before she moved swiftly to the stairs. She caught Moira's eye, a silent plea to not let Connal see this, then continued on. To the tower. She passed her own room, taking the narrow staircase leading toward the sky. A single door stood open, a place her son often went to play. Inside was a musty pallet tossed in the corner, a stool and chests of Tigher-an's garments. Gaelan stepped inside and ordered the guards to remove the trunks. Siobhàn surveyed the room, then moved to stand before him.

She pried a key from her girdle and held it out to him. "You would not be wantin' me to escape, would you now?"

Her lips bore an odd smile as Gaelan accepted the key, then stepped closer, unfastening her girdle full of keys and charms and jamming it inside his tunic. "Nay, I would not." He turned to leave.

"Do not take this out on them, PenDragon. Swear to me."

He looked back at her, his eyes as cold as the wind skating across her beloved home. "I swear to naught, princess. Until you do."

Siobhàn turned her back on him and he sighed, closing the door. Beyond it, Gaelan fell back against the wall, mashing his hands over his face. He did not want to do this, God above, he did not. But her compliance was a necessary part of turning the lands over to Henry's liege. He had to have her obedience. She was a proud, honorable woman and only an oath would bind her.

Yet even as he walked away, Gaelan knew one way to gain control without it—and the price was too high. Even for his king.

They spat at his feet as he passed, crossed themselves if they happened to meet his gaze. Little work was accomplished, the keep in utter chaos. Rhiannon was even less help, hiding off with Connal, he supposed. He couldn't find them. Gaelan recognized that the work progressed because Siobhàn encouraged them with her smiles and warmth and strength.

She refused him each time he came to ask for her oath, not

uttering a word, but simply giving him a blank look. On the second day he thought she would surely break her silence. She was hungry, he knew.

"Eat," he said to her back when the old man Davis brought her a meal.

She didn't turn around, staring at the floor.

"Think of your son then."

Her gaze jerked to his.

"Nay. I have not seen him." The alarm on her face was enough to bring him to his knees. "Rhiannon has taken charge of him."

Her shoulders fell and she moved to the only window, its shutter loose on its leather hinge and sagging pitifully. She sat on the window casement, her hands folded, and stared out the window at the yard below.

She looked the fairy queen Reese was so fond of describing, he thought. The sun blistered the floor around her skirts like a pool of water, dancing off the silver trim of her kirtle. The cool breeze lifted her hair across her face, shielding her from him in a veil of deep red mist, making the bells tinkle softly. Gaelan ached to go to her, to plead with her to give him what he needed, what he must demand, for the sake of preserving her people's lives. But she wanted naught of him and his kind. She hated everything about him, hated enough to refuse food and refuse to fight her imprisonment. He almost wished she would throw something at him, for her fire was preferable to this unending silence.

"Siobhàn, lass."

She shifted again, a move so subtle he might not have noticed. But he noticed everything about this woman. She'd paled, her skin a little less rosy. Guilt swam through him. He'd done this before, he'd forced submission from a dozen traitorous earls, Italian counts, even a moolah, but naught affected him more

than the wasting of this princess. Gaelan took a step inside
and, without looking, she sensed it and stiffened.

His anger flared. "Eat, princess. Or I will force you."

She turned her head. "When you leave, I will eat."

"Good." As he backed out of the room, he heard, "When
you leave Ireland, savage."

He hesitated, then shut the door and locked her in.

Siobhàn watched from the tower as PenDragon rode through
the gates, his destrier's powerful legs prancing majestically.
Her gaze followed him as he tossed the reins to Reese and
stormed across the yard. The lad darted out of his path, lest he
anger the man further. PenDragon yanked off his gauntlets and
dunked his head in the rain barrel, snapping it back, then shaking
like a dog. His hands braced on the barrel's rim, he tipped his
head back, and the yards separating them from ground to tower
and across the ward, closed.

Her heart did a strange twist in her breast. He looked
exhausted, dark smudges under his eyes making them look like
the caverns of a soulless man. His gaze thinned in a speculating
way she'd come to know and he arched a dark brow, asking
the question he'd put to her daily. She shook her head. He
flung himself away and strode to the armorer. Though she could
not hear his words, the thunder of them sent people scattering.

For the past three days he'd done this, riding out and returning
hours later in no better mood than before. And each time he
was alone. She knew he'd not found a village girl to bed, or
his disposition would hopefully be a sight less ferocious, and
she wondered what he did out there without a single man-at-
arms or knight in his company.

Not a soul passed through the gates who was not inspected,
nor was anyone allowed to leave. She might be in the tower,

but her people were prisoners as well and Siobhàn was terrified she'd push him too far. With one incident, he could slaughter them all. It was best to keep silent then, for everything she did, apparently, angered him. And there was only absolution in death.

In the darkness of the tower, she wondered if 'twas her pride forcing her against him or her heart. She did not think she could bring the man to his knees with a fasting or silence, yet he had to understand that he could not treat her or her people as if their wants did not matter. She rubbed her arms, the wood provided long ago burned to naught but white ash. She missed her son, wanted to hold him, but the Englishman denied her even a glimpse of her precious little prince. 'Twas worse than being denied food. She gained strength form Connal, from his unconditional love. And she needed it now. For her feelings for the knight were crowding the needs of her people.

"Nay. Do not bother to translate," Gaelan said tiredly, his hand up, his gaze flicking to the baker holding a stack of bread loaves and delivering a vicious glare that would normally grant him a thrashing, then to Siobhan's man Driscoll. "The Maguire."

Driscoll clasped his hand behind his back and nodded.

'Twas the talk and he only now had heard it enough to understand the meaning. *Pòsaim*, marriage, *grà*, love. If another soul mentioned the Maguire and his undying love for Siobhàn, he thought he would explode. It grated down his spine worse than the thought of her up in the tower without food and her family. Her silence was driving him mad, shoving him between anger and bitter regret. And he wondered—over and over until he could barely speak without growling—if she loved this chieftain.

Gaelan waved off Driscoll, who'd taken it upon himself lately to follow Gaelan about, especially when he visited Siobhàn.

Raymond strode to him. "When will you release her?"

"Never." A lie, he knew.

"She will die."

"She will bend."

"Sweet Jesu, Gaelan, can you not see by now how determined she is? She is protecting thousands of women and children. What do you expect from her?"

Gaelan stared, his gaze hot with impotent anger. "I expect her to see she cannot win and concede defeat. I expect her to value her own life as well as the others here. I expect her to obey and not present herself as a royal Irish pain in my arse!"

"Gaelan, listen—"

"Nay! If she wishes to die on mere principle of defiance to me because she loathes what has brought me wealth and respect, then so be it!"

"And you will kill her for an oath that when sworn would be meaningless." He stepped closer, his voice low and private. "You have the bloody castle. You can make them do your bidding. Yet you punish only her? You must earn her oath."

"I do not need to earn it. It is mine by right!"

"Not if you want it from her! You must find another way or kill her!"

God. He could not. Gaelan shoved past. "You are my second in command, DeClare, not my advisor. Hold your tongue!"

Raymond grabbed his shoulder, forcing him around, and Gaelan fumed with scarcely suppressed rage. "Fight someone who has a chance of besting you, PenDragon. Not a woman with only her pride left to bargain with."

Siobhàn stirred from one of several naps to the clash of steel to steel. Scrambling to her feet, she pried open the shutter. Her breath filled her lungs and she watched him wield the sword, slashing over and over, driving Sir Raymond back and being repaid in kind. In a human ring in the outer bailey, they were surrounded by his troops, and when she expected them to shout encouragement, there was only the deadly silence of concentration. The clang and clash made her wince, and her heart pounded, never having witnessed so honest a battle. This was not training. This was rage. And they wore no armor, no mail, yet only PenDragon was bare-chested.

He fought, his muscles gleaming with sweat, his exposed skin revealing a body honed in war, in the letting of blood for his bounty. It sickened her, this mad profession, but her breath still snagged in her chest when he came close to being hacked to pieces.

Sir Raymond, nearly as tall as his opponent, struck blow after blow, but PenDragon was fast and accurate, catching the blade and thrusting him back. Then with a growl of pure anger, Raymond brought his sword down in a smooth arch. PenDragon blocked it with the shield. The wood and metal fractured, the tip of Sir Raymond's sword slicing down the Englishman's side. They stilled and Raymond said something to Gaelan, jammed his swordpoint into the dirt, and threw down his shield before walking away.

Siobhàn saw blood running down PenDragon's side and staining his braies. She rushed to the door, pounding, and when none responded, she tried the latch, shaking it mercilessly. The ancient hinge gave and she blinked as the door swung open, then ran down the staircase at full speed, passing her guard, who was watching the fight out the arrow loop, and raced outside. Her people cried out in surprise but still she ran, her head dizzy from lack of nourishment, yet she gathered her skirts to her knees and pushed past soldiers and into the ring.

The area cleared for her and he looked up, scowling. His gaze snapped to the tower, then to her.

She took a step.

"Stay back!" he roared, his hand up, his rage at a dangerous level.

"Do you seek to kill your friend?" She glanced at Raymond, winded and angrily pacing off near the cluster of horses, then back to Gaelan. "When 'tis me you wish to hurt?"

Gaelan's gaze shifted, his stare leveling her from beneath a lock of brown hair. He looked tormented, a beast struggling with his private demons.

"You cannot wield a sword, or I would." It would be the only way he would win, he thought.

Siobhàn walked toward him, desperate to keep her feet steady when her head felt as if it were about to topple off her neck with dizziness. His chest rising and falling with exhaustion, he held his sword limply before him. Her gaze dropped to it, then rose to his face. She stepped closer, and his eyes widened as she carefully pinched the sharp blade and pressed the tip to the hollow of her throat.

The voices around them went silent. He tried to lift the sword, but she wrapped her fingers around the blade.

" 'Tis what you want, is it not?"

"Damn you, princess." A single move, Gaelan thought, and he'd slice her fingers off. "Let go."

"Drive it home, PenDragon."

"Nay," he said, as if she were mad.

She leaned, and a drop of blood wept on the blade.

His gaze shot between her eyes and the razor-edged sword. He swallowed thickly. "Siobhàn, lass, please." Gaelan's throat worked. "Step back and release the blade. You will lose your fingers."

"Will you be satisfied then? Will my blood, my hand, a limb satisfy you so you will not hurt those who care for your life?"

"You know that is not what I wish."

His wish she could not grant. "Have my folk revolted against you? Have they not bent to your presence? Have you been denied aught that comes from Donegal?"

I am denied the greatest prize, he thought in the recesses of his brain, his gaze on the blade and his focus to keep it steady. "Why do you test me like this, Siobhàn?" There was hint of pleading in his voice.

"I want only what we deserve, PenDragon. Respect for our home, our ways, our heritage in our surrender—before you bring more English."

His gaze searched her beautiful pale features. He'd never seen such courage in a woman before, so willing to accept punishment for an entire settlement. Had she done this to prove none would do aught to anger him with her life at risk? "You have gained it this day, Siobhàn O'Rourke. I will do what I can, for I can no more wound you than I can have . . ."

Her hand flicked open and she crumbled to the ground. Gaelan threw down his sword, catching her before her head cracked on the ground. Swiftly he lifted her in his arms and strode toward the keep, his gaze never leaving her pale drawn face. He willed her to waken as citizens followed, rushing to do his bidding as he called for water, bread, and broth. He carried her to her chamber, kicking open the door and laying her on the bed. Culhainn growled, snapping at his legs, but Gaelan ignored the beast and sat on the edge of the bed, pouring a cup of water and tipping it to her lips. She stirred, sipping, then sagged into the coverlets.

"You are an amazingly stubborn woman, Siobhàn." And brave and intelligent, and she made him feel insignificant, made him feel a tremendous need when he did not want to feel. Made him hurt when he thought he no longer had the capacity. He warred between wanting her so desperately his arms fairly throbbed to hold her close and hating her for showing him how ruthless he'd become when faced with such unyielding determination.

Her lashes swept up and his chest constricted at the turmoil in her eyes. Her voice broke as she whispered in a gravelly voice, "I am prepared to discuss terms, Sir PenDragon."

Gaelan sighed, dropping his head forward.

And in doing so, he didn't see the tear slide down her temple and melt into the pillow.

Nor her silently mouthed words—begging the forgiveness of her ancestors.

Chapter Ten

Bathed and freshly dressed, Siobhàn's stomach was full, her energy restored. Though she was not the least bit tired, having napped far too often in the tower for God to approve, she could not resist holding Connal in her arms and singing him into a needed rest. She was thankful he had not witnessed the scene in the ward, and laying abed with him, his little arms about her neck, his warm body pressed to her side, she was reluctant to leave. For the inevitable awaited her downstairs.

From her spot in the large chair near the window, Rhiannon cleared her throat. Siobhàn met her gaze, then followed the direction of her nod. He stood in the door frame, filling it with his height and width, and she was struck at once by how handsome and commanding he was. A shame, she thought, kissing her son and shifting out from under his hold. Connal sank into the bed with a deep sigh. Dermott wiggled into her warm spot and Connal slung an arm around the lamb. She smiled gently, touching her son's red-brown hair, then drew a breath before facing PenDragon.

"I am ready."

He dragged his gaze from her child to her, blinking as if in a stupor, then nodded sharply, stepping out and waiting for her to walk ahead of him. The instant she appeared belowstairs her friends rushed her, whispering what a brave woman she was, how proud they were of her, and what an awful beast PenDragon was to her.

She held comment on the last and they scattered like frightened mice when he appeared behind her. Ignoring the bitter amusement dancing across his features, Siobhàn walked to the solar, Tigheran's rooms, and thought it fitting that the end of her old life begin here, for in this same room her marriage contracts were signed, and in this room, he had announced his intention to go to Dublin to swear oath to the king. She knew it was not for the sovereign's greater power, but what the allegiance would gain Tigheran, that the king would grant him armies to crush her uncle Dermott MacMurrough—as if her marriage of peace meant naught. He, like PenDragon, preferred making war to his home. And wars like they made had taken her parents, her brother, her chance for happiness.

She swiped at the dust on the desk, reminding herself to clean the room, wash away what was left of her husband before the new lord attended. Suddenly, she sank into a chair in the corner, as if just realizing that yet another stranger would ride up to the gates and install himself in her home. She swallowed the thick knot in her throat. PenDragon might not cart them all off to who knows where, but this new lord could. She looked up at him, where he stood near the window, his arms folded over his chest, gazing through the precious glass Tigheran had paid a ransom's worth of silver to have shipped from France.

She wanted to be away from him, from this chamber and the memories it brought. She glanced at the old bed tucked in the alcove and shivered with revulsion, images of Tigheran, his body pounding hers whilst he called out another woman's name—of him taking maid after maid within earshot or even view of her. She jerked her gaze away and said, "I've five days' worth of chores to be done, PenDragon. Where is your list of terms?"

"He is coming with them."

She arched a brow, eyeing him from head to foot. Still wearing his sword, he was attired in naught but braise and a dull white lawn shirt, his boot cross straps laced over his legs to his thighs. The fabric clung like skin, offering the twist of corded muscle, and the mere sight of him moved strange feelings through her and her skin flushed hotter than usual. And when his breath escaped in a soft rush, she sensed all was not well with him.

"Are you not satisfied with my compliance?" She really shouldn't test these waters again, she thought.

"Aye." Then why did he feel as if he was beating it from her?

Sir Raymond entered, immediately taking his seat, rolling out a piece of parchment, and at Gaelan's gesture began reading off the dictates of King Henry, her fallen position, how many of her men were expected to attend him in battle, the tenant paid to his liege; who could marry whom without royal approval. It made Siobhàn ill to hear it.

"Why does he speak this misery aloud?" she interrupted, jumping to her feet. "I can read."

"I cannot."

She blinked up at him and blurted, "I can teach you whilst you await this new lord."

He turned, his gaze on the floor, his arms folded. "I am a bit old to learn."

"Codswallop." He looked up and oh, sweet Mary, the tormented regret in his eyes made her wonder if he was at all pleased that she was signing away her life. Then she gasped, "You're bleeding." She rushed forward, pushing back his arm and tugging the shirt from beneath his sword belt.

Raymond stood, his face gone a bit paler.

"It needs attention."

Gaelan glanced at the top of her head, frowning at her concern. "My squire will see to it."

"Like he has with that." She pointed to the jagged scar running up his forearm. "Or that?" She nodded to the scar inches from the one bleeding where the stitches had broken during the healing and he had not bothered to have it resewn. "Sit, sit," she commanded, shoving the tall carved chair back with her foot and forcing him into it.

"Gaelan . . . I . . ." Raymond started.

"Be useful instead of stuttering, DeClare." Raymond's lips pulled into a thin line she didn't see. "Ask Meghan for my herb basket, cloths, and a bowl of warm water. Quickly!"

Raymond left, the hated parchment left on the table.

"Take off your sword and shirt."

Gaelan smirked with amusement and did.

Siobhàn inhaled and slid to her knees. The three-inch cut steadily seeped blood. "Did you not think to cover it to stop the bleeding? Mary mother, PenDragon." She pressed his shirt to the gaping slice. "For a man with such prowess on the battlefield, you act the fool."

Gaelan scoffed to himself, unable to take his eyes off his latest source of foolishness.

Meghan entered, stopping short at the sight of the bare-chested man, then rushed to her mistress, depositing the items on the desk and nearly tripping to get out.

"God's bones, but they act like scared rabbits around me."

She pushed his arm back out of her way, and with a fresh cloth, washed and examined the wound, prying at it with silver tongs. "Mayhaps if you did not look as if you wanted to snack on them, this would change."

"It does not matter."

"If it did not, then you would not make comment."

Irritated with the truth, he snapped, " 'Tis a scratch, woman."

"I gave you a scratch in the field, sir. This . . . 'twould not bleed so well if it was—ahh, and this is why." She plucked a sliver of metal, holding it up to him before tossing it aside. "I think Sir Raymond will need a new edge to his weapon."

"That will please him," came bitterly.

She threaded a needle. "Something must, for your swordplay did not."

" 'Twas . . . a bit of practice."

She heard the falsehood in his tone and paused before saying, "From the look of your scars, sir, you could use a bit more of it."

He chuckled softly and her gaze flashed to his. For a second they stared, frozen, Gaelan recalling the rage in himself, at her stubbornness that pushed him to battle his dearest friend. She broke eye contact and looked down, taking a stitch, blotting the wound as she did.

Gaelan continued to study her.

"Siobhàn . . ."

"Hum?" She took another stitch.

"I . . ." What did he want to say? That he regretted locking her away, regretted pushing her to the point that she would lay down her life for a few words. Or that he wanted her, what this land, these people had when he still did not know what it was? *Ahh God, why do I torture myself like this?* Her warm cheek pressed to his ribs, jerking him from his thoughts as she wrapped a strip of cloth around him.

"Heavens. You are huge," she muttered, stretching her arms to reach around him, then tying it off. Gaelan caught her chin, tipping her face to his.

"My thanks, princess. I have never been tended by one of royal blood."

She scoffed and tried to pull away, but his hold refused.

Gaelan stood, grasping her upper arms and pulling her to her feet.

"Careful." She pressed her hand to the wound. "You will open up again."

"Open up to me, Siobhàn."

She stiffened with understanding and flattened her hands to his chest. The feel of his skin, cool and smooth beneath her palms, was exquisite, fogging her senses. "Nay," she managed.

"For a moment, lass, you are not the Irish princess. I am not the invader. For a moment, we are as we were in the field, in the barn . . . strangers."

She gazed into his liquid dark eyes, seeing the heat of his desire before she felt it against her body. Beyond the partition, the hall was filled with people, their noise coming to them, the clank of platters and the cry for ale and food.

He gathered her against him.

"Nay, PenDragon. This will not help." Her voice wavered and Gaelan would swear she was close to tears. He tipped her chin and found her eyes glossy.

"Why not?"

"You are the enemy. I cannot betray them all for my feelings. Not now."

"And what are these feelings?"

Desire, whispered through her mind. " 'Tis useless to speak of them."

Gaelan's throat tightened sharply. His heart, thundering at her touch, now raced and heated his blood further. "You loathe all that I am."

Her shoulders shifted. "Aye."

"But you desire me."

"Nay."

He read the lie in her eyes. "Say it, Siobhàn. Once afore I leave here, say it."

"Aye," she choked, refusing to let tears fall.

Gaelan bent, his head nearing. She was still, a little helpless sound escaping. He swallowed it, drank it into himself, his lips moving in slow deliberation over hers. The sound came again, a fracture in her shield, and it left him weak to hear more. He tasted her, sweeping his arms tightly around her slender form and pressing her to his length. She moaned, a telling sound of a passion she kept capped and away from all who knew her, all who only saw it when she defied him and denied a king. Her hands shifted, rubbing over his bare chest, her thumbs rasping across his nipples. Gaelan's knees buckled and he slumped to the edge of the desk, pulling her between his thighs.

His hand swept down to the base of her spine, pressing her softness to his groin, and she shifted against him, restless, impatient. A tiny bit of surrender. Gaelan thought he would lose control right then, twist about and take her on the dusty desk. Instead, he tore his mouth from hers, his lips searing over her face, her throat, bending her back over his arm and nipping at the swell of her bosom. Her fingers sank into his hair, and suddenly she brought him back to her mouth, kissing him with all the heat she held, all the moments of desire she'd crushed. Her tongue pushed between his lips and he clutched her, wildly mapping the contours of her spine, her buttocks.

In the privacy of the solar, whilst the world moved on around them, Gaelan savored the delight of having her for one brief moment. He was not good enough for her, undeserving. She hated him, hated all there was about him, yet here, she desired. Here, he could touch the purity of her and feel clean and untainted by the blood on his hands. Here, he was worthy of her. She was innocent and giving and warm in his arms, her fingers singing through his hair, touching his features with a wildness that ached for release.

Screams filled the air, tearing them apart. Gaelan frowned, releasing her, grabbing his sword and moving to the partition. He shouted for silence, searching for Raymond or Driscoll. Then a trumpeter hailed, the sound quivering through the walls from the gates and towers. Her eyes flew wide and she looked at him. He was already at the doors. She ordered everyone inside and the keep doors sealed before she grabbed her cloak and followed.

Gaelan ran, his sword slapping his thigh as he barked orders for the inner gate to close behind him. Siobhàn slipped through, lifting her skirts and dashing after him. A patrol crossed the stone road, hooves clattering until they met the ground of the outer ward. Sir Owen slid from the saddle, slipped off his helm to address Gaelan.

"An army comes," he managed, winded.

"A garrison?"

"Nay, but enough, sir."

Five knights surrounded him, awaiting orders. "All troops to arms. Send men on horseback to gather the folk living outside. Take them, if they protest." There were hundreds living in clusters beyond the outer curtain, serving the needs of the village and castle, and he would not have a single soul harmed when he'd sworn to protect. Ordering the tower watch doubled as well as the archers at the arrow loops and along the parapet, he ran to the parapet, foregoing the staircase in the stone tower and climbing the scaffolding. He surveyed the area. With the sea at their back, they were vulnerable on three sides.

"PenDragon!"

He turned and peered over the wood rail. "Get into the keep, woman."

She reached for the wood ladder. "I can take the stairs, but then, I will be very angry by the time I reach you."

Gaelan smiled to himself and as she climbed, he caught her about the waist and lifted her to the ledge. "Your stubbornness will get you killed," he said gravely, still holding her waist.

"Then mayhaps you should leave Ireland."

"Mayhaps you should simply obey me?" His lips curved, the smile too genuine, pricking through her ire.

The devil take him, she thought, throwing off his hands even as her heart tripped. "Who is it?"

"An invader."

She sent him a side glance, her lips twisting wryly, then moved to the edge. She squinted, unable see aught but the rolling green hills.

Gaelan walked the parapet, relaying orders, and as the carts and horsemen rode inside, depositing villagers, Siobhàn hailed them by name, motioning them to the inner ward. The gate closed like a snapping jaw and she looked at Gaelan. Already donning a shirt and leather-padded tunic, he spoke to his knights and soldiers as Reese helped him into his armor. Where she expected him to garb himself completely, he donned only the breast and back plate, shoulder and vambraces, as he had in the forest. He placed his helm on the ledge, its fountaining plume noticeable for a half mile, and she expected 'twas his intention. The face shield was down, molded in the fierce snout of a dragon. It made her skin crawl. Today she would see him as he truly was, a man who lived by the skill of his sword, spilling blood to earn his pay.

He loaded a crossbow, the muscles in his forearms and hands flexing as he pulled the bolt into position. He had the strength to snap her neck in those hands, she thought, yet those same rough, scarred hands had been gentle on her body, in her hair. Unfamiliar feelings tripped through her body, sympathy and understanding for his harsh life crowding with the price she would eventually pay—they would all pay—for the sake of his fee and King Henry's greed.

She turned back to the wall, cursing her weakness. Torches flamed to add light before the sun fell too deep. Then she saw them. Riders. Over a hundred at least, cresting the hilltop. No banners flew. They neared and she gripped the edge of mortar and stone, praying the PenDragon lived up to his reputation.

He moved up behind her and felt her fear. "Who is it, Siobhàn?"

"The Maguire."

Gaelan squinted. "I will have O'Niell's head for this!"

She twisted a look up at him, yet his gaze lay on the

approaching army. "Lochlann had no time to warn him. Maguire lands are to the south. He had to have ridden for two days to get here now."

He met her gaze. "Why is he here? He is sworn to Henry, princess." Her crestfallen look kicked him in the gut.

"You lie!"

"I will give you the chance to ask yourself. Before I kill him." He moved away, ordering the archers to load weapons, the doors secured.

If Ian had not sworn, PenDragon would open fire. If he was Henry's man now, Ian would be, at the least, severely fined and, at this tender state, could lose his lands. The Irish warriors rode down one hill and up another, spreading out around the entrance to Donegal castle. With the crossbow, Gaelan stood atop the wall, making himself a target.

"Sweet Mary mother, PenDragon, get down."

He looked at her, smirking. "Careful lass, one would think you care if I live or die."

She scoffed. "Go ahead then. God pities fools."

The leader pushed his cloak back off his shoulders.

"Why do you come, Maguire?" Gaelan called.

"I speak with the princess."

"You speak with me or die now. As a sworn vassal of Henry, you break your oath coming here armed for battle."

"I have sworn to no one."

Gaelan could feel her I-told-you look.

"I come for the princess, not to attack, PenDragon."

"That did not stop you three days ago."

Ian's brows drew down. "What do you accuse, English?"

Gaelan withdrew a scrap of fabric from inside his tunic. "Deny this is your plaid?"

"What are you talking about?" Siobhàn hissed but Gaelan ignored her. "Is that from the day in the field?" She tried to get a look at it. "For if so, I will tell you now, 'twas not Ian's men."

"That time they were masked as well, Siobhàn."

That time. The blood on his armor, his sword the day he arrived, she realized. " 'Tis a mistake. I know these people!"

Gaelan shot a bolt at his horse's feet.

The horse reared, and as Ian sought control he yelled, "You know 'tis mine."

"I could have told you that," Siobhàn snapped.

Gaelan fired a heated look at her and motioned her into silence. The fool woman was pushing a wood box close to stand on. "Stay back," he warned. She didn't, leaning over the edge.

"Ian Maguire!" The man's gaze jerked to her and his relieved smile was blinding, killing Gaelan's compassion. "What have you done? 'Tis true? Did you attack his men?"

"I am not a fool, Siobhàn. I cannot defeat Henry's army and neither can you."

"I do not have to! I did not raise arms to him. I swear you are still so reckless."

"Siobhàn," Gaelan warned. She waved him off like a bothersome child, and his patience at an end, he hopped down and strode to her.

"I would not risk your life, Siobhàn," Ian said.

"You risk it now, all of ours." She waved to encompass her lands. "Why are you all so willing to die?"

"For you, love, I would."

"Oh, Ian," she moaned, and beside her, Gaelan's scowl turned black.

"Let him have Donegal, Siobhàn. Come home with me, marry me. I will see you safe."

Yanking her back, Gaelan leaned over the wall and shouted, "If she weds anyone, Maguire, 'twill be me!"

Chapter Eleven

A hundred pairs of eyes snapped to him, stunned by his declaration.

"What?" Siobhàn gaped up at him. "But you leave!"

Gaelan heard the horror in her voice, felt the shallow depth of his station, yet kept a careful watch on the man below as he spoke. "Did I not tell you the situation could change?" Gaelan had never allowed his emotions to rule him, but greed pushed him. Greed for more than his worth, unexplainable to a man who'd needed no one, had wanted no ties, especially to a woman—for she, this rebellious princess, was beyond anything he imagined. Yet he'd known what he wanted the moment he'd laid eyes on Siobhàn O'Rourke and laid his mouth to hers.

He would not be denied.

Ian's expression turned molten, his hand on the hilt of his sword. "She won't marry the enemy."

"You challenge me, Maguire?"

Archers took careful aim.

"Ian! Nay! Do not!" She gripped the stone ledge. His men would all die!

"You wed him and you betray Ireland," Ian warned, his voice steely with suppressed rage.

She gasped, deeply stung. "I wed no one and you risk the king's anger."

"I do not bring the enemy into my bed and his blood into our clans!"

Siobhàn reddened, her gaze thin and pricking. "I have not, Ian." Curse men and their foolish pride. "I choose whom I wed, Ian. You should know that by now!"

Ian's handsome features stretched taut.

"Enough!" Gaelan hauled her against his side.

"Let her go, PenDragon!" Ian raised his arm, his archers ready to return fire.

PenDragon's men aimed. "I give you one warning, Maguire." He looked down at Siobhàn, his voice low. "War or peace is in your hands, princess. Agree to wed me or there will be blood shed. The Maguire's the first to spill."

His ultimatum infuriated her. His threat to her oldest friend tore through her very soul, scraping away the tenderness she'd experienced in his arms only moments before.

She stared up at him, her world teetering on the brink of war. To submit to him in wedlock would bind her forever to the enemy, forcing her to obey his commands and his desire. And to reveal her secrets. Yet she'd already sworn to take any punishment there was to give. Marriage to the beast would be enough to assure her place in heaven, she thought maliciously, then thought of Connal, his future so uncertain, his inheritance lost until this moment.

His arm flexed at her waist and her gaze flew to his.

"I want no other, Siobhàn." His lips quirked with a touch of arrogance. "And your body tells me what you desire."

His gaze flicked down to where her hand rested on his chest, her fingers unconsciously moving over his armor as if 'twere his skin.

She quickly dropped her hand. "Aye, Englishman. For the sake of my brethren, I will wed you." And he will live to regret it.

Gaelan schooled his features, the venom in her tone slicing him like a blade, but there was no turning back now. His future was set. "Tell him." He inclined his head to the Maguire.

Stoically she pushed out of his arms and stepped onto the wooden box, gazing down at her friends. It took every ounce of will to speak the fatal words. "I wed the PenDragon."

Ian cursed, his despair palpable. A rumble of discontent filtered through the keep, from the warriors prepared beyond the walls. "He threatens you, doesn't he?"

"He would not have had to, Ian, if you had not come to war."

Ian's expression fell into utter sadness and regret.

"Say no more, Siobhàn." Gaelan watched, alert for the slightest signal.

She looked back over her shoulder. "There will be stipulations to the marriage, PenDragon. Do not look so pleased."

He studied her for an instant, wondering what she had brewing in that sharp mind of hers, but as his wife there was little she could do to him. "We will discuss them later." He looked back at the Maguire.

"Let him go unharmed."

The broken plea in her tone was unmistakable and he could not look at her, could not bear to see the tenderness she bore the chieftain, and for an instant thoughts of her heart belonging to the man, sharing kisses with him, or mayhaps a bed, plagued him. Gaelan nodded gravely. "For the sake of my bride, you may leave unharmed, Maguire. But arrive again armed to do battle and I will give you what you wish."

Ian's gaze shifted from Siobhàn to the warlord, his expression defeated as he nodded once and wheeled his mount toward

home. Siobhàn watched him until he and his army were naught
but darker shadows on the night-blackened land, then, without
a word, she turned away from PenDragon and walked to the
west tower, descending the narrow stone staircase leading into
the outer ward. She stilled when knights bowed to her and she
glanced back over her shoulder to the man on the parapet.

"Give me time to tell my son."

His features shifted, as if just realizing she did not come to
him alone; then he nodded. Siobhàn walked toward the keep,
soldiers and her folk stepping back to allow her passage. Villagers whispered prayers and sympathy for her. Suddenly she
grabbed handfuls of her skirts and ran, to the home that was
no longer hers, hiding the tears she ached to shed.

Two hours later, Gaelan entered the solar, his brows rising
high. The room was scrubbed clean, the furniture arranged. In
the far left, near the hearth, stood a large bed. Did she think
to keep him sequestered here?

Raymond cleared his throat and Gaelan glanced, motioning
him inside.

"I have sent for the priest." Gaelan frowned. "He should
witness this, be prepared to gainsay any demands."

Demands. Siobhàn had made enough already, as if he did
not hold her life in his hands. "Have her man Driscoll attend;
Brody too, if she desires."

"You do not wish to speak with her alone first?"

"Aye, I will," Gaelan said, with a glance at the bed.

Raymond made himself a place at the desk, setting inkwell
and sand carefully to the surface. He racked the papers and
dipped the quill. "Mayhaps now you will have the time to
learn to read."

"I don't need to."

"Ahh, but you will, for you have to appoint a steward, a
sheriff, and it would not harm Reese to be schooled a bit more."

Gaelan twisted, arching a brow. "You are pleased with this,
I see."

Raymond looked up, laying the quill aside. "Aye."

Gaelan studied his somber expression, detecting a hint of laughter in his eyes. "You may leave Ireland, if you wish. I cannot stop you from earning your keep as we have." He turned his gaze to the window, a tinge of regret inching through him, wiped away with her image.

Raymond had no intention of going anywhere. Ireland pleased him and more so, to see what transpired between his friend and his new bride. "Will you be happy as lord of Donegal?"

Gaelan scoffed nastily. "The only one who will be pleased is King Henry."

"You lie," Raymond said softly and Gaelan's gaze snapped to his. "You have all you need and more here."

"Aye, a people who issue prayers to God when they see me and a bride who loathes the man I am."

Raymond propped his elbow on the desk surface, his chin on his fist. "She did not appear repulsed in the barn, Gaelan."

Gaelan's lips tugged a fraction. Nor was she here earlier. But much had changed. He was forcing her into this marriage. And though Gaelan had never in his life expected to wed, and certainly not Irish royalty, he knew there was no other way to gain control. Possess the princess and her people would follow. He returned his gaze to the window, to the little garden he could see behind the kitchens. Neat rows of seedlings struggled to push through the rocky soil and he could tell the garden was tended with a loving hand. Could he find that caring for this pile of stone and wood? Would he grow tired of the mundane and thirst for battle again?

In the silence of his mind he admitted he'd garnered more of his share of doubts since his declaration, and though he did not regret it, he questioned his ability to be lord and master over villagers and families when he'd commanded only coarse, violent men for so long.

And to do all this with a bride he had forced?

You are the worst kind of man, PenDragon. Letting the blood of others, for others.

Would she change her mind now that any fighting he did, he did for her and her folk? And what, God help him, would she do when she discovered he had killed her husband?

A rustling sound drew his attention and he turned his head. She stood on the other side of the room, Driscoll and the priest behind her.

"I wish to speak with you in private, my lord."

My lord. God above, he hungered for the moment when she would say his given name.

Raymond stood, inclining his head to the others.

"You mentioned stipulations, princess." Gaelan flicked a hand toward the bed. "Is this one of them?"

"Aye."

"Nay."

She moved around the desk, closer to him, her fragrance spiraling up to greet his senses with heather and spice. Soft and womanly she was, but her eyes, her posture, were layered with northern ice.

"You have me by threat, PenDragon, and no other reason, understand this well," she hissed in a low voice. "I swear to perform my duties as chatelaine, offer the people a united front, but I will not share your bed and—"

"Nay," he interrupted. "That is unacceptable. We *will* share a chamber and a bed." She winced at the words. "And what transpires behind the sealed doors is our concern alone, yet afore your clan and my men, you will appear the wife in *every* sense." His meaning could not be more clear. "I will not bring shame to this castle nor my name."

She scoffed, "Any more than pillaging across the country has?"

Damn her! "I do not pillage, steal or rape! I am paid well enough to lay siege and ride away."

"Not anymore, PenDragon. This county and castle offers

little fortune for tributes to your king, men for battle, and now you must see no others lay siege. For now—'tis yours.''

Slowly he shook his head, her gaze trapped in his. She was still, her spine so stiff he thought it would snap. " 'Tis ours, Siobhàn. *Ours.*"

A flutter started in her breast as he neared, his eyes glowing with an emotion she wished she could decipher. Jager me, she knew so little of this man she would call husband. But in marriage, she could watch him, curtail any injustice to her people.

"Your marriage vow binds you to me more than an oath to Henry." And he would gain it, he thought, someday, he would. "Now what say you to my stipulations?"

She stared at his chest, feeling helplessly trapped, her words barely audible. "I will share a chamber, but I ask that you not take me as . . . as your true wife"—she lifted her gaze—"until I am ready."

The fear in her eyes slapped him. "I am not ruled by my lust," he snarled, turning away.

"What rules you then, my lord? For 'tis not your heart."

He jerked a look at her, stung. "Do you think I have no feelings, Siobhàn? Do you think that because I live by the sword, I cannot feel the loss of a comrade? The pain of a wound?"

Instantly contrite, she moved to him, laying her hand on his arm. His hard flesh flexed beneath her touch, the lines bracketing his mouth tight.

"I beg your forgiveness." He melted a little. "That was thoughtless of me. I know not what is in your head or your heart—"

"You swore afore I did not have one."

"The subject is still in debate, m'lord." Her lips twisted wryly. "I know being strapped with a bride you did not want—"

"Who said I did not want you?"

Her heart skipped at his softly growled words. "You do so for compliance."

"Do I?"

Her eyes sparked with anger. "Do not play games with me, PenDragon." She put distance between them. "Raymond tells me you have always had this choice, that the king wanted you here as border lord."

"Raymond should hold his counsel." Gaelan had a dozen reasons for not wanting to remain, the foremost his part in her husband's death.

"At least he is honest to me. Had you done so, then—"

"Would you have wed me willingly?" Her hostile expression warned him not to seek what was not there. "Would you believe me when I say that I am tired of warring and wish to cease?"

"Nay."

He scowled.

"You were quick to threaten war on Ian."

He loomed closer. "I replied to his threat, Siobhàn."

"Ian is trustworthy, my lord, but I will argue that at another time." When she told him of the raid before he arrived, she agonized, stepping away.

As much as he wanted to gather her in his arms and tame her with a kiss, he did not, his thoughts centering suddenly on the Maguire and what he meant to her. He dismissed the uncomfortable notion. She was his prize and he would keep her.

"Are we in agreement now?"

Reluctantly she said, "In this private matter, aye."

"You have more?"

"There is the honor price, my lord." She stepped beyond the partition and motioned. In moments Raymond, Driscoll and the friar stepped in. Friar O'Donnel was a round little man, red-cheeked and thick-fingered. He clasped them around a stack of books, grinning hugely at everyone, even Gaelan.

The friar dropped onto a tall stool and reverently opened the books. With Driscoll near the entrance as if to guard against a fleeing bride, the friar read the contracts of marriage and the price Gaelan must pay to have her, brehon law strangely blended with the church's rule. Then he learned Tigheran O'Rourke had been married before and put his wife Devorgilla aside for her betrayal with his enemy Dermott MacMurrough, Siobhàn's uncle.

"Do not look so disconcerted, PenDragon. I have been the price of peace afore."

He arched a brow, a sick feeling working through his chest.

"Devorgilla was kidnapped by Dermott MacMurrough, but the truth was, she summoned him to take her away. Tigheran put her aside, as was his right by brehon law, but he was not satisfied, warring with O'Connor on MacMurrough. To stop the killing of my clansmen, I married Tigheran."

A sacrifice. A hostage in wedlock, and the similarities twisted his gullet. "By this brehon law, you could have refused."

"Oftimes the church and the needs of the whole shadow such choices," she said in a dead voice.

Once again she was atonement. But now that the wheels of his future were in motion, a thought occurred. "Siobhàn?"

She lifted her gaze from where she was reading over the friar's shoulder.

"We will be bound in a marriage of Christian law. Do not think to end this sacrament on the whim of ancient rules."

The friar grinned, his eyes merry, but the look evaporated the instant his gaze swung to Siobhàn's.

"I would have your agreement now, lady."

'Twas his voice that bruised her, like a mortal blow through her breast, and though his expression was sharp and carved with impatience, his tone bore the entreaty of a man asking for more than ecclesiastical sanction, but a weary voice filled with deep longing and afraid—aye, she assessed again—afraid to voice it. It touched her to her very soul, this emotion she never thought he possessed, and she wondered how deep it ran and what else lay hidden beneath his coarse exterior. Yet with the request, the tiny spark buried inside her flamed, the same burning ache she had when she'd come to Tigheran with the hope of something more than a marriage of bargains and peacekeeping. Though she was well and duly trapped by PenDragon's authority from the king, and had been, she admitted, from the moment he set foot in Donegal, she clung to the prospect that mayhaps in this marriage they would one day find even ground to stand upon.

"Forever in the eyes of God, then."

Gaelan's shoulders relaxed, yet he remained wary. God and her heart were not one in the same, he knew, just as he understood this woman was not so easily won with words. And in that instant Gaelan wanted her respect more than he wanted Donegal.

He gestured to the priest to read on. O'Rourke had paid her and her family *coibche*, bride price, and a sum to her each year until the twenty-first year of their marriage. Naught was returned to his family if the marriage did not survive on his account, half returned if 'twere Siobhàn's fault. And since Irishwomen owned land, and Tigheran's bride gift to Siobhàn was half of Donegal, he unjustly swore to the king with his portion.

Gaelan's lips quirked. "You are an expensive bride. Are you worth it?"

Her eyes narrowed. She found no humor in this. "The judgment will be yours, m'lord." Siobhàn waved to the priest and he read her assets. He'd listed no more than household goods before Gaelan cut him off.

"I do not care what she brings to this marriage."

"My lord, other than her lands," the priest said. "You gain a great deal—"

"Nay," he said and moved to stand before Siobhàn, gazing down at her. He could see the confusion in her eyes, in her beautiful upturned features. He liked it. "I care only that she brings herself."

Her breath skipped into her lungs, a soft sound caught behind her lips. "We must discuss Connal, his future—"

Fear. Untold fear lay in her eyes and he realized she thought he would foster him off to an English lord. A discarded bastard himself, he could not steal from the boy all that was stolen from him. "He stays with his mother."

Siobhàn's eyes burned, her relief so tremendous she thought her legs would fold beneath her. Was he conceding to her demands save one because of his sudden need to have Donegal for himself? She still was not certain why he chose to remain and become the king's border lord, for it would bring him little wealth and much work. Jager me, this man confused her. He could scowl like the devil and threaten lives one instant and grin like a child with a mouthful of comfits the next. He rattled her composure so often, she was in a constant battle with her mind and her body. But knowing that Connal would grow up around her, she wanted to throw her arms around his broad neck and kiss him daft.

And the look on his face said he knew it.

His smile was slow, sultry. His eyes were bright. He raised his hand and touched the tip of her nose, letting his fingertip slide down to peel her lower lip open.

She nipped it. His eyes flared, and beyond them Driscoll exchanged a frown with the priest, then looked at Sir Raymond. The dark-haired knight set down his quill and folded his arms.

"When will this marriage take place?"

"On the morrow."

Her eyes flew wide and he lowered his hand.

"On the morrow," he warned, then leaned close to whisper in her ear, "Have this one night of privacy, Siobhàn. When the sun sets again, you will be mine."

He bowed to her, made his mark on the contracts and left.

* * *

Her rooms had been penetrated last night.

"PenDragon!"

Siobhàn stared at her chamber, then down at Culhainn. "You have gone soft for him that you did not alert me?"

Culhainn hung his head in shame.

"Betrayer," she said, and pointed to the door. Culhainn slunked out, his fluffy tail dragging the floor. She moved to the piles spread about her room, lifting a length of the most beautiful cloth she had ever seen, the darkest red shot with gold threads. She sanded it between her fingers, imagining a kirtle made from it or a tunic for Connal. Her gaze slipped over the trunks spilling with spools of thread, extravagant fabrics and trims, the tiny chest of gold coins, another of jewels in colors and gems she'd never seen before. The foot of her bed was weighted with a stack of ermine and fox furs as tall as her son.

"You screamed?"

She spun about, clutching her dressing gown to her throat. His cat-with-a-mouthful-of-bird look irritated her. "What is this?"

"Your bride price, my lady."

She smirked. " 'Twas to be in milch cows, PenDragon." Her people could not eat the fabric and gold.

"I did not think you wanted dung littering your floor, and the braying would have woken you." And she'd looked so damned inviting then, he thought. Naked, and quiet.

"Oh for the love of St. Patrick, PenDragon." She flicked a hand at the chest of coins. "This is too much."

He was surprised. He'd never met a woman who made such a fuss over too many gifts. " 'Tis *coibche* for the next twenty years, Siobhàn." And it would never be enough, he thought, letting his gaze linger over her thinly clad body, her hair wild from sleep, her dull worn dressing gown too large and slipping off her shoulder. He imagined waking up tomorrow morn and seeing her like that. "I would hazard this is all worth more than twenty cows."

She scoffed, her lips curving. Aye, 'twas worth Donegal and the lands beyond, she thought. And he knew it. "What am I to do with this?" She gestured to the coin. "I have nowhere to spend coin."

He wasn't going to mention he would take her to England to spend it if she desired, for the subject was too tender to prod. "Then store it in the tower room for Connal's future. He will need to be educated, and tutors cost money."

Her expression softened for the briefest of moments. " 'Tis your fees."

His brows furrowed. "Do not refuse, Siobhàn. I cannot change the king's proclamation any more than I can change the man I am, nor the manner of my living."

"I know that," she said, vexation in her voice. " 'Twould do well for such blood money to do some good for the less fortunate."

His lips flattened into a thin line. 'Twas a reminder that though she might be wedding him in a few hours, she still loathed the past he carried.

"Do as you will, Siobhàn. I do not care." He should have known a few trinkets would not soothe the strain between them. Gaelan only wished he knew what would.

At dusk, Gaelan knelt beside his bride as the priest laid his hand over hers, sprinkled them with holy water and recited vows. Clad in the deep green of her land, she took his breath away. Her head was circled in silver, the cape of her heritage draping her slim shoulders. He watched her face, the eyes that could not lie, and though she spoke in a clear strong voice, absolute rebellion lit her magnificent eyes. Yet this time, it amused the bloody hell out of him.

And when he stood and faced her, taking her hand and

slipping a band made of rare bluish green stones so like her eyes on her finger, he knew this was only a small step in laying claim to his wife. She stared in awe at the ring, then frowned up at him. He did not give her a chance to speak, a truly wise decision considering the sharpness of her tongue, and in a hall filled with English and Irish, he swept her into his arms and kissed her until she sank against him and drove her wonderful fingers into his hair.

Ahh, he thought, this she cannot fight. And Gaelan Pen-Dragon, Lord Donegal, knew exactly the path to travel.

Chapter Twelve

Rhiannon watched her sister kiss the English knight, her eyes widening at the heat the battling pair emanated. Sweet merciful, she thought, blushing for her sibling's sake. She had never seen Siobhàn act so, never knew that, in her always-with-matters-in-hand sister such fire lurked. Her gaze darted to Driscoll, his openmouthed look bespeaking his shock. She nudged him. His jaw snapped shut.

Raymond DeClare grinned from ear to ear. Friar O'Donnel rocked back on his heels, bending a fraction as if to see daylight between the pair, then laughed to himself. The couple parted sharply, but the Englishman held her close still, and although Siobhàn blushed, Rhiannon recognized the look in the PenDragon's eyes. Pure, raw desire. She had seen it once before in a man and directed at herself. And the like had boded ill for her own life. She prayed it did not for Siobhàn's. She deserved so much more. She glanced down at Connal, tucked at her side, but close enough to touch his mother's skirts.

His hatred for PenDragon was palpable, his tiny fists clenched at his sides and thumping his thigh. She bent to him.

"Oh sweetling," she whispered. "This anger will do you no good."

His gaze jerked to hers, hard and pinning for one so young. "I hate him. He makes Mama marry him when she does not want to."

"She has no choice, Connal. King Henry is stronger than all of us, and PenDragon is his power. If he declares it, it will be. Besides, the church gave him the right to come here."

"Then I curse the church."

She inhaled, squatting. "Dare you blaspheme, child?" she hissed. "What will your mother do?"

"She has *him* now," he sulked.

"Nay, love, nay. She needs us now more than ever, for she is forever bound to the PenDragon. And so are we. Do you understand, if she loses us, she will be alone and heartbroken?"

Connal's expression fell into shame. "I still hate him."

"Aye, and 'tis your right. But do not let your mother feel she has not done justice to us. For 'tis she who will gain his wrath. *Tuigim?*"

"Aye, I understand." He bowed his head, and when next he looked at her, he showed himself the true prince of Ireland with his trembling smile.

She straightened. "Ahh, that's my favorite nephew."

Glancing up, he eyed her from beneath a shock of hair the shade of baked apples. "I am your only nephew."

"Are you now?" She looked shocked. "Then I supposed that's why you are my favorite." She tickled him under his arm and he giggled, cringing, then looked up at his mother.

She reached out and touched his hair as she always did, and Connal made himself smile for her, loving her with all his heart, and when her sad face turned happy, he knew his aunt was right. He would be good so the PenDragon would not hurt her, he promised. If he did, Connal would find a way to kill him.

Siobhàn tried moving away from him, but he clasped her hand and brought it to his lips. She was fascinated with the play of his mouth over the back of her hand, and the shameful desire stirred in his arms—renewed through her body, coloring her cheeks.

"Wife," he said, thoroughly possessive and sending a tingling skipping merrily down her spine. "United afore the people," he reminded her, and her features sharpened a fraction.

Gaelan did not push his fortune and faced the crowd.

Siobhàn looked up at him, then to the hall filled with familiar faces, and smiled brightly. A cheer rose, mostly from his soldiers and knights, and the latter swarmed them, wishing them well as she was passed from man to man and kissed, then deposited with great flare before Raymond DeClare.

He grinned hugely.

"Your smugness irritates, sir."

"I know." Catching her shoulders, he lightly kissed her cheek. "Patience; he is new to this lording life," he whispered before stepping back.

She glanced at PenDragon, thinking he "lorded" over her rather well, then eyed DeClare. "Codswallop." He chuckled deeply as she turned to PenDragon. He took her hand, leading her back onto the dais, the tall carved chairs of lord and lady replacing the priest's altar. She and her husband stood before it. Then she noticed his knights assembled along the west wall, then their dress, long belted blue tunics bearing the PenDragon crest.

"What goes here, PenDr—husband?" she corrected at his warning look.

"You will see," he tipped to whisper.

Raymond DeClare unrolled a sheet of parchment, and from

her position Siobhàn could see the flowing signature of the king and his great seal. Reese brought a small table and took up the dipped quill, holding it out for Gaelan. Siobhàn leaned out to watch.

Bending with quill in hand, Gaelan looked at Siobhàn, sketching her slender form from the obstinate tilt of her head to the dainty tip of her slippers, and prayed to God that she was worth his freedom. The quill hovered; then he put his mark to the paper, sealing his future.

The knights roared with applause and cheers.

Siobhàn blinked, shocked and confused.

Sir Raymond stepped forward and read the script. "By the will of his royal highness Henry Plantagenet of England, Wales, Cornwall . . ." Siobhàn listened carefully as DeClare listed the king's holdings. "Hitherto, Sir Gaelan PenDragon places his mark upon this, he accepts the duties of liege lord to King Henry the second, to protect and serve the good of lands Tyrone, Coleraine and Donegal to the north, to secure the border to the sea, the duty and position in reward for saving the life of his sovereign." Siobhàn inhaled and her husband glanced down, a look of scattered pain passing over his features. "Hitherto he is instructed to pay tribute . . ."

As DeClare read on, Siobhàn crooked her finger to her husband. "You did not truly need me as a wife to gain Donegal for yourself, did you?"

Gaelan caught only a hint of bitterness lacing her words, and although he knew a great deal more lay beneath, he chose to ignore it. During the night he'd mulled his decision a hundred times, recognizing the price of his freedom—to battle for whom he chose and not be at Henry's beck and call—against the responsibility of so many families, so many futures. Previously, only men moved in and out of his ranks at their own will, and in his service they risked their lives willingly. Now these people depended on him to keep them fed, housed—safe.

His mercenary life had ended when he claimed her for his

bride, and though at the time it seemed a rather simple solution—command her and command her people's loyalty—he could not let her know that he wanted Donegal because he wanted her. He did not understand it himself, this emotional chaos he felt whenever he was near her, thought of her, but if she knew she had sway over him in the basest of ways, he would be lost. He reminded himself that, with the exception of a few shared kisses, she detested him and his past, and staring down at her, said the words he knew would make her see the benefits of marriage to him.

"I am a different man than O'Rourke, Siobhàn. I bid you give us a chance afore you judge me."

Siobhàn blinked, rearing back a bit. His softly whispered entreaty made her aware of passing quick judgment and mayhaps a bit harshly, but her feelings were of little consequence right now. Maintaining the health and future of Donegal was. She looked down suddenly, thinking of the time she'd be forced to reveal her deceptions, and fear slipped over her skin. Would he cast her out then? Would he take his reaction out on her folk?

". . . referred to as Gaelan PenDragon, Lord Donegal. And should he take a bride . . .".

Siobhàn's brows rose and she leaned out to look at DeClare. "She, Lady Donegal."

Gaelan glanced. "A princess to a lady, I apologize for the step downward."

Siobhàn's smile was faint with determination. "It matters only to me that we rule as I have."

"We?"

Her eyes narrowed in a side glance. "Do not start with me, husband."

Gaelan grinned. " 'Tis the beginning, lass."

The Irish folk mumbled among themselves as they sought Driscoll to translate DeClare's words. A single knight moved before them, withdrawing his sword. At her questioning gaze, he smiled reassuringly, then nodded to the knight. Sir Owen went down on one knee, his sword hilt clasped, the blade point in the rush-covered dirt floor.

He bowed his head. "As a vassal of King Henry, upon this weapon, I swear before God and my liege, to honor and serve my lord's wife as I will my lord. And lay my life down to protect hers."

"Let us hope it does not come to that, Sir Owen."

He looked up and smiled as the other knights laughed among themselves. The priest blessed him and he stood and bowed. Another, then another filed past, swearing to her so easily she was stunned. Then came DeClare. He withdrew a tremendous sword, the top third of the blade serrated, the hilt glowing with gems. He knelt, head bowed and hand's clasped, recited his vow.

Gaelan stepped forward, laying his hand on his head. "All within these walls and to the end of the province, hear now, Raymond DeClare of Pembroke is my voice when I cannot speak, my sword when I cannot wield." He glanced at Siobhàn, his features gentle with hope. "And when I cannot, he holds the honor of my lady's champion."

Siobhàn's throat closed, her gaze shooting between Pen-Dragon and DeClare. Her husband's men showed their loyalty to her when she had not earned it, vowed to protect when she would have rather seen them banished from Ireland. With the speaking of vows and a mark on parchment, they were now her people. The gathering of English and Irish touched a bruised spot in her. Was she holding her fealty from PenDragon simply because he was not Irish? She'd already lost her power in wedding him, for through him, she was obligated to the king. Was she withholding her oath to protect herself? For without a barrier, she would fall vulnerable to his charming smiles, his handsome face and magnificent body her fingers craved to touch. She jeopardized more than her heart in joining with this man. She could easily lose her soul.

Before she could think on it overlong, Driscoll stepped forward and spoke to her in her native tongue. Gaelan's eyes flared briefly.

"We are one clan, Driscoll. This we must accept as they have." She waved to the knights.

Driscoll met Gaelan's gaze. "I have been the princess's champion since she was ten."

"And you will continue, if that is your desire."

Confusion lit his features as he glanced at DeClare, standing to Gaelan's left.

"I had planned though, since these are your friends and folk, to appoint you high sheriff, but if you wish—"

Siobhàn looked wide-eyed at her husband. "I thought you trusted no Irish?"

He met her gaze with steely intent. "I must begin the healing sometime, wife. Driscoll speaks my language too, and DeClare cannot issue my orders if your people cannot understand."

Siobhàn nodded, appreciating the wisdom, then looked back at her man. "The choice is yours, Driscoll."

Driscoll turned his attention to his lord and nodded.

"Swear to me, then."

Driscoll's gaze snapped back to his princess's, but she did not acknowledge it, leaving the matter to his conscience. Driscoll knelt, and in a language so beautiful Gaelan wished he understood, spoke the words. "As a son of Ireland, a clansman of the princess of Donegal, I swear my life and heart, my home and family to your care," Siobhàn translated. "I accept the duty of high sheriff, and swear fairness and honesty"—Driscoll looked up—"to all."

Gaelan nodded, then followed Driscoll's gaze to Siobhàn. A single tear moved down her cheek. "Siobhàn?"

She waved, looking at the floor.

Driscoll came to her. "Princess?"

"I wish I could do so with such ease, my friend," she

whispered tearily in Gaelic. "God knows I would mayhaps please him as you have."

Gaelan frowned. "Siobhàn" Did she feel betrayed?

"Is there more, my lord?"

The quaver in her voice tore at his heart. "Nay, lass." He gestured, and the fiddlers' music filled the air, Driscoll still close, frowning at her as she sat. Gaelan called Brody forward and he spoke in low tones, appointing him steward and entailing his duties.

He looked wide-eyed at his lady. "That has been her duty, sir."

Gaelan arched a brow at Siobhàn. She was looking at her lap. "Wife." Her head jerked up. "What here do you not do?"

"Wield a sword."

Fortunate for him, he decided, his lips quirking. "You will not have the time to maintain such tasks." His wave meant every task she'd done before their marriage.

Siobhàn looked him up and down, refusing to acknowledge how much pleasure the simple act gave her. "You speak as if you take a grand amount of care, English."

"I plan to keep you busy," he murmured huskily.

"I have plenty to tend, sir." She huffed at the silky innuendo in his tone. "I thank you for taking a burden." Overbearing clod, she thought, smiling approval at Brody and thinking her life had returned to the fetch and carry of her marriage to Tigheran.

Gaelan detected a fraction of resentment and smiled. She was more readable than she imagined and did not like giving way to his authority, even in marriage. But then he'd known that from the moment he'd kissed her in the glen.

"Begin the feasting," she said, nodding to a servant holding a platter. Gaelan frowned, confused. "They will not dine until you are served." He nodded and accepted a bite of mutton from a platter, popping it into his mouth.

'Twas clear, Gaelan thought, that there were a few things of castle life he'd yet to learn. "Come," he said, taking her hand and choice from her. As the musicians painted the air with lively tunes and feasting began in earnest, he guided her through introducing his knights, pages and squires. "I can recall faces, but I admit that beyond these men, I can rarely recall a name."

She met his gaze and with his hand at the small of her back, he led her back to the dais and the trestle table positioned before their chairs. "You should try now that you do not have to go off a'warring." She waved to the servants to serve his lordship, trying to ignore the warmth of his fingers on her spine.

"But you would rather I did," he said, tipping his head close to whisper before she sat.

She would rather he vanished into thin air, but 'twas moot now. " 'Tis your way, my lord. You know no other."

He slid into his chair as she poured wine into silver goblets. "Now I war for Donegal. Surely in that you approve?"

She was taken aback, offering him the wine. "You do not truly want nor need my approval."

But he did. Deep inside, in a place he rarely delved, he needed it. "Would you even believe otherwise of me?"

Her lips pulled into a tight line. "What do you want from me, that you have not already taken?" she hissed, aware of listeners. In the middle of the revelry, he leaned indecently close, staring deeply into her eyes, his hand slipping to her waist, his thumb stroking over the fabric of her gown as if she was bare and brazen to his touch. Their agreement made her stay when Siobhàn wanted to shove his hand off. Then his fingers moved, slow circles, and Siobhàn experienced the same unaccustomed rush through her blood, the weight of his touch amplifying the sensation as he plucked a dried apricot from a platter, a contribution from his army's stores, and poised it at her lips.

"I want only that you remain true to our bargain, my lady."

She nipped a bite of fruit. "I will *act* the proper wife." He caught the inflection, watching her eyes. "You will allow my people to live as they have under your protection, yet no matter what comes atween us, you must not shame me with another, PenDragon."

She looked him directly in the eye with the warning and Gaelan's brows furrowed. "I am a bastard, not an adulterer." Did she think him so baseborn he would behave without a shred of decorum? His gaze thinned. "Is there another reason you ask?"

She simply stared.

"Is there?"

She was not about to reveal that Tigheran was a whoremonger, not above taking a maid within plain sight of her, then demand his wife service him moments later. It was a humiliation she refused to suffer again, even in the telling. Yet regardless of the passion simmering under the surface, the memory brewed a distrust. "Though you have promised to wait for me, you are a lusty male—"

" 'Tis only a recent discovery—"

Without missing a beat she said, " 'Tis the way of men—"

Although he could surmise what stirred her distrust, he'd plenty of time to discover where it began. He finished off the apricot. "You are judging again," he warned in a teasing tone whilst his broad hand moved slightly higher, brushing under her breast. Her eyes flared and he adored it, longing to uncap her hidden passion. "Why would I want another when I have you?" He tipped his head close, brushing his lips to the spot near her ear and whispering, "Should I worry over you and the Maguire?"

"Nay. I give you the same fidelity, my lord." Her fingers flexed where they wrapped his biceps, and she closed her eyes. "But Ian is special to me," she managed when his lips were kneading her lobe like that.

He tensed. "How so, Siobhàn?"

"I was betrothed to him."

Gaelan's head jerked up, something gripping hard inside his chest. "By choice?"

"Aye." She met his gaze. "When I was seven and ten."

She'd loved him. He could see it in her eyes. And his heart sank. "Then why did you not wed him?" God above, he did not want to hear this!

"Our people were being slaughtered, by O'Rourke's."

She made the sacrifice sound so simple, dutiful. "Why not after Tigheran died, then?"

" 'Twas a long time ago." Her chin tipped up, her expressive eyes naught but pools of green-blue glass. "My reasons are private, my lord." Siobhàn could not drag Ian into her sea of lies. "And no longer matter."

Gaelan ground his teeth. It did matter. She was hiding more than unrequited love, and it was a wonder Maguire did not launch a full attack this night. He'd lost his woman twice to the enemy in the name of peace. Men had warred for less.

"Have you ever done aught for yourself, Siobhàn?"

"Aye," she said, and her gaze slipped to Connal.

Gaelan's gaze lit on the boy, the child's resentment and hatred felt from across the hall. A horrible thought flickered in his brain, wounding his hope. Did O'Rourke and Maguire own a piece of her heart still? If so, what was left for a life with him? He sat back. "Go abovestairs."

Siobhàn's head snapped around, her brow furrowed.

"And do it with a smile."

She searched his features, glacial, sharp, the thin-lidded look of his eyes. What happened to the man who was nibbling on her earlobe a moment ago and begging for a chance? "Ordering me about will not win me, PenDragon." She stood abruptly, rounding the chair and moving into the crowd without a backward glance.

Gaelan glared at her back, filled with an impotent blend of anger and helplessness as he realized he was no closer to understanding his mutinous bride than he was the day she opened the gates and let him into the keep.

Chapter Thirteen

Her figure nearly disappeared into an unlit corridor before he came to her, lightly catching her elbow. Siobhàn gazed up at him, awaiting punishment for her insolence. His hand rose and she winced, and though his lips tightened, he simply brushed the back of his fingertips across her cheek, pulling her deeper into the dark.

"We are wed, lass, forever. Why do you fight me so hard?"

"You have demanded instead of asked, husband. You have taken, not earned."

He folded his arms and stared down at her like a sultan to a slave. "Did you earn the right to be princess?"

"Aye. My bloodlines do not give me the right. I am no different than them." She inclined her head to her folk. "But for two decades, my family fought to keep the *tuath* free and rule justly. When the clan cannot provide food, shelter, protection, for loss of men and land to raiders, or stolen by an *ard-ri,* a high king, then this privilege of leader is lost. We all lose." She craned her neck to look up at him. "Many have tried, but none have proven themselves by helping their clansmen. There are those who take from the people, the land, and give back naught. My mother, father, and the elders, taught me that to reap without sowing new is rape of the soul. And to make a body feel less than his rightful place and freedom in a *tuath,* whether they are indebted or nay, is to make a person feel less of his worth.''

How wise she was, he thought. ''Yet you continue, even after vows that change our lives, to see me as the taker, the thief.''

''You have come hidden behind the banner of a king who knows none of us, who believes we are filthy wild heathens in need of English guidance.'' Bitterness tainted her words, though her expression remained gently patient. ''His assault was sanctioned by the church, but his teachings are here.'' She gestured to the friar, deep in his cups and nodding off, and her lips twitched. ''For those who wish to join.''

''Do you believe in the almighty God?''

She was shocked he had to ask. ''Of course. But I also believe in the old ways, and respect them. You would be surprised to know how many Christian customs came from pagan beliefs.''

''Really?''

She eyed him. ''Ahh, you do not believe.''

''Nay.''

''I will show you.''

She took a few steps farther down the hall he'd yet to investigate, and with her keys, unlocked a thick door. He helped her push it open. The cool scent of age and ill use hit him as she moved into the room without benefit of light, rummaging. Suddenly the chamber filled with light as she set a thick tallow candle on a small table, then opened a chest and carefully removed a book, bringing it to the table and untying the bindings. She pulled a small stool beneath her.

''My lord?'' She looked up, motioning.

"I cannot read, Siobhàn, only bits." 'Twas the first time it shamed him, made him feel less than he was.

"This, even Rhiannon cannot read. 'Tis old Gael."

He moved closer to her, going down on bended knee. She tipped the manuscript to the candlelight and read a passage. "What does that festival sound like to you?"

"Easter." She read another and he responded in kind. "Advent. And the other, 'tis All Saints."

"Sain' Patrick's doing, I'm thinking." She started to rack the loose pages and close the book, but he stayed her with a gentle hand.

"Read this." Hiding a smile, she began. "Nay, in the language."

Siobhàn read to him, relaying the story of Patrick driving the snakes from Ireland. He settled to his rear, bracing his arms on his bent knees and listening. Gaelan did not understand a single word but was entranced with the sound of the words on her lips, her beautiful mouth shaping the strange syllables. She paused abruptly, meeting his gaze.

His brow marred softly at the soulful look in her eyes. "What ails you?"

" 'Twas a book of my grandfather's and very precious to me." She exhaled a slow breath. "I am suddenly thankful these will remain with my family, my lord. All of this will." She waved to the chests filling the room, age wafting in musty scents of herbs and old cloth. "This is my heritage, and that 'twill not be burned or tossed aside comforts me greatly."

"Are you saying you are seeing a benefit of wedding me, princess?"

She lifted her gaze to his. "Aye."

Her smile was slow and genuine, and if Gaelan was not sitting he would have been knocked to the floor. His heart jumped in his chest and he wanted to see it often and directed solely at him. In that moment, he wanted naught more than to win this strong woman's heart. Yet so much stood between them.

"Connal will be thankful when he is old enough to appreciate it."

His expression turned sour. "That is doubtful." She frowned, and he regretted his discouragement. "Your son cannot even talk to me."

"He is a child." A fraction of sympathy for him lit her features. He had a stepson he did not know how to reach and Siobhàn knew Connal's anger was festering, and even she would have trouble staying mischief and maligning if he chose to vent it. "He understands only what he is told and unfortunately, he heard naught but a jaded view of the English."

"Where might he have gained that, Siobhàn?"

Her chin tipped, rebellion shadowing the private truce. "Mayhap when I told him an Englishman took his father's life and he would never see him."

Gaelan's features tightened criminally as he stood. "Has anyone given you an account of his death?"

"Nay, none of his retainers returned, dispatching to other *tuaths,* I'm thinkin'."

Nay, he thought, most were executed for their part in Tigheran's attack.

"He is dead and that is all I needed to know then."

Gaelan could do no more than nod, guilt falling through him like hot oil, burning away his urge to tell her. He could lose even this small moment, and he was not ready to relinquish this truce even for a moment. Suddenly he wanted to keep the truth at bay with the force of his legions, though he knew 'twas a hopeless wish. He held out his hand and she accepted it, rising to her feet. With one hand, he took the book, placed it in the chest and closed the lid.

"One day I shall clean it out." She looked about the room, to the chest filled with her son's baby things, with her girlhood. "I am sure there are some things another could use."

"Leave it, if you choose, Siobhàn."

She smiled slightly, her eyes suddenly dancing with humor. "All the bridal gifts need a place to hide, though."

That reminded him. "I want you to fashion garments for yourself with the fabrics and trims, Siobhàn. They've been in my possession so long, I feared they would rot. And I want to see you attired befitting your rank."

"I try not to. The flow of riches afore the less fortunate show how little others possess and a wish for more."

"I wish it."

"I will think on it."

"Must you defy even the smallest request?"

" 'Twas not a request, but another order."

He sighed tiredly, releasing her hand and raking his fingers through his hair. "By God. I never knew a woman who did not want new clothes."

"Those women are not me, my lord."

He laughed, softly and to himself. "Of that, wife, I am most certain." He cocked a look at her then, his gaze lingering over her fitted bridal garments, the deep green of her homeland, the Celtic marks of her ancestors in the circlet banding her head. "But then, we have years to learn of each other."

Siobhàn stared at him, this man who was her husband, this man she was bound to by Christian law, by her people and his. He was all things she disliked in a man, tyrannical, arrogant, a slayer. She did not trust him, nor did she believe he was committed to Donegal or to her. Their marriage was a bargain, a price. For land and power. She held no fairy-filled notions of more, for she'd done the like before and would not bare herself for such disappointment again. Yet her heart did a strange spin in her breast every time they touched, every time she met his steely gaze, and she found herself searching for the vulnerability she'd witnessed when he asked her to wed under Christian law. 'Twas a moment she would never forget, for it stole a piece of her then.

She stepped, her intent on the door, and was not at all surprised when he caught her to him, his hands on her waist. Her heart suddenly pounded, a furious beat of unnamable proportions. He was merciless and strong, great in size, a seasoned warrior, yet when he touched her . . . oh, sweet believer, when he touched her he did with the tenderness of uncertainty, as if she was fragile and cherished. No man had ever given her that.

"I ask for a kiss, Siobhàn. I do not take, nor order. I ask."

Her gaze searched his and she found a flicker of unguarded humility in his dark pools, a breath of fear. It endeared him to her, and without pause, she placed her hands on his wide chest, smoothing her way up to his neck and tipping his head down. " 'Tis no portrayal for the people this," she whispered against his lips and swore she felt him tremble. "Deny me naught, husband."

Her mouth pressed against his and the passion exploded. They moaned as one, sinking into the kiss, a kiss blistering in heat and untamed desire, heads shifting to take more and still more. Standing a hand's width apart, his fingers flexed on her waist, and Gaelan felt a quiver rake him down to his boot heels, his muscles at once, tensing and turning to water under her touch. She was voracious and womanly, a radiant power releasing on him, and he could bare no more of being parted and slid his arms around her, crushing her against his length. And she melted into him, soft breasts to his chest, hip to hip. Her finger sang deep into his hair, holding him, marking him her willing prisoner as her tongue pushed between his lips.

Gaelan came undone, groaning his pleasure. Never in his life had he felt such energy in a single kiss, yet this woman unmanned him, mastered him with her untutored touch, her lush body. She had in the glen, had in the barn, and Gaelan felt that only in private did he see the true woman he'd wed. And in private he wanted to keep her.

"My lord—oh, forgive me."

Slowly they parted, gazes locked. Together they sagged

through a heavy release of breath, not looking at the man standing in the hall.

"If you value your life, DeClare, the enemy had best be knocking at the gates."

"Well, not exactly."

Gaelan cocked him a look. That grin was going to split his face in half, he thought.

"The men want to wish you well."

"A drinking game," Siobhàn said, sliding her arms from around his neck. Patting his chest, she took up the candle and moved to the door, waiting.

Gaelan waved at DeClare and he moved away, and when Gaelan met her at the threshold, he blew out the candle and set it back inside.

"I must oblige them."

"Of course you should."

He pushed her hair off her shoulder, exposing her slender throat. He watched the spot at the base, where her heartbeat pulsed, then lifted his gaze to hers. "I would accept your offer to teach me to read."

She nodded, keeping her expression schooled, a feat when he was running his finger over her collarbone in whispery strokes.

"I would not have the keep know."

" 'Tis naught to be ashamed of, husband. Apparently you never had the time to learn."

"Apparently." She was seeking a bit of his past, he could tell, but he could not spoil the erstwhile moments with the ugliness of it. The telling would lead to how he gained the king's favor, and he could not stomach seeing the gentle moments turning to vapor. He leaned, pressing a kiss to her forehead, then guiding her into the corridor and back to the hall.

Every pair of eyes focused on them and Siobhàn blushed, a ridiculously maidenly thing to do, considering her age and past.

"Get to our bed, wife. I come anon." Then, for her ears alone, he said, "Sleep, Siobhàn. I swear this night I will not demand a thing from you." She had given up her home, her people to his threats, and now her freedom. Knowing her as he did, she would not have done so without some thread of hope stringing between them. And although he'd never been so frustrated in his life, he was not willing to break the twine with husbandly demands. Not from a woman who could too easily look upon him and show her loathing.

Slowly her lashes swept up, blue-green eyes gazing deeply into his. Her confusion was succor to his hungry soul. "But they will know—"

He touched her lips with his finger. "They will not."

Siobhàn searched his gaze, dark eyes suddenly soft and comforting. Lord above, she prayed their life together would not be this constant puzzlement listing between total command and a tenderness that left her hungering for peace with him.

His gaze shifted past her and his handsome features sharpened. Siobhàn twisted and her heart nearly shattered to find Connal, standing alone and forlorn near the solar, his fists clenched, his eyes boring into the man at her side.

"Go to him," Gaelan urged. The boy's hatred lay on his sleeve for all to see. "He needs his mother this night." He could see the relief on her face and kissed her lightly. She fairly ran to the boy, scooping him up and hugging him. The child wrapped his arms around her neck, his look biting as he stared over her shoulder at him.

Gaelan sighed. Another Irishman he must battle for his wife, he thought, and watched until she left the hall before his comrades immediately dragged him off, thrusting a tankard in his hand.

Siobhàn slipped out of Connal's room, blinking back the burn in her eyes. He hated the new lord of Donegal so much, she was afraid this marriage would scar her son beyond repair. Closing the door, she pressed her head to the wood, praying she could find a way to make his young mind understand that they must accept the new life King Henry thrust upon them, that she would try her best to see that the tide of England felt like only a ripple in Donegal.

"Siobhàn." She spun about, blinking unshed tears, to find Rhiannon and several women standing close. "We've come to prepare you for him."

Was that envy she saw in Rhi's gaze? "I have wed afore, my friends. A man's ways are not new to me." Though this one's were, she thought. "Find your beds." The women departed, their quickness telling her they wanted no more to prepare her for the sacrifice than she wanted to be the lamb of his feasting. Her sister remained.

"Go drink some wine, Rhiannon. You look as if *your* bed would house him and not mine."

Rhiannon blinked, still wringing her hands, her gaze darting to the doors below.

"Who do you expect?"

"None," she snapped, and Siobhàn's gaze narrowed. "I am sorry," she offered an instant later. "But drunken knights in the hall bodes ill, I swear."

That was not it, Siobhàn thought and stepped closer, her voice low. "What know you of Ian's men attacking my husband's?"

"Naught." Rhiannon frowned deeply. " 'Tis true, then?"

"Ian says he did not."

"You do not believe him?"

"His view is a bit jaded of late."

"If he attacked, 'twas for you. He still loves you."

Siobhàn made a sour face. "He lets his head full of sweet dreams and poems rule him, Rhi. PenDragon could have killed them all last eve."

"You side with the English?"

Siobhàn took a step back. "There are no sides, Rhiannon.

Ian has not sworn to Henry and would have good reason to war, but only in his eyes. I am not worth the wrath of my husband, be assured. Yet PenDragon is right to suspect. The day we met we were attacked, and the riders cared naught who they slaughtered. PenDragon was ambushed again afore he arrived here. Think you 'twas the same that burned the herder's shack and killed his family? Or mayhaps 'twas the Fenians?''

"*Fianna Eirinn* would not do such a thing," Rhi insisted.

"To keep the English out, I think they would."

"They are too few."

"Small armies have been known to tip the scales of war." Siobhàn knew her sister was hiding more than she spoke and she wished she could see into the soul as Rhiannon could. "And PenDragon's army is more than enough to put any rebels down."

"Then you must make certain he does not war on the Fenians."

"Impossible."

"I saw you kiss. You can sway him for our people."

Her knowing smile irritated Siobhàn. "Becoming a whore for Ireland is not a choice I choose to make!" Siobhàn snapped. "These raiders are outlaws. They are killing Irish and English alike."

Rhiannon reddened with shame. "I am sorry, but you will share a bed; why not use the advantage?"

"For the love of Patrick, you are asking me to betray him!" Siobhàn gripped her arms, giving her a quick shake. "Hold your tongue, for if he hears such talk, you will find yourself wed to DeClare and sent back to MacMurrough castle."

Rhiannon paled. "I would rather die."

"That could be within his power, too." Siobhàn let her go.

Rhiannon licked her lips nervously. "Siobhàn, you know my heart lies elsewhere."

Arms akimbo, Siobhàn leveled her an exasperated look. "Your heart lies with a man who will never return. These past years should have widened your closed eyes.'' Rhiannon looked away, her mouth in a flat, rebellious line. "Find a future, as I have, in what is availed to you." Siobhàn didn't add the comments lingering on her tongue and turned away, heading to her chamber alone.

She paused at the sound of laughter, looking down into the hall from the squints.

Evidently his men had started the toasting without him, for they were weaving pitifully, and a tinge of resentment rose as she noticed Driscoll and Brody were in the thick of it, with half the men still able to lift a cup without dumping it on themselves. To the rhythm of his knights pounding on the tables, PenDragon drained the mug, swiped the back of his hand across his mouth and, amid the cheers, tipped the tankard in salute to her. She rolled her eyes and shook her head, not wanting to see him fall so deep into his cups that they had to pour him into her bed.

Her breath skipped suddenly.

Her bed.

Regardless if he kept his promise this night, she would share a bed, bare their bodies and slip beneath the bedclothes. The thought drove a fresh blade of tension over her skin and she looked back at him, her gaze lingering over his broad shoulders, his magnificent chest. Siobhàn admitted their kisses were exciting, his interest in her giving her back something she'd long ago lost beneath duty and her place in this clan—her femininity and the power behind it.

Still, did he think because she offered herself in a single kiss, that she would join her body with his this night? It would be just like a man, she thought, to see more than was there and take more than she wanted to give.

More than Rhiannon's attitude grated on her frayed nerves, and although her maid, Meghan, had seen to the fire, food and honeyed wine, Siobhàn loathed the darkness and went about the room furiously lighting candles. She could not believe her

sister asked her to sway him with her body. Did she think the
man was stupid to not see through such a ruse? With angry
moves, she pulled the bells from her hair, wincing at the hair
leaving her head by the roots, then tossed them on the commode
table. Kicking off her slippers, she was halfway off with her
gown and shift when her forgotten circlet of silver clattered to
the floor. With a gasp, she scooped it up, placing the crown of
her heritage carefully in the chest. No longer a princess of
Ireland, she thought with a tired sigh, but Lady Donegal. She
lifted out a pair of thin spiral bracelets, the swirling knots and
curves so delicate they reflected lace. They were rumored to
have been created by a Druid. Her fingers whispered over the
markings, her eyes burning for the women who wore it centuries
before her, for the loss of her quest to keep Donegal as it had
been for decades, and for the purity of her Celtic blood that
would one day run with English.

She tipped her head back, too practical to allow the tears to
fall, to overwhelm her. Those ancestors gave her strength, her
belief that she was right in fighting PenDragon, remaining true
to her soul, just as wedding him was the only way to spare
lives and make certain her brethren were treated well. 'Tis all
his in the King's eyes, and she was thankful PenDragon had
not burned everything. At least now she had something to offer
Connal when he came of age and took a bride.

In a moment of weakness she sank to the floor, murmuring
an ancient prayer over the old bracelets and slipping them on,
pushing them high on her arms. She rose, naked, and moved
to her bone comb, working through the snarls, and was searching for her robe beneath the piles of bridal booty PenDragon
thought to soften her with, when the door rattled with a fierce
pounding.

Siobhàn snatched up a length of russet velvet and had scarcely
covered her nakedness when the door flung wide, banging
against the wall. Gaelan stumbled in, DeClare and his remaining

knights, the ones who were not facedown in the rushes, staggered in behind him. They froze, gaping at her.

"My God, Gaelan." DeClare's gaze raked her bare shoulders, the cloud of deep red hair falling over the velvet. "I envy you this moment."

"Me too, my lord," another knight slurred.

Gaelan swallowed, his mouth gone dry. The red-brown velvet clutched to her breasts, she stood near the bed, the fire's glow bending the hue of the expensive fabric with the shade of her hair. His gaze swept her hurriedly, from the swell of her breasts against her fist, the silver snaking her upper arms, to the dainty toes peeking out from the uneven hem.

"My velvet becomes you."

Siobhàn stared. For the love of Saint Andrew. He was stripped down to his braies and boots, the leather thongs wrapping his powerful thighs and accenting the bulge between. A bulge no woman could ignore. Heat flamed through her blood. The men continued to gape at her as if she'd grown new breasts, likely waiting to witness the bedding, an English custom she loathed. She'd no intention of joining with PenDragon this night, especially since he was drunk. But regardless of his promises to remain celibate, an argument of strength with him would be no contest.

She met his gaze and did not know what possessed her as she teased, "You may have it, if you wish." She loosened the fabric a fraction, exposing skin to her nipple. His eyes widened. An instant later, he turned, shoving the others out and closing the door.

Relief swept through her.

Gaelan pressed his head to the wood door, praying for patience and willing the thickness in his groin to subside. But her tart threats earlier, that he had land and a castle but not his bride, still stung, and he knew he would not have drunk so much if he wasn't feeling so inept at this marriage thing. The problem was, strong drink had done little to dull his desire and he could scarcely keep his thoughts from possessing her completely. But Gaelan knew, if he wanted this woman willingly, he must grow some patience.

Facing her, he bent and untied the thongs, toeing off his boots, then padded barefoot to the table, pouring wine and taking up a bite of cheese. He stared at her, munching, offering her a goblet. Siobhàn nodded, moving near and accepting it. She drained the wine, a drop dripping from the corner of her mouth. Gaelan watched her tongue snake out to catch it before she thrust the goblet into his hand and turned her back on him. Moving to the foot of the bed, she stared at the pile of bedclothes, her shoulder on the bedpost, and he wondered what was running through her quick mind.

His gaze slid over her. "You are very beautiful, Siobhàn."

"I am well past—"

"You are beautiful, Siobhàn. And it matters only to me."

She rolled around the post to look at him. It had been a long time since anyone had complimented her on aught but her efficiency. "My thanks, husband."

He scowled, truly irritated that she would not call him by his name. "I've made a fair amount of bargains and promises in this marriage . . ."

"As have I."

He went on as if she hadn't spoken, ticking off his justices to her. "Not to bed you until you desire it, to remain faithful, not to kill your precious Maguire," he said, his tone tight with jealousy. "I think you could at least look upon me without fear."

" 'Tis distrust, m'lord."

"Ahh, that I know. But 'tis there, the fear. I see it." And the distaste he wanted to banish.

"You are too drunk to know the difference." She was not afraid of him, yet she feared her unmistakable need to be touched and petted and kissed by this giant of a man who'd come into her life and stolen everything she held precious.

Gaelan walked toward her, and to drive his point home, Siobhàn stepped back, her grip on the velvet tightening.

He paused, arching a brow, withholding comment. "Now," he began in an uninvolved tone, "in the morn you must look thoroughly ravished or they will suspect we have not consummated this marriage rightly."

"Ravished?" came in a squeak as she dropped to the bed. "But—"

He was near, grasping her arms and pulling her to her feet. She struggled to cover her breasts as he bent, rubbing his bristled cheek across hers, then looked at his handiwork. "Almost." He repeated the process, working his way down to her throat.

"What are you doing?"

"Marking you for the eyes of the keep," he said against her skin, the hum of words driving gooseflesh down to her nipples.

"Oh."

Gaelan smiled against flesh, his mouth trailing over her slender throat. He liked keeping this woman off balance, he thought as he licked and suckled her skin, scored her delicate shoulders with his teeth. Her breath panted softly over his hair, her head lolling as his mouth plucked, his beard leaving a blushing path. Ahh, she was damned sweet, he thought, trying to remember his purpose.

Siobhàn caught her lip between her teeth, tipping her head back as he rubbed his face back and forth, nudging the covers lower. Without thought to what she was doing, she let the fabric slide downward. His tongue arched the skin above her nipple, then dipped, flicking it. Her entire body clenched at the flash of heat snapping through her. He seemed to ignore it, then lowered to his knee, parting the velvet and scraping his teeth over the flare of her hip, his hands splayed over her belly and back as he sampled the curve of her buttock.

She leaned into his touch and Gaelan smothered a smile as

he rose and took her mouth beneath his. His arms slid slowly around her, the coverlet between them, her hands fisted there, yet the weight of her bosom, her nipples brushed his chest, building the fire burning inside him. He wanted her. Now. Her restless motions, her little whimpers tested him, his fingers flexing on her back, itching to slip between her thighs and stroke her, feel the gush of her desire, taste it beneath his lips. His restraint nearly snapped when she arched a fraction, her hips pushing against his, his arousal heavy and filling the space between. The velvet did little to shield the incredible heat of her skin from his thickening groin, yet instead, he called himself honorable and valiant as he drew back, examining her face with a critical eye as her lashes swept up. The liquid glaze in her eyes nearly undid him.

"That should suffice until you are seen again," he said and let her go.

Siobhàn stumbled back, clutching the velvet, feeling bereft and hungry for more, and realized that if he had played her a bit longer, she would have lain beneath him quite willingly. Jager me, she would have demanded it. Numbly she crawled onto the bed and under the covers, cursing her feeble effort to resist. Her body humming with something akin to pain, she warred between spreading herself for his touch and conking him on the head with a chamber pot for making her feel as if she were cheating herself out of something glorious.

Gaelan smiled to himself as she slapped the velvet on the floor, then huddled under the bedclothes as he moved to the table. He poured another goblet full of wine and dropped into the stuffed chair near the fire, nibbling on a crust of bread. He shifted in the seat, his soft groan of discomfort carving the silence. She rolled over, meeting his gaze.

"Go to sleep, wife."

"You do not come to bed?" For pity sake, was she mad for tempting him?

He spared her an indifferent glance he wasn't feeling. "Nay." He did not trust himself. Not with so much wine in his belly, for her beauty struck him with a mortal blow, her hair a river of deep red against the white sheets, the silver armbands intriguing him, lending her an air of seduction, especially since it was all she wore. He looked away from temptation and stared at the heavy fabric draping the grand bed, thoughts of her husband bedding her, of her crying out for his touch and crying over his death torturing him. His stomach clenched, threatening the stability of the wine laying there.

He'd pushed the memory of O'Rourke's death out of his mind, not wanting to address the ramifications once she found out, yet crossing the room and lying next to the man's wife brought home how much Gaelan had altered Siobhàn's life. And she his. If not for her and his unaccustomed feelings, he would be riding to the shore and England right now. If not for Henry, and the threat of war, she might have married the Maguire. Between the two chieftains and their need to champion his wife, it was enough to leave him burning with morbid suspicion and distrust.

What ghosts would he battle to win his own bride?

His gaze slipped to her, so lovely in sleep. She shifted, the coverlet slipping to expose the swells of her breasts. He swilled back more wine, images of her rolling on the bed, naked and hot for the Irishman, drove an unaccustomed jealousy up his spine. Curse the Maguire, she was his wife now. His.

And he would be damned if he'd let her forget it.

"Bargains or nay, joining our bodies does not make a marriage, Siobhàn. Never forget who possesses you—will always possess you," he warned to the sleeping woman. "Never."

Silence stretched, the fire popping and hissing with the burn of peat and wood. Her lashes swept up and across the room, she met his gaze. Her soft voice startled him, sounding wounded and more forlorn that he'd ever imagined.

"Vows or nay, having my body does not make you my true husband, m'lord."

With that, she rolled over and fell asleep, leaving Gaelan to wonder why he tested calm waters and that she wanted just that, for him to be her true husband. Now, if only he knew what that meant.

Chapter Fourteen

Ian Maguire stared at the fine glass he'd brought from Dublin, watching the dark liquid coat the sides, the firelight flicker off the cuts in the crystal. She would have loved it, he thought, would have told him he should not waste his coin on something so fragile. But she'd have loved it anyway. A wedding gift to his betrothed.

Now she lies beneath the enemy—again.

His stomach rolled at the thought of her submitting to Pen-Dragon, of the bastard mercenary taking her beautiful body, planting his seed in her. Ian groaned, an agonized sound. He feared for her life, that the new lord of Donegal would beat her or worse, for her tart mouth tested the best of men.

She could have fled with him if not for her people, and Ian knew that if the PenDragon wanted them dead, naught she could do would stop him. Damn her for being so righteous, he thought, and brought the glass to his lips, tossing back the whiskey in one swallow. The warm liquid seared to his belly, seeped through his limbs, doing naught to ease the torment of losing the one woman he loved more than his life. Siobhàn always did what was expected for the good of the whole, a human sacrifice for peace. It made her a great leader, he admitted.

Ahh, Siobhàn, my love, Ian thought. What happened that you would not accept me after his death? What did Tigheran do to you to make you shut out the love we had? He refused to believe she never loved him. Hadn't she kissed him once whilst she was wed to Tigheran? And what a fiery sweet kiss it was. Ian did not want to remember how she had scolded him for taking it, did not want to hear her tell him she was wed to Tigheran and that was that. Why, when she had the chance to leave the PenDragon's clutches, did she not come to him for help or leave with him?

Why couldn't she think of him first, instead of the clan? The thought shamed, but he was in a selfish mood and brought the glass to his lips, found it empty and hurled the precious glass into the hearth with the other four he'd destroyed. The crash didn't bring any attention, the servants staying away from the solar unless summoned. Ian slumped in the chair, elbow on the arm, shielding his eyes with his hand.

He could not go on like this, he thought, his days unending, his nights filled with drink and pounding into women who were faceless vessels for his pain. He had to find a way to bring her back to him, to destroy the English lord and free her.

Siobhàn stirred awake, abrupt and sharp, and shifted to her side. Her gaze searched the darkened chamber, lighting on the man in the chair, then the empty goblet rolling over the floor. Throwing back the coverlet, the blast of cold did not affect her, her skin always unnaturally warm, yet she reached for the velvet, wishing she knew under which pile of treasure her robe lay. Wrapping herself, she padded to him, bending for the goblet. Setting it aside, she stirred the fire, adding peat and logs to warm him, then glanced back over her shoulder. Sleep did little to soften his features, his jaw square and strong, his bones chiseled as if by a masoner's hand. But still so very handsome.

He shivered, shifting in the chair, and she considered waking him, coaxing him to the warmth of the bed, then decided that would come soon enough and took up a blanket, covering him. She smoothed the edges over his scarred shoulders, marveling again at the size of him and the power she tested so regularly of late. 'Twas exhausting, this battling, and Siobhàn knew she could have done worse for herself. He could have warts and little hair and smell as unappealing as an overripe turnip, she thought with a small smile. Or a cruel beast like Tigheran. Instead she had a strong husband, brave and commanding, and she did not doubt he could protect Donegal. He could have taken her defiance once and burned the castle to the ground, yet he did not.

He could have forced her beneath him as a prize of the siege, yet he'd bent to her rank, wed her right and true and showed her last night how a simple brush of his mouth over her skin could ignite the very heat in her soul. What would it be like, sharing her body with this man? Would she find that pleasure she never attained yet knew to reach for? She glimpsed it only in this man's arms, felt it whisper out of her reach, but, oh sweet lady, how she yearned for it.

But hasty vows and her stipulations forbade it.

She could not take pleasure with him, come to him as his true wife till she was certain he was committed to Donegal, to them all. Withholding herself from him, like withholding her oath, was the last vestige of her own free will remaining out of his control.

If she gave one, the other would follow, and then she would surely be lost.

* * *

Gaelan met the last step and searched the hall, his gaze falling on his wife. He was not surprised to wake and find himself alone, though the blanket neatly tucked about him left him comforted that his misspoken words last night had not completely estranged her. And yet, a light sleeper, even after a night of drinking, he wondered how she managed to dress and open the huge wood door without making a sound.

Her son beside her, she was wiping his mouth, encouraging him to drink his milk. Connal beamed at her, wrapping a lock of her hair around his little fingers, listening whilst she instructed Brody and the cook's assistant Bridgett with the day's labors. He crossed to her, smiling at the knights cradling their heads before he stopped beside Siobhàn.

He bent and in a low growl said, "Go change your clothes."

Siobhàn paused in taking the trencher from Bridgett. "These are me workin'—" The fierceness of his gaze stopped her.

"I can provide for my wife well enough, Siobhàn, and I will not have you parading about in rags. Wear an apron if you must, but you are Lady Donegal and will attire yourself accordingly."

She nodded mutely, but made no move to obey.

"Must I strip that hideous thing off you myself?"

"Must you order me about?"

His features pulled taut as her reminder sank home. 'Twas such a trivial thing, her garments, and Gaelan's lips twitched. "Will you humor a man who imbibed too much and change, my lady?"

Her lips pulled into a small smile that was both wrenchingly sweet and wholly false as she rose from her chair and with a secretive touch to his chest, tipped her head back. "As you wish, m'lord."

Gaelan almost laughed at the tightly gritted compliance and caught her against him, softening the request with a gentle kiss.

For the briefest moment, her lips shaped his, and he heard the sighs of the women around them and could not resist patting her behind. She yelped, lurching back, muttering something in Gaelic as she fled to the stairs.

Gaelan turned back to the table. Connal sat a couple of spaces beyond him, digging his spoon into a bowl of meal and milk, shoving it into his mouth between glares. Gaelan was at a loss as to what to say to one so young—and so filled with anger.

"Connal, would you—"

The boy threw down his spoon and scrambled off the bench, stomping to the doors. Gaelan sighed, taking up a slice of bread and cheese.

"Give him time, sir."

Driscoll stood off to his right, watching the boy's retreat. He did not tell him he'd no intention of pressing the child, since he had no notion of what to say to soothe his aches. Gaelan popped the cube of cheese into his mouth, then gestured to the seat nearest him. "What have you to tell me, Driscoll?"

The man's face showed his surprise.

"I didn't believe you waited in the hall to see if your princess survived a night in my bed. What is it?"

Driscoll nodded to the solar. "I feel there is a need for privacy in this."

Gaelan frowned, the bite of bread halfway to his mouth. He stood and, taking a goblet of watered wine with him, they headed to the solar. Five minutes later Siobhàn stepped inside and he rounded on her.

"Why did you not tell me the raids had been going on for over a fortnight now?"

Briefly her gaze spilled past him to Driscoll and his face reddened. " 'Twas not your concern, husband, 'twas mine." Siobhàn flicked a hand and Driscoll departed. "And when was I to tell you—when you threatened Ian, when we settled the contracts or mayhaps during the ceremony?"

Her condescending look angered him and he crossed to the

chest, throwing it open and withdrawing his sword. "That will change today. Driscoll reports to me alone." He fastened the weapon in place. "You will not handle affairs of war."

"Aye, you are best at that."

At her biting tone, he twisted and met her gaze. "You expected different?"

This is who I am, he was saying, and yet Siobhàn detected a plea for understanding. She took a step closer, yet he grabbed his gauntlets of chain mail and left the solar, calling for Reese, his armor and for DeClare and his wondrous sword.

Gaelan reined up. "Sweet Jesu." He had seen carnage before, been the maker of it, scented the stench of death, but this— these were not warriors. They were herders and woodsmen— families. His gaze moved over the bodies strewn like rag dolls on the ground, bent back over carts. A child no older than Connal lay under a bench, the wood shattered where a broad sword hacked through the child and speared the earth. Gaelan pulled his gaze away and met Driscoll's.

"My suggestion is to burn it; do you agree?"

Driscoll blinked, shocked at being consulted. "Aye." He started to dismount, but Gaelan stayed him with a wave.

"We will tend to it, Irishman. Are there villages nearby, anyone who would have seen this?"

Driscoll frowned in thought. "A small one, half this size. 'Tis but a half day's ride."

"Take ten soldiers and seek information." Gaelan looked at Sir Mark. "Join him, and answer to Driscoll's will."

Sir Mark nodded gravely and, with Driscoll, wheeled about and rode off.

A half hour later, Gaelan watched the flames consume the tiny village, his men standing by to see that the fire did not leap to the forest. There was no reason for this. The livestock was butchered along with the owners, so it was not a raid to fatten a man's pens. The few citizens were too far north of the castle to know Gaelan had married Siobhàn yet, therefore it could not be a retaliation on him. Or could it? Could this be the Maguire's doing? Would he take his jealous vengeance out on these innocent people?

Gaelan walked the perimeter, his hands on his hips, his gaze on the hoof prints. Firelight flickered off something shiny and he bent, digging in the damp earth. His scowl turned black and he shoved the item inside his breastplate, then headed to his horse.

Siobhàn stared out the window, searching the landscape.

"I hope he is dead."

Siobhàn gasped and twisted to look at her son. "Do not say such things!"

"I do!"

"Connal O'Rourke!" She marched over to his bedside and knelt, tucking him in like a bun in a basket. "I am shamed to hear such talk. 'Tis mean and a bad omen to wish death on a body."

"Then I wish it twice!"

She sighed heavily, calling on patience and smoothing the blanket over his tummy. " 'Twill not change matters."

"If he is dead, it will."

"Nay. Another nobleman will come and the king will order me to wed him, too. And without an army, we are weak, Connal. Why do you think I let him in without a fight? They are too many, too strong. I could not risk our lives, laddie. Would you?"

Connal was quiet for a moment, then muttered a stubborn, "Nay."

"Good. Besides, we have what we need, a roof, food on the table, in your belly," she said, tickling him. "And we are protected from invaders, my sweet. Wed to him, I can make certain all are treated fair. With another, I might not. *Tuigum?*"

Connal turned his face away and nodded, yet she knew her son, knew there was something else on his mind he was not speaking. Unwilling to press him, she kissed his forehead and left.

Siobhàn entered her chamber, the emptiness of it making her feel more alone than before. They had been gone for two days with no word. And though she'd busied herself with storing the gifts and providing space for his things, she admitted she was growing worried. She snapped her fingers and Culhainn slunk from the bed, taking his position on the floor at its foot. Stripping off her clothes and crawling tiredly beneath the covers, she wanted to believe her worry stemmed from Driscoll being with them, that if aught happened to them, she would be facing another of Henry's knights and she was just growing accustomed to PenDragon's face.

She rolled to her side, punched the pillow and sighed. *I do not miss him,* she vowed.

A minute later she flopped on her back, then kicked off the covers, uncomfortably hot despite the cold spring air.

Fine, she thought. She missed the big oaf. She missed sparring with him, the way he teased her, held her as if she would shatter like fine glass in his arms. Missed his kiss and the scent and taste of him.

Leaving the bed, she moved to the window, throwing open the shutters, the blast of cold bracing to her hot skin. No man here spoke to her so candidly. No man looked upon her and made her feel like a woman instead of a leader. And she'd lain awake the past night tormented with thoughts of what had happened to him. Had they been ambushed again? Was Ian out there, laying in wait for just such a chance, for her husband to venture out with only forty men? She would not put the matter past him, considering the jealousy she'd witnessed. Had Lochlann defied the king's edict and joined her former betrothed against PenDragon? Nay, she thought. O'Niell and Maguire rarely saw eye to eye on aught, but the thought of them warring on her husband made her shiver. It would be a bloodbath.

The guards called out; the trumpeters hailed. Siobhàn strained to see in the dark, then dashed to the chest, flipping it open, forgoing a shift and wiggling into a fresh gown. Jamming her feet into her slippers, she paused at the oval looking glass PenDragon had given her and finger combed her hair.

She made a face in the glass, quickly fastening her girdle. "I am pitiful, aye, Culhainn?" She looked at the wolf in the glass, but the animal's only response was a shift of his eyes. The trumpets blasted again. "Come, beast."

Lifting her skirts, Siobhàn raced to the stairs, waking the household and flinging orders for a bath and food brought to her chambers before heading outside. Culhainn barked at her heels as she crossed the inner bailey, excitement and relief clenching her stomach. The gates of the outer curtain swung wide, the thunder of hooves and clink of weapons and armor coloring the air. She stood back, her gaze searching the faces, the mounts, for the familiar. Her heart slammed at the sight of the dead man slung over the horse. His soldiers.

Oh, God.

She heard her name and her gaze swept the squad of knights and soldiers again. Then she saw him, his face blackened with smoke, his hand bleeding, and she darted between the jumble of horses and men, rushing forward.

She froze a few feet from his mount. Her eyes misted. She did not know why, the devil take the man, but she was relieved he'd survived.

Culhainn settled beside her on his haunches, his blue gaze moving between the two.

Gaelan slid from the saddle, leaning back against it and simply looking his fill of her. God's bones, she was like a breath of spring air in the black of winter. "Greet me proper, wife." She lurched into his arms, her breasts mashed to his cold armor, and Gaelan tipped her head back and kissed her deeply, hungrily, her response weakening him in the pits of his soul. He did not question her greeting—they had a bargain in this marriage—yet she was all he could think about on the return, all he longed to touch, to feel her softness after so much death and destruction. The carnage had never bothered him before, yet this time, his only thought was, it could have been her.

Drawing back, he kissed her once more, then tossed the reins to Reese and swept his arm around her waist, guiding her toward the inner bailey and away from the captured prisoners. He did not want to answer questions right now. Culhainn barked and Gaelan looked back, inclining his head, and the dog leaped, barking a greeting before dashing ahead to the keep.

She caught his hand, examining it. "You are not injured elsewhere?"

He shook his head, unable to find a bit of intelligent thought with her so close.

"Alan, wake the dairy maids to bring three pails of milk to the hall," she ordered a passing servant, then to another said, "Ask Bridgett to warm the mutton from supper, and the bread." Inside the hall, Gaelan let her lead him through the maze of folk stirring from sleep and the knights filing tiredly inside.

At the staircase, she stepped from his side and clapped. Attention swung to her. "Driscoll, 'twas unsafe to leave your wife and children alone. They are in the solar." He smiled brightly, glancing to the entrance as his woman emerged and with a cry, flung herself into his arms. "Stay here the night and rest, my friend." She looked at Brody, crooking her finger, and he joined with them to take the staircase. "Let Davis sleep, but see a tray is provided for Driscoll and his family. Have a cask of wine opened and tell Nova to lay out this evening's fare for the men. I know there was plenty, so send a portion out to the soldiers." Brody nodded as she mounted the steep steps, unconscious of her arm around her husband's waist. "Have I forgotten aught?"

"Your husband," Brody said, leaping forward to push open the chamber door.

Siobhàn tipped her head and met Gaelan's gaze.

He smiled, the flash of white teeth against his sooty face looking sinister. "You are a bossy wench."

"And you may scold me later, husband. *You* need a bath." She gave him a push inside, and after ordering Culhainn to remain with Connal, she closed the door. Gaelan halted where he was, his gaze moving around the room. The fire was high and glowing gold into the chamber, and a large tub sat near, water steaming the chilly air. Candles filled the room, showing a platter laden with dried fruit, bread, meat and cheese on the table with a pitcher of wine; the honeyed wine, he hoped. The bridal gifts were stored except for the carpet covering the stone floor, the tapestries on the walls, the mirror, a jewel box and chest of coins, the latter on an old carved desk, one from the mansard, polished and tucked in the corner, the back to the window. A tall chair stood behind it. His gaze swept farther and a knot thickened in his throat. His trunks were here, his extra sword on the mantel, his battered goblet having a place beside it as if 'twere made of gold and not tarnished pewter.

He dragged his gaze to her.

"Siobhàn?"

She looked away, briefly. "Since Brody has my duties . . . I was . . . bored."

He faced her, his armor scraping as he lifted his hand to her face. He drew a line across her cheek, down to her lips. Gaelan was so deeply touched he could not speak. No one had provided for him like this, seen to his comfort, and he was beginning to understand the true benefits of a wife—save one.

"You are my husband," she confessed under his probing gaze. "I saw no reason not to treat you as I would any other of my folk. I apologize for my neglect."

"My thanks, Siobhàn." He bent to steal a kiss and she pushed at his chest, turning her face away, then cocked a glance.

"You reek, my lord."

He smiled. "You do not. By God, you smell like flowers." And home, he thought as she wiggled out of his arms.

"And you may too, if you wish. Come sit." She toed a stool to the center of the room and he guessed her intent.

"The armor is too heavy. Send for Reese, if you like."

"He is currying your horse. I can do this."

" 'Tis not necessary, Siobhàn. I can remove it."

Her look doubted, yet he unbuckled his sword belt, laying it in the open chest, then loosened the leather straps hinging him into the metal suit. She watched as with practiced speed, he removed the vambraces from his arms, the greaves covering his shins and thighs, then reached behind his head and lifted the breast- and backplate. He held it out to her and Siobhàn grasped it, the weight of it driving her backwards. Gaelan leapt to catch her, taking the metal shield and setting it down carefully.

"You did that a'purpose."

He grinned. "There are somethings a woman cannot do, Siobhàn."

She eyed him. There was a message in there somewhere, but with his arms around her, his eyes looking so soft and tender, she could not find it.

"Sweet Mary, how do you walk under that mammoth weight, let alone climb astride your horse?" She scooted away from his touch and crossed to the table, pouring wine.

"Practice." Gaelan dispatched his boots.

"The Irish fight wearing only a tunic." She glanced up, smiling. "The Scots do it naked."

"Godless heathens," he muttered on a smile. "No protection."

"Ahh, but quiet." She smiled a bit smugly. "You likely alert the entire countryside clanking about in that."

Gaelan watched as she came to him, offering him the goblet. He accepted, draining it without stopping, soothing his smoke-dry throat before handing back the cup. "Is that for me?" He nodded to the tub, pulling off his chain mail.

"I am not the one who stinks."

He sent her a false scowl, then walked toward the tub, stripping off his clothes as he did, and Siobhàn sighed, following the trail of hauberk, leather tunic, sweaty shirt, stilling when she scooped his braies off the carpet. She straightened, lifting her gaze to him.

"Jager me," she whispered, and he looked up, peeling muslin trunks down. Bare, Gaelan stared at her, his body reacting to her perusal with amazing swiftness.

Her gaze swept him, remaining briefly on his arousal, and her expression turned almost eager.

"Do not look at me like that, Siobhàn, or I will break my promise."

Her gaze snapped to his and she brushed past, refusing to look down again. She'd already garnered an eye full of his masculine attributes. And my stars, he was huge. Yet she could not get the image out of her mind and she thanked God for the reprieve when he stepped into the bath, sinking with a groan. Gripping his clothes, she smothered one of her own. Every inch of him was honed with muscle, his chest sculpted, his stomach ribbed, his arms and legs like long twists of thick rope. Even his hips were sinewy. And between . . . oh lady, spare me this aching, please, she thought, her breasts suddenly throbbing to be handled, the wool gown rough against her nipples. Her skin grew hotter than usual and, dropping the clothes, she moved to the window, throwing open the shutters. She told herself she would find no pleasure in bedding with him, that he would likely rip her in half when the time came, yet her body refused to listen, rushing with blood. She wrapped her arms about her waist, trying to smother her sudden trembling.

Gaelan scrubbed the soot from his face, slicked back his hair, then settled deeper into the hot water. He could feel the tension building in her, as if he wore it and the connection comforted him. Closing his eyes, he listened to her move about, rattle the shutters.

"Siobhàn."

"What!"

He suppressed a smile. "The draft."

"Oh, forgive me." She bowed her head, closing off the wind, then faced him. Crossing to the hearth, she took up a cloth and, swinging the iron arm out, tipped the kettle to a pitcher. The hiss of droplets hitting the fire drew his attention. He opened one eye.

The firelight cast a silhouette to her drab worn gown, showing him she was bare beneath. His body clenched with the temptation of her. Her breasts peeked against the fabric, yet he could see perspiration blistering her temple. He remembered the heat of her skin when she was in his camp, the mist rising from her like a fairy vapor. He ached to feel it, see if 'twas as hot as he remembered.

She set the pitcher aside to cool. "Hungry?"

His gaze lingered over her body before rising to meet hers. "Starved."

She pulled the platter within his reach, sampling an apricot as he slapped cheese and mutton onto bread and ate.

"Tell me what has transpired since I left."

I missed you, she thought, then smiled a bit. "Naught. Jana birthed her child, a fat, healthy boy." Her smile widened, delighting him in ways he could not describe "He arrived screaming to Coleraine. Mayhaps his father might hear him and come for her."

Gaelan glanced, the remains of the mutton halfway to his lips. "The father is not here?" That shames Jana, he remembered. None to pay the honor for the child.

She shook her head. "She was captured whilst she visited

her mother in west Antrim.'' She sighed, slow and long, looking off. ''Jana will never confess if he raped her or nay, but I could not let her stay a captive.''

''You?''

She sent him an arched look. ''Aye, me. And Driscoll and ten warriors.''

''You just walked into the camp and took her back.''

Clearly he didn't believe it possible. ''Nay, I confronted him. When he chose not to release her, we stole her back.''

''Without being seen?''

''Aye.'' She smiled to herself, privately, mysteriously. '' 'Twas a bit of fog that night.'' She stood, taking the platter away, then dipped her finger in the water. '' 'Tis cold, and you will wrinkle like a dried apple.''

Gaelan did not think aught on his anatomy could shrink with her so close, then jolted when she poured the hot pitcher full between his knees. ''You seek to ruin me, woman?'' he said with a dry look, stirring the water.

Mischievous fairies possessed her then, she swore, when she peered down at the water barely covering his arousal. ''Will hardly do damage, I'm thinkin'.''

''A good wife would check.'' Hope colored his tone.

She arched a brow, the temptation daring her to call his bluff. ''I'm sure you'll be risin' above the discomfort, my lord,'' she said, and he choked a laugh as she ladled water over his shoulder, then held out soap and a rag.

Gaelan took it, not daring to let her wash him, yet as he lathered the cloth, she spooned water over his head and soaped it. Naught in this life compared to her strong fingers in his hair, he thought, closing his eyes, feeling her body brush his back as she massaged and played with the suds. He cast a look over his shoulder and she grinned. His gaze swept up and he could see horns fashioned in stiff soap.

''Brat,'' he muttered, and she shoved him forward and dumped a fresh pitcher laced with cold over his head. He came up shaking like a dog and she shrieked, lurching back and nearly falling in the fire. Rising half out of the tub, Gaelan snatched a fistful of her gown, hearing it tear as he yanked her forward. She slammed against him, knocked breathless, her hands flying to his shoulders for balance.

Gazes met and locked.

Suddenly he scooped her in his arms and brought her down into the tub with him.

Water splashed on the stone floor. "Oh, for the love of Michael! Husband!" She tried getting up, but he held tight.

"Look at me."

She did, shoving her hair from her eyes and trying to ignore the hard shaft wedged against her hip.

"You had this tub made for me, didn't you?" He gestured to the freshly coopered wood, large enough to fit his bulk well.

"Aye." Her lips curved playfully. "Don't want you stinking up the castle, do we now?"

"Ahh, Siobhàn, I love it when you smile for me." He traced the shape of her lips with his fingertip. "When you show me the wild girl still locked inside you." She looked confused for a moment. "There is a part of you that hides, especially from me."

"Is not."

"Is too." His smile softened to a somber look that robbed her breath. "No one has ever done such for me, lass." He glanced about the room, his place in it. "Not like this." He brought his gaze back to hers, his hand moving over her back.

Oh, sweet believer. The pleasure on his face was worth the effort. " 'Twas naught."

But it was, for it wasn't part of the bargain, and that burrowed deep into his heart. His hand slid over her legs, dangling over the lip of the tub, and he watched her eyes glow darker. " 'Tis a bit of hope that we could be civil." His hand slipped deep beneath her hem.

She covered it. "Civil, is it now?"

His smile spoke volumes as he tugged at the sopping fabric. "That gown is not fit enough for Grayfalk's back."

"Then he does not have to wear it, does he, now?"

A devilish light filled his dark eyes. "Mayhaps you should remove it?"

Bracing her hands to his chest, she heaved from the bath, but he was fast, rising, catching her about the waist and tossing her over his shoulder.

She shrieked. Water dripped. He took several steps and pitched her on the bed.

She bounced, shoving hair from her eyes. "I am not a sack of grain, husband. Cease this nonsense."

"Take it off." He stood before her, brazen bare and rampant.

And destroying her composure. "My lord?" She scrambled off the opposite side of the bed, the sight of his body, his erection prepared for pleasure, arousing her into madness.

"Off." He bent a knee to the mattress. She skipped out of his reach. Gaelan stepped back, rounding the foot. Siobhàn lurched past, sliding over the bed. "Come here, woman."

She had the make-me look in her eyes he was beginning to adore.

Gaelan pressed his knee to the foot of the bed and when she tried shooting past, he leapt, throwing her on her back and covering her with his body. He smiled down at her.

"Surrender."

His arousal lay heavy against her thigh, the heat of it making her squirm. "Never."

With a diabolical chuckle, he clipped her wrists in one hand above her head and slipped her dagger free. Her eyes flew wide as he rolled off her just enough to catch the blade tip in the neckline and rent the gown to her waist.

"Husband," she gasped.

"Now 'tis a rag." Gaelan tossed the blade aside, laying a long look down her body, her rapidly rising chest before he kissed her, taking her mouth ferociously. She responded with equal fervor, battling back, straining against him, and he thrust his knee between her thighs, rubbing, spreading her, trapping her with his leg to the gown and leaving her vulnerable to his touch. And he would touch, just as he knew he must control his own passion, suppress it. Battle had taught him that, and this was a little siege he planned to savor—and win.

A whimper worked in her throat as he spread the gown and Siobhàn did not know if she was struggling against him or to him. Then he touched her, his callused hand molding her flesh, diving beneath the torn gown to stroke her belly, her hip. She wanted more and nearly shouted for him to touch lower.

He left her mouth, holding her gaze as he bent to draw her nipple between his lips.

"My lord," she breathed.

"I swear I will make you say my name."

"Hah," came in a choke as his tongue circled and flicked; then he drew deeply again on the delicate peak before he paid homage fit for a sovereign to its mate. By then she was arching into him, jerking on his hold, and he released her wrists and moved lower, licking her ribs and parting the gown as he did. The rip of old fabric stirred her. Siobhàn felt her insides shift and loosen, her flesh damp and aching. His moves were deep, unhurried, staggering her will, and she wanted to watch, to see his mouth on her, see his face, but pride bade her nay. She gripped his shoulders, her body slickening.

Then he tore the gown to her knees, his weight gone, and as she looked up, he quickly spread her thighs and covered her softness with his mouth. She cried out loudly, and he chuckled, parting her flesh, probing the dewy fold with his velvet tongue.

She squirmed, trying to bend her leg and ease the throbbing.

He refused her. "Say my name."

"Nay."

Falling back on his haunches, he caught the tattered fabric and yanked her to her feet, stripping off the remnants of the gown, loving that she swayed unsteadily, and before she could pull away, he caught her hips in his broad hands, tipping her to the heat of his mouth.

He licked.

"Oh, my stars." Her legs threatened to fold and she caught the bedpost, his lips and tongue giving her pleasure she never knew existed. "This is madness," she muttered, her fingers twining through his hair. Her hips rocked.

"Say it."

She looked down, the sight of him, his head between her thighs horribly arousing.

Then he drew her leg over his broad shoulder. "Say my name."

"My lord."

His tongue snaked, flicking the core of her. Her knees buckled and she reached above and held on to the bedpost.

"My name."

"PenDragon."

He smiled, smoothing his hands up the back of her thighs and dipping his fingers between. Her breathing quickened deliciously. "Say my name, Siobhàn."

Tasting her still, he parted her, plunging two fingers inside her.

"Oh—oh, sweet mercy." The beat of her desire throbbed through her, quick and blazing. He could feel it, in feminine muscles flexing and pawing against his touch, in the flesh quivering with the coming peak.

She rocked.

He moaned encouragement, withdrew and plunged deeper. "My name."

"My lord," she gasped, grinding to him, shameless, unbridled in pleasure.

Siobhàn accepted it, let it shower her like hot rain, her body reaching for the undiscovered rapture just on the edge. Always on the edge.

He tortured her, demanding his name again in surrender.

She refused, and his tongue circled the bud of her desire over and over. She cried out in her language. Cursing him in one long moan and still, he mastered her body.

Still, he tasted her desire.

Her passion-slick muscles clamped and pulsed, and Gaelan lifted his gaze, watching her climax spread through her, her head tipped back, her fingers deep in his hair. Her lips parted in breathless pants, her eyes closed against the tension trying to escape.

Suddenly she inhaled, bowing from the bedpost like a silken banner caught in the wind.

He drank her ecstasy, felt it rip through him with a ruthlessness that unmanned him, fractured his control and made him spill his seed.

Her pleasure was his.

He took her to the edge and over it and when she sank boneless, Gaelan rose, gathering her in his arms and laying her gently on the bed. Her lashes swept up and he saw tears. He knelt, and she touched a trembling finger to his cheek, his jaw, then across his lips. There was no shame in her expression, only satisfaction and a bit of confusion. "Siobhàn?"

"I never felt that afore."

"I know." He wanted to flex and roar just then. "You liked it, aye?"

"Me moanin' like the banshee tell you that?"

Gaelan loved how her voice rose in questioning pitch at the end of a sentence.

"Where do we go now?"

He shrugged, yet his eyes held a plea that had little to do with contracts and bargains or making love. "Wherever you like."

Chapter Fifteen

Siobhàn stretched, arching like a cat, and Gaelan's gaze followed the slip of the sheet exposing her beautifully pale breast. Breasts he'd the pleasure of loving last night. Along with a few other delectable parts. The memory of her abandon, her taste, made him hard and hungry to discover the rest of her.

Siobhàn blinked awake and turned her head. He was on his side, elbow bent, his head propped on his fist.

"Good morn, wife."

'Twas odd, she thought, to see a man in her bed after so many years. Her gaze slid over him, his thick arms and his carved chest, to the sheet pooled at his waist. "Good morn, husband."

His eyes, so dark and filled with mischief, glowed. "What else must I do to get you to say my name?"

Her face flamed to the roots of her hair. "You did not get it last eve, did you now?"

"I am most willing to try again." He reached.

She gathered the sheet to her bosom. "I think not." Though she was not ashamed, she felt defenseless to him now, stripped of her guard, and she needed distance to rebuild it. Letting him touch her again, though her body cried out for more, would not help. She still did not trust him. Looking away, she glanced at the window, then inhaled a sharp breath. "Oh, for the love of Saint Michael!" The sun was already high in the sky!

Leaving the bed, she pulled the sheet with her, wrapping herself, but Gaelan caught it, giving it a quick jerk that landed her in the bed, on her back. He loomed over her, half upside down and smiling.

"Where think you to go this morn?"

She cocked her head a bit. "To my duties, my lord. And I am well past showin' meself belowstairs. They will think—"

"You were taking your pleasure of me," he interrupted, bending until his lips met hers, his kiss slow and wet and stirring the embers hidden under her skin. Her hand rose, almost hesitant, then finally cupped his jaw and tasted him back, racing her tongue over the line of his mouth. His breath shuddered raggedly as he drew back.

"You are in a surprising mood for a man who did not get any hisself." Her eyes flew wide at her own impertinence.

His brows shot up. "Wishing I'd break my promise? For I can accommodate her ladyship—" He threw back the covers.

She looked. "Jager me," she whispered, then rolled and scooted off the bed.

Gaelan laughed. No matter how much she abandoned herself to him last night, she still feared her own desire and him, apparently. It was comforting that she was not so resilient, that she had weaknesses, beyond her people. He'd begun to think she was invincible.

She flung open a trunk and rummaged, selecting a gown and a shift. Her back to him, she slipped on the shift.

"I saw you bare last night Siobhàn; why hide now?"

" 'Twas a moment of— ah, I don't feel—'' She sighed, dropping her head forward. "Humor me, my lord.''

"Shyness now, after you rode my mouth like a wave?" She inhaled and spun about, eyes wide. He grinned, loving her blush and watching it spread down to her breasts. "Intriguing.''

Siobhàn snapped her mouth shut. "Oh, you big ox, cease lying abed and dress.'' His laughter filled the chamber as she went to his trunks and retrieved fresh garments, flinging them at him. "Don't you have men to train or—'' She frowned, his tunic in her fist. "What happened that you were covered in soot?'' She rushed to the bedside. "And your hand.'' She grasped it. The bath cleaned it well and it was crusted with healing. "You need a salve and wrap on that. And to remove your stitches as well.'' She dropped her gown on the bed and went to her cabinet, pausing to search for her girdle and the key. She gathered clean strips of cloth and a small pot stoppered with a fat cork. She sat on the bed beside him, plucking out the stitches in his side, and though the wound on his hand was minor, Gaelan let her tend him.

"Tell me," she said in a firm voice as she gingerly spread the salve.

"A village to the north, 'twas attacked.''

Her head jerked up. "The people? Grainne and Elric, little Muirgheal and Teague?''

God above, she knew them by name and the hope in her beautiful eyes nearly destroyed him. "Dead, lass, all of them.''

She looked at her work, wrapping the bandage, tying it off neatly and collecting her things. Crossing to the cabinet, she replaced the items, locked the cupboard, then moved to her gown, pulling it on over her head and fitting it about her hips.

Frowning, Gaelan stood and dressed quickly and was looking for his pouch when he heard her choke. He glanced and his expression fell into utter sadness. Before the mirror, she combed her hair, tugging angrily at the snarls. Her lips quivered with her effort to hold back tears.

"Ahh, sweetling." He came to her, wrestling the comb from her tight fist. She shoved at his chest, then shoved again and again, and Gaelan let her, holding her close as she pounded out her grief. Then she cried, sinking to her knees and folding over, rocking.

"Oh Lord above," she sobbed, and he knelt. " 'Twere three new families there. Grainne and Moreen, they'd just had their first child. Babes, my lord, babes who won't see their first birthday." Gaelan wrapped his arms around her, holding her warmly, pressing his lips to the top of her head. Nearly an hour passed before she was silent, telling him of the children, the friends she'd lost, and still he held her. Then he saw his pouch under the table and reached for it, tucking it discreetly at his waist.

" 'Tis a mystery, Siobhàn. The livestock was butchered." He blotted her face with his sleeve and helped her to her feet. "There is no sense in it."

"As in the south. So far apart from the other, why?"

"We rode for miles, lass. Driscoll found another village, in the forest." Her breath skipped. "Nay, no one died, but they'd been raided recently. Little more than half their livestock was gone."

Her delicate brow furrowed. "But 'tis not the same, then."

He shrugged. "Who is to say the villagers did not anger the raiders and refuse to give up their stock?" She agreed with that. "The second village did not fight, but for a young lad who took a hit to the head." A pause, and then he added, "We captured two men just beyond the hamlet with the livestock."

"Irish?"

He shrugged. "They've refused to speak a word."

That marks them with guilt, she thought as she went to the basin and splashed her face with cold water, dried, then took back her comb. She freed the tangles as she spoke. "I had nary a clue afore, either. I could only bring the villagers closer to the castle or inside."

" 'Twas your wisest choice until now.'' She twisted a look at him. "I have men already out on patrol, Siobhàn. And will send more when they know the area and have a guide we can trust.''

She nodded, suddenly seeing the benefit of his legions. She could never spare so many men for fear of leaving the ones here unprotected. "Allow Driscoll to select the guides, my lord. I trust him. And let Brody go with you if you need him.'' Her lips curved a bit. "He will find castle work tiresome after a bit and he is very accurate with a javelin.''

"I will find them, I swear.'' Gaelan's stomach rolled with the memory of the child beneath the bench.

"I know you will.'' She saw it in his eyes, his lethal determination, and she came to him, gazing up into his handsome face as she braided her hair, weaving the bells. The sound made him smile softly. "Come below and break your fast.''

"When I find my boots.'' He glanced around, and Siobhàn walked straight to them, plucked them from the floor and dropped them in his lap.

"Hurry.'' She offered a weak smile. "I will need someone to blame for my tardiness.''

"Lay it fully on me, wife.'' He slid his arm around her, dragging her close for a warm kiss. "And aught else you'd like.'' He wiggled his brows.

Smothering a smile, she scoffed, playfully shoving him back as she passed to the door. Gaelan enjoyed the sway of her hips as he donned his boots, then, straightening, he peered to see she was gone before he withdrew the pouch, spilling the contents into his hand.

He stared, scowling, for glittering from the center of his palm was a silver spur.

A knight's spur.

* * *

"I am ready for my lesson."

On her knees in her herb garden, Siobhàn looked up. He stood at the far end, a book she'd never seen before tucked under his arm and a basket in his hand.

"You wish to learn to read now? But—" She waved to the garden overrun by weeds.

"Everyone else is taking a meal and a bit of rest, Siobhàn." He walked toward her, careful not to crush her seedlings. "So should you."

"I am not tired."

He squatted and she looked up. "I could make you tired." Those brows wiggled and she shook her head, her smile soft. He looked much the boy pleading for an extra comfit, and she sat back on her haunches, dusting her hands on her apron.

"Come dine with me. Then teach me."

She cocked her head, aware again of what it took for such a proud man to ask for her help. He pulled her to her feet and they moved to a tree growing flush against her herb house.

Gaelan knelt, giving her the book, then pulled the cloth from the basket. He uncorked a jar of watered wine and handed it to her, then forged for the meal he'd asked Bridgett to prepare. He was starved, but more for Siobhàn's company, and after the teasing they'd suffered this morn from Raymond, he knew why she'd hid out in this secluded place. The outer curtain, one wall of the keep and the herb house made three sides of a square, the kitchen closing off the fourth nearly completely, except for a gate to keep out the animals. There was serenity here, where the sun shone well enough over the low herb house, whilst the walls offered shade. He'd watched her from the solar before coming out. She looked like a serving woman, with her apron and the kerchief covering her hair. It was an English custom for women to cover their hair, but here, the ladies wore their manes like crowns and he found he liked it. As did his men.

Hair as beautiful as that of the Irishwomen should never be concealed.

Siobhàn watched as he solicitously laid out the fair between them. It was the first time a man had ever done aught like this for her. And sipping wine, she settled to the ground to enjoy it, pulling her kerchief from her head. With his eating dagger, he cut portions of meat and goat cheese, sliced bread and fruit she had never seen before.

"Pomegranates," he said. "I'd fear they'd rot, for the men do not care for them."

"You have women in your groups, husband."

"Aye, but I gave all the choice to remain or not and most left with the few men who set back to England on their own."

"When?" She hadn't noticed a lessening of his ranks.

"The morning of our wedding."

She blinked.

"I sent word to the king then. We should hear from him in a month's time."

"Would he not approve?"

He glanced up from cutting food, spearing a chunk and holding it to her lips. "Hoping he will recall me and rescind his edict?"

"Hah, he would never do the smart thing." Smiling, she nipped the meat from his fingers, drawing back and chewing.

"I think he will be in shock but well pleased." He relaxed against the tree, removing his sword and laying it aside.

She held a cube of soft cheese for him. "Because he knew you had every intention of leaving me to the hands of another lord?"

Gaelan met her gaze. *Leaving me.* Not her people, but her. *Ahh, lass, you're letting me into your heart and unaware of it,* he thought, grinning. "I would not do aught so foul to another Englishman. You are hellion enough."

"Oh! You—" she gasped and shoved the next bite into his mouth. Gaelan chuckled deeply, and they fed each other; she sucked the soft cheese from his fingertips and he the crumbs from her chin. In an instant, he was leaning over the meal to kiss her and could stand no more, urging her closer.

"This is not a lesson in reading," she said, yet made no move to stop the kiss, her hand lightly on his jaw.

" 'Tis more fun, I wager."

"I do not think you need any more practice."

"Compliments, my lady?"

She smiled against his mouth and leaned back, taking the book and shifting beside him. "Where did you get this?" It was bound, the pages stitched secure in a spine.

"DeClare." Gaelan folded the remnants of the meal into the basket. "It comes from the east."

" 'Tis beautiful." He watched her eyes skip over the pages, aching to know what they said. " 'Tis a book of poems. Did DeClare translate these?"

Gaelan looked where she pointed to Raymond's scribbling between the lines and shrugged. "He was going to be a scholar, you know. Into the priesthood." She looked at him, shocked. "Aye. But he found he liked getting under a woman's skirts more than God would allow."

"He's been under a few already," she said with a nudge, and his brows shot up. "Tell him to be careful. 'Tis worse than the danger of a battlefield here, with so few men." He fished paper and a quill from the basket, and Siobhàn gave him an old piece of wood she used to mark the rows as a firm surface. "There are a few girls who would like to snag a man as handsome as DeClare."

Stretched out and settled on his stomach, he looked up, eyeing her with a cheeky grin. "Handsome? Should I be jealous of that?"

"Be whatever you like," she said, tapping the book.

She pointed out the letters of his name, instructing him to re-create them again on the paper. Over and over he repeated the writings, learning the sounds to the letters, and though

Siobhàn was not surprised with his quick absorption, it was his handwriting that stunned her. Strong and fluid, it was beautiful. He learned the alphabet and was reciting the letters with each sound when he stumbled over one or two. She slid down on her side near him, propping her head in her palm. They repeated together.

"*K*, as in kiss?"

"Aye."

"*P* as in passion."

She smiled. "Aye."

"*E* as in . . . intercourse."

Oh, the rogue, she thought. "Nay, 'tis *i*—"

"—who would have some with me?"

"Husband!"

"Nay?" God above, he loved it when she got all indignant. "Then I will settle for a kiss."

She eyed him, then darted forward and pecked his cheek, but Gaelan snagged her at the base of her neck and took the advantage. He kissed her languidly, their bodies apart, yet his hand rode the length of her from shoulder to hip, a light caress that turned her insides to syrup. He offered naught more. But it was enough, enough to make her want, enough to make her remember that tongue playing elsewhere, and when it swept the line of her lips, dipping deep and retreating, she wanted the power of him, the weight of him crushing her deliciously. But he did not give it.

Ahh, Siobhàn thought, her hand slipping to his jaw, her thumb smoothing over his cheek. 'Twas a courtly kiss, soft yet restrained. He was showing her in his own way that he would abide her wishes, yet she heard his breathing grow rapid with hers, felt his fingers flex ever so slightly at her hip. The wind rushed over them, the scent of mint and foxglove, Solomon seal and penny royal sweetening the moment. She wanted to feel his hands on her, feel the same stroking fire of last night.

Yet he leaned back, his gaze searching her features. He licked his lips, as if to sample her again.

"That part of you tastes quite different."

She turned ten shades to red and stuttered, yet said naught.

Gaelan laughed and kissed her once quickly, then rose, gathering up the writing implements, the book and the basket. "I will leave you to your work as I have mine." He walked from the garden, leaving her body hot and stirred, and she watched him close the gate and wink. She flopped back on the dirt. Oh, for the love of Saint Michael. She could deal better with his open assaults, but this . . . ahh, this was hard to fight.

Gaelan stared at the prisoners. They were guilty. Found with the stolen livestock and blood on their clothes, there was no question. "Speak or you will die for your crimes."

The men simply stared. Gaelan noticed the marks on them and glared at his soldier. "Beating them is forbidden."

The soldier colored and nodded, his posture stiff. Gaelan considered dealing with them immediately, but he needed information, a clue, and mayhaps a day or two without food would bring it.

That night she waited for him to come to their chamber and when he did not, she went looking, yet found Connal wandering the halls in his nightshirt. She scooped him into her arms and took him back to his room. "Where is your aunt?" Rhiannon shared a room with Connal of late, giving hers up to DeClare and two other knights.

He shrugged, and Siobhàn realized he was feeling cast aside but would not say so. She crawled into bed with him, hugging him close, toying with his thick hair. He tossed and twisted for an hour, and no amount of coaxing could get him to tell her the root of his discomfort, though she knew. He hated Gaelan.

Hated that he was here, hated that he shared her bed, for her son had never seen a man there. Was he mayhaps jealous? She regretted not keeping him with her more often, but even a sorrowful boy got into trouble and underfoot when he was bored.

"Shall we take a ride together on the morrow?"

He cocked a look at her through sleepy eyes. "Just you and me?"

"Nay, poppet, we must have an escort. There have been bandits in the hills."

"Will *he* go?"

She shrugged. "PenDragon has much work to do."

"Good." He closed his eyes. "I would rather DeClare join us then."

Siobhàn looked up to see Gaelan moving away from the door, his head bowed, his wide shoulders drooping on a heavy sigh, and her heart went out to him.

Gaelan had slept alone that night, leaving Siobhàn to comfort her son, and in the morning he stood back and watched them ride through the gates, Connal tucked in front of his mother, an escort of no less than fifteen men accompanying them. He had not kissed her good-bye, nor touched her when she mounted the palfrey, but he had wanted to, for he'd missed spending the evening with her more than he thought possible. She twisted in the saddle, meeting his gaze, and he felt a sense of companionship with her, for although he'd made no indication that he'd heard Connal's words last night, he'd not balked at the request. After all, they'd been wed only days. The boy needed time.

But he'd allow only so much time to pass before he let Connal come between them.

Chapter Sixteen

Gaclan frowned when Siobhàn and the group rode back inside the gates but an hour later, hardly enough time for a decent run. He strode quickly to her, glancing at DeClare, who looked a bit scuffed and dirty for a simple ride, then Driscoll, both men's expression guarded, before bringing his gaze to Siobhàn. She put up her hand, halting inquiry, then slid from the saddle and reached for her son. Connal came to her stiffly and she set him to the ground, bending to his ear.

"Get yourself to your chamber, laddie. I will be up in a moment's time to have a chat with you." Connal glared first at Gaelan, then his mother, and Gaelan's brows rose as he watched the child stomp toward the keep.

Siobhàn's shoulders slumped and Gaelan stepped closer. "Is there aught wrong?"

"Not that a good paddling won't cure."

Gaelan frowned. He never thought to see her so angry with her child.

"He put a thistle under DeClare's saddle and he was

thrown.'' Gaelan's gaze shot to Raymond and the knight shrugged. ''Sweet Mary, I don't know how he reached that high, but the devil is in the child this morn.''

Gaelan looked at the ground, his shoulders shaking suspiciously, and she moved closer, tipping up his chin.

Her eyes flew wide. ''You think 'tis funny? He could have been killed!''

''You have to admit, Siobhàn, the boy is tenacious.''

''That *boy*''—she pointed, in case he forgot which one— ''is going to spend a day in penance, and do not let him see you laughing about this.'' She swatted his chest in warning. '' 'Twill only breed more mischief.'' Still, PenDragon chuckled. ''Know you he cut the girth to your saddle?'' Gaelan's laughter died and his gaze narrowed. ''Ahh, see, 'tis not such a lark, now, eh, husband?'' She looked at DeClare. ''Please accept my apology, sir.'' He nodded and she bobbed a curtsey and strode off.

Gaelan watched her go, pitying the lad a bit.

''Being birthed in an abbey did little to sanctify he'd be an angel, eh?''

Gaelan swung around, frowning at Driscoll.

''Aye, my princess had left to join Tigheran in England when she discovered she carried the prince in her belly and was forced to remain at an abbey in Wales till his birth. The weather being bad about then.'' Driscoll's voice turned soft and melancholy. ''The day she rode through those gates with that bundle, I swear her smile melted the snow, for 'twas the only time I ever saw her truly happy to be here.'' Suddenly he shook himself and cleared his throat, his cheeks pinkening. ''Then word came of her husband's death. And, well . . .'' He shrugged, as if that said what he could not.

Gaelan digested this as he ordered them to get off their arses and come look over his plans. Yet as they hovered over the diagrams spread on the table, Driscoll's words nibbled at the back of his brain, and during the remains of the morning Gaelan tried to understand what bothered him about the tale, then dismissed it. He had much to do before luncheon and his reading lesson with Siobhàn.

Rhiannon leaned back against the stone wall in the garden. Above her sunlight refracted through the colored glass, spilling red, yellow and blue on the opposite wall twenty feet away. She tipped her face to the sun, letting the warmth dry her tears, and she stared at the trees, the wind turning the leaves back. Then she slunk to the ground, covering her face. She sobbed, quietly, privately, ashamed of herself, of her heart's desire and the betrayal of it.

Castle folk cleared a path for her, aware of her ire, and Siobhàn was thankful for the small courtesy. She hated disciplining Connal so severely, but the child's behavior was growing worse by the day. She did not want to inform her husband of the bed ropes he'd cut and she'd discovered, much to the objection of her rump, just now. What did he think to accomplish with all this mischief?

Siobhàn froze at the inner gate, her gaze moving over the outer ward. She'd never seen so many men inside the castle walls. His men, his soldiers, footmen and archers slammed hammers, used muscles for war, to build. Not a soul stood idle, and already this morn carpenters worked to expand the armory and accommodate the cache of weapons. Pages and squires sat on a log like birds, polishing and repairing armor and tack, the line of deadly crossbows and bolts sending a shiver down her spine. Archers strung new bows and along the east wall another group of soldiers—*his* soldiers—lifted a finished wall off the ground and pushed it into place, extending the barracks. Carts rolled between the yawning doors of the outer curtain, thick-chested war horses put to work to pull the heavy load of stones.

Masoners chiseled and oversaw the mixing of mortar in great vats. Then she recognized the kettles were from the kitchen! Her best ones!

Irritated more than her share this day, Siobhàn's gaze searched the congestion for her husband. Her breath shot into her lungs when she saw him, using his broad back to help lift a huge stone into a break in the curtain wall. Above him on the parapet, three men struggled with ropes to pull the chiseled boulder up into place. Siobhàn called out to her people, for the largest to come help before he was crushed under the weight. A few men gave her a belligerent look before complying, and the many hands hoisted the rock into place. With a growl, her husband straightened, flexing his bare back and arms, then clapped a hand on the back of an Irishman, thanking him.

The man merely nodded and went off to tend his chores.

Siobhàn met her husband's gaze, then crossed to him, offering him the rag looped in her apron. "You seek to ruin my pots and kettles?"

Gaelan smiled. By the Gods, she was a combative female, he thought, stepping closer, loving the way she cocked her head as she awaited an answer, adored her hands on her hip and her tapping foot.

" 'Tis all we could find."

"Had you asked I would have shown you the tar vats in the herb house."

"Using them to brew potions, were you?"

"Aye, you'll find that Englishmen make a fine stew," she bit back. "The vats are useless for aught else, since 'tis difficult to get tar to fill them. Tigheran wanted a castle better than any in France and England. Unfortunately"—she glanced at the ill-placed buildings and gates—"he knew naught about building one."

"Ahh, but I do."

Her gaze thinned a bit. "Only because you know how to find their weak spots and tear through them."

His look was sultry, a reminder that he'd found his way beyond her defenses two nights past.

"Do not speak of it," she warned with a finger in his face.

He grinned, wiping the sweat from his chest, and Siobhàn's gaze unwilling followed the path of the cloth, aching to touch his sun-bronzed skin.

"If an enemy penetrates the strong, Siobhàn, what do you think he can do to the weak? They must be prepared."

"We are not totally inept, sir. Know you how to throw a javelin? I would wager even I could manage farther than your finest bow man."

"Is that a challenge?"

"If you feel the need for one, aye."

Damn but she was spoiling for a fight, he thought, smothering a grin she would not like. Standing this close to her, he could feel the energy running through her, heightening her color, making him eager to feel it explode on him in ways other than anger. Obliging her, he called out a man, ordering a javelin brought forth. The Irishman cast him a guarded look, his gaze flicking to Siobhàn. Discreetly, she nodded, and Gaelan sighed, realizing that lord or nay, when she was near, airing her defiance, her authority undermined his. Working as one, as true partners in this marriage instead of circling adversaries, was not just theirs but her people's only hope of survival. Yet short of beating the lot of them into submission, he recognized that wedding the princess of Donegal gained him naught but a mutinous wife and an unsatisfied ache in his groin. And it was time to change that.

The clash of swords drew her attention and Siobhàn turned. Near the stables, knights were instructing several Irishmen on swordplay, a huge tree stump the target. Beyond them, the gamekeeper, the cooper and their assistants worked to lift a wooden horse to a track. A quintain. Her castle was quickly turning into a training field.

"My folk have duties, PenDragon. Use your own men for such tasks."

His eyes narrowed and he leaned close to whisper, "They are *our* folk, and for a woman who was rather compliant in the garden"—she inhaled and blushed prettily for him—"you are in a most difficult mood."

Siobhàn's gaze flew to his. "Hush." Her gaze darted to DeClare not but a few feet away.

"I think you need to be kissed."

"Nay." That was the last thing she needed.

"Thoroughly. All over," he growled explicitly.

"Husband!" His look told her he would get her to say his name any way he could, and Lord above, tension and heat filled her with just the thought of his wondrous torture. She could scarcely look him in the eye without thinking of the ecstasy she'd experienced under his practiced touch, and it seemed like an eternity since he'd held her against him last. Bedding with Tigheran had held little pleasure, for he'd ignored her needs, yet that night her pleasure was her husband's only concern. It weakened her to the very roots of her soul. Sweet believer, her knees shook with the memory of his plying her with her own passion, yet the worst was, she knew there was more; for if his mouth could bring her to such heights, joining with him would surely ease this thickening desire she craved to explore. And Siobhàn was more than a bit irritated that she'd put herself in such a corner, for her body fairly screamed for this man's touch. And to add to it, he knew it.

"Nay?" He swept his arm around her waist and pulled her flush against his bare chest. "You would deny me even a kiss after I tasted your sweet—"

She slapped a hand over his mouth, her eyes warning him, his dancing with mischief.

"You are an insufferable creature, PenDragon." His tongue toyed with her palm. " 'Twas difficult enough to withstand the looks and whispers during the morning meal—"

He peeled her hand off and kissed the damp center, his gaze hot and velvety on hers. "What occurs in our chamber is not anyone's business."

"Still they talk. And bedding me does not make you my husband true," she said, repeating the words from previous nights.

"And joining does not make a marriage, Siobhàn. Trust does."

"I have little reason to trust an Englishman." Her eyes clouded briefly and her gaze faltered. "But I am trying," she said in a small voice, so unlike her own, and Gaelan crumbled a little inside. She was over four years alone, carrying the burdens of a leader and trying to hold her clans together, and though he suspected she wanted to trust him enough to share more than the defense of the castle, war and England had taken too much from her.

"Then I can only wait," he said, pressing a kiss to her forehead and wondering when he'd find the will to reveal his part in those changes.

Someone cleared his throat and they looked.

"The javelin, my princess." Her smithy offered the sharpened spear.

Siobhàn glanced at her husband, a little deviltry in her eyes as she scooted out of his embrace and took the javelin, propping it on her shoulder and walking toward the gates. Gaelan followed, unaware of the audience gathering behind them. Siobhàn took little time to prepare, yet lifted her skirts and tucked the hem in her girdle.

"Siobhàn!"

Pulling his shirt over his head, Gaelan gaped at her legs, bare to the knees.

She smiled, wondering what he'd think if he saw her in the braies she often wore on a hunt. "My target is that tuft of grass," she told him, then faced forward.

"A wager on this?"

She met his gaze, tipping her head thoughtfully, and when he sent her a slow smile and a glance down her body, she recognized the vein of his thoughts and warned, "Do not push me this day, husband, I am in no mood."

"Luncheon with me over there." He pointed to a cluster of trees and shrubs near the creek.

"And if I win?"

He bowed regally. "Your heart's desire."

Her gaze swept him briefly and before her imagination went amuck, she focused on the target. She arched back, the javelin near her cheek, then took three quick steps and with a heave, hurled it into the sky. Gaelan, Raymond at his side, watched the spear glide through the air, far beyond the camp to plunge into the grass cluster. The Irish cheered as the pole quivered. Siobhàn freed her skirts and curtsied to the crowd.

"Another," she called, and Irishmen raced to do her bidding. She handed the spear to PenDragon, arching a brow in challenge.

He did not bother to call his bowmen, focused on the target, then hurled the spear. Though it sailed higher, it missed the target by yards. Gaelan blinked, then looked at her. With a great flourish, he bowed.

"I am humbled afore your skill."

"Hah! Naught humbles you, my lord."

She did, he thought. "Your desire?"

She folded her arms over her middle, looked first at the keep, then the glen. Siobhàn was terribly irritated with her son, and her sister, for her constant disappearances lately, and needed a reprieve. "A private swim in the creek."

His brows shot high. "'Tis freezing, woman."

"I did not say you had to join me, did I now?" She unfolded her arms and stepped closer as Raymond ordered the people back to work.

"'Tis dangerous to be so far from the keep."

"You cannot protect me?" She patted his bulging biceps

significantly, then lowered her voice. "Then I will give you your lesson, aye?"

He merely smiled, pleased to have his way.

"But you must feed me, too."

His eyes darkened. "I had planned to do more than feed you."

Siobhàn's entire body lit with the sweetest of tremors. "Ahh, but I only asked for a guard and a swim." She stepped back and motioned him. "Be about it, my lord."

Chuckling at her impudence, Gaelan twisted and shouted for his page. In moments young Jace struggled with a fat basket, Reese not far behind him with his sword and his mount.

Siobhàn blinked. Well, the little sneak, she thought, and wondered if he threw the contest. Donning his sword, he checked the saddle's repaired girth, glancing wryly at her, then swinging onto the beast's back. He held out his hand. Grasping it, she hoisted her leg onto his instep and he pulled her onto the saddle before him.

He took the basket from Jace and tucked it to her, and she wiggled into the curve of his body. Gaelan groaned at the sweet agony of it.

She looked back over her shoulder. "A run, my lord, please?" Her eager smile pierced his heart.

If she would only smile at him like that every day, he thought, and heeled the horse. Grayfalk bolted. They rode, the cool wind biting and pungent with newborn grass, her dark red hair spreading across his chest like a warrior's shield. To lengthen the ride, he made a wide berth, skirting the outer edge of the barracks under construction, the small camps of soldiers. Her laughter spilled like crystal water from a fall, showering him, and she glanced back, her bright smile carving a hole in his heart. Gaelan tightened his hold around her waist and let Grayfalk have his head. The black destrier plunged over the low hills, climbed the mounds of turf, and his master guided him around to the west slope where the creek ran clear, the rare sun glowing over a dale with trees and wild stubby bushes.

With the castle still in sight, he slowed the mount. Before he stopped completely, she slid from the horse's back and raced to the creek, dropping the basket under the trees and kicking off her slippers. Yanking off her hose and flinging them aside, she dipped her toes in the water, then lifted her skirts, gathering them in her girdle.

Gaelan dismounted, ground tethering his horse and walking toward her. She looked like the wild girl he'd met in the forest, bare-kneed, holding her hair back, searching the stream for fish. Once she shoved her hand into the water for one, then cursed. Gaelan leaned back against the tree, simply enjoying the sight of her.

"You do not have to forage, Siobhàn; I have food here."

She looked up, holding her hair from the water. "Ahh, but 'tis the skill I must hone."

"I hunt for Donegal now."

She studied the fish moving under the water. "Want you a wife who cannot take care of herself? And you will not always be here, husband."

He pushed away from the tree and came to the water's edge. "I know you can take care of this fief, but can you not see that the burden is no longer yours alone to carry?"

"I know this, PenDragon."

"Nay, you do not." She met his gaze, straightening. "Not well enough to show your people. Think you I do not see that they obey me only at your discretion? Would you like to see them beaten for defiance?"

"Of course not!"

"Then you must cease airing your . . . prejudice afore the folk."

"I want them treated fairly."

"Name me once when they were not."

She was stumped completely and her shoulders sagged. He

was no longer the mercenary, his purpose so obvious in the construction he ordered on the castle, the coin she knew he would pay for the labor and supplies. She was suddenly terribly ashamed of keeping him at arm's length when he tried so hard to please her, bending to her, but . . .

"I do not trust you . . . completely."

His heart grabbed onto her hesitation and longed for more. "I know," came sadly.

"I do not know when I will." She left the creek, stopping on the soft bank before him.

" 'Twill come in time, Siobhàn. And by then, mayhaps, I might trust your motives as not a part of our *bargain*," he said with obvious distaste. "We have come by this alliance through much hardship to you, but you must understand that unless I am called by the king, I will not leave." His voice lowered to a husky pitch. "Donegal is my home now too."

'Twas his tone that snagged her, lonely and rarely heard.

"My only home ever, Siobhàn."

Her throat constricted. "Ha—have I not made you feel welcome?"

"You have made a place in your chamber, aye."

Her brow furrowed. "But not in my bed."

"Our bed."

It hit her then, the division she'd marked without realizing how it affected him. Hadn't she pitied his solitary existence before they'd wed? Yet she'd denied him the chance to alter his situation by keeping him from her bed, by battling with him, when he'd conceded all he could in his power.

"You cannot expect me to believe you have changed from war maker to settled lord in a sennight's time, husband."

"Nay, I am a warrior, Siobhàn, yet—" He looked off to the side. "I am learning, this I swear to you. But . . ." He shifted from foot to foot, his voice barely audible, almost shy. "I need your . . . help."

Something broke inside her then, slicing through the resistance. The moment offered a glimpse of his life, how difficult being inside the keep instead of burning it down must be for him. And she had done naught but keep him on the other side of the wall, sheltering her heart at his expense and denying the life he obviously craved, the life he'd earned for saving the king's.

"Oh, my lord husband," she whispered, fingering his hair off his brow, and his gaze snapped to hers. His features were brittle and carved with anxiety. "Forgive me."

"I could forgive you aught but your hatred of the man I am." His hands hovered over her shoulders, then settled there with a gentle weight and his tired sigh. "I cannot help my past, Siobhàn. 'Twas all I had until now." He swallowed heavily, staring deep into her eyes. "That man is fading, yet if I anger you with orders, 'tis because I've known no other way. But now I have more than a bastard has a right to possess and I find I want more."

"What else is left that you do not have, my lord?"

"You."

Her brow furrowed. "But we are wed—"

He touched his fingertip to her lips, silencing her. "The other night in our chamber I felt truly wed to you, but the morn brings the terms of our bargain to light. I am weary of living on the outside of real lives—your life, Siobhàn—when I belong on the inside." He neared, his body brushing hers, and Gaelan scented her like a stag scents its mate, hungering with a fierceness that robbed him of his will, his pride. "Donegal and her lands were the reason I wed you, Siobhàn." The slight narrowing of her eyes made him want to shout. "But you alone are the reason I wanted Donegal."

You alone.

"For the sake of a passion," she gasped, wetting her lips and searching his dark eyes. "You have relinquished your freedom?" She could hardly believe it.

"For my want of you, Siobhàn. Of the woman who challenged me like a warrior even when her life was at risk. And for a place to belong as you belong here.''

Over her head, he sketched the verdant land, and in that instant, Siobhàn recognized how deep his longing ran, brimming with the fierce determination to be a part of Ireland, a part of something more than war. The unguarded moments of the past week filled her mind, the turbulence in his eyes when he asked for a marriage under Christian law, when he found his possessions in her chamber, the tub made for him; when he asked her to teach him to read and begged that none be aware of his shortcomings. He was a man struggling with a new life, a new people and a position he hadn't needed from the start, and that he wanted to be a real part of her life unfolded hope inside her, the hope she'd had but could not share.

How many times had she dreamed of having such a mate? How often had she wished that she and Tigheran could have made more of their marriage? She was a bride of peace with the chance for so much more, and aye, she admitted, she liked this man very much, ached for him in ways she never thought existed. He'd carved a spot in her heart for himself that day in the field, and he was pushing his bulk inside with his bold teasing and the incredible tenderness hidden beneath his grand power.

She was losing her heart to him, and it left her vulnerable, pitifully so when he looked at her as he was now, with expectation and want and hunger.

He lifted his hand from her shoulder, let it hover near her jaw, and she slid her hand over his, pressing it to her skin. His dark eyes softened, and he whispered her name, reverent on the breeze.

"I did not know."

"I did not want you to."

"Why?"

"I am weak for you, Siobhàn. You did not need another wound to pluck open."

She need not ask if it was a weakness of the flesh, for she understood well there was more to this man than bedding, more she'd yet to discover.

"I can only promise to honor you well, PenDragon. And if I vent my feelings, 'tis because they have been smothered for so long." His features tightened a fraction. "I know not how to share them, for to show them was to appear feeble afore the people, and they needed my strength."

"You can yield them to me, wife, and I will not see you weak." He sighed and slid his fingers into the hair at her nape, tipping her head and brushing his mouth over hers. "I will keep them private, Siobhàn, for I cherish the sharing."

His confession touched her heart, piercing it with the strength of an arrow. A whimper worked in her throat, tears burning behind her eyes as he took more of her lips with each passing moment. He wet them, tasted and licked and kissed, and her heart escalated with the warmth of her body.

"Oh, husband," she gasped, her voice fracturing. "Hold me."

Gaelan slid his arms around her, a slow motion, as if afraid she would run from him and what he was experiencing was naught but a dream. He felt new ground beneath his feet, his walking into her arms a step into her mysterious soul. His guilt faded under the heat of their kiss, the pain that would come hovering beneath her spell, and with her mouth moving over his, she came into his arms, pressing her softness to his hard length and leaving him trembling. He'd tried to win her with gifts and deeds and it was the baring of his soul that brought her here. So simple. Yet there was naught simple about this woman.

He drew back, yet his mouth still whispered over hers, nipping and tasting.

"I need you, Siobhàn, not just in our bed. I . . ." He swallowed. "I need you to keep my secrets too."

"I will," she promised and pulled him harder to her, hurting inside for him, to be the wife he needed, to have a mate who would listen to her private worries, to care when she was troubled, and give her tenderness and passion without making her feel ashamed of her desires. Again, she marveled at the complicated man unfolding before her eyes. He was more than she expected and Siobhàn craved him, his companionship, his touch. He made her feel feminine and beautiful and deliciously wicked with his daring words and seductive threats.

Lost in her kiss, Gaelan felt her fidget and looked down as she removed her girdle and tossed it on the grass.

"What are you doing?" His words came tightly laced with tension.

"Taking me a needed swim." She retreated enough to pull her gown up to her hips, her intention clear, yet Gaelan stopped her, glancing around at the terrain, at the fortress off in the distance.

"Are you mad, woman?" She smiled, her body tempting him more than her grin. "A swim you said, not to parade the countryside naked!" God above, he could not look at her like this and not want to have her.

"I'm not paradin', my lord. And did you think I would swim in me gown?" She jerked the garment off and flung it in his face. Spinning away, she dove, and Gaelan dragged the garment from his head and searched the water. Only the flow from the mountains rippled the current and his heart pounded. He stepped into the water and she burst through the surface like a fish, her shift clinging to her skin as if she was bare. Smoothing her hair back, Siobhàn smiled at him, splashing him once, twice. His eyes warned her of more than a water fight coming.

And Siobhàn wanted it, wanted him.

Like a water sprite, she walked from the water, each step revealing her splendor until she stopped before him. Gaelan's gaze searched her features, her smoldering eyes, and she took a step farther, bringing another fracture in his armor. He did not touch her, afraid he would hurt her, his need of her clenching his muscles, laboring his breathing. His hands folded into fists as he stared at her. Her pale skin was rosy, her breasts peaking hard against the wet shift. A feathery mist swirled over her skin and his gaze raked her over and over.

Gaelan felt himself come apart, the courage and restraint he'd learned in battle splintering. "I cannot look at you and not want you, Siobhàn. Why do you torture me like this?"

"I do not seek to torture you, my lord." She moved past him, dragging her gown from where it hung on his shoulder and moving to the seclusion of the trees and shrubs.

He still stood on the banks, his back to her, his hands on his hips.

"Come to me, husband."

He whipped around, his stare scorching over her as she lowered to the ground, her figure hidden by the trees and bushes.

Gaelan swallowed, his mouth dry. She lifted her hand and he walked to her on unsteady feet, then sank to his knees with a jolt. He stared, his gaze raking over her, the wet muslin shaping her beautiful body in a veil of seduction.

Water pearled on her skin.

"I do not have to trust you to want you, PenDragon." She inched closer, her hands flattening over his chest, the threadbare lawn shirt. "Come to me," she whispered, leaning to touch her lips to his throat as she pulled the fabric from his braies. "Give me again what you gave me two nights past." Her lashes swept up, revealing blue-green eyes snapping with hidden fire. "This time I take from you." Her hands slid under the folds of his shirt, mapping the contours of his chest, her nails rasping over his nipples as she pushed it up. "For I wish to taste you."

Gaelan searched her face. "Out here?"

"Aye." She helped the shirt off over his head, dropping it to the ground, and Gaelan was seeing the hunger she'd suppressed, the need for him she'd smothered in aloofness. Her eyes looked everywhere, pleasure giving and taking in one sweep, her hands moving over his chest with a fascination that stirred him beyond thought. Then she leaned close, her tongue circling a flat coin nipple and he gripped her waist, dropping his head back as heat ground through him.

"We could be seen and I would want to savor this." Gaelan's hand moved over the slope of her hips to cup her buttocks, knead the soft flesh.

"But I want now," she pleaded, her fingers hovering at the edge of his braies. His muscles convulsed beneath her touch. "I want to touch you as you did me."

He met her gaze, his body pulsing savagely, blood rushing through his veins. "You do and I will not last, Siobhàn." His touch rode wildly over her buttocks, her spine, palming her breasts.

"But can you stop me?" Her small hand dipped inside his braies and enfolded his hard flesh. Gaelan jerked and moaned, crushing her to him as she stroked him warmly, her fingers slicking over the velvety tip of him. He trembled violently, his groan almost an agonized roar.

"Oh, God."

She manipulated his hard flesh as she whispered hotly against his mouth, "I find I have an appetite for the dragon, husband." She licked his lips and his ragged breath tumbled into her mouth. "Come. Satisfy it."

Chapter Seventeen

The seams of his hungry soul split at the softly spoken demand. An eternity of unbridled pleasure passed before he gathered his thoughts and met her gaze, snatching her hand away from his arousal. "You are certain of this?"

"You tease me for days and ask that?" She nipped at his lips, his throat.

His eyes slammed shut, his breathing ragged. The anticipation would surely kill him. "I do not want what you do not wish to give me, Siobhàn."

"I plan to take, PenDragon—" Her tongue snaked over his nipple as she loosed his hold. "Mayhaps I was not clear?" Her hand dove again, her fingers sliding mercilessly over his erection.

"Aye—oh, sweet Jesu, woman." He pried her hand from him, a warning in his eyes. "Want me to slam into you and not please you?"

His excitement was hers, coating her, arousing her with the power of it. "You please me with your trembling, my lord."

Without hesitation she climbed onto his lap, her moist flesh pressing hotly to his hardness, and Gaelan caught her jaw in his broad palms, the threads of his restraint snapping as he kissed her, a dark plundering of lips and tongue that ignited the passion to glorious heights.

She rocked against him, her body begging for more, and his hands rode down her shoulders, her arms, sweeping around to cup her buttocks and grind her to him.

"Someone could come upon us," he said, even as he hurriedly peeled her wet shift off over her head. Her arms above her head, he looked his fill of her swelling breasts, her naked belly and the dark red tuft between.

"I know." Her smile was catlike, wicked, as her hands floated to his shoulders. He cupped her breasts, kneading them, and she leaned back, offering him more. Gaelan bent to wrap his lips around her nipple and suck the tender tip deep into the heat of his mouth. She arched and gasped, her fingers digging into his broad shoulders. He held her suspended, bent back over his strong arms, his mouth torturing her bosom with heated kisses, his teeth scoring lightly over the soft cushiony underside.

The velvety tip of him slicked her and he growled like a beast, pushing her to her back, his hip spreading her.

Still she played. "I want to taste you as you did me."

"Nay, Siobhàn, and if you do not cease your squirming I will come now."

"Come where?" she teased.

She rolled him easily onto his back and straddled him, her hair a red veil of privacy as her mouth played over his throat, his chest. She suckled and stroked, molding the carved muscles of his chest, the ridges of his stomach. She met his gaze, her eyes darkening with seduction as she pushed his braies farther down, releasing him fully.

"Siobhàn. Siobhàn, nay, lass." He pleaded, even as she bent to him, taking him into her mouth. He flinched violently, curling up to watch and feel and absorb this woman unleashing her passion on him. His heart thundered so hard he swore she could hear it, his body bleeding with fiery sensations, demanding that he toss her to the ground and pound into her. But her pleasure, the feel of her flesh brushing over his, was a prize he would savor and cherish, her surrender a step to winning her trust.

Her mouth played. He thickened and hardened, and he called her name over and over, begging her to cease and let him pleasure her. But she refused, her tongue sliding, her lips pulling until he was too near exploding to care, yet he did. He wanted her, *her,* and caught her beneath the arms, dragging her over him, thrilling at the feel of every inch of her laid bare to his touch.

Her skin was on fire, pure heat against the cool air.

His broad hands mapped her contours, hands coarse with calluses, fashioned to wield a sword and crossbow, an ax and a javelin—hard, unyielding. Yet when he held her, the sensations of war turned to vapor and he knew he held a woman, ripely shaped, soft, with skin of silk and tasting of honey. His life was battle, survival and conquer, yet here she was the victor, leaving him vanquished and weak.

And he cherished it, wanted more of it, a willing prisoner to her power.

No woman had ever touched him as she did. No woman gave of herself in a single kiss, in a tiny stroke of his flesh, and Gaelan knew he would do aught to keep this woman his, close and private and in possession of his soul.

In the seclusion of a tiny dale, she abandoned the cloak of her position. Hidden beneath the shade of trees, the wall of shrubbery still thin from the winter's cold, she spread her thighs, toeing his braies further down with an eagerness that stirred him to explosion. When she rose up, sliding, slicking him, Gaelan could stand no more.

He sat up sharply, grinning at her started look, his arousal pushing between her thighs, seeking the warm nest, and he reached between their bodies, his gaze never leaving hers as he guided himself deeper into her. He filled her, loving the flare of her eyes, the way her tongue passed over her lips, the breathy pants . . . and the feminine muscles flexing wetly around him.

"Oh—oh—husband," she repeated over and over and threw her head back, gripping his shoulders and he shoved upward, sheathing himself to the hilt. Gaelan groaned, his body quaking.

Suddenly he pulled her hard against him, chest to breast, taking her mouth with all the heat and raw desire grinding through him. Her arms wrapped his neck and he gave her hips sweet motion, lifting her and lowering her, obliging the impatient whimpers of his bride. He could feel her body pawing his. He heard her whispers of encouragement, the telltale signs he was just beginning to know; a tuck of her hips, a fractured breath.

Then she spoke, whispering how delicious he felt inside her, that she could feel him throbbing, his blood pulsing, her words bold and meant to drive him mad. And they did.

He yanked her legs around his hips and pushed her to her back on the soft mossy earth, bracing his weight on his arms. He shoved and withdrew, his mouth whispering an apology, yet she gripped his hips and demanded more of his long torturous strokes. Her heels dug into the cushiony ground, her hips rising to greet his. The cadence buffeted, smooth motion, and Gaelan gazed into her eyes, watching her rapture climb to a peak.

Her eyes never closed, looking over him, watching his body disappear into hers. And each time, she bit her lower lip to hold back a cry.

"Let me hear you, princess."

She did, her gasps coloring the air, her emotions cresting with the tightness peeling through her undulating body. Delicate muscles gripped him.

Gaelan plunged, taking her mouth, wanting to taste her pleasure on his lips.

"My lord!"

He chuckled and she pounded his shoulders, then cupped his buttocks and drove him deeper. He retreated and plunged, tight and hard and spearing.

Gaelan conquered, only here, only now.

Siobhàn surrendered, receiving him, skin to bare skin.

Carved bronze against ivory silk.

Seeking, seeking, hastening toward the prize.

Then they found it, the clash shattering, swelling.

He drove her across the earth and touched her soul, and she arched, bowing beautifully beneath him, her fingertips digging into his chest as he slammed into her, once twice, and she cried out, scattering birds from the trees and begging for more. Gaelan gave, unable to contain even a shred of restraint and threw his head back, pleasure roaring through him like a caged beast set free.

Siobhàn felt his climax skip through her, every cell breaking, his throbbing arousal elongating to spill his seed into her. The hard base of him pressed and rubbed, sending exquisite convulsions down to her toes and she flinched over and over, taking all he had and finding her rapture in his release. She held his gaze, watching it, the flutter of his lashes, the softening of his creased features, the blaze in his eyes as she held him vulnerable inside her.

Suspended on the edge, Gaelan couldn't move, wracked with tremors trapping him in the grip of desire. He stared at her, his chest heaving for air, sweat rolling down his temples and the center of his chest as he took in every detail of her. A vapor simmered over her hot skin, her red hair spread in a halo around her exquisite face. God above, she was beautiful, headstrong, rebellious, yet here, in his arms, beneath him in loving, she was a magnificent savage, her release as untamed as she was, as if capped for too long.

Then she reached, playing with his nipple, outlining the contours of his breast before her fingers curved his neck to bring him down to her mouth. Her kiss was probing and turbulent, stirring him deeper than before, and with a groan, he sank onto her, rolling to his side and taking her with him. Her calf rubbed over his, her fingertips drawing patterns on his damp back.

He was still lodged inside her and her hips pushed deliciously to his.

"Did I hurt you?" He'd never pounded into a woman with such ferocity before.

"You did not hear me complainin', did you now?"

He grinned. "So then, you are still hungry for the dragon?" he teased, stroking her hair from her face as she tipped her head to look at him.

"You would deny me the pleasure now?"

He chuckled, kissing her again. "I would indulge you all day, but we will be discovered soon." His gaze swept meaningfully to the lowering sun.

"I do not care."

He scoffed, running his hand over her slender back, enjoying the peace and the feel of her skin. "You will when the entire keep sees your bare behind." He patted the tender area. "I am surprised Driscoll did not come a'running to see if I was killing you, your cries were so loud." Her gaze snapped to his, searching for the admonishment, but found only a tender humor.

"My cries?"

He arched a brow.

She shoved at his chest. "Oh, do not look at me as if you were not roaring like a beast too long in a pen."

He grinned, his eyes sparkling with mischief. "You opened the cage, woman, and let the dragon out."

Her gaze lowered briefly to where their bodies joined. "When one knocks long and hard enough," she said with a moan, thrusting softly against him, "one must answer the door."

Suddenly Gaelan rolled her to her back, plunging deeply and gazing into her eyes. "Knock, knock."

* * *

Siobhàn watched him walk from the stream, his naked body glistening with water like fairy dust. The sight of him made her heart skip, and she tipped her head as he neared. Truly a beautiful man, she thought, proud he was hers. Their marriage was unbreakable now, sealed before God, and Siobhàn did not have a single regret. She had kept them from being truly husband and wife. *She* had drawn a battleline between them, and the needs of her body and her heart had melted into one and she recognized hours ago that if she wanted a new life, she had to break from her own rebellion and give into the sweep of it. There had been no question that she'd wanted to be physically loved by him. 'Twas a pleasure she would never forget, a pleasure that would be remembered with a look and a touch. Her gaze followed him as he dressed, constantly astonished at the power he harnessed for her this afternoon. Muscles rippled and flexed as he stepped into his braies, then pulled on a poorly made lawn shirt, the cuffs and sides gathered. She could not take her eyes off him as he laced the boot thongs over his thighs and fastened the leather, unadorned codpiece over his manhood. Even flaccid, 'twas substantial, she thought, desire for him stirring through her again.

"Siobhàn," he warned. "That look is dangerous. Want to find yourself on your back?"

"I would prefer my knees," she said tartly, and his head shot up, his eyes flying wide. She nibbled on a cube of cheese, looking at him through a curtain of hair. "I have shocked you, I see."

"Aye," he admitted.

"Forgive me."

Squatting, he reached, tipping her face up, frowning softly. "Spare naught from me."

Her brow knitted and she shoved the cheese into her mouth, then studied the samplings. "Tigheran was unfaithful," she blurted. "To him bedding was a weapon. No matter how I tried, he saw me as a cruel second to Devorgilla. The enemy's niece." She scoffed rudely. "He did not believe a woman should have any desires."

Gaelan dropped to his knees before her, then snatched up a bite of food. "I am most glad you have them."

She glanced up, her smile slow, trembling a bit. He could not know what his tenderness, his coaxing and the freedom she felt in his arms meant to her. Her eyes burned for the giant of a man who hid this side of himself and gave it only to her, for letting her be herself and discover all she'd suppressed. Making love with him was new, fresh, and she felt almost virtuous. He gave her more than she gave him. And she knew she'd denied them both these past days for the mark Tigheran left on her, for the hateful words he'd say to her when she so much as patted his arm. But this Cornish knight craved her touch, and when she gave it, he wanted more. Siobhàn was most willing to deliver.

"So am I, my lord."

He sank down beside her, cupping her delicate jaw, his thumb rasping over her lovely lips. The glossy look in her eyes nearly destroyed his composure. O'Rourke was mad to turn her away, he thought. "Touch me when you wish, Siobhàn. Call to me and I will come to you." His gaze darkened, smoldering velvet and filled with promise. "Know you by now I would rather be touching you than eating, drinking, sleeping, riding, fighting, building . . ."

Her mouth moved lightly over his as she said, "Yer saying you be thinking of getting beneath me skirts a good deal, then?"

He groaned, his hand sliding under the aforementioned skirt and stroking her bare thighs. "Aye."

She caught his hand, stopping him. "Think on it a bit longer then. Write," she said, with a wave at the quill and parchment. With a look that was almost childlike in disappointment, he took up the quill. Lying on his stomach, he practiced whilst she hovered over the cloth laden with food, popping piece after piece into her mouth.

"Worked up an appetite, have you?"

She looked up sharply, eyed him, her cheeks full as she chewed, then swallowed. "Nay, you did it."

He grinned, smug and itching to roar, then focused on his writing. They dined, he wrote and Siobhàn fed him the picnic meal, correcting his work, tasting his mouth in reward.

"We've been gone a bit," she said with a glance at the sky as they gathered the items and wrapped up the uneaten portions.

"I will simply tell them that you stripped to your bare butt and threw yourself at my feet, begging to be had."

"Oh!" she gasped, then laughed, shoving the basket at his chest as she mounted the horse. He lashed the basket to the saddle and she waited until he climbed up behind her before wiggling into his groin. He groaned softly, his body responding with amazing swiftness. "Now we will see who'll be doing the beggin', my lord."

"Sorceress," he said on a grin.

"Nay, that's Rhiannon."

He scowled.

Her brow knitted a touch and she looked surprised. "I thought Driscoll would have told you." His expression said otherwise. "She is not a conjuring one, but a seer. She can . . . feel things," she said with a shrug. "I advise you not to let her touch you too long, if you be having a secret to keep."

"I won't."

Gaelan kissed her suddenly, his arm around her waist, her body tight to his front. His mouth molded, the reminder, his sudden fear of losing her driving him to put all his mastery in the single kiss. Grayfalk shifted beneath them. Siobhàn whimpered, the little sound of eagerness he recognized as she twisted in the saddle, diving her hands beneath his shirt and stroking his warm flesh. She was breathless and panting when he drew back.

"Oh, my lord," she moaned on a rush of air, sinking into his embrace.

Gaelan curled her to him, her head resting beneath his chin, her arms around his waist. They rode slowly toward Donegal castle, sated in body, hearts wishing for more and both fearing their past would destroy the feelings budding like spring heather on the moors.

Every head turned, a thousand pairs of eyes watching as the lord and lady of Donegal rode between the gates. Their ease with each other was apparent, and Raymond DeClare folded his arms over his chest and awaited their approach. A maid rushed to take the basket, her expression warring between a frown and a smile. Gaelan swung down, then turned for his wife, and Raymond could not help but notice the look on her face when he let her slide down his body. Gaelan touched her hair lightly, tipped her chin and kissed her, murmuring unheard words. She nodded and, with a lingering stroke to his chest, moved past him. Raymond followed her retreat, the way she kept looking back at Gaelan, smiling, and he did not need any clearer an image.

"The work is going well, my lord."

Gaelan dragged his gaze from Siobhàn's sweet behind and glanced at the walls. " 'Tis getting dark; cease for the day."

He nodded. "Did my lord have a good time at the creek?"

Gaelan slid him a glance. "You've a comment to make, make it, DeClare."

His gray eyes widened. "Me? Abhor the thought. Although . . ." Gaelan eyed him, waiting. "The knights are already speculating on the arrival of your first child. . . ."

"I will wager you will be a father afore me, DeClare."

Raymond paled.

"Watch yourself." Bidding to see him at the evening meal, Gaelan headed toward the keep, his steps quick.

Driscoll moved up beside him, watching Gaelan for a moment. "Think you he's impatient for the day to end so he can be alone with her?"

Raymond's glaze slid to the side. "You noticed that, eh?"

"Everyone has. Makes him seem a bit more human, that he sniffs after the princess—her ladyship"—he said with a sour look—"like a panting boar."

"I think he is falling in love with her."

Driscoll glanced, his brows high, doubt in the look. He knew the princess better than most and she never gave herself such a luxury. "And you are an expert at love?"

"I've been in love many times"—he grinned—"though briefly."

"Aye, as long as it takes to bed a wench. 'Tis five of the dairy maids, last I heard."

Raymond reddened. "Great Scot."

"Nay, sir, lovely Irish lasses." He patted his chest dramatically. "Steal a man's heart right out from under him." He chuckled at DeClare's not-me look and strode toward the stables. Raymond looked back at the workers, calling an end to the day and ordering the guards to seal the gates at sundown.

A figure caught his attention, the setting sun glinting off a cloud of light red hair, and he recognized Rhiannon as she moved across the outer ward toward the chapel, ignoring everyone, her head down. Now that one was cold as the Irish wind, he thought, for although he'd tried to get to know her, she would not bestow even a smile on him. She was beautiful; golden red hair, fresh face and comely as any other. Yet there was something odd about her, a supremacy he could not get beyond, even in casual conversation, and though he would love to see if her lips tasted as glorious as they looked, her recent behavior made him suspicious. She was constantly looking over her shoulder, searching the crowd as if she waited for someone to appear and name her a killer or aught as ridiculous.

Raymond watched as a figure came forward, cloaked in

Take 4 FREE Books!

Zebra created its convenient Home Subscription Service so you'll be sure to get the hottest new romances delivered each month right to your doorstep — usually before they are available in book stores. Just to show you how convenient Zebra Home Subscription Service is, we would like to send you 4 Zebra Historical Romances as a FREE gift. You receive a gift worth up to $24.96 — absolutely FREE. There's no extra charge for shipping and handling. There's no obligation to buy anything - ever!

Save Even More with Free Home Delivery!

Accept your FREE gift and each month we'll deliver 4 brand new titles as soon as they are published. They'll be yours to examine FREE for 10 days. Then if you decide to keep the books, you'll pay the preferred subscriber's price of just $4.20 per title. That's $16.80 for all 4 books for a savings of up to 32% off the publisher's price! What's more...$16.80 is your total price...there is no additional charge for the convenience of home delivery. Remember, you are under no obligation to buy any of these books at any time! If you are not delighted with them, simply return them and owe nothing. But if you enjoy Zebra Historical Romances as much as we think you will, pay the special preferred subscriber rate of only $16.80 each month and save over $8.00 off the bookstore price!

We have 4 FREE BOOKS for you as your introduction to
KENSINGTON CHOICE!

To get your FREE BOOKS,
worth up to $24.96, mail the card below.
or call TOLL-FREE 1-888-345-BOOK

monk's robes and blocking her path. When Rhiannon tried to step around, the person followed. She stopped, her hand on her hips, her impatience for him to move aside ringing from her slim body. The figure—Raymond could not tell if the body housed breasts or not—stepped closer to her, and yet the sudden fear on her face sent the knight rushing forward.

"My lady," he called, his hand on his sword.

Her head snapped around, her eyes flaring wide. "Nay. I am well," she said with a staying hand, then spoke sharply to the intruder before turning about and heading back to the keep.

Raymond watched her, frowning and when he looked back to the monk, he was gone. He spun, his gaze raking over the area. Damn. There was no place to hide, not that quickly, he thought, looking to the gates. He strode to the tower, calling out and asking after the visitor. The guards reported no one in robes entering or leaving the keep today. Raymond sighed and turned back to his duties, reminding himself to inform Gaelan of his sister-in-law's strange behavior.

Chapter Eighteen

Gaelan watched her with her son. Although the boy pouted, she kept up her smiles, her gentle touches to his hair. Connal scarcely looked at him, if not to glare and twice this evening had tried to speak with him, without success. Gaelan wondered how old the child would be before they would find even ground. Impatience for the meal to end, for the moment when he could take his wife abovestairs and make love to her, rode him and he tried to smother it.

But when she looked at him, he could think of aught but her expression when she touched him, when she took him inside herself, the abandon she gave only to him this day. Beside him, his wife looked regal and poised, the lady she was, but Gaelan knew better, and he was delighted that no other man experienced loving her.

No man living, a voice corrected. His dark thoughts turned to Ian, the man's jealousy dangerous, and now he understood from whence it came. For if Siobhàn were in the Maguire's arms, he would kill again. And enjoy it.

She turned to him, her brow knitting. "What ails you? You look ready to devour a body whole, husband."

His features smoothing out, he leaned close to whisper, "I want to devour you."

Her skin pinkened softly and her hand slid over his. People stared and smiled, but she did not see them. Connal folded his arms and pouted harder, but she had no notice of it. Her heart skipped at the look in his eyes, the memory of their play steaming her skin warmer.

Rhiannon approached, clearing her throat. Siobhàn turned.

"I will take him." Her gaze slipped to her brother-in-law. "Be with each other." She inclined her head toward the stairs.

Gaelan's features tightened. How did she know?

"Rhiannon," Siobhàn said with a concerned frown, "tell me you did not—"

"Nay," she said with a smile. " 'Tis too obvious to everyone that all has changed." Rhi leaned down, careful not to let Connal hear her. "I am pleased you made this match work, brother, sister," she said, her gaze moving between them. "He will come round soon enough." Her gaze flicked to the child. "As will the others."

Gaelan's gaze bounced off Connal, then to the folk dining around them. He could easily pick out the Irish who were not pleased with their princess, the damning looks obvious and irritating enough that Gaelan wanted to say something, yet did not know what. Loving Siobhàn's body was his business, private, and to the folk, naught would change. He was the invader, the enemy still, and he'd hoped Siobhàn's acceptance of him in bed would have made some mark toward their allegiance. Apparently, it was not the case, and he hoped they did not rebel against her, for she was his only tight link to gaining their loyalty. None of them would survive in this torn land if even one sought to betray her.

Gaelan's attention turned to Rhiannon as she lifted Connal in her arms. Connal twisted in her hold, reaching for his mother, and Gaelan nudged her, nodding. Siobhàn rose and carried her son to his chamber herself. The boy smirked, so adultlike, over his shoulder at Gaelan. It had little effect and he recalled a time when he'd been likewise pleased to have the attention of his own father. Saroan PenDragon was a benevolent man, pleased to find he had a son, an heir late in his life, but his treatment only extended to his blood, for Gaelan's brother, by a different father, was ignored. Gaelan had asked him to help Stephan, but . . . anger threatened his mood and Gaelan swilled back the remnants of his wine and stood, determined not to allow the past to interfere tonight. It would come soon enough.

He left the dais, ignoring Raymond's smirk and Driscoll's heated looks as he headed toward the stairs. He found her in their darkened chamber near the fire, her body draped in the russet velvet she wore on their wedding night, arms folded over her breasts. Again the bands of silver wrapped her arms, and Gaelan thought she'd never looked more beautiful, more the princess she was.

As he stepped through the door, she tipped her head to look at him.

Gaelan frowned, the sadness in her eyes unmistakable. "What ails you, love?"

Siobhàn drew a breath, exhaling slowly. "My son is growing angrier by the day."

"Has he done more mischief?"

"Nay. But I have raised him better, my lord. Someone is feeding this rage."

Gaelan crossed the chamber, gazing down at her. "Who would do this?"

She shrugged bare shoulders and his gaze swept her, realizing she was naked and prepared for him. Oh, God. He tried to focus on the conversation.

"Children mayhaps?" he said.

"A child will contradict other children, yet youth follows what their elders tell them."

"Who's judgment would he trust?"

"Anyone's here, my lord," came sullenly.

"It hurts you, doesn't it? That your folk could be saying hateful things to Connal."

"Would it not you?"

"Nay." Her brows rose a fraction. "I am accustomed to being loathed and called aught but my name." His shoulders moved restlessly. " 'Twas the price of my profession."

"Those who speak so are of little minds, my lord."

His lips quirked. "You called a few choice slurs afore."

Her chin tipped a fraction higher, her features tight with memory. "Most of them were truth, PenDragon, at the time, but I apologize if I wounded you."

"You did." He caught her shoulders. "Only you can, I fear."

Siobhàn's expression softened with her body, and he pulled her flush against him, his arms sliding around her waist. She gazed up at her husband, her feelings for him growing by the hour. He confessed his heart so easily, a habit she never expected from a man, any man. She opened her arms, letting the velvet pool at her waist, exposing her breasts and loving the way his eyes greedily absorbed her. She never felt more of a woman than in his arms. Her hands slid up around his neck, drawing him down for a kiss. He trembled, and it aroused her more.

'Twas something special, making such a powerful man quake like this, and she rewarded him with a slow wet kiss, a seduction of patience, lacking the urgency of this afternoon. Though she'd thoroughly enjoyed loving him by the river, this night she would savor ever nuance. Her desires were in control, his pleasure the outcome. Here, she trusted him; here, in his arms, she felt whole, safe and wonderfully complete. Her fingers pushed into his hair at his nape and he groaned, tightening his embrace. He tasted her as if she were a fine dessert, teasing her lips, and when she drew back, she was aching for more of

him. She pushed out of his arms and stepped back, smiling
devilishly.

"Strip."

Gaelan's heart skipped. "An order?"

"Aye. I want to see all of you." She sank into a nearby
chair, wrapped in velvet and watching him with a patience she
did not feel.

Gaelan nearly tore his clothes off, dropping his wide belt to
the floor, yanking off his tunic. Her gaze followed every move,
and when he stood in naught but braies, the look of anticipation
on her face nearly undid him. He peeled the hose down and
she shifted in the chair, silently begging him to come to her.

He didn't.

The velvet lowered a fraction, exposing her breasts above
her nipples.

Still he remained near the fire.

Her green gaze marked him like the slash of a blade, stroking
over his body, lingering enough at his arousal to make him
grow for her.

Distracted for weeks over this woman, Gaelan wanted to
make good his promise to have her begging for him. And by
the look on her face, she was not far from it.

"What do you want, Siobhàn?"

"You," she said plainly, and his manhood flexed.

Siobhàn loved it, seeing him straining not to jump on her.
She was well prepared to have him, her body slick with desire,
her skin dampening. The firelight glowed off his golden skin,
the contours of muscle and man shaded and revealed in the
flickering light. She let the velvet drop to her waist, her hair
webbing her breasts.

"How much?"

Her brow furrowed, then smoothed. "Very much."

"Enough to beg?"

Her lips curved. "Who will be doing the beggin', my lord?"

He chuckled, a low sound telling her he would be the last to fold.

She arched a russet brow, tipping her head back, her hands smoothing over her breasts, enfolding them.

Gaelan's entire body clenched.

She closed her eyes, her head back, her body arching off the chair. Russet velvet pooled around her waist, hiding her treasures, one slim leg exposed at the calf. Her fingertips toyed with her nipples. "Do you want me, my lord?"

"Never doubt that, Siobhàn."

She looked at him, sinking into the chair, her hand sliding beneath the velvet, between her thighs. She gasped, eyes flaring.

Gaelan stepped closer, gazing down at her. Her gaze fell on his arousal, and he wrapped himself, watching her twist and toy. She reached, her hands sliding around the back of his thighs, pulling him near.

He tilted her face up and her tongue snaked across the tip of him.

Air hissed in through clenched teeth and he folded to his knees. "You are devious."

She simply smiled and relaxed back into the chair, her gaze locked with his.

Gaelan spread the velvet, looking his fill, then leaning out to drag his tongue over her nipple. She shuddered hard, a soft *ahh* slipping from her lips.

"More?"

She had that make-me look he loved.

His hand slid to her spine, coaxing her to the edge of the chair. He nudged her thighs apart, wedging himself between. He suckled her with a consuming heat, keeping his body from her, his weight. She gripped his shoulders, offering her breasts to his feasting, her delicate pants filling the darkened chamber. His hands smoothed over her thighs, up and down, dipping between, but never touching her womanhood, and she whimpered, impatient, restless.

"More?" he whispered against the tip of her breast, then drew it deeply into his mouth. His tongue circled and flicked and she bit her lip to keep from crying out, from begging, the game weakening her. Slowly, his fingers curled around her knees, lifting one, then the other to drape her slender limbs over the arms of the chair. He sat back, his gaze savage as it ripped over her. Siobhàn writhed, lavish, abandoned. A dew-kissed offering for his pleasure.

He buried his face in her belly, the roughness of his beard stimulating already sensitive skin. He nipped at her ribs, the curve of her waist, and she flinched. He nuzzled harder and she jerked, her little laughter escaping into the warm room. He ground his mouth over her hips, the join of her thigh, scenting her. His fingers neared her center, touching all around, and she shifted, excited.

His hand slid beneath her buttocks, lifting her toward his mouth. Her gaze flew to his, his hot breath fanning her softness. "More?"

"I surrender."

"Remember that." He tasted her.

She shrieked, bowing off the chair, and he drove his tongue deeply, mercilessly. Her breathing, rapid and on the brink of a scream, was the only sound. Gaelan stroked his wife, her climax luxuriously near, and when she flexed deeply, a low groan tumbling from her lips, he pushed two fingers inside her and felt her explosion grip him, claw and steal and when she started to sag into the chair, he began a new assault, circling the bead of her sex.

"Enough! Nay, oh cease, cease!" She twisted in his grasp and he chuckled against her flesh, the sinister sound vibrating through her body. "I beg you," she cried, and slowly he let her fall to earth, lowering her legs, then sampling her tender breasts. She caught her breath and was on him in an instant, retribution in her bright green-blue eyes.

She kissed him, ruthlessly, gripping fistfuls of his hair and tasting herself on his chiseled mouth as he dragged her off the chair and onto his lap. She tipped his head back, her chest working for air as she sucked his earlobe, whispering what she was going to do to him, and then did it. Her thighs spread over his, she rocked against his hardness, refusing him peace, her breasts rubbing his chest, and Gaelan could take no more. Then she wrapped her fingers around his arousal and slid off his lap, taking him deep into her mouth. He fell back and she came with him, offering him a view of her shape yet not a single touch. It was too painful, his want of her, and on the river of velvet, he forced her to her back. Siobhàn grinned up at him, her hair tangled about her throat and shoulders.

"You said something about your knees?"

Her brows furrowed, then relaxed, and he realized she'd meant straddling him. He would show her more this night and rolled her to her stomach, drawing her back against his chest, his erection between her thighs.

"Oh, husband, aye," she moaned, pushing into him. His hands swept her body, her breasts and belly, then dipped between her thighs. She pushed against, and he stroked her dewy flesh. "My lord, please."

"Please what, my wife?"

"Give me."

"What, Siobhàn?"

"Your power, this power," she moaned, reaching between to guide him.

He flinched at her touch. "Sweet mother, you are the hottest creature." Her skin felt burned by the sun, her silken depth wet for him. Gaelan groped for the chair, dragging it close and bracing her hands on the arms. He entered her swiftly, plunging deep, and she threw her head back, her hair, the bells, sliding over his shoulder like silken threads.

She rocked and he gave her control, his hands free to tease and pleasure. She undulated like a wave against him, her motions stronger, harder, and when Gaelan did not think he could withstand another instant, she slammed back into him, reaching back to cup his buttocks and urge him.

"I will hurt you."

"Nay, nay." She shook her head.

He wanted to see her face and left her, pulling her to the floor and driving into her. Her legs locked around his hips, his hands threaded with hers aside her head, arms braced. He withdrew and thrust, long and hard, and she watched him fill her and retreat. It was enough to make his climax arrive too soon.

"Look at me."

Her gaze flew to his, locked and held.

His tempo increased. Her hips rose to greet him, take him. Every fiber of him throbbed with the rush of blood and sensation, feeling everything about her, her fingers flexing in his, the claw of feminine flesh, wet and slick and possessing. He drove and she accepted, the slow torture long forgotten in the thrash and slaughter of passion.

Bodies surged in extravagant rhythm. Smooth and wet and savagely raw.

Firelight spilled their primitive indulgence across ancient stone walls.

With her, he had no patience, no command.

He was at her mercy, and when her breath skipped, her body tensing, gripping, her pleasure ground through him, unleashing his seed.

He shoved and they strained against each other.

She curved off the velvet, exposing her throat, displaying herself a siren of womanhood in the throes of carnal rapture. A keening sound of exhilaration and surrender spilled from her lips. Her body groped luxuriously and he shoved and shoved, a tremendous shudder raking his body to his heels. He pulsed inside her and she felt it, felt him touch her womb and prayed for the gift.

They remained so, poised for a fraction on the edge of mindless desire. She sucked in gulps of air, sinking to the floor, and Gaelan crumbled onto her, only his shaking arms supporting him. He released her hands and her arms enveloped him; this woman, his woman, cradled him against her heart, stroked his damp hair from his temple.

"Ahh, Siobhàn," he murmured into her throat, trying to catch his breath. "You are the sweetest torture."

She smiled against his hair, sifting his dark curls. "My thanks, my lord."

He chuckled, shaking against her, then managed to lift his head. He brushed his mouth over hers, loving her easy response, her lips shaping his.

"Oh, husband." She sighed softly. "You may do that all night if you wish."

He cleared his throat. "Ahh, give me a few moments."

"Oh? The dragon sleeps?" She laughed, wiggling, and he groaned, holding her still, a warning in his dark eyes.

She was bloody damned smug, he thought, adoring it.

Slowly, Gaelan shifted back, leaving her body in small increments. The separation was almost painful and he smoothed his hands over her from breast to thigh, then looked about for a cloth. Without a word she rose and went to the bowl and pitcher near the hearth, spilling water into the basin, and with a cloth returned to him.

On her knees she bathed him, her strokes gentle and without teasing, and Gaelan savored her touch, her consideration for him. Then he took the cloth, dipped and wrung it, rinsing his seed from her. Her breath hitched when he dragged the cloth between her thighs, and Siobhàn lifted her gaze to his, feeling suddenly, ridiculously, defenseless. For weeks she had been on her guard and now so little remained concealed from him, save one thing. *Ahh, merciful Lord, do not destroy this,* she prayed. *I have coveted these feelings, the fragments of hope for so many years.* Then he leaned and rubbed his mouth over hers, intimate and now familiar, his dark eyes soft with affection, and her unease, her fears faded to a place she cared not to visit.

She rose and held her hand out to him. "Come to our bed, my lord."

His features tightened for an instant, in surprise or pleasure she did not know, yet he accepted, climbing to his feet and walking to the grand creation. When he hesitated, she looked back at him, half on, half off the bed. His gaze was on the mattressing, a frown marking his brow.

"He has never lain with me here, my lord."

Gaelan's gaze shot to hers. How could she read his thoughts so easily? he wondered.

"Only in the one belowstairs in the solar."

His gaze glazed her round bottom, the drape of hair as she climbed onto the bed, slipping beneath the covers, then tossing a portion back for him. "Nor has any man till now." She patted the space beside her.

Gaelan all but leapt into the bed.

She laughed softly, snuggling into the curve of his body, feeling sheltered and free. "Would it matter? For I do not ask of the women."

"Nay, but I have no women, Siobhàn. Only the kind bought with coin."

She met his gaze and clearly thought this a falsehood of the first water. "You chose no wife, ever?"

His lips twisted wryly. "Women do not flock to wed bastards."

"Codswallop."

He chuckled.

" 'Tis English thinking"—she waved airily—"the church and its harsh ways. You are in Ireland now; think like the Irish."

"God forbid."

She elbowed him and he made a great show of folding over.

"Of course," she conceded, "a lass would go a'running when she thought of bedding with you."

He met her gaze, arching a brow.

"You are a rather substantial fellow." Even as she said it, her hand rode over his shoulder, fingers tracing the sculpture of his thick arms. "Then again, the name is enough to send the fainthearted to fleeing."

He hovered over her. "Oh?"

"Aye, all those strange PenDragons," she said dramatically. "A history you have, of betrayal and treachery, incest, wife-stealin', brothers wedding to half sisters." She tisked, her lips quivering.

He grinned, for 'twas obvious she cared less for his lineage. "Are you asking after my family. Now?" His gaze swept her body, then ended on his ring banding her finger.

Her teasing faded. "You do not want to share it?"

" 'Tis not pretty."

"I did not think it would be, for you've been a mercenary for so long," she said with a sour look and a shove back. "I want to hear of the child." When he did not speak, she rose up on her elbow, puffing pillows behind his head and shoulders. "Your mother; where is she?"

He shrugged, sinking into the down. "The last I saw of her I was mayhaps eight." He rubbed his back on the softest of sheets as she snuggled close to his side, tangling her legs with his. "She left me and my brother to work for Pembroke's army. I did naught but carry water, food. I made myself scarce, for one so small garners a cuff on the head for the slightest indiscretion."

"Small?" Her gaze slid pointedly over his chest, so wide she felt she looked up a mountain.

He smiled down at her, brushing her hair off her face with the backs of his knuckles. "I didn't grow till I was nearly ten and three. By then our mother had returned often enough to see we elevated ourselves to page, then squired for a man she bedded a few times.''

The bitterness in his tone made her wince, and Siobhàn realized why he insisted on a Christian marriage and her promise of fidelity. His mother was a whore.

''Your brother?''

''He is dead, killed in battle,'' came crisply. ''I was my father's retainer then, though I did not know who he was nor our link until Mother arrived, asking for money. Saroan Pen-Dragon was most pleased to know he had an heir.'' His lips twisted with the cruel memory. ''Stephan had another father, and Saroan sent him to the stables. He died squiring for me.''

'' 'Tis not your fault.''

He reared back. ''How would you know?''

So defensive, she thought. ''You wanted him near you, aye?''

''He should have been left behind. I was newly knighted, only a year or so older than Reese, hardly skilled in so ruthless a battle, and for that reason alone, he is dead.''

Oh Lord above, there was pain in those words, she thought as he closed his eyes, his features taut.

''I could not protect him.''

Siobhàn saw beneath the tightly gritted words, understanding his fierce need for the Irishmen to be prepared, for the keep to be adequately defended. ''You cannot be all things, my lord,'' she said, turning his face to hers. ''Yet you became the seasoned warrior, cloaking yourself in a reputation of fear and loathing, so oftimes you would not even have to lift your sword, hum?''

Gaelan flopped back onto the pillows, staring at the ceiling, and Siobhàn curled over him, half across his chest, her hands folded there, her chin on her fists.

''Aye,'' she pressured.

His gaze swept to hers. ''I suppose.''

''You know I am right.''

His lips quirked. ''But you are such a pain in my arse when you are.''

She smiled brightly, rising up to kiss his sour mouth.

"Though 'tis a sweet pain," he growled, his hand smoothing over her behind, then up her naked spine.

"You do not fool me, husband," she said. "Here." She laid her hand over his heart. "Is a gentle soul trapped in a fierce warrior." He scoffed and started to turn away, but she held him down, staring deep into his eyes.

Gaelan felt something shift between them.

"Show Donegal the knight you are, husband, but me, I want only the man."

His fingertip traced the curve of her jaw, grazed her lips, and in a voice holding a slight tremor asked, "And what will you do with him, Siobhàn MacMurrough O'Rourke, wife of PenDragon, lady of Donegal?"

She stroked a lock of hair off his brow, watching her moves before meeting his gaze. "Hold him when he desires, feed him when he hungers, teach him when he needs it." His lips quirked at that. "And accept him, no longer the enemy."

"Does this mean you trust me?"

"Hah!" She shoved his chest. "Do not be pushing your good fortune with m—"

He kissed her, silencing her, loving her sass and rolling her to her back, his mouth molding hers with dark hunger and neverending possession. 'Twas more than he expected from her in this lifetime, more than his unworthy carcass deserved, and he prayed he survived the days ahead, for his heart was no longer his to rule.

Chapter Nineteen

"Woman! You are in the way." Slapping his arm around her waist, Gaelan yanked Siobhàn back from the table of plans just as a mason turned and nearly bashed her in the leg with a spade.

"I want to know what you are doing to our castle."

He smiled at the "our" reference and let her go. "I would tell you if you'd asked. 'Tis dangerous." He lurched forward, catching a plank and glaring down at the man who'd swung it around without looking.

"Forgive me, me lord," the man gasped, his gaze shooting between lord and lady.

"Be watchful, Egan."

Egan nodded and carefully lowered the plank from his shoulder, carting it off. Gaelan looked back at his wife, folding his arms over his chest.

"Fine," she huffed at his I-told-you-thus look.

"Do you not have enough to do?"

"Of course I do."

"Did you mayhaps miss me?"

Her chin tipped. "Nay."

"That is not what you said last night."

She reddened, breaking eye contact, and Gaelan chuckled lowly. He'd fallen into bed the past few nights, too tired to even speak for the work going on about the keep. Until she started touching him, wiggling her bare body against his, her little hands stroking and teasing until even his fatigue was forgotten under her spell. Once the door of her passion opened, he thought pleasantly, there was no closing it. A delight, of course, to him, since he'd rather be loving her than arguing with her.

Siobhàn tossed her hair back over her shoulder, fidgeting. Heaven help her, she felt like an untried lass before him, his gaze moving over her with such slow deliberation she thought of naught but his hands mapping the path. 'Twas shameful, this insatiable urge for him, and didn't know why she was here, for she could scarcely get a bloody thing accomplished with him about.

She was pitiful.

"Siobhàn?"

Her head jerked up and she found him close, close enough to catch the scent of rare sandalwood he put in his bath, close enough that she had to crane her neck to meet his gaze. Close enough to want.

"I will show you the plans now."

"Oh." She wanted him to show her something else, blast him. "Nay," she sighed, disappointed and half ashamed of her behavior. "I've a child to teach."

Gaelan nodded, his seductive thoughts fading. Connal had grown more uncontrollable by the day and neither of them knew what to do, since the boy refused to speak to Gaelan and punishing him only made him more rebellious. He bent and kissed her softly, her arms immediately slipping around his waist. Around them, English soldiers and Irishmen and women worked, hammers pounded and horses drew carts pulling loads of stones across the inner ward.

And Gaelan sank into the kiss, into her. Folk stared and smiled and they were oblivious.

Then the soft crack of strained wood brought his head up.

His gaze scanned the area, then abruptly, he pushed her aside, lunging toward the shifting scaffolding, Connal sitting but a few feet from beneath it. Gaelan ran and dove, grabbing the boy, tucking him to the curve of his body, his urgency slamming Gaelan into the wall. He ducked, enveloping the child, and an instant later, the scaffolding fractured, wood planks sliding free of rope and spilling stones on his back.

Siobhàn cried out, racing to them, but Raymond stopped her. Rock tumbled. Wood fell. Dust clouded the air as men hurried to clear the wreckage. Siobhàn shifted from foot to foot, her heart pounding with fear. He was a big man, strong, but the planks were heavy and supported a dozen huge stones for the wall. Two men hoisted a foot wide rock off the broken plank, then tore the wood away. Siobhàn darted forward, pushing people from her path.

"Speak to me, speak to me!" She heard Connal whimper for her and released a trapped breath. But Gaelan was not moving. "Husband!"

Crouched, he shifted, and Siobhàn sank to her knees, tears in her eyes. "Where does it hurt—oh, nay, do not move!" Slowly he released Connal and the boy flung himself into her arms. She ran her hands furiously over his little body, inspecting him for injuries, and found naught but a scrape on his elbow.

Cheers and praise rumbled around them, people shuffling to see if their lord was dead for saving the boy.

"Husband," she gasped, sniffling, her trembling fingers skipping over his dusty hair. He tilted his head back, then sank to his rump on the ground. Clutching Connal, she looped her arm around Gaelan's neck and hugged him. He groaned in pain and she jerked back. "Oh, forgive me."

Gaelan caught his breath, then raked his hands through his hair. "What were you doing so close to the work?" he hissed at Connal, and the boy cowered.

Siobhàn nudged her son forward. "Answer him."

Connal's gaze shifted between his mother and her husband. "Playin' in the dirt," he sobbed. " 'Tis me spot."

"What!"

Siobhàn put up her hand, pressing her lips to the top of his head and rocking him. "I forgot. He plays there by the chapel wall often." She gestured and Gaelan twisted, the motion driving an ache up his back as he looked at the cluster of wooden toys, a discarded spoon and a pail near the wall. Scowling with concentration, he glanced at the destroyed scaffolding, then the workers, before bringing his gaze back to Connal.

Reaching out, he forced the boy to look him in the eye. "Until the construction is finished you must find another *spot*."

Connal looked at his mother, obviously expecting her to defend him.

"He is right, child. You could have been killed if not for your lord."

Connal's lip quivered pitifully, his gaze lowered. "You saved me life," he muttered, as if he could not believe it.

Over Connal's bowed head, Siobhàn and Gaelan exchanged a look, and when Siobhàn opened her mouth to speak, Gaelan interrupted in a gentle voice. "Collect your treasures now, boy." He stood slowly, dusting himself off. Connal glanced uncertainly between the couple and Gaelan reached for him, pulling him from his mother's lap and ushering him toward the pile. He turned back to her, helping her to her feet.

"I apologize for—"

"Don't, love. He's but an innocent and I am simply glad he survived." Gaelan looked again at the destruction, then moved past Siobhàn to the foot of the framework. He inspected it, calling Raymond near.

Gaelan nodded discreetly at the scaffold post lodged in the ground.

Raymond's features tightened with understanding. There was a rope fastened about the base, buried in the ground, and Raymond tugged it, his gaze following the path to a horse hitched to a cart in the distance. The rope was caught on the wheel.

"An accident?"

"Of course it was."

Gaelan flinched around to find Siobhàn hovering over them. He yanked her to the ground and showed her the rope, intentionally buried.

"Keep him close to you," he said in a grave tone. "If the child played there often enough, then someone knew he would go there."

She inhaled, eyes wide. "You do not think one of our folk tried to hurt him? Why?"

"Someone who does not want me here or hates me enough to hurt your son because it would destroy you and the blame would lay with me. Someone who does not want us to make peace in this castle." He shrugged. "I cannot speculate for so many possibilities. There are unfamiliar workers coming in and out of the castle lately." He shifted closer to her, trapping her gaze with his. "Do you not see why I need their total allegiance, Siobhàn? Without it, things like this"—he lashed a hand toward the rubble—"will breed discontent I might not be able to control without retribution."

"I know, but what can we do?"

He helped her to her feet, gathering her close, recognizing that the fright had not left her, and kissed the top of her head, rubbing her back. "We will think of something. But do not allow Connal near this mess again." She tilted her head back and nodded, patting his chest. "Go, see to the boy." She left them, hurrying across the compound.

"Who were they after, Gaelan, you or the child?"

"Me, I would wager. Connal is no longer the prince awaiting his throne. He is little threat to anyone."

Raymond's lips pulled in a flat line. "And here I thought we were making progress."

Apparently, Gaelan thought, the only progress he was making was with his wife.

Like phantoms out of the mist, they hovered in the darkness, ancient chants simmering in the cool night air. Moonlight glinted off hatchets and axs, off bolt tips and swords. The leader scanned the armed warriors, the finest and strongest of the clans joined in revolt. Proud men. Angry and sworn with determination. His features distorted under the dyes and rubs, he stared down the hillside at the sleeping village. Rage twisted in him, for this night, like the many before, marked him outlaw, murderer to his woman, his people, his land.

God forgive me.

He pulled the hood over his head and dug his heels into the horse's thick sides.

They rode, a thunder of death across the green moors. In minutes the village was silent of cries and pleas for mercy, every clansman left homeless and hungry—and some dead. The leader wheeled about and rode into the forest alone, dismounting, shoving the horse away. He stumbled, seeking solace, and then stilled, ripping off the hood and staring up at the night sky, his face wet with tears as he sank to his knees. A horrible pain-filled howl tore from his throat, startling night creatures from burrow and hollow. And when the echo died, he folded over, his bloody fingers digging into the earth as he vomited.

Rhiannon bent and dug beneath the goose for fresh eggs, placing her find in the basket at her feet. She sidestepped and reached for another collection. A hand slapped over her mouth, a strong arm clamping about her waist and jerking her back against the hard frame of a man. She struggled, clawing at his fingers, and the hold tightened mercilessly, squashing her breath from her lungs.

"Be still!" the voice hissed. "Meet me in two nights' time."

She shook her head and he squeezed harder.

"Meet me or I will reveal your lies, woman."

Rhiannon's eyes widened, her denial a low moan and renewed fight. Suddenly she was free, stumbling forward and tripping over the basket of eggs. She whirled about, gasping for a clean breath, and found herself alone with the geese and doves. She darted to the dovecote's entrance, searching the inner bailey for the intruder. She knew she would not find him and turned back inside, hugging herself.

Meghan ducked into the dovecote and Rhiannon turned, at first thinking her Siobhàn, their hair so close in hue.

"Oh, my Lord," the woman gasped, rushing to her side. "What has happened to you?" Meghan caught her hands, holding them for inspection.

"What?" Rhiannon snapped, wondering if the woman saw her assailant but not daring to ask.

"Look at you." With the hem of her apron, she swiped at Rhiannon's face.

And the white cloth came away stained red with blood.

Rhiannon snatched the hem, wiping her face over and over. She felt ill, her skin suddenly too hot for her clothes. Oh, Lord our Father, what had he done? she agonized, then looked down at her plain gown. The mark of his hold left an imprint of red.

"Say naught of this to anyone," Rhiannon warned.

Meghan frowned. "But, my lady—?"

" 'Tis naught. I broke an egg and it must have been fertile." She nodded to the eggs crushed when she'd tripped, then bent to gather the remaining finds. She fled, leaving Meghan to stare after her, her eyes flaring wide at the bloody stain on her lady's back.

"Fertile eggs, my eye," she whispered.

"I cannot find him, sir."

Gaelan nodded to the squire, fanning his fingers beneath his beard. His glance moved over the people in the hall, dining.

"You are concerned?"

He looked at his wife and smiled. "Nay, but he's late for his duty." It was unusual, for if anything Owen was prompt and this was the second time in two days. A sound pierced through the din of the hall and Gaelan scowled, twisting toward the corridor behind him.

Meghan appeared, her face pale as she rushed to his side. Siobhàn stood, touching her shoulder. "Meghan, my word! What is it?"

Her gaze shot to her lord. "Come, please come." The servant turned away, heading back the way she came, and Siobhàn and Gaelan followed, his motion bringing two soldiers with him. Gaelan met the last step of the staircase leading below to the dungeon and cursed.

"Oh, Lord." The two women crossed themselves and Siobhàn ushered Meghan back from the hideous sight, sending her above.

The two prisoners dangled from the barred door, naked and strangled. It was an effort to do this, Gaelan thought, for the ceiling was low and they had to make a rope from their clothes.

Gaelan flicked a hand to the dead men. "Cut them down and bury them." The soldiers did his bidding and he turned away to find Siobhàn gathering the broken remnants of the prisoners' meal onto the tray. He bent, helping. Her hands were trembling. Behind them, the thunk of bodies to the wet stone floor made her flinch.

"I wish you had not seen that."

"I have seen worse, just not in my own house." She hated the dungeon. It spoke only of death and dying. Tigheran had been notorious for keeping it full for the meanest infraction.

"Why would they kill themselves rather than talk?" he said more to himself, then caught the scent of . . . "What is that smell?" He frowned, meeting her gaze.

Siobhàn sniffed, her back to the dead. "Mint, I think." 'Twas hard to tell, with the stench of death lingering in the air. Together they rose, Gaelan taking the tray from her and escorting her up the stairs. He handed it over to Meghan.

"Did you see anyone go belowstairs afore you went to deliver the meal?"

"Nay, my lord."

"Not Sir Owen?"

She shook her head and Gaelan dismissed the woman, his features creased. Siobhàn whispered to her friend to take a break and have a bit of wine before returning to her duties.

Gaelan strode toward the doors, stepping out into the sun and crossing the inner ward to the gate. He bid a soldier search for Sir Owen, yet as the man moved off, the knight came around the corner of the cookhouse and stopped short.

"You're late. Where have you been?"

Owen stood straight and tall, his eyes ahead. "I was . . . indisposed, sir."

"Where? What was so important that you are tardy for your duties?"

He inclined his head toward the garderobe, yet the man's guilty flush and breathlessness didn't escape Gaelan's notice. "See me after you return. And if this continues, Owen, I will fine you."

"Aye, my lord," he said, ducking his head and moving past.

Gaelan stared after him, then turned back to the hall and his wife. He slung his arm around her waist, tucking her warmly to his side and hating the distrust brewing in him.

* * *

Siobhàn woke to find him standing near the window, the breeze fingering his hair. She rose up on her elbow, gazing at him, his regal profile, his knee bent, one foot on the bench. Then he sighed heavily, rubbing his face, and she frowned, slipping from the bed, naked. He turned his head, holding out his hand to her, and she came to him without hesitation, sliding up against his body, circling his waist and resting her head on his chest. For long moments they stood there, one shadow, two hearts beating in time. His arms tightened and Siobhàn tipped her head back to look at him.

Defeat mapped his handsome face.

She reached and he met her gaze as her fingers smoothed over the lines deep in his brow, the downward curve of his mouth. "Tell me what wars in you, husband. I will keep the secret, as I promised."

He hesitated, pain flickering in his eyes before he sighed, resigned. "I feel this land being torn apart beneath us."

"You will protect us."

He arched a brow.

Her chin tipped. "*I* have always trusted your strength and skills as a warrior, PenDragon. 'Tis your loyalty to the Irish I have doubted."

"Do you still?" His hand glided over her bare hip, her smooth skin silky beneath his palm.

Siobhàn searched his troubled gaze, his dark eyes begging for a word from her. "Nay, my lord. I cannot ignore your willingness to be fair and keep us all safe."

Gaelan's lips curved, his smile not reaching his eyes, and Siobhàn realized there was more there than he was offering.

"I cannot succeed if I do not know my enemy," he said wryly.

"You still believe Connal's accident was deliberate?"

"If it was not, then the culprit is inside these walls."

Siobhàn frowned. "The raiders?"

He debated telling her suspicions, then reached beyond her to the sill, coming back with the spur. "I found this at the first attack, buried in the ground." He dropped it into her hand.

Her breath caught. An English spur. "It could have been there for some time."

"Aye, but if not?" He shook his head, confused, staring out the window. "This all lacks reason. If I could understand what they wanted, I could fight them."

"What are you not telling me?"

"Sir Owen is unaccounted for twice these past days. And he refuses to tell me exactly where."

"Surely you do not suspect him of killing the prisoners, my lord. 'Twas suicide."

"Aye, but with or without help?"

She shook her head. "I do not believe it, not of Owen. He may have a distaste for the Irish, but he would not betray you."

"Even I am not certain of that." He tapped the spur, then took it from her, laying it aside and pulling her tighter into his embrace.

"There are the Fenians, my lord."

Gaelan's gaze snapped to hers, his frown dark with sudden irritation.

"*Erinn Fenian.* They are a clan of warriors, sworn to defend the land and old ways. To keep Ireland pure."

He scoffed, irony in the sound. "You are not part of this group?"

She reared back, trying to smile. "Nay. I would never survive the test to join, regardless. But mayhaps they have something to do with the attacks. The raiders on the livestock—they are not one in the same, I fear."

"Why did you not tell me of this afore?"

Her bare shoulders moved restlessly. "The Fenians have been secret for centuries. Never seen, and none know who belongs to the clan. And they are not oftimes violent." She lowered her gaze to the center of his chest, tracing the curve of muscle, toying with the smattering of hair dusting his flesh. "Lately the Fenians raid to even the fight atween feuds. Taking a bit of livestock or returning it to the owner. Harmless foolery."

"This is no game, Siobhàn."

"I know," she snapped.

He nudged her chin. "What are *you* not telling me?"

"There is no way to discover aught about them, my lord. They live in the wild, on the land, and would rather die than give their identity. Gaining their confidence is near impossible—even for a princess."

Gaelan frowned, searching her eyes, then leaned his head against the stone window casement, staring out the window. They were surrounded by enemies, he thought. Outlaws, feuding clans. Ian Maguire was not to be trusted, and neither was the O'Niell, and now these Fenians had made themselves suspect. But Gaelan could not help but look for more, and the spur pointed fingers at his own men, for there was not another English army this close to Donegal.

These attacks were sparse yet deadly, weakening confidence and defenses. Did they not see that battle would destroy more Irish than English, that they were unmatched? Who, other than Maguire, was willing to risk their own to see him fail? Was this all directed at him, Siobhàn or an old dispute with Tigheran?

Dark memory reared in his mind, of a solitary battle that changed his life. Gaelan recalled Tigheran's face, bearded, his eyes wild, his expertise formidable. But winning was Gaelan's life, the sport of single combat rare, and he'd provoked the man, told him he'd burn his castle to the ground but not before he'd have his wife lying beneath him. Amusement had shaped Tigheran's craggy face then, yet his fight was as brutal and skilled as any he'd encountered. Though Gaelan was now ashamed of his cruel taunts, he understood why the Irish king had fought so valiantly.

Siobhàn was not a woman easily claimed, and to do it, a man paid with the price of his soul.

He looked down at her, tilting her face up, his gaze searching hers. The fact remained that she was still keeping things from him, and he realized that though he might have vanquished her body, he did not possess her heart.

Nor her complete trust.

The crush of it almost made him confess his sins, clear the rubble of his past before it could butcher the relationship building between them. Almost. He could not risk losing her to the truth. Not now. Not when the thought of being without her made him want to die. He'd been alone all his life, and now that he knew there was another life he could lead, he could not bear the loneliness again. She was his wife, his mate, for eternity, and his need to mark her, brand her his in every way possible, surged through him.

He ducked and kissed her, devouring and strong, pushing his tongue between her lips, his knee between her thighs. His hands charged a wild ride over her bare body, enfolding her buttocks and pulling her hard against his groin. She strained for more and the heat of her sex moistened his thigh, the scent of her commanding him, driving him.

He twisted, pressing her back against the stone wall, his kiss ravenous, desperate. He shaped her body, rubbed and dipped, tasted her on his fingertips and ceased his assault long enough to step out of his braies. Then he nudged her thighs wider, stroking her wetly, teasing her with the tip of his erection until she was reaching for him, until she whimpered and arched and clawed for him to fill her.

Then he did, lifting her legs around his hips and shoving himself inside her with a force that mashed her to the wall.

She gasped in pleasure, clamping her arms around his neck, rocking.

He imprisoned her hips to the wall, his thickness pleasuring her in smooth deliberation, his dark eyes watching her, smoldering with an almost sinister obsession.

"You are mine, Siobhàn," he murmured into the curve of her ear, his hands palming her breasts, circling her nipples. "Mine."

Siobhàn could not wonder over the desperation in his voice, the rough texture of it. But his motions spoke more, his touch, his taste of her frenzied, anxious, his every move designed to thrill and excite beyond her limits.

In the darkness of the chamber he possessed her, bodies undulating in rhythmic cadence, skin slick with sweat and desire. He drank in her pants and sobs of rapture and then when she could take no more, begging he cease, he refused, greedily delivering her into a summit of mindless passion and leaving her dangling over the edge.

He was tender with patience, then at once, savage and erotic, bringing her to a shattering climax before the looking glass with only the touch of his hand. Her wild response drove him insane with lust, her ecstasy spinning through his being and penetrating deep into the hollows of his corrupt soul. He tried to take her into himself, smother doubts, win her heart so firmly naught could shatter them apart. Yet near the witching hour, when they sank into the soft bedding in a seductive tangle of arms and legs, Gaelan realized the demon he chased lay within, and even in the comfort of her soft arms, he could not fight it.

Standing in the inner ward, Gaelan brushed his mouth over Siobhàn's, the memory of the evening before, of the love play they shared, blossoming in the kiss. She was an inventive creature, making their nights more interesting than he thought possible.

Gaelan felt the sting on his shoulder and drew back, turning sharply in time to see Connal dart into the barns, his lamb a bit slower and giving clear evidence to his presence. What did the child think to accomplish with this daily attack?

"I apologize, my lord."

" 'Tis mischief." And he does it only with his mother near.

" 'Tis meanness." She started after him, but he stayed her, then strode calmly after the child to the barns. After a quick scan, Gaelan noticed the haystack moving and stepped closer, digging to the timothy and pulling the child free. The lamb bahhed, working its head through the stack.

Gaelan held out his hand.

Connal scowled and slapped the slingshot in his palm.

Leaving the barn, he strode to his wife, depositing the boy at her feet.

Siobhàn tried not to laugh at the look of horror on Connal's young face as her husband crushed the slingshot in his fist. Connal wailed.

"Silence."

The boy's lips quivered and he looked to his mother for support. Siobhàn simply folded her arms, frowning disappointedly down at him.

"When you learn that I am not the enemy, you may construct another." Gaelan looked up, searching the inner yard, then calling out to a dairy maid. "Connal will assist you today. Report to me his behavior."

The maid blinked, her gaze shifting quickly between lord and lady, then to the boy. She bobbed a curtsey, inclining her head to the milkhouse. Connal trudged off to the duty, a little smile curving his lips as he pulled another slingshot from inside his tunic.

Gaelan frowned at the gaunt man, suspicion breeding through him. Several carpenters and masoners moved in and out of the castle whilst the construction continued, and though he'd come to know the closest villagers, at least by face, this man had not lent a hand. Only a coward did not come forth, yet the man's looks bore an unquestionable hatred. He strode toward him and the thin man straightened, meeting his gaze.

"Who are you and what are you doing in my castle?"

"I've come for you, PenDragon." Disgust thickened his voice.

Gaelan, his hands on his sword hilt, studied the man. "I have seen you afore."

"I am the only one who survived."

Recognition dawned, and Gaelan's heart slammed to his gut. Tigheran's man. He was at the field when he slew the Irish king. The ramifications of his presence swelled through him, fueling anger, stripping his compassion.

"You should have died with your betraying master."

The Irishman, slim and undernourished, straightened. "Prepare to die, Lord Donegal," he spat, drawing his sword.

Gaelan snatched his wrist, twisting the blade away from his chest. The fragile bones snapped under his grip, yet the proud man did not show a flicker of pain. Soldiers and guards rushed forward, but Gaelan waved them back, his gaze on the Irishman.

"Lay down your weapons and I will spare you. As his retainer, you should have paid the price with your treasonous king."

"And what is your price, PenDragon, for warring on Ireland?"

"I war only *for* Donegal now. For my wife and my folk. You may join us or leave, but speak no ill of me and mine here or you will die." He thrust him back, tormented with the thought of Siobhàn learning his sins from gossip. He glanced at a nearby soldier. "Alert Driscoll of this man's presence, but first escort him to the kitchen, see that he has all he wants to eat and a bed for the night. Do not harm him, Markus."

The soldier nodded, impressed his lord knew his name, and walked alongside the thin man. Gaelan watched his retreat, proud that Markus tried to talk with him. Mayhaps some wounds will heal, he thought, and be stronger for it.

"My lord?"

Gaelan jerked around, his chest clenching at the sight of his wife. *Oh God.*

Siobhàn's gaze slipped past him to the Irish soldier, her frown deepening. "Who was that? He is familiar."

He sighed heavily, the weight of his misdeeds crushing him. Denying now would only delay the pain. "He is—was Tigheran's retainer."

She hastened toward the Irishman, but her husband caught her. She met his gaze.

"Nay, wife. Do not talk with him."

Her brow knitted delicately. "Why not? I wish to know what happened. A detail, at least."

It took every ounce of his will to say, "I can tell you that."

Her expression filled with trepidation, her voice but a whisper as she said, "How—how can you?"

"Because, love—" He swallowed, his Adam's apple grating like stones in his throat. "Tigheran died by my hand."

Siobhàn simply stared at him, searching for the lie in his beautiful eyes, and when she found only harsh truth, her own filled rapidly with tears. "Deny this," she insisted in a broken whisper. "Say you did not put your sword in my husband's chest and came here only to take what was his in reward."

"I did."

"Oh, Gaelan," she cried softly. "How could you keep this from me after all we have shared?"

Why, he agonized, was this the first time she called him by name? "Would you have even let me inside without a fight? Would you have wed me, Siobhàn, shared your bed?" Made me love you, he despaired.

"I had a right to know!" Her desolate look severed him in half.

People paused, staring, and he caught her arm, handing her into the stable. She jerked from his touch.

"Do you not think I would like this to be a lie? Tigheran tried to assassinate the king and he died for it."

Siobhàn paled. "Nay. Oh, nay!"

Gaelan's expression tightened with quick anger. "I speak the truth," he said even as she shook her head.

"He would never go against Henry like that. He went to swear to him, to gain an army to put down Dermott."

"Henry took his oath but refused him the army. Dermott MacMurrough's holdings were larger and of more use to him. Tigheran returned at night to beg his favor and whilst ten of his men assaulted the king's camp, he threatened Henry. His men were caught and executed and I entered the king's tent in time to halt the assassination." Gaelan swallowed, watching her beautiful face crumble with each word. "Because of Tigheran's rank he had the choice of single combat and he accepted. His majesty awarded me the duty of his champion."

A court battle, viewed like a slaughter. " 'Twas unmatched! Tigheran was neither powerful nor skilled. You, PenDragon, are naught but the king's mur—"

"Do not say it!" He caught her arms, holding her when she was wont to flee. "He tried to murder the *king of England!* He had to die, by my hand or an executioner's ax. It did not matter if O'Rourke had succeeded. Had I not won, Donegal and all you loved would have been burned to the ground, your people massacred, their bodies dragged through the streets of London. England would have cheered and none would have been spared." His fingers flexed. "Not even you!"

Her breath choked and he released her.

She stared at him, a turmoil of anger and regret and guilt slamming through her. His words rang with the truth. God above, hadn't she wondered why it took the English so long to come to Donegal? But all she could see was the lie—and how she fell so easily for her want of this man. How he'd smiled at her, loved her body, opened her tired, lonely soul whilst he hid the truth, knowing he'd slain his way into her home, her heart.

"See me, PenDragon." She thumped her chest, shame in her eyes. "See the woman so trapped in her passion that she let her husband's killer into her bed!"

He advanced. "I am your husband!"

"And I am your fool."

Gaelan grabbed her arms, his gaze black and pinning. "Nights ago you swore to keep my confidences and this is one I *order you* to conceal." When she looked to rebel, he snarled in a harsh voice, "More rests on this than our marriage, wife."

"Aye," she hissed, prying his hands off and throwing them back at him. "You imprison me with your lies in a Christian vow." Gaelan's expression fell into complete misery as she fought tears and anger, her lip trembling. "I trusted you, Gaelan," her voice fractured, her words choked on a sob, "and I wanted so badly to love you." She shoved past him, covering her mouth with her hand and racing out into the ward.

Gaelan's shoulders slumped and he stared at the straw-covered floor. Sorrow ripped through him, the agony of loss and the swell of guilt burning like black fire in his chest. Alone in the stable, he raked both his hands through his hair, then rubbed his face.

Oh, sweet Jesu.

Chapter Twenty

She wept like a motherless child. Falling to her knees on the dirt floor of the herb house, she did not cry for a husband she'd preferred dead. She wept for the cut Gaelan's lie left on her heart, and the lie she must conceal despite her turmoil. His lie wounded only her. Hers would destroy Donegal.

"So, you have discovered the truth."

Siobhàn twisted sharply, then climbed to her feet, swiping at her cheeks. "What are you intoning, sister?" But she already knew. 'Twas the dark secret she'd seen.

Rhiannon crossed the dirt floor, reaching out to her, enveloping her in her arms. "Ahh, Siobhàn," she soothed, her words tight in her throat. "You cannot blame him for defending himself."

Siobhàn choked on a sob. "I blame him for lying to me."

Rhiannon's features tightened. And what lies do we all hide, she thought, then said, "PenDragon spared you the humiliation. You would let Tigheran's destroy you now, after all this time? The man was cruel and unjust to you."

"Nay, I was the enemy—"

She held her back. "Great lady above." Rhiannon rolled her eyes. "Must I remind you of the rape of your body each night, and half the women here, or of a princess fetching and tending him as if he were a child?"

"I know, but, oh, Rhi—I cursed him to die." Siobhàn hated herself for saying those words, hated the memory of watching him ride off and hoping he did not return.

"So did half the castle folk." Rhiannon's lips twisted wryly. "You have done your duty to his memory. His bitterness sent him to England, and call him fortunate to have met PenDragon on the field and taken a swift death."

"How can you say such things! He was our king."

"He was his own enemy. Did one of his retainers return to your side?"

She shook her head. "All but one was executed."

Rhiannon turned away, moving to the kettle steeping with herbs and stirring down the boil. " 'Twas a crime, Siobhàn, and justice metered. If not PenDragon, then another would have done it."

Siobhàn loathed that she was right, and worse, repeating Gaelan's words. "Swear this to secrecy."

Rhiannon stilled in her stirring. "I have told no one, but do not believe word will not reach the folk. I am not the only one who is aware, I fear."

Siobhàn sank miserably into a nearby stool, gazing down at her hands. "Connal can never know."

"Aye." There was no question in Rhiannon's tone. Connal had to be protected at all costs. She turned to her sister, frowning softly at the desolate look on her beautiful face. It was rare to see her so low, the fight gone from her eyes. She sank to her knees before her. "Brew in this and more will suffer, Siobhàn. PenDragon did as his king bid him. Mercenary or nay, he is knighted English and had no choice. We both know he did not want this castle, the responsibility—he wanted only you."

Siobhàn opened her mouth to speak and Rhiannon hushed her. "He spared us because of you. He bent to your demands because of his feelings for you."

The truth soothed through Siobhàn with an odd comfort.

"A man with a dark past, with blood on his hands, came to destroy us, and yet he showed compassion and sacrifice. Do you forget he saved Connal's life? That you have lain in his arms these weeks past and found pleasure?"

Siobhàn's eyes softened with memory, yet a tear rolled down her cheek. "You could have tried a bit harder to warn me."

"You are too stubborn to listen to reason oftimes." Rhiannon scoffed and stood. "PenDragon has proven himself more the lord than Tigheran, that ugly beast of a man, ever bothered."

Siobhàn's lips quirked. Rhiannon had detested Tigheran, had delved into his thoughts often to prepare her sister for his moods, for the lust she could not avoid. Her only pleasure was that Tigheran feared Rhiannon. "I would not have thought you to defend Gaelan."

Her lips twitched. "Neither would I. But I cannot let you lose so much over a dead, selfish fool. 'Tis no wonder Devorgilla refused him."

"Dermott is no better."

"Our uncle knows how to love and forgive. Be wise and do the same." Rhiannon eyed her. "Cease your stubborn pride and do something for yourself, Siobhàn—not for the rest of us. Forgive and repair the damage I know you did."

"Me? You accuse me—"

"Siobhàn!"

Both women turned to find Gaelan filling the doorway. His gaze shifted to Siobhàn, half angry, half worried, flicking only once to Rhiannon in confusion. It told her he'd heard most of the conversation. Rhiannon glanced at her sister, then hurried to the lord of Donegal before he stepped inside.

"Leave her be, my lord." Gaelan dragged his gaze from Siobhàn. "For this day, do not press her."

Gaelan scowled, and Rhiannon motioned him out of the thatched house, pulling the door closed.

Gaelan slapped a hand to the wood, stopping her. "I will take care of what is between me and my wife, sister." He started to push past, but she snagged his arm, her grip stinging through his skin to his bones and rendering him motionless— powerless. Her eyes glazed for an instant, a smile curving her lips, then fading.

"I know you will, but . . ." She paused, her brow knitting, her look perplexed. "Prepare, brother . . . there is a darkness coming here," she whispered suddenly, as if divulging a secret long kept. "Great pain to many people. And only you can heal it."

Peeling off her hand, Gaelan scowled, his gaze darting to Siobhàn as she rose from the stool, frowning at her sister. Rhiannon's words were so contrary, he wondered if this was one of her premonitions?

Rhiannon blinked, then smiled gently, her wisdom revealed in the single glance. "You must give time for her to see the benefit of your deeds."

"Do you?"

Her lips quirked a bit. "Oftimes I see more than I would like."

For an instant Gaelan wanted to ask her what she saw for he and Siobhàn, then dismissed it. He did not believe in such rubbish and he would not let his future be jaded by witchery.

"Nay, I am not a witch," she said into his thoughts, "though there are times I wish I was."

Gaelan scowled. Such a peculiar woman.

"And your temper is not malleable right now."

Gaelan looked at the half-open door, the profile of his wife poised on the edge of a stool, her hands clenched on her lap. He never thought to see her so ravaged and the blame rested at his feet. If he had not lied, if he had told her from the start, fought that war first, before he had lost his heart to her, he would not be risking his future now.

"I will see you this evening, wife, in our chambers," he said to her profile, and she nodded solemnly.

Gaelan did not think aught could hurt as much as her passive response and he longed for the combative Irishwoman who baited him at every turn. He exhaled a hard breath, leaving the little cottage. A half hour later, astride his horse, he charged through the gates, sending workers and soldiers darting for cover.

Tired, sweaty and hungry, Gaelan strode toward the keep, pausing long enough at a rain barrel to scoop water and douse his face, then slake his thirst. He scanned the inner ward, swiping the back of his hand across his mouth. Folk looked at him strangely, and though his argument with Siobhàn was in seclusion, gossip spread in this place as fast as the wind. Deciding that talking with his wife, even fighting with her, was preferable to silence, Gaelan headed toward the keep.

Passing the dairy, he heard a scuffling, the distinct sound of grunts and a short cry. Scowling, he strode behind the building, and when he expected to find a pair coupling, he found Connal and a boy nearly a half size larger beating the stuffing out of each other.

Gaelan bent and pulled them apart, holding them off the ground by the scruffs of their necks. They blinked at him, breathing heavily. Connal dragged his sleeve beneath his nose and Gaelan realized he was weeping. He looked at the other boy, nearly three years older, two hands taller and sporting a bloody nose. He set them down, a hand on either shoulder when they tried to escape. "Explain."

Connal looked at the other boy, his breath hissing in and out between clenched teeth. "Auggie lies."

"Shut yer mouth, brat!"

"You lie!" Connal leapt on the other boy, bashing him in the gullet.

Gaelan sighed and pulled them apart again, kneeling. "What did he say, lad?"

"He called me mother a Sassanach whore."

Gaelan's eyes flared and looked at the opponent. Auggie stared at his bare feet, shamefaced.

"Do you know what that means, Connal?"

"Nay," he confessed, sniffling. "But he said it mean." Connal gave him a decent imitation whilst glaring at the other boy.

Gaelan pulled Auggie close, meeting his gaze with a look meant to strike terror. It did and the child swallowed, his lips trembling. "Speak so again, boy, about *any* woman, and I will see you punished." Fear flared in his eyes. "I will have a few words with your father." He released him. "Now go home." The child dashed around the wall out of sight.

Straightening Gaelan took a rag hooked on the wall, dipped it in the cistern and turned back to Connal. The prince remained where he was, the top of his head barely passing above his knee.

He knelt and swiped the rag over his dirty face.

"I hate you."

"I know."

"I want you to leave us alone."

"I am married to your mother and will not abandon her."

"She does not need you."

I need her, he thought. "I suppose you will hate me forever."

"Aye. And when I grow up, I will kill all the English."

Gaelan stilled, eyeing him. " 'Tis a great lot of people, lad."

"I do not care! I will kill until I find the man who killed my father."

Gaelan paled miserably and dropped his head forward. Sweet Jesu. "Come, sit." In a shadowed corner between the dairy and the stone wall, Gaelan settled to the ground, gesturing to the spot beside him. His shoulders drooping pitifully, Connal joined him, plopping like a sack to the ground. They sat there, quiet for a moment.

"That word," Gaelan said.

"Whore."

Gaelan winced. It sounded even uglier coming from innocent lips. "It means—it names a woman who does not care for aught but her own pleasures, a woman who is free with her body to all men and asks for pay. Is that your mother?"

"Nay!"

"Then you know Auggie was wrong."

"But 'twas bad and about me mama." Connal's lip quivered and his eyes filled with fat tears. Gaelan never felt so helpless in all his life. He looked as if he would fight the world alone for her honor.

"I know, lad." His hand hovered near his tiny shoulder, uncertain and half afraid he'd hurt the child, then settled gently on Connal's back. That the boy did not move away was a comfort. "If we let every cruel thing a person says wound us, we will spend our lives fighting."

"You do."

"I did for pay, aye, and I did not fight for myself. That way I fought with skill and not rage."

"What is rage?"

"What you felt when Auggie spoke ill of your mother."

"Oh." He drew a shuddering breath, sniffled juicily, then sighed. "You do not like me, do you?"

Gaelan's brows rose. "I have little reason not to like you."

Connal dug in the earth near his foot, aware that his streaks of mischief should have garnered a spanking at least. "I am sorry for hitting you with me sling."

"Forgiven." A pause, and then, "You are an excellent shot."

Connal sighed, too heavily for one so young. "Do you . . . like my mama?"

Gaelan's throat tightened. "I would not have wed her if I did not, Connal."

"You touch her too much."

"I like her. People who like each other touch."

Connal lifted his gaze. "But you locked her in the tower!"

'Twas only one of Gaelan's regret. "That was before I liked her."

"Oh."

Gaelan's lips quirked. "Did you ever want something so bad you would do aught to have it?"

"Aye. You. Gone."

Ahh, he was so much like his mother, he thought with a smile. "I won't leave, ever. I suggest you discard this quest of mischief and sour moods." He eyed him. "It troubles your mother, and I have only so much leather left to repair Grayfalk's girth."

Connal flinched, obviously thinking he'd gotten away with that one. "She does not care about me; she has you now."

Sympathy and sudden understanding sparked in Gaelan. "You know that is untrue, Connal, and she spoke to me of her worry." Connal colored with shame. "I am not here to steal her from you. I want only to share her." He leaned down to whisper, "She will always be *your* mother *first.*"

Connal looked at him and smiled, sighing with relief, and Gaelan felt something kick him in the chest then. So changeable was the mind of a child, he thought, nudging him. "I am not even English, you know."

Connal cocked his head, inspecting him as if it would show in marks.

"I'm Cornish."

" 'Tis almost as good as bein' Irish."

Gaelan smiled and Connal returned it. An uncomfortable silence stretched before Gaelan spoke. "You and I . . . we—ah." He swallowed, uncertain if he should approach the subject. "We have a common thread in our lives." Connal eyed him, looking wary and distrustful. "I did not know my father, either."

"Sir Raymond said you were knighted in his household."

Raymond needed to keep his own counsel, he thought. "Aye, but not when I was young like you."

"Was he pleased? Did he like you? Did he teach you things a man must know?"

Gaelan heard the eagerness in his voice, the same he'd had when he'd arrived at his father's house, the need for approval, to meet a standard, and to mayhaps find his place and have the chance to succeed. "Aye, he was pleased, I think." Gaelan shrugged. "He did not pat me on the head or aught like that. I remember, though, when I mounted the quintain and managed to keep my seat, he smiled"—his gaze slid to Connal's—"once."

Connal made a pitying sound. "*My* mother smiles even when I drinks me milk." He drew in the dirt and Gaelan peered, seeing the shape of a horse. "Your father, he let you have a horse?"

"I was older than you and could already ride, lad."

The boy sighed, his shoulders sagging, and Gaelan realized how sequestered his life was, and though he envied the love that surrounded the child when he needed it most, Connal was feeling left out, mayhaps even cast aside to a new marriage.

"Would you like to tour the barracks when I inspect this night?"

Connal's head jerked up, his smile blinding, then falling. "Mama will not allow it."

"I do not need her permission, Connal." Not that she would speak to him now, regardless.

"Then aye, I would."

"Good. Off with you for now," he said. "You may make another slingshot today, if you wish."

Connal blinked in surprise, then stood, brushing off his rump.

"As punches go, lad," Gaelan said, and Connal cast him a wary glance, "you've the makings of a fine warrior."

Grinning, his little chest puffed out, he swaggered out the door.

"Connal."

The boy turned.

"Cause your mother heartache again, son, and *I* will discipline you . . . severely."

Instead of fear, Connal nodded, then dashed out of sight.

A smile ghosted across Gaelan's lips as he leaned his head back against the stone wall. If only your mother was so easily won, he thought, then stood. He came around the edge of the dairy and found Siobhàn stepping out of the building. She looked up, her eyes suspiciously bright, a pail of milk in her hand.

"My thanks, Gaelan," she whispered, her lower lip trembling.

He took a step closer and she retreated. Gaelan stiffened. "I will teach him to ride, Siobhàn. 'Tis time he had duties and not so much time to cause trouble."

"He is a child."

His gaze thinned. "He is a prince, the stepson of a lord, and will take Donegal in his care one day." His words bit with finality.

Her throat worked. He could see it, and the rift between them seemed to stretch to unbearable length. Finally Gaelan strode off, wondering how a woman with so much compassion for her folk could not find a smattering for him.

Siobhàn frowned into Connal's chamber. Her child slept soundly, yet Rhiannon was nowhere about, her bed mussed. Her gaze shifted to the wall of pegs. Her cloak was gone. Cursing under her breath and quitting the room, she started for the stairs to search the hall, but something told her Rhiannon was not in the keep, and taking time to search would give her naught. Siobhàn turned into her chamber, grabbing her fur cloak and donning it before striding to the west wall, sliding the trunk to the right. With both hands flat on the wall, she pushed. It gave, mortar and rock grinding as it swept back to reveal the steep tunnel. She ducked, then stilled, glancing back in indecision. Gaelan would be here in less than an hour and she wanted to talk with him, apologize for the harsh things she'd said, but Rhiannon's behavior warranted her immediate attention.

She advanced into the tunnel, using her shoulder to shove the wall back into place. He would see the chest had been moved and discover the tunnel, she thought, and cursed herself for not telling him sooner. 'Twas how she left the keep whilst his men were in the hall that first night, she remembered with a smile. And how she got back inside after discovering Gaelan in the stables. 'Twas Tigheran's wisest triumph in constructing this castle, except that both of the two tunnel exits should have ended outside the walls, not one in a stand of trees beyond the castle and the other at the dovecote. She emerged quietly from behind the cistern, scanning the area. A figure moved at the postern of the inner ward, and Siobhàn stood, walking briskly across the yard. Most were still in the hall eating and only a gaggle of geese peppered the grounds. At the wall, she paused, looking down at the soldier asleep, a mug in his hand. She bent, taking the mug to her nose and sniffing. Oh, Rhiannon, she thought. Drugging the troops!

Laying the cup beside the young man, Siobhàn retraced her steps, taking the tunnel into the bowels of the earth. Pushing the hatch open, she blew dirt and grass from her face, ruffled it out of her hair and searched the area. Her eyes widened at the sight of her sister riding off to the north. On Siobhàn's horse.

She did not consider the repercussions and ran to the closest camp of English soldiers, slipping quietly into the horse pen.

She whispered to the animals in a low voice, patting and soothing until she found one small enough for her to mount without notice. She led the animal out, away from the campfires and into the twilight of the hillside, then swung astride, riding slowly. She prayed Rhiannon had a good explanation for this, for when Gaelan found out, she would be punished. And in his present mood, it would be severe.

Gaelan could not find her anywhere.

He'd told her to wait for him in their chamber, and a horrible feeling slipped over his skin when he found it empty. He'd seen her enter, so where was she? Immediately he checked Connal's room, then strode belowstairs and out of the keep. After searching the herb house and every space between without success, he headed to the outer ward and found Raymond and his vassals gathered, preparing to head out on the next patrol. The men grew quiet as Gaelan approached and Raymond parted from them.

"Have you seen Siobhàn?"

Raymond sighed, looking at his feet for an instant before meeting his gaze. "Sir Owen saw a woman near the south end near Maguire lands."

Gaelan frowned, then gestured to Sir Owen to come forward. "You did not detain the female, question her? God, man, brigands do not always wear braies."

"My lord . . ." Owen hesitated. " 'Twas the princess."

Gaelan's scowl turned menacing.

"At least it looked like her."

It couldn't be. It was growing dark, he reasoned, and what would she be doing outside the keep? The risk was insurmountable. "All the more reason to detain her or follow, Sir Owen." His gaze jerked to Raymond. "We ride, now."

"My lord," Owen called.

He paused, turning, his gaze bouncing between Owen and Raymond and not liking the pity he saw there.

"She was not alone."

Gaelan's features yanked taut.

"I swear she was speaking to a man, and he wore a plaid like the ambushers who attacked us on our way here."

Gaelan's eyes narrowed before he turned toward the stables, bellowing for Reese.

The ambushers wore the Maguire's plaid.

Chapter Twenty-one

Darkness fell sharply, clouds blocking the rise of the spring moon.

Wind ripped hard and quick over the land, snapping with cold and a coming storm.

Siobhàn huddled in her cloak as she rode, skirting the edge of the forest. Ducking beneath the low branches of Blackthorn trees, she hoped it was the spot where she'd seen Rhiannon disappear. She directed the animal carefully around the gnarled woods, and like the soft call of spirits guiding her, voices drifted, a low hum on the air. She dismounted, lifting her skirts high and wishing she'd worn braies. But there was no time.

Jager me, when Gaelan hears of this Rhi will be sent away for certain, Siobhàn thought, her delicate slippers sinking into the mire. Nor did she want to think what he would believe of his wife. She stilled, the voices growing stronger, and squinted in the dark. Siobhàn spied Rhiannon, her figure cloaked and hooded. She spoke with an unfamiliar man and an instant later, when he tried to touch her and Rhiannon thrust away, her hood slipped back. Wrapped in furs, the man stepped cautiously close, as if calming a wild animal. Siobhàn could not hear the conversation, yet recognized her sister's characteristics. She was furious with this man.

When the conversation grew more heated and he caught her by the arms, giving her an angry shake, Siobhàn decided 'twas time to make herself known. She advanced, but Rhiannon was not a weak woman, shoving the man aside and fleeing into the trees.

The man called to her but did not follow.

Siobhàn walked forward, and as he turned, she pushed back her hood.

"Princess." His voice held surprise and a touch of awe.

Suddenly the forest was alive, warriors dropping from the trees, emerging from the darkness. Cloaked in furs and coarse tartan fabrics, their faces painted for ancient ritual, she did not recognize a single man—but she knew who they were.

Fianna Eirinn.

The Fenians.

"You trespass," she said to the leader.

He folded his arms over his chest. "No part of Ireland is beyond us."

"When you murder my folk, Donegal is forbidden!"

The leader's features tightened and he looked away, briefly, a portrait of quick agony. Yet when he returned his gaze to Siobhàn, a dark hatred settled in his eyes. "We raid the land for food, princess. Whilst you spread yourself beneath the enemy and betray your people!"

Siobhàn inhaled a sharp breath. "You raid for food and slaughter innocents. And you break tribal law, insulting me, Irishman," she snapped, the past day's turmoil falling on her shoulders like a hammer, sending her forward.

The outlaws raised their weapons, javelins and arrows aimed at her heart.

"Do not test me this day, sons of Erin," she hissed, glancing at each man and bringing her point home with a glare meant to maim. "Your vows to protect the *tuath* and its folk is false. People are dying, and the only ones skilled enough to slaughter are you."

"What of your husband's army?"

Her gaze jerked to the leader, tall, russet haired and brawny. "He would not kill his own people. Nay!" She slashed the air, her body growing hot with rage. "He would not! You are either the cause or part of the strife, Fenian." She gestured to the mismatch of tartans, then noticed more about them. Although Siobhàn had never seen a Fenian, they looked bleak—defeated.

The leader clenched his fists, his body tightly coiled. "You cannot stop what is to come, princess."

"Neither can you! You cannot defy the will of King Henry. I have tried!" Her body and soul responded to her outrage, heat simmering over her skin. A blue-white vapor rose around her, smoking the trees. The leader slowly unfolded his arms, watching, wary. "Mark another village, Fenian, and I swear on the blood of my ancestors . . ." She drew a deep breath and spat, "I will *beg* my husband to destroy you!"

Warriors scowled, weapons faltered, expressions clouded with awe and sudden fear as the mist curled, enveloping her like blue flame, protecting her. Approaching hoofbeats trembled the earth, black clouds overhead colliding.

The beasts of thunder roared.

The leader's gaze locked with hers. "*You* I do not fear. A reckoning is coming, princess." His tone cracked with threat and knowledge. "Beware."

Siobhàn's eyes narrowed. "Be warned," she returned. "Naught will save you from his wrath, Fenian."

The splinter of branches drew her around as PenDragon emerged from the forest like the devil from a darkened womb, a silver giant against murderous black. Siobhàn's features slackened as he fired a bolt into the forest. She whipped around, but the Fenians were gone, their retreat cloaked in the mist.

Controlling his eager mount, Gaelan waved sharply, and dozens of soldiers and knights bolted into the forest, giving chase. He rode to Siobhàn, stopping, staring down at her as he lashed the crossbow to the saddle, a mix of rage and relief bleeding through him. White vapor permeated the edges of her fur cloak, whispering from beneath her garments. The sight made her all the more elusive, untouchable.

"Did you meet him?"

Him. Ian. Fury lit through her at the accusation. "After what we have shared, you think me ready to run to another man to give you pain? You disgust me, PenDragon." She turned away, heading back toward her mount in the forest, but Gaelan did not give her the chance, riding closer, flinging from the saddle. She turned and he grabbed her by the arms, driving her back against a tree.

"Why were you here?" he roared in a tortured voice.

"I followed someone from Donegal and beg you let me confront them myself first."

"Who betrayed us, Siobhàn?" His tone warned, his fury barely suppressed.

She looked down, unable to reveal her sister's part before she spoke to Rhiannon herself.

"I see."

Her head jerked up. "Nay, you are blinded by jealousy."

"Like the Maguire?"

"Ian had reason to be jealous. You do not."

"Why? Tell me why I should not seek the man and sever him limb from limb?"

"He is not part of this." Gaelan scoffed and she jerked on his hold, demanding he listen. "I would never betray you. I am *your* wife, yours alone." His brooding gaze scraped over her features and Siobhàn saw his doubt, his wretched thoughts. "Even my disappointment over your falsehood this morn—" She touched the side of his face and his hard gaze softened a fraction. "I would never do aught to hurt you, to destroy us."

"You drug guards and leave in secret, refuse a name, risk your life . . . how can I believe you?" came in an anguished whisper.

Her brows rose. "For I say 'tis so."

"What you have said thus far does not warrant such a trust."

Hurt bloomed deeper in her green eyes and she shoved him back. "You demand from me what you do not offer! I ask for a few hours, not a lifetime."

"You help him out of pity. He will not thank you for that." Spinning on his heel, he swung up onto Grayfalk.

"Gaelan."

"God," he said, gripping saddle leather, rain drenching his back, "oftimes I prefer you call me aught but my name. It hurts to hear it."

She stood near the horse, her hand on his thigh. "Only *your* suspicions hurt you, husband. I love Ian like a brother, an old memory. You have naught to question in that and those men"— he tipped his head back, meeting her gaze—"they were the Fenian warriors, and I did not recognize even one of them."

Gaelan digested this for a moment, staring at her beautiful upturned face, smooth and rain splattered. For the ride here, he'd imagined the worst, imagined finding her body mangled or without life or not at all. Battling with the demons riding his spine, he could say no more than, "Get on your horse."

Sighing defeatedly, she turned away, led the horse from hiding and obeyed. When she was mounted, he rode close, taking the reins and lashing them to his saddle.

"You are forbidden to leave the castle."

Her lips tightened. "That will not change what rots atween us, Gaelan."

"Mayhaps 'twill keep you alive a little longer, then." He looked at the forest, the mist cloaking the ground, and knew somehow, she created it. "My loyalty is with you and Donegal, Siobhàn." He turned his head to look at her, his expression wounded and angry. "If you cannot give me your trust, then

I . . .'' He swallowed. "I will lock you in our chamber to keep you safe, I swear it.''

" 'Tis you who withholds trust, husband.'' Siobhàn gripped the saddle horn as he turned his back on her and rode out of the forest.

They were drenched to the bone by the time they reached the castle walls. Gaelan dismounted and turned to aid his wife, yet she shoved his hands away and dismounted easily, brushing past, joining her maid, Meghan, and striding across the outer ward. Gaelan called to her and she stilled, waving Meghan onward, yet did not turn to him. Gaelan stepped around to face her, rain saturating her hair as she tilted her head to look him in the eye.

"Give me something to believe, Siobhàn," he begged softly.

"You have accused me falsely and I have naught but me word, my lord.'' Torment lay like an open wound in her eyes. "And you have naught but your doubts to comfort you.''

He reached for her and she flinched away, moving around him and running toward the keep. Gaelan sighed, his shoulders drooping miserably. He stormed to the walls, waiting for the patrol to arrive, pacing furiously, his mind haunting him with images and distrust that would not rest.

"Damn you, Rhiannon. Damn you! You should have told me before now!''

Rhiannon's eyes widened at her sister's reaction.

"My husband believes I have betrayed him. That Ian was in those woods and *I* was meeting him.''

"What? Why Ian?''

"Because he did not see you a'tall and the Fenian wore a Maguire plaid. A Maguire attacked his army. A Maguire was betrothed to me and nearly started a war for his stupid jealousy." She threw her hands up. "Choose a reason!"

"Siobhàn, calm down." Rhiannon reached for her sister, but she jerked away.

"How can I? You have defied his rule, and I have defied him for you. Sweet Mary mother," Siobhàn said. "He thinks I drugged the guards."

"Then you must tell him 'twas me." She could not allow Siobhàn to pay for her crime.

"You think he would believe me? Hah!" Siobhàn moved to the fire, searching for a solution in the flames.

"I will tell him myself."

Siobhàn darted, catching her arm. "Nay."

"Aye." Rhiannon's expression softened, and she tipped her head, stroking a strand of hair from Siobhàn's cheek. " 'Tis mine to fix this time."

He will not listen, Siobhàn thought. He sees what he needs to see to justify his harsh words. "He will punish you, you know that. And I will not be able to convince him of leniency this time. He is trapped in jealousy."

"For your sake . . . if you must, sister, reveal—"

Siobhàn instantly pressed a finger to her lips. "Do not speak of it. You know we cannot." She tipped her head back, a single tear falling. "But he is my lord, my *husband*," Siobhàn said on a gasp, her voice fracturing. *And I love him. I love him,* she thought, and fresh pain flooded through her. To protect the future of her people, she had to keep her silence, and she knew it would someday destroy her marriage.

"Raymond tells me a stranger approached you," Gaelan said coldly.

She glanced at the knight, her expression clear of emotion before she looked back at PenDragon. "Aye. He was a messenger, asking me to meet with the Fenians. I refused."

Behind her Raymond nodded.

"They came again and threatened my family. I had to go."

Gaelan propped his elbows on the chair arms, fingers steepled, tapping his lips. "You could have come to me, Rhiannon. I could have sent men to protect you."

"That was a condition. And they would not have harmed me."

"Sister, they were Maguires—"

"Nay. They are many clans, my lord, and renounce their tribe to become *Fianna Eirinn*. And tartans are similar. For warmth, I would even wear your banner."

Gaelan almost smiled, and if the situation weren't so grave, he might have believed her. "You still have not told me why they summoned you."

"They wanted knowledge that would destroy you." She waved her hand over his and Gaelan scowled as the tingling sensation began. His fiery glare sent her back a step.

"You gave it."

She shook her head. "On the grave of my father, I did not."

"It appears to me that these warriors will not let this matter rest."

"In that, at least, you are right."

Her tone implied other matters and his gaze flew to hers.

For an instant, Rhiannon saw the wounded beast inside him, clawing at his self-made cage. Her heart wept for his pain, false and unjust, and she could hold her tongue no longer. "Hear me well, my lord." She sank to the floor at his feet, uncaring of the men who looked on, uncaring of the price to her dignity. "Siobhàn has reason to distrust—"

Gaelan glanced above her, inclining his head, and Raymond, Driscoll and Andrew departed the solar. Gaelan looked back at his wife's sister.

"Siobhàn is loyal to you. To us all. You have already experienced how hard she can fight for her allegiance. Do not make her fight for you."

Gaelan could not mistake the sincerity in her eyes, yet he found Rhiannon's explanations for leaving the castle in secret weak. He admitted he understood why Siobhàn kept Rhiannon's identity from him. He would have done anything if he could have protected his brother.

"Ian Maguire was the love of a young girl, my lord. Siobhàn was forced to set it aside and hence grew away from it. Ian has never forgotten nor forgiven because she *chose* to break with him and be the armistice of this land to the O'Rourke. And he will forever resent that another man won again. But this is not atween you and my sister . . . 'tis atween you and Ian.''

Gaelan looked away, wanting to hold on to his anger, for it kept other thoughts at bay. He had by no means set about to believe this woman, for she was odd to start, but Gaelan could not dispatch what she'd said either.

Moments passed in silence and Rhiannon stood, gazing down at him where he sat in his big chair. "I accept whatever punishment you deem.''

Without looking at her, he said, "In that, woman, you have no choice.''

Gaelan waved a hand and Rhiannon left him alone with his thoughts.

He stepped into the darkened chamber and found Siobhàn on the floor near the fire, staring at the blaze. She did not acknowledge him, and although the food lay untouched on the table centering the room, she had taken leave of the bath. He walked to his chests, removing his damp tunic and boots, then donned a fresh shirt. Taking his boots, he moved to the fire, propping them close to dry. He stared down at her, her hands clasped on her lap, her hair shielding her face.

Then Gaelan noticed the tears splattering her fists and he

groaned. Her head jerked up and he sank to the floor. "Ahh, Siobhàn, please talk to me."

She lurched into his arms, clinging to him, fingers digging into his back. "Oh, Gaelan," she cried. "Cast me aside if you must, but keep Connal safe."

He blinked. This was the last thing he expected her to say. "Aye."

"Promise me, swear to it," she pleaded, tipping her head back to look at him, her eyes bright with fear. "Promise me, if aught happens to me you will raise Connal as your own, protect him. Please!" she begged when he simply stared.

"I—I swear, love, I swear."

Her gaze searched his for a moment longer, as if seeking the truth before she sank bonelessly into his embrace. Her vehemence troubled him, like her sister's premonitions. She spoke as if she would not live to see the child grow. Such a valued trust she gave, the life of her child, and even as he cherished it, Gaelan tried to piece together the puzzle of this woman, frowning as his mind pulled together the fragments that now included Connal. Driscoll said she'd birthed Connal in an abbey, detained there for the winter snow.

But Tigheran was killed in the spring and she'd showed no sign of pregnancy, according to Driscoll, before she left. Gaelan counted months to weeks, then came to a troubling conclusion.

Connal was not Tigheran's son.

Siobhàn found Gaelan in the tiltyard the next morning and her heart skipped at the sight of Connal astride Grayfalk. She raced to Gaelan's side, but he did not look at her, his eyes on the horse and boy. He held a lead rope and rotated as the horse circled in a perfect ring.

"Do you not think Grayfalk is a bit large for him to take his first ride upon?"

"I trust the mount, Siobhàn. And look at him, he has a fine

seat.'' Siobhàn did look and Connal smiled, his mind and body concentrating on keeping in the huge saddle, posting with the jolt of the horse. He looked like a leprechaun atop a mountain of horseflesh.

"Do not let him see your fear," Gaelan warned. "It took me all morn to get him to even approach the animal."

" 'Tis no wonder."

Her son looked so proud of himself that her heart clenched, and with each turn about the ring, he sat a little straighter and with more confidence. Soldiers and Irish warriors applauded him and Connal beamed. Ahh, she thought, it had been a long time since she'd seen him smile like that.

"Aye, that's it, lad. Good, good. With your knees," he called, then lowered his voice. "Think he is tired? I do not want him so sore he will never get on again."

"He looks so happy."

His gaze darted to her and Gaelan frowned. "Why do you weep?"

"I do not weep." She swallowed, blinking back the burn of tears. "I did not realize how much he would enjoy having a man's attention."

Gaelan's shoulders sagged. "He is a good boy, Siobhàn, but coddled by women, he will be too soft for the reins of Donegal."

"I know."

Gaelan halted Grayfalk, striding quickly to Connal and lifting him from the saddle. "Enough for today. Walk about and stretch your legs. Do not sit for a while or you will not like sitting here"—he patted the saddle—"in the morn."

"I can do it again?"

Gaelan knelt. "Aye and someday, when you have practiced, I will see you have your own mount. But," he warned, when Connal looked ready to explode with joy, "you must first learn to care for it." Connal nodded and Gaelan motioned to Reese, unclipping the lead rope and coiling it before handing it to the squire.

"Show Connal how you clean hooves and curry. But he is not allowed near."

"Aye, my lord." Reese looked down at Connal. "Come along, then." He thrust the keel of lead rope at Connal. "Do yer part." Connal smiled as he took it, and Siobhàn and Gaelan watched him go, his short little legs desperate to keep up with the strapping squire.

She dragged her gaze from the stable and met his.

He simply stared, his mind working over his discovery of last night. "Siobhàn . . ."

"Aye." She waited and waited, a strange look passing over his features. "My lord?"

All Gaelan could think, all he could see in his mind was Siobhàn in Ian's arms, her body growing large with his child. Did she have an affair with him after Tigheran left or before the man died? Or was the boy in truth O'Rourke's and he was tormenting himself over naught? There was only a few weeks' discrepancy and he knew that with births, he could be wrong, for of all the things he understood, the least of which was women and pregnancy.

"Never mind."

"You are certain there is not something you wish to say? Since you departed this morn afore I woke—" Her voice lowered. "Would you not like to accuse me of betraying you afore the entire keep and not just within earshot of your knights?"

Her tone held the sting of a wound, and no matter what he was feeling, Gaelan experienced the uncontrollable need to soothe it. "Siobhàn, I did—"

"Nay," she cut in, too hurt to hear even an apology right now, especially not in public. "Just keep your promise to Connal."

She turned away, scarcely noticing the completed barracks, the extension to the stables and new roofs to most of the outer buildings. Nor the archery targets and quintain, or the masoners slavering mortar and mud into the gaps around the fitted stones.

She noticed naught, except the breaking of her heart, piece by piece.

For two days they went through the motions, wooden around each other, fragile. Speaking when spoken to and no more. She tended him as any wife would: at meals, his bath, seeing his clothes prepared, his wine sweetened. Yet her smiles were brittle and false and each one cut through to his soul.

Siobhàn festered in hurt, waiting for his apology.

Gaelan wallowed in doubt and suspicion, hating himself for it.

Each night they lay in their bed, together yet apart, hungering but not taking, neither willing to reach out and touch, longing hidden in stony silence and shadows.

Siobhàn rushed to Gaelan's side as the gate swung open.

"We spotted them an hour ago. 'Tis the O'Niell."

"You would let him in?"

"He comes with a gift from the king."

"Lochlann?"

He smirked but did not meet her gaze. "Startled me too."

"Why would Henry send a gift?"

Gaelan glanced down at her, expecting her to be eager and finding only mild curiosity.

Lochlann O'Niell rode between the gates and slipped from his mount, opening his arms to her, expecting her to throw herself at him as she had before. When she merely stepped forward and pecked his cheek, he frowned, his gaze shooting between husband and wife.

Stepping back, he said, "Imagine my surprise when I was in Dublin and bid bring this to the PenDragon's new bride."

Lochlann gestured, and a soldier led a beautiful honey-colored mare forward.

"For me?" She looked at Gaelan and he nodded.

"Did I not tell you Henry would be pleased?"

"Aye, you did, husband," she said, then looked back at the horse, stepping closer. The mount was cloaked in the king's banner, bright red ribbons woven into the mane and tail.

"For you, Lord Donegal." Lochlann handed PenDragon a missive bearing the royal seal. "And there is this, Siobhàn." He gestured, and his man presented an ornate saddle. "I told him you preferred astride."

Gaelan chuckled without humor. "Only Henry would answer the whims of a woman," he said, and Siobhàn's gaze shot to his.

"You have."

"Lately to my contrition," he muttered.

Siobhàn felt struck across the face by his words. Gaelan instantly regretted his callousness and reached for her, yet she back stepped, her eyes burning between hurt and anger. Instantly she turned her back on him, moving to Lochlann as Gaelan barked for Reese.

Siobhàn looked wistfully at the creature as squire Reese drew it away, then to Lochlann. "Come break bread with us, brother."

Lochlann glanced between the two, wondering why Siobhàn did not mount the creature and test her head now, but kept his mouth shut and walked beside her to the keep.

'Twas obvious to him, the alliance of O'Rourke and Pen-Dragon was not a happy one.

"You must destroy them all," Lochlann insisted.

Gaelan shook his head. "You seek a bloodbath. To what end, man?"

"My lord," Lochlann said, hitching his rear on the edge of the desk, "four villages have—"

"Five," Driscoll added.

Lochlann's expression grew more grave. "They hide like vultures. I suggest we position about the villages as yet unhit and catch them."

Gaelan sighed. "We have done that without success. They vanish into the hillside and leave no trail." God above, Gaelan thought. It was as if they sank into the earth and were covered by trees. The trails simply ended. "Half were left untouched, only the livestock taken."

"And three have been left bloodied to the ground!" Lochlann shouted, straightening. "You are lord here now. Do something afore there is naught left of Donegal or—"

"Or what, Lochlann?" Siobhàn said from the doorway, and heads swung around.

"Or the price will be your keeps on the borders."

"What!" Gaelan said, lurching to his feet. "What keeps?"

Siobhàn smothered a smile and the men gathered in the solar stood as she stepped inside with the tray. Depositing it on the scarred desk, she offered her husband the first mug of ale, then Lochlann, before serving Raymond, Driscoll and the remaining knights and newly appointed Irish retainers littering the outer edges of the room.

"You said that you did not want to know what came with me in this marriage, my lord." She bent over the table, laying a trencher of freshly roasted mutton, boiled pigeon eggs and onions before Gaelan, and when she lifted her gaze, she found him staring at her bosom. At least he has not dismissed me completely, she thought.

"Surely you jest?" Lochlann said, clearly appalled. "Were there no contracts?"

"I had Donegal. What other lands come with the princess was not a concern at the time."

Siobhàn swept around the edge of the table to stand near

Gaelan. "I should say so," she muttered under her breath, and he tipped a look at her, his lips quirking a fraction.

He ordered Raymond to bring the contracts and unfolding them, Gaelan gave them a quick glance, pleased he could now read. He looked at his wife, brows high. "Three more? You have three more? Sweet Christ, Siobhàn!" He dropped into a chair. "These people have been unprotected!"

"Nay, the Maguire sees to that, and Lochlann. 'Tis their duty to the *tuath*. Their fee paid in cows."

At the mention of Ian's name Gaelan's expression darkened. "Maguire is not sworn."

"Swearing to the lord of Donegal will not stop Ian from protecting his clan, Gaelan. Nor our keeps." There was a bite to her tone none could mistake, and Gaelan's eyes narrowed on his wife. " 'Twill be a matter of time afore he understands he cannot fight the English."

Gaelan did not believe the Maguire was anywhere near swearing his oath to Henry, and that Siobhàn failed to mention that the man was still connected to her in clan debt, festered inside him.

Siobhàn laid her hand to his shoulder and he snapped a look at her. For an instant she frowned softly, searching his dark, brooding eyes. "If you are worried, I suggest you send some of those men lazing about in the camps to the other keeps. Or Fallon O'Donnel"—she glanced at the Irish retainer—"since his kin live there."

Gaelan leaned forward, forcing her to release him, and rolled the parchment, tying the ribbon thong with such care Siobhàn grew nervous. He lifted his gaze and said one word.

"Leave."

Siobhàn flushed with anger, yet she kept her mouth shut. He had no right to speak to her thusly, treat her as if she had not ruled this land for years without his army and his bloody damned guidance. Yet she did not want a scene—not now—but there would be one, she thought. Jager me, there would. She bobbed a curtsey, quitting the solar. Outside the entrance, she sagged against the wall.

"My lady?" Brody paused on his way into the solar.

Siobhàn blinked at him, then forced a smile. "You're looking fine in your English garments."

The man grinned. "Fits me better than furs and rough cloth." He patted his chest and the PenDragon shield there.

Siobhàn frowned at it for a moment, then nodded to the solar. "Go, they talk of battle. I am certain you are interested." She pushed away from the wall, quickening her steps, trying to escape the hurt of being cast aside.

First by her husband, now by her clan.

Chapter Twenty-two

Siobhàn cooed to the horse, running the brush over her golden honey hide. "Ahh, you're a bonny lass," she whispered softly. "Such pretty legs, so dainty, m'lady." The stallions in the stables stomped and snorted, scenting the female among them. "Beware of that one, eh?" She nodded to Grayfalk, the other knight's steed lining the freshly timbered stalls. "He's got a head as thick as his master."

The horse bobbed and Siobhàn smiled, laying her cheek to her mare's wide neck, smelling animal and leather. And freedom. She longed to race, to be the wind and lose herself in the ride. To be anywhere except in this keep, now.

"Mama?"

Siobhàn looked up, smiling and motioning Connal closer, Culhainn at his heels. The dog plopped near the door, not daring to come close to the jumble of hooves as her son looked up at the grand charger with wide eyes. Siobhàn lifted him in her arms, setting him gently on the mare's back.

"Did the king of England really give this creature to you?"

"That is what Lochlann says."

Connal toyed with the ribbon in the horse's mane. "She is pretty, Mama."

"That she is. What shall we call her?"

Connal looked thoughtful, bending around to look the mare in the eye and nearly tumbling from her back. Siobhàn laughed, catching him, holding him before the animal's face. He petted the mare's nose carefully.

"Riona. It means royal, aye?"

"Aye, lovey. Riona, then."

Connal looked at the creature, his expression serious, and Siobhàn frowned softly as he stared into the animal's eyes. "Riona, you're a king's gift to my *maither*. Serve her and only her, aye?"

Siobhàn smothered a laugh at his adult behavior, that he tried to deepen his voice a bit. Yet when the horse nodded and then dipped its head low, stretching out one leg, suspicion raced through her.

"She understands," she whispered, clutching her child away from the horse.

"Aye, of course."

Siobhàn smoothed his hair back, staring into his eyes. "Keep this secret, son."

"Why?

"Those who would harm you, would use it against you."

"Like my father did with the mist?"

Her eyes flared. "Who told you that?"

"I heard the soldiers speaking of it. But Uncle Lochlann told me. Will you conjure the mist for me?"

"Nay! 'Tis not a toy to be played with at the whim of a child!"

His lower lips curled down, and Siobhàn regretted her sharpness, hugging him, apologizing as she pressed his head to her shoulder. His arms swept tightly around her neck, his legs around her waist. Tigheran forbade her to leave the keep in winter and remarked often enough that he'd married into a family of witches. Thank the Lord he never said such afore witnesses, she thought. And now this talent of Connal's would grow as he did, just as it had in her and Rhiannon.

"Do not be afraid, Mama," he said softly. "I will protect you."

Siobhàn's eyes burned. Oh, how she loved him and she tightened her embrace for a brief moment. He leaned back and kept leaning until he hung upside down, giggling. Siobhàn twirled for him, tickling her son, and dizzily they sank to the straw piles. Connal tickled her back, trying desperately to make her laugh.

"Cease, oh cease, child. Your fingers are bony and I am not ticklish."

He muttered a curse, a funny one of toads and larcenous rats.

"Go ask Nova if the meal is ready, then come back to tell me, aye." He nodded, scrambling off the soft pile and running to the doors. Siobhàn snapped her fingers for Culhainn, yet the dog whined for an instant, sniffing the ground along the walls, then looked at her.

"Go, follow him." The white beast finally lumbered off.

Siobhàn laid there alone in the timothy, her thoughts growing sad and dark. She was furious with her husband for the way he'd treated her in the solar, for accusing her of giving her sympathies to Ian. Neither man recognized that if she'd truly loved Ian those years back, naught would have stopped her from being with him. It reminded her that Gaelan had little love in his life, a slattern mother, a cold father, and had lost the only person he'd ever cared about, his brother, and blamed himself. It was a wonder her husband managed to be such a tender lover after so harsh a life, and Siobhàn understood where his feelings brewed. But his past did not give him the right to insult and shame her.

She rolled over, catching a pipe of straw and chewing on

the tip. She really should be helping with the meal, seeing to Lochlann and his men. But she did not want to be near Gaelan feeling this way. She was afraid she would say something she'd regret.

Damn him.

His doubt would not hurt so much if she did not love him. Siobhàn closed her eyes, laying her cheek on the straw and remembering the feel of his arms around her, his teasing smiles and their sensual game of saying his name. Her heart constricted painfully. She missed him, missed the man trying to win her, the man who looked upon her with affection and tenderness. She missed his bare skin pressed to hers whilst they slept, the way he watched her when she bathed, as if his eyes were the water, coating her body with a sultry look.

She could not hold tight to her anger over the death of Tigheran. It dissipated as quickly as it had come, for she knew, in her heart that Tigheran had been desperate enough to put down Dermott to attempt an assassination. And Gaelan was doing as his king ordered. Winning.

Would Ian be the same kind of fool as Tigheran to try to defeat Gaelan? For her?

Oh for the love of Saint Patrick, she prayed he had more sense than that. Yet, who's to know a man's heart anyway? She wed a man whose unfounded jealousy stole his trust in her. And she'd no way to repair it. Long ago the mastery over her heart had been his. From the moment she'd met him, Gaelan possessed part of her soul, held it in the palm of his hand, and with a single glance and angry word, he could wound her. Over and over.

Climbing to her feet, she finished currying the horse, returning her to the stall and smiling at the stable hands and pages asleep in the corner of the tack room like a pile of puppies exhausted from play.

She frowned at the entrance.

Connal should be back before now, she thought, and walked

to the doors. Torches lit the yard, offering little light and more shadows. People milled about, some finishing up chores before the evening meal. Two maids flirted with the English guards, one man stealing a steamy kiss and taking the girl deeper into the dark. Bowmen lined the parapets, ever vigilant on the land surrounding the walls. It was so quiet she could hear the shuffle of the guards walking their posts.

She squinted and saw her son pop through the inner ward gate, skipping his way toward her.

A noise came, crisp and loud, like the crush of stones beneath heavy boots, and Siobhàn sketched the area for the source. A cart rolled away from the wall near the armory, its weight shooting it like an arrow across the slanted grounds.

And Connal was in its path.

Running, Siobhàn shouted for him to turn back and he stopped, frowning at her. She pointed. Guards raced toward the wagon and Siobhàn watched in horror as her son tried to dart out of the path, but the rocks and terrain jolted the cart in a new direction, as if following him. She bolted, screaming for Gaelan.

Out of the darkness, a figure appeared, running, diving for Connal, tucking him to his body as he rolled and rolled out of the wagon's path. The cart crashed into the chapel steps, shattering and spilling rocks and wood onto the ground.

Then, just as suddenly, Connal flung himself into her arms. Sinking to the ground, Siobhàn sobbed into his shoulder, checking him for wounds and hugging him.

"Oh my sweet child, oh dear God."

"I am well, Mama, really," he assured her, patting her. "Where did he go?"

Siobhàn sniffled and held him back to look at him, then the area around. They were surrounded by castle folk. Standing with her son in her arms, she glanced about, then ordered a guard to search for the man who'd saved her son.

"Did you see his face?"

"Nay, he was hooded, but he smelled like . . ." Connal frowned, thoughtful. "The herb you put in your bath."

Mint, she thought. "Whoever you are," Siobhàn called above the crowd, "I am in your debt."

The crowd parted as Gaelan rushed forward, his glance at the rubble telling him much. Frozen, he stared at mother and son for a moment, and when she looked at him, her face stained with tears, he came to her, enveloping her and Connal in his arms and assuring himself they were unharmed.

"Go inside."

Siobhàn met his gaze, her tone imperial. "I wish to speak privately with you." She didn't wait for a response, marching toward the inner gates, refusing to let Connal travel on his own power when he insisted he could.

Gaelan turned, his soldiers a'ready. "Find him." His soft tone bit with the force of a blade across tender flesh and troops scattered. An hour later, unsuccessful at finding Connal's rescuer, Gaelan stepped into their chamber. Siobhàn paced before the fire, straw-dusted skirts swishing, bells jingling.

"This was deliberate," she said without looking up. "Connal was with me in the stable and I sent him to Nova, and whoever released the cart heard me tell him to return to me and simply waited."

"Aye."

She stilled, her head jerking up, her eyes hard with anger. "What do you plan to do about it, husband?"

The cold distance in her tone scratched the air between them. "There is little I can, except to keep anyone who has not lived here afore out, make rounds assuring that carts and scaffolding are secure, and keep Connal inside, in his chamber. Under guard."

Imprisoning her son when he was just learning his freedom seemed terribly unfair when he'd done nothing wrong. "You can question everyone."

"I have."

"Then do it again."

"Siobhàn—"

"Nay, do not think I will take this lightly, PenDragon. Someone in this castle deliberately tried to kill my son!" She choked on a breath and sank into a chair, covering her face with her hands. Gaelan came to her, sinking to one knee but not touching her. She cried, her hands shaking, and more misery settled in his chest.

"I was helpless. I could not run fast enough. I could not reach him. Oh Lord, my child would have been crushed."

"He wasn't," he soothed softly. "He is fine and laying abed with his lamb and Culhainn at his side."

She looked up slowly, her hands falling away. "Culhainn?" she whispered. "He was at the wall, sniffing the ground and whining."

Gaelan scowled. "Likely chasing a bug."

"Nay, he does not venture into the stables, husband. He's had a paw or two stepped on and does no more than sit at the doors."

"You think someone lay in wait outside?"

"It is a solution."

"Then why did he not alert you?"

"Mayhaps, they walked away. Connal said he smelled mint, like we did in the dungeon. Mayhaps the scent was familiar to Culhainn. I do not know!" When his look remained impassive, she stood abruptly, the motion sending the chair scraping back. "Do as you must, but if my son is not safe crossing the yard, then he is not safe in this castle, PenDragon. And I will take him to another until he is."

He stood. "You are not going anywhere."

"Then Connal goes with Rhiannon to the shore."

"Nay." If she left with Connal, there would be no chance of regaining the peace between them. "I will see he is protected and post more guards on the unfamiliar villagers, but the boy stays here." He was not about to hand his wife and her son over to the care of O'Niell and certainly not the Maguire, and he folded his arms over his chest, his hard gaze snapping over her features. "Rhiannon, however, can be wed by morn and packed off to where she can cause no more trouble!"

Her eyes flew wide. "What! You cannot force her to wed, husband."

"I can do as I please, *wife*."

Her gaze narrowed, a dangerous fire glittering there. "Aye, you can. You can accuse me of disloyalty, to you, to my *own* people"—she struck her chest—"when you have no right or reason," she hissed in an ugly voice. "You can insult me afore the retainers and a man I think of as a father. You chose to believe your jealous thoughts instead of *my* word. Aye, my lord PenDragon, you can do as you please. And be assured, for my son, so will I!"

She shoved past him, heading to the doors, but Gaelan caught her in a gentle grasp, forcing her around to meet his gaze. She was crying without sound.

He loathed that he'd brought her to this.

"I do not like you very much right now, husband." She jerked on his touch. "Release me."

He didn't, pulling her closer even as she tried to twist out of his grasp. "Siobhàn . . . ahh, my sweet, what has become of us?"

"You have doubted me word and there is no way to assure you," she muttered and stood woodenly as his arms slid around her. She pressed her forehead to his chest. She would not touch him, she could not. She was so bloody mad and wanted to keep it fresh and on the surface.

"I did not mean to insult you afore Driscoll and the O'Niell."

"You shamed me, husband." Disappointment rang in her words and Gaelan sighed and lowered his arms, stepping back.

"I was angry."

She scoffed, staring off to the side.

"I felt like a fool."

Her gaze flew to his.

"I would have seen that the contracts spoke of the keeps, and the Maguire's obligation to you . . . if I could read then. Yet 'twas a matter I should have known. I was careless."

The admittance softened her posture. "Raymond did not tell you. Why?"

He shrugged. "Likely he knew my feelings for the man and did not want to test the water."

"If you did not have your nose so far up mc skirts, you might have known."

He hated the bitterness in her voice, knowing that he put it there.

" 'Twas unwise, for all of us, to allow that to happen," she said. "And by English law, Ian is already bound through your possession of Donegal and its fiefs."

"He is his own chieftain. By his laws he is not, and that is what matters in Ireland." Gaelan crossed to the fire, bracing his right forearm on the mantel. He did not want this conversation, avoided it out of sheer fear of losing her completely, yet he could not tolerate this agony a moment longer. He stared at the blaze, wondering exactly how he'd grown so foolish.

He loved her.

Ahh, therein lies the sorrow, he thought.

He could scarcely breathe every time he looked at her lately, her thinly veiled venom knifing him to the core. He would rather die than suffer another day of this constant bleeding each other until there was naught left to save.

"Why do you doubt me, after all this time?" floated across the separation, without the rage, without the sting.

"I slew your husband. I broke the trust you gave me. I knew you were angry with me. . . ." He shrugged, almost boyishly. "I . . . I thought . . . angry enough to go to him and give him your sympathy."

"And help him war on you?" Her lower lip trembled despite the hard tilt to her chin. "I am not your mother. And I under-

stood why Tigheran had to die, my lord. Not your lie of it.''
She saw him wince and moved closer. ''For the love of Michael,
I have lain in your arms night after night, how could you think
me so base as to turn against you like that?''

''Because I am a bastard, a thief of lands, and I did not
deserve you!'' He plowed his fingers through his hair, frustration and self-anger in his voice. ''And all I knew is that you
loved him once, Siobhàn, you *chose* to marry him once, and
for the second time in your life''—he straightened, facing her,
like a man awaiting execution—''you were forced to wed a
man you did not want.''

''But I did marry you,'' she cried. ''I entrusted my folk to
you and shared my body with *you.*''

''Aye, aye, and I knew in my heart you would never betray
me. *I knew,*'' he said, shaking clenched fists in front of him.
''But when I saw the Maguire plaid on the Fenian, I could not
forget that Ian was the man you truly wanted . . . the man you
deserved.''

''Oh, Gaelan.''

His name on her lips made the muscles in his chest clamp
like a vice.

They stared, prisoners in each other's gaze.

The uneasy silence tightened like scorched skin over brittle
bone.

His throat worked. ''I have ruined everything, haven't I?''
came in a tortured rasp.

Sorrow crushed through her. Gone was the seasoned warrior
and before her stood a man stripped bare of his rough exterior,
his title and rights. Uncertain, defenseless. Unused to faith and
loyalty. He craved a chance, a small portion, so desperately
that he laid his soul at her feet like an open wound for her to
crush or soothe.

She stepped closer, and Gaelan felt the impact of her stare
down to his boot heels, his anguish twisting through every inch
of him. Her scent permeated the air with spice and flowers as

she reached, delicately fingering a lock of his hair off his brow. Briefly, he closed his eyes, her touch painful and sweet and making him tremble with his need to hold her.

"Naught is ruined that cannot be repaired."

His hopeful gaze searched hers, rapid and greedy. "You can forgive me, then?"

The expectation in his voice made her heart skip. "I must."

His brows worked.

She inched closer, laying her hand on his chest and feeling the incredible strength of his heartbeat. "I have no choice but to forgive you, Gaelan. I need you so much more than I need my anger."

His tense shoulders drooped and he covered her hand with his, bringing it to his lips. God above, he was damned unworthy of this woman. "Siobhàn . . ." He exhaled a hard breath. "I *am* sorry. I—"

"Shh, I know, I know. 'Tis done." She cupped his jaw, loving the way he turned his face into her palm, the texture of his skin. Her gaze sketched and absorbed. "I have—" She swallowed, slipping closer. "I have missed you so, Gaelan."

His big body trembled, his one hand framing her waist with a gentle weight. "I am so mad to hold you," he gasped uncertainty. "I fear I will crush you."

"Crush me. Please."

He did, sweeping her in his arms and burying his face in the curve of her throat. Her arms locked tight around his neck and she sobbed, driving her hands into his hair. Gaelan groaned, relief spilling through him like hot wine. Sweet Jesu, he needed her, and he tightened his embrace, his eyes burning. How could her warm body against his make him feel unmanned and powerful in the same instant?

"I've been such an imbecile," he mumbled into the curve of her throat.

"Aye. You have."

He chuckled unsteadily, kissing her neck, his hands racing

up and down her back, getting lost in her hair, before he tipped her head back and took her mouth with exquisite tenderness. He felt the dampness of tears on his fingertips and said naught. A hard tremor shuddered through his big body and she was silent, kissing him back, offering him the love roaring through her heart. She gave and he drank, peace and pleasure filling him like an overflowing goblet, and when he drew back, pressing his forehead to hers, together they sighed.

Then they smiled, choking on unspent tears.

Cradling her beautiful face, he rained kisses over her eyes, her cheeks, taking her mouth again and loving the way her body yielded to his. She caught his hand, bringing it to her breast, and he molded the soft flesh, throbbing to be naked and rolling with her on the bed, for the chance to show her how much he loved her, needed her.

A knock sounded and Siobhàn made a frustrated sound, covering his hand briefly before she called out. Meghan responded, asking if she should have a meal sent up.

"Nay," Gaelan said, his gaze never leaving hers. "We come anon." He rubbed his hands up and down her arms. "We cannot ignore O'Niell."

"Aye."

He wanted to shout for the disappointment in her voice. "But we can retire early."

"How early?"

His smile was slow and wide. "The sooner you are changed . . ." His glance touched on the dirt and hay stuck to her gown.

Quickly, Siobhàn moved away, wiggling out of her gown as she did, then searched her trunks for a fresh one. Gaelan dropped into a chair to wait and watch, her bare round bottom displayed as she bent over the trunks. She tossed the dark blue gown on the bed, then stood before the mirror, plucking straw from her hair, combing.

The door rattled softly and then, "Mama?"

Siobhàn twisted. "Aye, lovey?"

"I am hungry. Are you coming?"

"She could be," Gaelan muttered, and her eyes flew wide. He smiled, his gaze glazing over her thinly veiled body with a force that sent her heart racing, his desire lying plainly in his dark smoldering eyes.

Gaelan stood.

Siobhàn stepped.

Connal rapped again.

Siobhàn sent him an apologetic glance, then moved toward the door, but Gaelan put up a hand.

"I will see to him." He took a step, then turned back. A heartbeat later, he had her in his arms, his mouth crushing over hers, his tongue stroking, his hands finding their way beneath her shift and palming her warm flesh. She clung, responded with all the passion denied over the past days, and cupping her bottom, he ground her into his arousal.

"Knock, knock," he whispered into her mouth and she made a frustrated sound, aching to feel his fingers, his arousal, inside her, and too aware of the child on the other side of the door and the hall full of folk waiting for them.

He released her, loving her freshly ravished look. "Be quick, woman." He patted her behind, then left.

Siobhàn sighed, heard him speak to Connal, adoring the tenderness in his voice as she turned to the commode and washed quickly, rubbed crushed flowers over her skin, then dressed. At the chamber door, she stilled, then glanced back at the chest tucked before the tunnel wall, reminding herself to tell him of it, then crossed to it, throwing open the chest and taking the fabric off the top, tucking it beneath her arm before leaving the chamber. She passed Meghan on the staircase, toting fresh sheets and blowing her nose.

"You do not look well, Meg." Her eyes were watering and her nose was red.

"A bit of the ague, I'm thinking."

Siobhàn grasped her hand, examining the red scratches. "Go rest." Meghan took a step away. "Nay. In here." Siobhàn retraced her steps and pushed open the door to her chamber.

Meghan's eyes grew wide. "Nay, my lady."

"Aye, no one will disturb you here. There is a salve on the mantel for those scratches."

"Me cat, my lady. She does not like bathing."

"Not unlike my son." They smiled, then Siobhàn inclined her head to the room. "Go. I will come wake you later."

The maid thanked her, sniffled, then ducked into the chamber as Siobhàn headed to the hall below. To her husband and the fresh start she would give him tonight.

Chapter Twenty-three

Lochlann O'Niell watched the couple, the strain he'd noticed before now gone, replaced with subtle glances and soft smiles. Their presence immediately changed the mood of the hall, and he suppressed the thread of envy springing through him. He'd no right to it. She'd never looked upon him more than a brother, but he could not help but stare. Siobhàn looked radiant in the deep blue gown, the silver threads edging the neckline and sleeves sparkling in the dim light. His fist tightened around his goblet before he drained the wine. Tigheran was a fool to turn her away, to hold his love for Devorgilla when he could have had a ripe woman like Siobhàn.

He would credit her with the fine meal and could not complain over his reception, for he was treated well, a room prepared for his use and an invitation to remain as long as he desired, a stark contrast to his last visit. And he would remain, if aught but to understand why the new bride and groom had been at odds, and to convince PenDragon to annihilate the outlaws.

PenDragon spoke mostly to him, yet neither ignored nor

coddled the woman beside him. Siobhàn focused on Connal, the accident earlier obviously leaving behind a dose of fear. But the boy would not have it, making impatient faces at her and finally leaving the table. He walked around behind his mother and went straight to PenDragon.

Connal tugged on his sleeve, and when he twisted in the chair, PenDragon's smile was surprisingly tender.

"Tired, lad?"

"Me bum's a bit sore." Gaelan smothered a chuckle. "But I am fine. My thanks for the lessons, my lord."

It was the first time he'd called him that and Gaelan felt his throat clench. In a heartbeat, he knew that if Connal was not Tigheran's son, it did not matter, and he was mortally ashamed for thinking ill of Siobhàn. In this and his suspicions of distrust these past days. His own parentage was never a concern to this lad's mother, and Gaelan understood what he'd always known—blood did not make a family. And for a man who'd detested having children about for years, he discovered he truly liked this child and recognized all he'd missed. They were inquisitive, as easily pleased as they were wounded, and by God, this lad spoke his mind. Gaelan found it refreshing, as he had in his mother.

In his line of vision he could see Siobhàn's expression, pride and a tinge of sadness. And it felt like a dagger in his breast, for he wondered if she was thinking of Connal's father, then cursed himself for falling into the trap of his doubts again.

"My lord?"

Gaelan blinked, focusing on the boy. "Go on to bed, if you like, son."

Connal tilted his head. "Can I be your son, my lord?"

He heard Siobhàn and her sister inhale sharply and didn't think his throat could constrict any more. So innocent, he thought, swallowing before he spoke. "Is that your wish?"

"Aye," he said, as if there was no questioning the matter. "You are me mama's husband, so I think it right. Don't you?"

Uncertainty lay in the boy's voice and, unable to speak, Gaelan nodded, laying his hand on his little head. After a false start, he said, "Then you are the first son of PenDragon, Lord Donegal."

Connal nodded gravely, his expression precious and solemn before he looked up and smiled. "Good eventide." He bowed a bit, then took off toward the stairs, the slingshot hitching up the back of his tunic.

Gaelan followed his retreat, then turned his gaze on Siobhàn. She was trying desperately not to cry, he could see, and focused on her meal, though she'd already devoured most of it. Gaelan leaned close. "I could not deny him."

"I am pleased you did not, truly I am." She gulped some wine. "My thanks, Gaelan."

Gaelan speared a dice of meat with his eating knife, holding it out to her. She nipped it off, chewing slowly. "Look at me, love." Her lashes swept up slowly and Gaelan frowned at the turmoil there. "What?"

She swallowed. "I still have the sense that you do not trust me."

"I do."

"Why? Because I say you should?"

"Because I know you would never betray me," he responded easily.

Siobhàn's heart clenched, her green gaze searching his. "'Tis a fragile thing, this trust we have, Gaelan."

"It will strengthen," he assured her, concerned over the look on her face, as if something would rent them apart at any moment. His gaze flashed briefly to Rhiannon, sitting just beyond her, suddenly recalling her dark premonition. Gaelan knew he would die if he lost his wife, lose his mind if she did not accept him with his faults and, truly in her heart, forgive him.

"I know I have done you a disservice—"

She covered his mouth with two fingers, shaking her head. " 'Tis I who have done it."

He frowned with confusion and Siobhàn pushed her chair back and sank to her knees before him. The motion brought heads around, servants, retainers and knights freezing where they stood.

Laughter and music faded to a strange brittle silence.

"What in the devil's eyes are you doing?" Gaelan reached for her, yet she caught his hand, pressing it to her heart and holding it there.

"I am Siobhàn, wife of PenDragon, daughter of Erin." Her voice was clear and bright. "On this night, afore my clan . . ." She cast a quick glance at the familiar faces around them before meeting his gaze. "I swear my fealty to you, my lord husband, Gaelan of Donegal."

The air snagged in his lungs, his gaze raking her upturned face.

She leaned forward, staring deeply into his eyes, lightly brushing her fingertips over his jaw, his lips. "I give you my trust, my life and . . . my love. For this world means little without you—" She patted his hand. "This heart beats for naught without you." Her eyes filled with tears, her lips trembling. "I love you, Gaelan. For eternity, I love you."

Gaelan was stunned, his mouth open to speak, but no words came. His throat worked, his heart thundering so fiercely he thought it would explode.

"If 'twere me," Raymond said into the quiet, "I would kiss her."

Gaelan grabbed her about the waist and dragged her onto his lap. Her arms swept his neck and he stared at her, a single finger, trembling and rough, drawing a strand of hair from her face. "I love you, Siobhàn."

Her eyes watered and she smiled. "I was hopin' you did."

His mouth covered hers.

The hall erupted with cheers.

Raymond DeClare threw his head back and laughed. " 'Bout bloody damned time."

Lochlann stared, tossing back the remains of his wine, watching the couple devour each other in a kiss so passionate he felt himself grow hard. Rhiannon blotted a tear with the hem of her sleeve and across the distance nodded to DeClare, then looked at Driscoll, his smile wide enough to split his face.

A faint laughter spilled through the air and Siobhàn and Gaelan drew back, looking to the squints and finding Connal there, grinning and hopping up and down. Siobhàn waved and laid her head on Gaelan's shoulder.

"You did not have to do that," he said into her ear, rubbing her back.

"Aye, I did." She tipped her head to look him in the eye, her fingers lovingly tracing his features. "You deserved your right to my oath, Gaelan. I gave it once in marriage, I give it now in trust."

His eyes were unusually bright as they sketched her beautiful face. "I cherish it, love."

"I know you will," she said on a sigh as she snuggled in his arms. The revelry regained its former din, ale spilling to tankards, several toasts making their way around the room.

Siobhàn shifted on Gaelan's lap, sitting upright. Her gaze snapped to his, her eyes wide with surprise. "Husband?" He was hard beneath her hip, the strength of it shielded by his codpiece and tunic, yet she still felt the exquisite heat of him, and tried not to rub herself against it.

Gaelan shrugged, sheepish. " 'Tis your fault." Then he leaned up, his big hands framing her waist as he whispered, "And if this hall was not filled with people, I would have you on that table right now."

Siobhàn blushed, her body responding to the softly growled words. "You need to learn a bit of patience then. You cannot abandon the O'Niell. 'Tis improper and insulting." With a quick glance, she smiled at Lochlann, and he saluted her with his wine.

"I should find him his own woman to occupy him," he groused.

"You've someone in mind?"

His gaze jerked to Rhiannon.

"Nay."

He arched a brow.

"They dislike each other."

That was news to Gaelan, since they seemed amiable enough. "Why?"

"She does not trust him."

Gaelan sent her a neither-do-I look.

"She never has, not even when we were children. He sneaked into her rooms and painted her face with dye. It did not fade for a fortnight."

Gaelan smiled and wondered what it was like to grow up around the same people your entire life, know them well enough to call them all by name.

"DeClare?"

"Nay. And do not even think to suggest another knight. One Irishwoman wed to English is all they can tolerate for now."

Gaelan grinned, his gaze drifting from his wife to the folk surrounding him. "Are you sure?"

Siobhàn twisted on his lap, viewing the hall. DeClare stood off to the side with Driscoll's visiting sister, hand gestures accompanying Raymond's limited use of the language. Driscoll, freshly shaved like the English, kept a close watch on the couple, but his wife pinched him, pulling him away. Sir Andrew held Bridgett on his lap, his arm about her waist, his hand tenderly stroking her shoulder and fingering her hair whilst he conversed with several men over a tankard. And across the hall, in the far corner, the tall squire Reese and dark-haired Elaine stood a few feet apart, obviously in deep conversation, yet not daring to move nearer to the other.

But Siobhàn recognized the hunger in the lad's eyes.

"I expect petitions of marriage soon."

Siobhàn looked at him, smiling, and she leaned close, her bosom in full view. His gaze slavered over the lush bounty like a beast before a juicy meal.

"Damn but you tempt me before all and know I cannot have you," he groused.

"When you knock, love, I will answer."

His hand slid higher on her waist, brushing the curve of her breast, and she laid her mouth over his, taunting him with the dip of her tongue, the wet slide of it over his lips. His fingers tightened, and he was about to carry her abovestairs, regardless of the O'Niell and damned propriety, when the hall doors burst open, slamming against the wall.

Wrenching apart, Siobhàn stood, moving to Gaelan's side as a knight and a half dozen soldiers rushed in. Their clothing was blood soaked, lanced by swords—and they carried Brody. Siobhàn cried out, dashing around the dais as they laid him on the rushes. Opposite her, Friar O'Donnel knelt and began last rites as she sank to her knees, cradling his head on her lap, calling for bandages and herbs between her tears.

Gaelan was at her side, kneeling, glancing at the troops, the knights, then back at the man. He was dying, the wounds to his stomach and chest too severe, and when Siobhàn lifted her gaze to his, she knew it too. Bridgett brought cloths and Siobhàn pressed them to his wounds, bending to kiss his bloody forehead.

"Oh, my friend," she sobbed against his flesh.

He struggled to talk, his voice garbled with the blood filling his lungs. Crimson foamed his lips.

"Shh, you are home."

Brody's cloudy gaze swept unsteadily to Gaelan and he bent low, his ear near his mouth. He whispered, and Gaelan's features yanked taut. He glanced at the knights, the O'Niell hovering close, then down at Brody. "Rest, warrior," he said as Brody slipped into death.

Siobhàn smothered her anguish, hugging her friend to her breast. Gaelan stroked her back, joining her grief, then stood. "Husband?"

He looked down, at her tear-streaked face, at his new friend growing cold with death. "He said they wore the Maguire's plaid."

The hall erupted with denials. Lochlann cursed.

Siobhàn opened her mouth to deny it, but clamped her lips shut. For reasons she could not understand—Ian had turned against her.

Gaelan focused on the knight, questioning him mercilessly. "About twelve, sir. We killed two, but the rest escaped." Sir Mark's gaze shifted beyond him to O'Niell. "Some to your lands, sir." Gaelan twisted, eyeing Lochlann. "The two dead were in tartans." Mark gestured to one of the servants wrapped in the plaid cloth. "We saw soldiers too." Gaelan jerked around. "English. Armored," Sir Mark added, as if he could not believe it himself.

Gaelan's scowl turned hideously dark. The hall went silent. His gaze clashed with Siobhàn and they knew it was possible.

"At first I thought 'twas the mist playing tricks on my eyes . . ." Mark stalled, clearly unable to explain what he saw. "We followed the rest southward, but the darkness . . ." His spine stiffened and he shouldered the blame. "I lost the trail."

Gaelan gave his shoulder a commiserating squeeze as he met Siobhàn's gaze, then Raymond's, thinking of the spur in his chamber, and knew the man was not seeing a ghost.

After a quick scan for Sir Owen, he addressed DeClare. "Take account of all our men. I want to know who else was not here during the raid." Raymond's features sharpened, yet he nodded. Gaelan walked toward the door, his vassals quick on his heels. Lochlann ordered his men to arms, joining them.

Siobhàn stood beside Brody's body, watching Gaelan leave, and when he reached the entrance, he turned. For a brief moment they simply stared, and Gaelan experienced a horrible foreboding drip through his blood. Renegade knights on his land. The Maguire turning against the woman he claimed to love, the woman he was so willing to war to regain. And then there were the Fenians, and their connection to Rhiannon stirring the muck. But he was not so vengeful over Brody's death to ignore that a tartan implicated; it did not convict. He was confused and unprepared, and without more evidence, he could do little but what he had been—hunt them.

He held out his hand to her and his heart twisted in his chest as she ran down the aisle made for her, slamming into his arms. He led her briefly, tightly, fearing he would not be able to stop this war; then, with her tucked to his side, they crossed the inner yard, through the gates toward the outer ward. Gaelan kissed her once, then ordered his men to dispatch anyone who did not live here before he arrived. Siobhàn went about soothing hurt feelings as Gaelan ordered stores prepared for the journey, and it took time for the people to be escorted out, grumbling as they were roused from their beds, or stopped in a meal. Within moments the outer ward was nearly empty.

"No one leaves, no one enters until we return." He looked at O'Niell. "You and your men depart, now."

"I have every intention of seeing to my clansmen, Pen-Dragon." Lochlann accepted the reins of his mount. "But you would leave these people unprotected?"

"Hardly." Gaelan smirked, striding closer. "You have left yours without a chieftain for some time, O'Niell, and travel with a dozen retainers, why is that?" Gaelan arched a dark brow. "Frightened?"

Lochlann stiffened, delivering a condescending look just shy of insulting. "This is my country, my lord. I do not fear ghosts in the mist. Nor the Maguire."

"Neither do I. See to the fortification of my wife's property in the north. I will take care of these marauders."

Lochlann pressed his lips tight, his gaze drifting to Siobhàn, then PenDragon. "You will kill them."

"To stop the slaughter of my people, aye, every one of them, if I must," he said, and behind Siobhàn, Rhiannon paled and reached for the hitching post. Suddenly he crossed to her, gazing down with a full measure of rage. "Many could die this night, Rhiannon. How sits that with you?"

Her eyes teared, but she said naught to defend herself. He scoffed, looking around at the men, Irish and English assembled. Squires and pages scrambled to carry armor and saddle horses. Bowmen lined the battlements and parapets, sharpening tips and laying aim. Torches lit the yard like morning, glancing off weapons and armor. He brought his gaze back to Rhiannon, disgusted with her secrets.

"Lock her in the tower."

She gasped. "Nay, please!"

Gaelan gestured, and two soldiers grabbed her arms.

On a portion of wood, servants carted Brody out of the keep toward the chapel, Friar O'Donnel whispering prayers for his immortal soul, and Siobhàn crossed to her sister, halting the procession and grabbing Rhiannon's arm. She forced her to look at their old friend.

"He was our father's friend, well known to most everyone for a hundred miles, Rhiannon. A gentle, giving soul, and look what they have done! Will you wait until 'tis me lying there? Or Connal?"

Rhiannon choked on a sob, her gaze flying to her sister's and hating the anger lying there "Ian did not do this. You know he did not."

"It no longer matters who did it! And the man we knew is gone, Rhiannon. The Maguire we grew up with would not harm the man who taught him to throw a javelin. But see you the evidence!" She lashed a hand at Brody and Rhiannon flinched.

"And the sister I love," her voice lowered to a deadly hiss, "would not let her family die for a promise made in fear."

Rhiannon's gaze jerked from the bloody corpse to her sister's face. "Do not think to judge me, for I have no control over this."

"Your Fenian does. Tell Gaelan all, so my husband does not die tonight," she pleaded.

Rhiannon's lips tightened mutinously, and with an aggrieved sound, Siobhàn released her, turning her back on her and walking to her husband. He saw the tears, the worry and fear for him, the disappointment in her sister, and he bent to kiss the top of her head, shielding her as the guards led her sister away.

Around them, cooks rushed with sacks of food, skins of wine. Her grip around his waist tightened briefly and she nuzzled her face in his chest, selfishly taking the moment for herself alone, inhaling his scent, savoring the rough feel of his tunic against her cheek before moving out of his embrace.

Grayfalk pranced, scenting the wind and the coming ride into battle. Reese stood nearby, his arms laden with armor. Gaelan held her gaze as he changed from the costly wool tunic to the padded hauberk and heavy chain mail, the coif covering his hair. He pulled on the leather gloves, leaving the metal gauntlets on the saddle, and for the first time bid Reese to strap on the armor. He could not take his eyes off her, gauging her reaction as he was encased in the metal skin. She was afraid for him and the thought jabbed, made him recognize all he stood to lose if he was not cautious. Who would protect her and her people? Who would Henry send in his place? Would she be forced to wed another as he had forced her? The thought of anyone touching her sickened him and he wanted to take her abovestairs, make wild love to her, assure himself of their marriage, their future.

She loved him. Had said as much before witnesses. That she found it in her heart to forgive him, accept him, still stunned him to the core of his soul. "Come closer, wife."

She did, instantly. Siobhàn's gaze traveled over him as every semblance of the man she loved was locked behind silver. She tipped her head, forcing a smile. "Are you certain you would not want to hide in the trees and fight like the Scots?"

His lips curved with memory of the night he'd first tasted her body. "I would rather play the battling Scot in our bed," he whispered, gazing down at her, his gloved finger brushing down over her cheek. She caught his fist, pressing it to her lips.

"There, I surrender."

"Ahh, a victory, at last," he teased, brushing his mouth across hers, then turned to Grayfalk, grasping the saddle horn. An instant later, he turned to his wife, sweeping her against him and wishing they were bare and alone and showing their new love.

She laid her hands to the silver breastplate, gazing up at him. "I love thee, Gaelan PenDragon."

Gaelan took strength in her words and kissed her, quick and deep and greedy, then buried his face in her throat, inhaling her scent, remembering it. "I love you."

"Be safe and come home," she said, stroking her fingers through his hair.

He would. He had a wife and friends and a family waiting for him. He would vanquish these marauding bastards. And this time he warred with his heart.

A shrill cry split the air and Gaelan turned from her. Connal ran, slamming into his legs, hugging them, and he felt his insides soften to powder. No one ever worried over him before now, he thought, bending to lift the boy in his arms.

"I want to go with you."

"I need you here, to help protect the castle and your mother."

Connal's gaze shifted between them, his vision narrowed with the moments of youth. Finally he nodded and Gaelan, so moved by the child's heart, clutched him to him, then wrapped his arm around his wife, pulling her close.

"Arm yourself, my love."

"Here?"

"Please, for me." It was killing him to leave her, and if he did not think she would get hurt on the journey or want to jump into the fray of battle, he would take her with him.

"I will."

Culhainn barked, darting around the warriors and knights, whining to join the brigade. Gaelan forced himself to leave her arms, lowering Connal to the ground, ruffling his hair before he mounted the stallion and rode to the rim of the ward.

"You!" He pointed to Culhainn, and the dog stilled and sat on his haunches. "Do not ever leave her side. Understood?" Culhainn barked.

Siobhàn stared at the dog, then her husband. "When did you learn Gaelic?"

He flashed her a quick smile, of assurances and white teeth. "Whilst I was falling in love with you," he said flawlessly, winking.

Gaelan wheeled the mount about, ordering three squads to join him. He would not leave his wife unattended, nor would he depart until the O'Niell was out the gates. He remained back as Siobhàn bid Tigheran's half brother good journey, watching them.

"I must go, but I do not like leaving you alone like this."

She scoffed with a small smile. "I am surrounded, Lochlann." She hugged him, brushed a kiss to his cheek.

He studied her for a moment. "You are happy, aren't you?"

"If there were no one betraying us I would be more pleased, but"—her gaze swept past him to Gaelan as he donned his helm, the face guard up—"aye, I am well pleased with the outcome."

" 'Tis amazing how the death of my brother has brought such good fortune, eh?"

She didn't care for his brand of humor. "I wanted to love him, brother, but Tigheran saw me only as the enemy's child."

''And me as a nuisance,'' he said with a wry twist to his lips. He kissed her cheek once more and mounted, his men in a line behind him.

She stood in the center of the yard, gripping her son's hand.

With one hand and his knees, Gaelan controlled the high-strung mount, the blue plume shivering, and Grayfalk's power-ful legs cutting the earth as the destrier threatened to bolt. He beckoned Sir Niles and Andrew, entrusting them with the care of his family, and bid Sir Mark join them and show the location of the last ambush; then, with a quick glance at her, rider and destrier lurched, trotting between the torchlit ranks of soldiers and knights leaving the outer ward.

Slowly, guards pushed the gates closed and she stretched to catch a last glimpse of him before he led his army south. And she pitied anyone who crossed him this night.

Chapter Twenty-four

Siobhàn closed Connal's door, pressing her forehead to the wood. She was thrilled he and Gaelan had formed a bond, yet his innocent questions about Rhiannon were like blows to her heart. His aunt was hiding the truth, and if she did not know the root of the evil spreading across Donegal, she knew who did. For that reason Siobhàn did not go to the tower. Rhiannon chose to protect the Fenians with her silence. She could suffer the consequences alone. She'd been duly warned.

After peeking in on Meghan, who'd slept through the entire ruckus, she stoked the fire and cracked the shutters to freshen the air, then left the girl to rest, descending the winding staircase. The hall was empty but for the two servants on their knees, scrubbing Brody's blood off the stones and replacing the rushes. Her throat closed miserably, her mourning silent for the man she'd known since she was a child. Culhainn trailed her heels as she moved aimlessly into the solar, evidently taking Gaelan's orders to heart. Inside the room she sank into her husband's padded chair, curling toward the fire scarcely stirring.

Resting her cheek against the beaten leather, she inhaled the scent of him, of sandalwood and man, and prayed he would find the culprits swiftly and return by morning. But she knew he would not.

She feared Ian was at the root of it. Yet beyond the two prisoners who'd refused to speak, they'd no evidence beyond hearsay and some scraps of tartan. Was Ian so bitter that it would twist him enough to kill her clansmen to see Gaelan fail? Without fealty to the king, Ian could lose all he had. And the Fenians . . . by all that was holy, she prayed they'd naught to do with this but helping curtail the raids. Hurting the villagers and attacking patrols served no purpose but to brew hatreds and hasty reaction when regardless, the king and his lords would be the final hand of power. With the exception of fifty or so men returning to England, her husband's army was still formidable. And undefeated.

A reckoning is coming and you cannot stop it, the Fenian had said.

Was this the dark pain Rhiannon spoke of, or was there a grand attack on Donegal castle planned? Were these renegade English attacking simply to stir war or to push Ian into giving his fealty? Siobhàn wondered, rubbing her temple. The possible avenues were growing quickly.

"M'lady?"

Bridgett stood in the doorway with a goblet in her hand, a length of blue fabric under her arm. "Some sweet wine?"

Siobhàn smiled, nodding, and Bridgett came to her, offering the cup. She laid the blue cloth on the table close by and Siobhàn sighed, fingering it briefly and wishing she could have shown the work to Gaelan. "You love Sir Andrew?"

Nearly at the door, Bridgett stopped and turned. Her lips curved. "I like him. He's fine to look upon, but I know he sees me as naught but a serving maid and partner for a single night, not a lifetime."

The hopelessness in her voice caught her attention more

than her words, and Siobhàn's brows drew down. "Think you because he is knighted he cannot wed you?" She sipped, the warmed wine soothing the knots in her stomach.

"Aye, that." Bridgett glanced at the floor, worrying her apron. "And I'm Irish."

Siobhàn knew the girl was in love and since she, Meghan, Driscoll and Brody were the only people who'd come with her from her father's household, she would see that Bridgett was treated fairly. "Do not view each other on steps above or below another, Bridgett. Or he will. And if his heart is true, it will not matter."

Bridgett cocked her head. "You hated PenDragon when he arrived. How did you find your heart?"

Siobhàn's lips curved. "He showed it to me." Her eyes danced with mischief. "And he started with the kissing."

"Stole a few, did he now?"

She half laughed. "More than a few." Oftimes she could sense more of him than another, feel his gaze, his presence, as if she wore him like her skin, and constantly marveled at how deeply his touch sank through to her bones. She was forever bound to him, beyond her heart and into her soul, and she gloried in it. "I think I have always loved him but was afraid," she finally said. Afraid of its strength, she thought.

"After the O'Rourke's way of treating you, don't be thinking any of us is surprised."

Her gaze turned haunted, her tone bitter. "Tigheran planted more babes in a year than he planted crops."

Bridgett agreed. "At least you've got your Connal. Such a bright lad."

Siobhàn smiled tremulously, finished off the wine and stood. Culhainn perked up, alert and on his feet. "Tell the guards I go to my bed, will you? Meghan is ill and sleeps in our chamber."

Bridgett nodded, taking the empty cup, and Siobhàn bid her good night and crossed the empty hall, the fabric tucked to her chest. The sounds of people finding a spot to sleep were sparse, every able man on duty at the walls. With each step she mounted, she felt the strain of the day, her body demanding rest, and Siobhàn wondered where her usual stamina had gone. Culhainn trotted ahead of her, scouring the area for intruders that did not exist. She paused on the landing, staring up at the next level, where Rhiannon remained locked behind stone and was tempted to go to her. Gaelan would not be pleased over that, but that was not what stopped her. A night in the cold, dank room would likely push her to confessing aught she knew.

Overtaking the remaining steps, she turned toward her son's chamber, slipping briefly inside, nodding to the guard watching Connal sleep. They exchanged a nod, a whispered word that she would return there to sleep after she checked on Meghan. She turned to her chamber, frowning when Culhainn sniffed madly at the floor in front of the door. Pushing the latch, she let it swing wide, letting him in first. Culhainn's nose made a wet path over the stone floor, the carpet. Erratic, seeking.

"There are no bugs who wield swords, beast," she teased uneasily, withdrawing her knife. Was it Meghan's scent he sought?

Suddenly he growled, his white fur rising on his back like a blade. " 'Tis Meghan; cease." On the far side of the bed, he continued to growl, his hind legs crouched to spring. Siobhàn glanced back at the open door, aware of the guard close enough to lend aid, then moved to Culhainn, frowning into the dark.

The breeze struck through the partially opened shutter, bringing a familiar scent she could not name. She stepped, and Culhainn crossed her path, nearly tripping her.

He bared his fangs, his growl intensifying.

"Who's there?" Siobhàn held her dagger in front of her. "Meghan? Speak up."

The wind stirred the bed drapes, pushing open the shutter, and moonlight spilled, illuminating her bed. Her breath snagged, her eyes growing wider by the second.

"Mary mother of God." She dropped the fabric.

Meghan lay in a pool of blood, her face shredded.

The wind gusted, and her gaze snapped to the drapes. The next moments passed like a flash of light, quick and startling.

The figure, shrouded and hooded, moved. A thick hand, trembling, gripped a stained blade, and the familiarity of it rooted her to the floor. Her gaze jerked up. He stepped, and Culhainn leapt into the air with a vicious roar. A pain-filled grunt, the growling tear of fabric and a second later, Culhainn yelped, then dropped to the floor, motionless.

Siobhàn backed away, her dirk in her fist. The figure lurched and she turned to escape, calling out. But before she uttered a syllable, his body impacted with her back, sending her hurling to the floor. Her chin struck, her teeth cutting into her tongue, her small dirk jamming in the floor between stones and snapping off at the hilt. Blood pooled in her mouth as she struggled beneath his weight, trying to throw him off, trying to call out, yet his fist smashed into her temple, once, twice, his murderous blade clattering to the floor in his effort. Firelight flickered off the dagger, the crest, and she reached, crawling across the floor, knowing naught would save her from this twisted rage. But the intruder was fast and uninjured, on his feet and crushing her fingers beneath heavy boots, English boots, ripping the knife out of her reach, then driving his toe into her throat. She choked and heaved for air, her throat burning. She screamed, yet naught came but a dry croak as he dragged her to her feet by the hair. She drove her elbow into his stomach and twisted, trying to see his face. He slapped her away, sending her into the mirror.

The valuable glass cracked like splintering ice.

Siobhàn staggered, breathing hard against the pain. Blood trickled into her eyes. He shoved and she fell into darkness, her back, elbows and shoulders colliding with stone, the musty odor of dirt and dampness filling her nostrils.

The tunnel, she thought dizzily, an instant before blinding

pain erupted in her skull. Her legs folded and her world went blessedly black.

Rhiannon paced the small chamber, a thick blanket over her shoulders. *This night bodes ill.* Images flashed behind her eyes. A river of blood. A woman with no face. Connal crying. She dropped to the cot, holding her head in her hands and rocking, trying to clear the images, praying for guidance. A chill that had naught to do with the room crept over her skin and she lurched off the cot, moving to the window, yanking at the shutter. Cold air blasted her face as she scanned the yard below for aught unusual. She saw only guards and little movement, most of the inhabitants forced inside.

Who lurked, waiting to hurt her family? The choices were varied and vague, and fresh sensations of coldness drew her skin tighter. Panicked, she rushed to the door, calling out to the guard, pounding the wood when he did not respond. In a gentle voice, he told her to please cease before he would have to bind and gag her. Rhiannon pressed her head to the wood and sighed, helpless, blinking back hot tears, then returned to the narrow window. She continued to watch, praying God would give her enlightenment—before her premonition came true. Too many, too late, she thought, resting her head on the casement and cursing her foolish heart for believing in a man again.

Soldiers walked with torches, searching the ground for a clue. It was torn from battle, but the bodies of the dead had been carried away. To where and why? And why attack a patrol?

"Armor, swords, they are not easily come by."

"Aught can be forged, Raymond." A tense silence and then, "I found a spur when the third village was attacked."

That he'd not been privy to this showed in his dark look. "The one we had to burn?"

Gaelan nodded, gesturing for Driscoll to come closer. "Who knows this land better than the Fenians?"

Driscoll's eyes widened. "None, I'm afraid. They are our best."

Gaelan rubbed his chin, thoughtful.

"You do not think the Maguire did this, do you?" Raymond asked, eyeing him.

"I withhold judgment, but Rhiannon was right. Wearing a plaid only implicates. It does not prove the crime." He addressed the Irishman. "Know you well Ian Maguire?"

"Since he was a lad." Driscoll straightened in the saddle. "He loved her deeply since they were children, my lord," he said, as if apologizing. "And he never forgave her for giving herself to O'Rourke for peace."

"Or to me."

Driscoll shrugged his broad shoulders. "He wanted her to run away with him, even tried to kidnap her when she refused."

Gaelan's brows shot up. This was news to him.

"His family paid dearly for his recklessness in honor price and his parents sent him away in punishment." He sighed, tired. "His arrival at your gates was not a surprise."

"And understandable."

Both Driscoll and Raymond looked surprised. "Sympathy, Gaelan?"

"One does not walk away from a woman like my wife without feeling the loss."

Driscoll hid a grin.

Gaelan dismounted, taking a torch and covering the ground himself. The armor hampered, and without hesitation he stripped off all but the breastplate, vambraces and mail, harnessing it to the saddle. Driscoll smiled with approval, himself garbed in furs and padded tunic and braies. Gaelan continued his search, wishing for daylight. He rubbed his hand over the broken ground, coming back with bloodstains.

"Fan out and search for a cave, a cottage, anywhere they could have fled so quickly. Have a caution with the torches." The squads spread out immediately and Gaelan turned back to Grayfalk, swinging into the saddle. But again, they found nothing.

Continuing on, they rode into a border village, portions of homes crumbled black from fire and still smoldering. The inhabitants hissed at him, but fear kept them from flinging the stones they fisted. Gaelan scowled, twisting in the saddle to Driscoll, and bidding he question the nearest man.

"He wants to know why you sent men to attack them."

Gaelan guided the mount nearer and the man back-stepped, his expression fierce with rage, a pitchfork brandished like a shield. "Did they look like these men?" Gaelan gestured for two of his knights to come forward. "Tell me exactly what they wore."

The man started spouting, too fast for Gaelan to translate with what little he knew. He glanced at Driscoll. "I caught blue and broken."

"They wore blue tabards, my lord. And the armor was not as well tended as your men's."

Gaelan focused on the man. "Aught else? Did they take livestock? Women?"

The man shook his head, his bleak eyes holding more question than trust.

"I swear by God in heaven, I did not order this."

The man eyed him with hatred and disbelief.

"You must help us find who did."

The villager's gaze shifted between Driscoll and Gaelan. "We tried to follow, but they disappeared as quickly as they came," the man said, obviously uncomfortable. " 'Twas as if they walked into the sky. Just"—he shrugged thin shoulders— "gone, my lord."

It was clever, however they were escaping, he thought, and looked to the trees, remembering what Siobhàn had said about being silent and quick. But where would they hide the mounts? Gaelan raked his fingers through his hair, then down over his face. Above him the sky bled to a deep purple with the coming sun. "Driscoll. Arm the villagers. Spare whatever we can and leave a dozen guards here to protect."

Driscoll translated and the man grew even more frightened, shaking his head.

Gaelan looked down at the ragged creature, seeing himself as a lad; distrusting, for the lord of the land had done naught to help them better their life. In fact, the lack of coin sent his mother to whoring. His gaze drifted beyond, to the woman standing in the doorway of the charred cottage, bravely fighting tears. Gaelan twisted to his saddle bags, digging in the bottom, then leaning out to the man. He pressed something into his hand, closing his fist around it. "I swear you will be safe with my men," he murmured, then turned his mount away.

The villager unfurled his fist and gaped at the silver cross gleaming in the faint firelight. And beneath it was a king's ransom in gold.

He was alone in his crime.

He dragged her through the narrow corridor, slipping once on the seepage pooling on the ground. PenDragon and his bloody damned moat, he thought. He wondered if she knew this passage led beyond the grounds and into a stand of trees.

It was fortunate that O'Rourke had constructed the escape tunnel, though the fool didn't know a smattering of what it took to construct a decent fortification. Apparently neither did PenDragon, he smirked, ducking to accommodate the low ceiling. Or he would have found this tunnel by now. Mayhaps he had, or she'd told him, he considered, then mentally shrugged, pushing at the sod and peat ceiling. The wood trap door gave, delivering a gust of cold air. He moved it aside, then climbed, the incline sharp and unused. He took several steps away and pulled the horse close, removing the feed sack from its nuzzle and the leafy branches used to disguise the creature in the trees. He turned back to the tunnel and dragged her by the arm through the opening in the earth, then squatted to lift her. The scent of blood made his stomach roil and he swallowed, lifting and throwing her body over the back of a horse. With measured steps, he walked the mount away from the castle. The guards were focused on the front, never expecting someone to leave the keep.

They found fresh horse tracks heading away from the Maguire's stronghold, *Cloch Baintreach.* Gaelan sent a small squad to follow it, then left another to watch over the Maguire, discreetly.

"Well, unless you call him out," Raymond said as they gazed down at the fortress. "Then you will never really know if he is there."

" 'Twould not matter. He, like you and I, could commission anyone to do our bidding." Although the Maguire did not strike him as a coward. The man had already faced down Gaelan's legions with only a hundred warriors, and those poorly armed. Yet his castle appeared prepared for war. Even from this position, Gaelan could see the javelins lining the battlements.

"Without evidence you cannot take this to the king."

"I do not *want* to take this to Henry." By God, he would solve this himself before he called on the monarch for advice. "His majesty bids that I gain the Maguire's fealty, immediately. Before the royal armies advance from Dublin to Armagh."

"Great Scots."

Gaelan removed his helm, cupping it over the pommel. He shoved his coif back and ruffled his hair. "We have demons all around us."

Driscoll was on his left, silent until now. "I've a feeling Donegal is not the only land suffering."

Gaelan sent him an arched look.

"O'Niell has sustained losses," Raymond pointed out.

"Aye, but this could be those who did not want our lady to rule, ever."

Gaelan scowled, waiting for an explanation.

"Most of Donegal was once O'Donnel land, taken by O'Rourke in his battle with Dermott. Everyone knew Tigheran warred more for Devorgilla's betrayal than for land and accepted Siobhàn like a payment to punish." Driscoll's gaze clouded and he looked at the reins curled around his hands, still regretting that he could not protect her well enough. "She suffered much, my lord," he said, then lifted his gaze. "When Tigheran died, the chieftains weren't ready to usurp her with an uncle as powerful as Dermott. But there are still a few who would see a man in her place, preferably an O'Donnel."

"There *is* a man ruling."

"Forgive me, my lord, but you are not Irish."

Gaelan's look said he was painfully aware of that.

"I do not think the first attacks before you arrived had aught to do with any of the trouble now. Oftimes the villagers get a belly full of drink, and talk brews rashness. People die and the culprits must live with the regret. And if it was not . . ." Driscoll shrugged, rubbing his clean-shaven face and missing his beard. "Who's to say 'twas one clan or another?"

Gaelan stared out over the darkened land. "Therein lies the difficulty. We must catch them, and for that we must remain he—" Abruptly he twisted in the saddle, narrowing his gaze in the direction of Donegal.

Raymond guided his mount closer. "What is it?"

Gaelan still stared. "I do not know." O'Niell had been escorted off the land and the castle was a fortress now, but Gaelan could not shake the horrible feeling that Siobhàn needed him. "Something is wrong." *I can feel it.*

Raked with a moment of indecision, Gaelan wheeled about, riding back toward the castle. Raymond trotted the line of troops, issuing orders and wondering if Gaelan had somehow adopted Rhiannon's ability to see the future.

At the edge of the county he halted his mount, twisting in the saddle to push her from the back of the horse. Her body hit the soft earth with a dull thud, flopping back and revealing her bloody face. A sadistic smile curved his lips. Her death was his freedom. He'd tried to be rid of Connal, but the little brat was too heavily protected.

He gazed down at her, her beautiful face swollen and spattered with dirt and drying blood. For an instant he felt remorse at the ruin of so lovely a woman, but she was too belligerent, too independent, not asking him for help, not wanting or needing it. He wheeled the mount around and rode off, leaving her withering body to the creatures and the elements.

Chapter Twenty-five

Gaelan saw the soldiers riding hard toward him as he crested the rise. His heart slammed to his stomach and he jammed his spurs into Grayfalk's side. He passed the troops at breakneck speed and as the gates swung open, he rode through the outer ward, ducking through the inner gate, continuing up the steps and into the hall. The clatter of hooves rang in the keep, scattering folk. He flung from the mount, glancing briefly at the people sobbing, and his chest ached with unbearable pain. He searched the gathering for his wife and when he found neither her nor Connal, he ran to the stairs, taking them three at a time. At the landing his pace slowed, his mouth going dry as burned wood. Gaelan shoved open the chamber door.

His focus snapped to the bed and he crossed the room, noticing the fractured mirror before he stopped beside the bed. The drapes were drawn.

He swallowed over and over, his hand trembling as he reached and flipped the curtain back. His features burned tight.

"Oh mother of God."

She lay in a mass of sticky blood, her face carved from her bones. A deep gash opened her chest.

His big body trembled. Misery engulfed him. Gaelan clenched his fists, fighting the torment, the grief swimming through him like molten steel. He sank to his knees, tears searing his eyes. He thumped his thighs with his fists, pitiful choked sounds filling the chamber.

Oh God!

You take her when I just learned how to love her. Why? Why!

Rage and sorrow erupted and he flung his head back, his tortured howl shaking the stone walls of Donegal Castle.

At the horrible sound, the guards succumbed to Rhiannon's pleas, releasing her, and she overtook the stairs, dashing into the chamber, to the side of the bed. She froze, stunned. "Merciful God."

She covered her mouth with a trembling hand, turning her face away. Tears came, quick and burning with regret. *Oh, Siobhàn, forgive me.*

Gaelan was on his knees, his head thrown back, tears streaming down his face. "I knew something was wrong," he managed in a dry rasp. "I knew." Ten times he cursed himself for not following his instincts and returning earlier. Oh God above, save me from the misery, he cried silently.

I am lost. Lost.

Rhiannon forced her gaze back to the body, avoiding the tattered face and focusing on the clothing. " 'Tis not her," she said suddenly, rushing to the bedside.

Gaelan's head snapped up, his bleak gaze narrowing.

"The clothes, they are not hers. She was wearing blue."

"She's been known to don rags." Gaelan did not want to believe in the possibility. His heart was already dead and he could not bear a shred of hope, if it were taken again.

"Nay."

"But the hair—"

" 'Tis not her, I tell you!" She reached. "I gain naught from the dead, but . . ." She plucked at the bloody sleeve, taking the cold hand gently in hers and turning back the cuff. " 'Tis Meghan." She showed him the cuts on her wrist and the back of her hand.

Gaelan stared, unblinking, then staggered back, banging against the commode. Relief swept him in waves so heavy he thought he would be ill. Without a doubt, Siobhàn was the true target. "Use your sight, Rhiannon." He loomed close and predatory. "Find her."

"It comes from the touch of the living!" she cried, her helplessness bringing fresh tears.

"Where is my wife then?"

Rhiannon turned her gaze to the cracked mirror, the overturned candlestick. "She was here. She fought."

"But how did she get out and where the hell is Culhainn?"

A whimper came and Gaelan glanced around, then knelt, lifting the blood-soaked linen. His features yanked tight. Blood thickened on the stone floor under the bed. He ducked and spied the animal. "Come puppy, come." Gaelan put out his hand and Culhainn sniffed, then inched forward, his breathing shallow and rapid. Gaelan gently grasped the dog and drew him from beneath the bed. He was still protecting her, he thought, covering the gash in his side.

"I'll get my herbs." Rhiannon turned to go as Connal rushed in.

Rhiannon flung the drapes down to cover Meghan as Gaelan raced past her, catching him before he saw the condition of the body and the pet.

"Where is my mama?"

He held the boy's gaze and hated to break his heart. "I don't know, lad."

"But—" His lip trembled and he glanced at the blood on Gaelan's hands, then to the bed. "Mama!"

" 'Tis not her, nay. Nay! 'Tis her maid, son."

"But my mama," he muttered, trying hard not to panic. "She brought Dermott to me, said good night to me. She kissed me last night!"

Raymond rushed inside, Driscoll directly behind him. Gaelan lifted Connal in his arms, hugging the boy and finding strength in the tiny arms looping snugly around his neck. Over his shoulder, he inclined his head to the bed and both Raymond and Driscoll crossed to look. They turned wide eyes to Gaelan, their faces gone pale. When he offered the victims' identity, Driscoll nearly folded where he stood, grasping the nearby mantel for support.

"Gaelan," Rhiannon called. "He won't last much longer."

Gaelan turned and knew there was no way to shield the boy. "Culhainn is wounded."

Driscoll snapped out of his lethargy and came around to lift the dog, his white fur stained crimson. Connal cried out, reaching, kicking to be free, but Gaelan held him tight as Rhiannon followed the sheriff out. Moving to a chair, he clutched the child and dropped into the seat. Connal sobbed quietly into his tunic.

"There were too many guards for this to happen, Gaelan. It just doesn't make sense." Raymond glanced around for a clue.

"When does murder have reasoning?" He transferred his gaze to the bed. "That could have been her," he murmured, and fear spirited through him. He looked at Raymond. "Assemble every man, woman and child who was here last night." Gaelan stroked Connal's shoulder, the gentle motion belying the heat behind his words. "I swear I will flog the negligent guards—"

"Gaelan." Raymond crossed the room near the bed, squatting to pull the hilt from the floor. He met Gaelan's gaze as he rose, leaving Connal in the chair and coming to him.

"It's hers," he whispered, taking the broken blade, aching to feel the warmth of her touch and feeling only the coldness of death. His gaze scanned the floor. Blood spattered the stone, handprints, only three fingers, stained nearby. Gaclan's chest squeezed his heart as he thought of her fighting for her life after her maid and pet were slain. The killer had taken her with him, and he could not bear thinking of what he would do to his wife after the gruesome murder of her maid.

"He could not have gotten her past the guards, all those people in the keep, the yard. How did they get out of here?"

"I know." Gaelan jerked around as Connal scrambled from the chair and went to the large chest half ajar. "Behind here."

Gaelan quickly shoved the trunk aside and Connal barreled his shoulder into the wall. It gave slightly and Gaelan helped it open. He stared into the dark hole, instantly noticing the scrape marks in the dirt, then looked down at Connal, scowling.

The little fellow craned his neck to meet his gaze. "Mama swore me never to tell!" he insisted. "My fath—O'Rourke built it for his escape. The passage ends outside, near a bunch of trees, I think."

Gaelan eyed the child.

"I swore a holy oath!" he cried, and Gaelan crumbled inside, kneeling to his level.

" 'Tis all right, lad. I'm glad you told me now."

"Only Mama and I know, my lord. Not even Aunt Rhi," he added, as if to protect his mother's sister. Connal pointed to the leather straps at the base of the wall. "You pull those to close it from inside." Cautiously, he lifted his gaze, and Gaelan read the apprehension there. " 'Tis how Mama got in and out when you first arrived, I'm thinkin'."

Gaelan stroked a lock of russet hair off his brow and Connal's lips quivered. "I think so too." It stung that she had not told him but realized that when she was upset with him, there was no reason. And after she forgave him, there was no time. But one fact remained. The killer knew it existed.

"Where is she?"

Gaelan gripped his thin shoulders. "I swear I will find her, Connal. And I will punish the person who did this."

His lip trembled. "And . . . and if she is already dead?"

Such a brave boy to ask such a thing, he thought, swallowing back his own fears. "Believe she is alive, son. To think aught else, we steal all hope. *Tuigim?*"

Connal's eyes flared and he nodded, then suddenly threw his arms around his neck. He patted his back, and together the PenDragon men sighed.

Rhiannon entered the chamber, her hands folded in front of her bloodstained apron as she watched the pair, envy in her eyes. Her gaze shifted to the dark hole in the wall. "What is this?" She moved briskly forward as Gaelan rose to his full, imposing height.

" 'Tis obviously the escape route of the killer." Gaelan searched her expression. "Have you something to tell me, Rhiannon?"

Her gaze jerked to his. She stared briefly, then looked down at Connal. "Culhainn will survive. He is in the solar. You may go to him."

Connal twisted to look up at Gaelan, and he nodded his permission.

Rhiannon's lips tightened with irritation as she watched the boy leave. She glanced between Gaelan and Raymond. "I did not know of this." She flicked a hand at the tunnel. "Nor who killed Meghan."

" 'Tis the why of it I wish to know. Someone risked his life to do that!" He lashed a hand to the bed. "Who was the warrior in the woods?"

"A Fenian. I told you they wanted information to destroy you."

He grabbed her arms "You lie."

"They want to bring you down quickly. All English. They threatened this"—her gaze glanced off the bed—"if I did not comply." Her voice fractured with shame. "I did not believe they would get to her. Don't you see? We cannot stop them."

Gaelan scoffed, thrusting her from him so hard she stumbled back. "I will, woman, be assured." He turned to Raymond. "Get a small torch. We find where this ends." He gestured to the tunnel. "And I want a guard on her." He pointed, anger blistering his tone. "She does not piss unless someone is present."

Rhiannon gasped.

His gaze raked her. "You prefer the dungeon?"

"Nay."

"I do this because Connal needs you, not out of sympathy for my wife's sister. If I find you have lied, Rhiannon, I will banish you from this place forever." Gaelan flicked a dismissive hand, turning his back on her. Raymond nodded ahead and Rhiannon spun on her heels, her spine stiff as she quit the room.

Gaelan braced his back against the nearest wall and slid to the floor, cradling his head in his hands. Helplessness overwhelmed him. Siobhàn was alone, unarmed and likely injured. *And if I do not find her, if she is dead?* He swallowed over and over, smothering his fear until it left a dull throbbing ache in his chest.

Wherever you are, my love, submit and live.

Sliding his fingers down his face, Gaelan stared at naught, planning his next moves. His gaze fixed on a pile of fabric on the floor and he reached, bringing it close, shaking it out. It was a banner, his banner, yet without the bar sinister cutting it diagonally. And in the claw of the dragon was the thistle of Donegal. His eyes watered and he blinked, then buried his face in the cloth, catching her scent in the weave.

"Gaelan?"

He tilted his head back to find Raymond near, an unlit torch in his hand.

"Driscoll has them all under guard." His expression said it

was useless since the discovery of the tunnel. "And Owen is here and was at the gates the entire time."

Nodding, Gaelan climbed to his feet, laying the fabric carefully aside. Raymond struck a flint to a torch and together they ducked into the tunnel.

He was as ruthless as he'd ever been, Raymond thought. Combing through Donegal with the precision he exacted in a planned attack, a siege. Men walked in lines, overturning brush, digging through clusters of trees, shrubs. But there was no way to cover every inch of land. And that fact was bleeding him dry. When Gaelan came to the villages, he approached with quiet care, his voice losing its angry bite. He removed his armor, the battleax and fierce dragon helm left in the camp. He came with only his sword strapped at his side. As humble as Lord Donegal could be.

Gaelan smiled, and Raymond knew there was no pleasure in the gesture.

He spoke softly when he wanted to rage.

He offered coin when he would have offered his soul for a morsel of information.

He touched the crown of a girl-child with long dark red hair, and Raymond saw pure agony flash across his features, instantly hidden from prying eyes. He'd seen it often in the past days, when he thought no one was watching. Gaelan would not allow a single soul to witness his pain, to see him weakened by it, and maintained the stoic expression as he had through a hundred other battles. Yet in the darkness of the evening, when they stopped to make camp and Gaelan retired to his pavilion, Raymond heard him beg God for her life, tears in his voice.

If this faceless enemy wanted to bring him to his knees, Raymond knew he was nearly there.

Not knowing where his wife was, if she was alive or injured, or buried under the very ground he trod, was unbearable torture, and Raymond hated to see him suffer, hated that he could do naught for him.

I never want to fall in love that hard, he thought. 'Twas not worth this slow death.

He swallowed the stone of despair every time he thought of the slaughter left in the lord's marriage bed and how Siobhàn would fair against one so lethal. What kind of man carved a woman's face from her skull, he wondered for the hundredth time. To what purpose? It was clear Meghan was mistaken for Siobhàn, her hair and coloring and her location obvious, yet even Gaelan did not know the maid slept there. Had the killer realized his mistake and in rage cut the false face off?

It was madness. Raymond suspected that if they found her, and if she were, by the grace of God, alive, she would be abused beyond hope. He hated himself for his weakened thoughts and refused to show them to Gaelan. The resolution of his troops was hard enough.

Raymond watched Gaelan walk toward him from the crofter's hut.

Gaelan paused at Grayfalk's side, gripping the pommel, fighting the urge to destroy everything around him. He met Raymond's gaze and shook his head, then swung up into the saddle, guiding the mount away from the solitary home on the edge of the border lands. They rode in silence, pausing just outside the encampment. Irish and English shared the warmth of fires and meals, the lines, so clearly drawn between them for weeks, faded with the need to find their princess.

My Irish princess.

Gaelan raked his fingers through his hair, his stomach clenching painfully. "On the morrow send them back."

Raymond blinked, at the sound of his voice in the stillness and the command. "All of them?"

"Aye. I go alone."

"How can you think to cover so much land?"

"We are nearly in Maguire's *tuath*, Raymond. Any further

and we threaten a war with this many troops. Henry needs time to woo his new cache of earls," he added bitterly.

Raymond could not disagree with that. "I ask to remain with you, Gaelan. Let Driscoll, Mark and Andrew go on ahead."

"Nay, my friend. I go alone. I need you at the castle." His tone brooked no argument and he wheeled around and rode to the edge of the glen.

Long moments stretched to hours as he sat there, looking over the land, staring at nothing. The muscles in his throat rubbed like grated glass, threatening his breathing, and Gaelan felt his world coming to a brisk end, for without Siobhàn it meant naught. Without her, land and home were just a roof and walls and earth.

It was near dawn when he returned to his pavilion, the loneliness leaving an ache so deep Gaelan didn't think he had the will to continue.

But he did. If only for the chance to kill the bastard who'd sent him to this hell.

Chapter Twenty-six

Open land surrounded him. The lushest green he'd ever clapped eyes on. Hours ago his troops forged toward the castle. Gaelan could not stomach the thought of Connal being alone in his worry, yet neither could he cease his search, not even to comfort the boy.

Squatting near the blaze, he drove his fingers into his hair, gripping his skull. It was as she had said, he thought, squatting and staring at the small fire. If he could not feed and protect his people, then he had no right to rule it. By the proclamation of Henry or the church, he did not.

The emptiness was swallowing him whole, leaving behind a barren cavern in his chest. She'd saved him from a desolate life, from feeling this emptiness again. It did not matter that he'd wanted the coin Henry offered, and to leave here . . . nay, to hide, he corrected honestly, to secret himself away from feeling this much. He cursed Henry for sending him here, then blessed him for giving him the chance to know love, to earn her respect when she loathed the man he was. To be someone she was proud to love.

For an eternity, I will love you.

To be denied it, denied her smiles, her touch—her wisdom, because some band of Irish warriors hiding in the trees wanted to see him fail was—impossible.

And in a burst of rage, he lurched to his feet, her name tearing from his lips.

It echoed across the open land.

One by one, figures emerged out of the darkness, rising from the ground like beasts from pools of smoke.

Gaelan's sword was in his hand before the first one was upright. He sensed a familiarity in these men. The men Siobhàn met in the forest.

The attack came swiftly. Five warriors, hooded and agile, descended on him like locusts. Gaelan sidestepped and swung his broadsword, decapitating a man, his head rolling into the fire as Gaelan swung the sword around his back, switching hands and driving it into another's chest.

For an instant, the burning skull held them rapt.

"Where is she?"

A third man threw a short blade and it impacted with Gaelan's unarmored body, driving into his shoulder to the hilt and hitting bone. He flinched, yet advanced, fending off attack as he pulled the knife from his shoulder. With a sinister smile, he threw. The blade sank into an opponent's throat, piercing the jugular.

With shrill war cries, two men charged, but Gaelan was a man driven with vengeance, the need to vent his rage and helplessness swelling to mammoth proportions. He expelled it on the perfect targets. He lashed at one, then the other, so close his sword left a track of blood over one man's chest, his chin.

"Come," he growled, waving them close. "Bleed me more."

"If you must leave this land in a sack of pieces, then so be it, Sassenach."

A hooded man lunged. Gaelan did not bother with his sword and drove his gauntleted fist into one man's face, driving his nose into his brain and dropping him where he stood. Instantly he turned his blade to the other, the last, advancing, jabbing, pricking him like a pincushion.

"Where is my wife?"

The man went noticeably still for an instant, eyes flaring inside the black hood. "Your people will die, PenDragon."

"You concede they are mine?" Another jab, this one in the thigh and enough to draw a burst of blood. He'd bleed him to death without a single mortal wound, his rage was so tremendous.

"The English are yours."

A quick clash of swords, thrust, strike and thrust, and the two backed off, circling. "Ahh, so you do not think I belong for the blood in my veins when the blood of a traitor runs in yours?"

With a harsh growl, the man lunged forward to strike. Gaelan brought the flat of his sword down so hard the Irishman's arm quivered with the vibration. His aim faltered and Gaelan tucked the blade tip under his throat.

"Drop it."

The sword fell. There was not a shred of regret or fear in his eyes as he awaited his death, as if he expected no less.

"Who sent you?"

He remained silent.

Gaelan called to Grayfalk and the horse nickered, sauntering to him. Without taking his gaze from the survivor, he swung up onto the saddle. "Only a coward comes in the dark." With the tip of his sword, he pierced the top of the hood, slicing it open.

The hood fell to just below the man's eyes. Green eyes narrowed and Gaelan felt a sense of awareness, as if he'd seen those eyes before, yet knew he had not. Gaelan drew the razor-sharp blade over the man's cheek, laying it open. He did not move a muscle, did not flinch, and Gaelan admired his bravery.

"Where is my wife?"

"On Ireland, I swear I do not know." Desperation laced his voice with a weariness lending more than from this skirmish.

Gaelan scoffed, sheathing his bloody sword. "I'm to trust a vow from a traitor to us all?"

The man glanced around at his fallen comrades, then to Gaelan.

"You are not the master in this," Gaelan said with utmost certainty. There was too much to debate over this man's behavior. He did not know Siobhàn was missing until now and it left Gaelan with a new hole in his theories of who was trying to destroy this parcel of land. "I show mercy for one reason only . . . from what I've learned of the Irish loyalty and honor, your death will come at the hands of your countrymen, not from me."

Mortification passed over the man's features and Gaelan had his answer. He wheeled about and rode into the darkness, leaving the Fenian warrior to bury his dead where they lay.

Gaelan stitched his wound closed as best he could, cursing himself for not wearing his armor, but the metal skins made a bloody racket out on the moors, especially at night. Just as Siobhàn had said. The dull throb did little to draw him from the thoughts plaguing him as he ventured a few miles near the shore. He knew naught of this area, the people, only that it was a place he had not looked. Hidden in the rise of a small forest, he stared down at the village, scenting the sea, hearing the crash of waves in the distance. Dismounting, he lashed Grayfalk to a tree where he could nibble on the soft earth, then removed the armor secured to his saddle. He buried it with his bloody clothes, wearing little more than boots, braies, a coarse brown tunic and a fur belonging to Driscoll. He'd already experienced the prejudice of his station and after the first day would not risk a piece of information slipping through his fingers. His sword he could not leave behind, but buried the ornate scabbard.

Daybreak brought sunshine and warmer breezes as Gaelan walked toward the village. He paused at the edge, inhaling deeply, cleansing the impatient anger in him. His gaze moved over the ring of trees circling the village like sentinels, to the homes, thatched and low slung. Yards were neat, the street combed smooth of ruts. Children worked and played. Several women stood near the town well, drawing water. Two men sat on stools, mending fishing nets and talking, while across the way a father and son struggled to fashion an animal pen. Gaelan strode forward, trying hard to remember every bit of Gaelic Driscoll had taught him and wondering if there was a tavern or an inn. Gaelan had yet to pass through a village without a tavern at least. The Irish, he knew, loved their drinking and put his men to shame often enough. His steps faltered, and he wondered if Raymond had made it back yet, and what Connal was feeling. He took succor in the fact that Rhiannon was with the boy.

A sudden crack brought him around, his sword out. He watched as a tree tipped, splintering through the remaining cut in its base before slamming into the ground. The jolt sent leaves and dirt up in a puff. A pair—father and son, Gaelan assumed— laughed at the log as if the bloody thing were more than dead wood. Gaelan carefully slid the sharp sword into a loop in his waist belt.

"Ey, lad? Cum lend us a wee bit o'tha' muscle you've got just lying there."

Gaelan grinned. The father and son were trying to lift a fallen log that should be split before attempting it and Gaelan strode close, his hands on his hips as he surveyed the freshly felled tree.

"Where do you want it?"

"There. It fell the wrong way," the boy added, sheepish, and his father winked at him.

Gaelan nodded and moved to the end, the other two opposite him. He lifted, and even though it wasn't a strain, he felt his shoulder open again. He dropped the log in its appointed spot and clutched his shoulder. Pain burned through the torn skin.

"My thanks—ah, yer hurt! Why didn't you say so, lad?"

Gaelan smiled. "You'd have been all day trying to chop it up to move it." Blood seeped into his clothing.

The father, a slender, black-haired man, looked at his son, and Gaelan thought the resemblance between the two uncanny. "Go get the healer and be quick about it." The boy dashed off, and then to Gaelan he said, "Come sit and wait. She'll sew you back into your body right enough."

Gaelan dropped to a stump and the man brought him a cup of water. He sipped, and though the wound did not offer enough pain to warrant so much attention, he would not dismiss it. Irish hospitality was a way of life, and he knew this man would give his last slice of bread to a stranger, if he needed it. And Gaelan needed these people. He needed a friend right now and introduced himself as simply Gaelan.

"Paddy, I am. Me boy is Flynn." They chatted amiably about crops and fisheries, little of which Gaelan knew, whilst Paddy whittled on a branch, obvious to Gaelan he was cleaning it for an arrow.

"I'm searching for a woman."

Paddy jerked a look at him, his eyes narrowing.

"She may have been injured."

"What would this lass be to you?" Paddy kept working his knife, disinterested.

Gaelan didn't know if telling them they were husband and wife would be helpful right now. "She is my betrothed."

"She run from you?" Paddy's eyes thinned. "You the kind to beat women?"

Gaelan scowled. "Of course not. What woman would survive?" He put up his hands, palm out. "Have you seen her? She is rather tall, dark red hair, green-blue eyes, with a bit of yellow in them, especially when she's in a temper and—"

Paddy's lips curved in a slow smile and he patted his uninjured shoulder. "You're fair well tucked and put away with her, aren't you, lad?"

Gaelan's heart slammed against the wall of his chest. "Have you?"

Paddy's nod indicated somewhere beyond him. "You mean looking like that one?"

Gaelan leapt to his feet and turned. "*Siobhàn.*"

Far down the road she walked, leaning on a dark-haired woman, and he wanted to shout for the sheer joy of finding her alive, yet his throat closed over with heart-ripping emotion. All he could do was stare. Sweet Jesu, what had the killer done to her? Her steps were shaky and slow, her gaze on her feet. Her hair, oh, God above, that glorious hair, was unbound and wild with curls, yet naught could hide the blackened bruises on her temple, throat and chin. Nor the angry cuts along her jaw.

"I have prayed and searched . . ." he said aloud without realizing it and took several steps, his relief so tremendous his legs nearly folded beneath him. "Siobhàn!"

Her head jerked up. "*Gaelan.*" Her smile blinded, quick tears blooming. "Oh, Gaelan!" She shifted away from the woman and Gaelan rushed to her as she staggered into his arms. They clasped tightly, and for a moment they simply held each other, Gaelan's face buried in her cloud of hair, hers snug in the crook of his neck, inhaling his scent.

"Oh my love, my princess," he choked, and Siobhàn heard days of suffering, of not knowing if she lived, fracture through his deep voice.

"All will be well now, my husband, shhh."

He met her gaze, raw agony shaping his expression as his gaze slipped over her battered face. "God above," he moaned miserably. *"Look at you."* His trembling hand hovered near her wounded jaw and he feared to touch and harm her more.

Yet she pressed his palm to her face. " 'Tis not so bad," she whispered, her lips quivering as she gazed into his dark soulful eyes, his tears cutting her to the quick. "I have truly missed you, my love."

"Me too, oh, me too. Oh, God, you cannot imagine—sweet Mary, Siobhàn"—he paused to tenderly press his lips to hers—"I thought I'd lost you forever."

"Nay, nay," she soothed, swiping at his tears whilst more fell from her own eyes. "I never doubted that you would find me. Never. I simply waited until you did."

Her absolute faith unmanned him and he moaned, holding her gently when he wanted to crush her, clinging to her and shedding the torturous place he'd lived in for days with each passing moment. He chanted her name, over and over, wanting only to feel her heart beat strongly against his and tell him, he too now lived again. And in the center of the little hamlet, the villagers looking on as he tipped her face to the sun and kissed her bruises and cuts, apologizing for not protecting her from this horror.

" 'Tis not you fault; don't be taking the blame," she scolded softly and, curling her hand behind his neck, she brought him to her mouth. "I love you," she whispered against his lips, then kissed him.

He moaned, sinking into her taste, lifting her in his arms and carrying her to privacy.

"I guess that means she's your woman," Paddy said as they passed.

Gaelan drew back enough to say, "She is more than that." He could not take his eyes off her. "She's the center of my soul."

"And his wife," Siobhàn added happily, her arms looped around his neck. "You needn't head into the forest, Gaelan."

He stopped, a little frown marring his brow.

"I have a cottage." She grinned. "And a bed."

Chapter Twenty-seven

Between kisses, he spoke of his love, their son and his brave little heart. In the low-slung cottage, Gaelan laid her to the bed of furs, kissing her as he impatiently stripped off her clothing.

"Gaelan."

"I want to see what this bastard did to you." He stilled suddenly, meeting her gaze. "Who was it?"

"I didn't see his face. 'Twas too dark, and he was hooded."

Disappointment made his voice harsh. "Even then he hides like a coward." In one motion, he pulled off her plain dress and shift, his gaze raking her body as he sat on the side of the bed. Sympathy swept him and he moaned, bending to press a kiss to her bruised shoulder, her ribs.

She sank her fingers into his hair, loving the feel of his mouth on her skin. "I'm a bit sore in other spots too, husband."

His gaze flashed to her, his smile slow and seductive. "Here?" His tongue snaked across her nipple and she gasped, arching, offering, then hurriedly unfastened his belt, letting the sword drop, before helping him off with his shirt.

At the sight of his wound, she inhaled, covering it as she sat up. "Why didn't you tell me?"

"Because 'twas unimportant." He ducked, taking her nipple into his mouth and loving her soft sighs.

" 'Twill become infected."

" 'Tis a price, for I want you badly." He laved and tasted instead, ignoring her pleas to let her tend him and dragging his mouth over her soft belly.

"Oh, for the love of Michael, Gaelan, cease!" she said, pushing him back.

He eyed her. "You will not let this rest, will you?"

Her look said he was silly to even ask as she gingerly swung her legs over the side of the bed. "Who attacked you?" She slipped on her shift, and as he told her about the men on the moors, his gaze followed her as she bustled about the little hut, gathering cloths, a blade, and herbs, then set them on the table and prepared her cures, darting to the fire for water. Gaelan's attention was so fixed on her breasts jiggling beneath the thin cloth that he didn't hear her.

"Gaelan? You think 'twas Fenian?"

"Aye, even if you do not."

She smiled. He could read her so well.

" 'Twas the man in the glen with Rhiannon. I swear he was more willing to die than fight."

She stilled for a second, chewing her lower lip, then said, "Mayhaps they know you will catch them."

She motioned him to a chair and he sat as she cleansed the blood from his shoulder and chest, the dull throb of worry and fear and rage he'd carried for days flooding away as he watched her.

"The villagers do not know who you are, do they?"

"Fionna does." At his darkened look, she said, "She is my cousin, Gaelan, and the only reason I breathe. Death was calling me, that I remember, my love." His expression twisted in agony and she touched the lines. "She wielded the elements to save me, fought for me."

His eyes flared. "A witch?"

"Aye, love, like no other of her kind. Believe me when I say she can be trusted. She burned my clothes afore any could question the fine garments, though they were ruined beyond recognition with dirt and blood." His features tightened at the image. "The rest of the villagers know only my name. I feared there could be betrayers here and after—" A shaky breath shuddered past her lips. "After what happened to Meghan, I thought it best."

"We must keep it that way and pray none have heard the news of the princess's marriage. This is the safest place for you right now." Suddenly he gripped her waist, pulling her between his spread thighs. "Why did you not tell me of the tunnel?"

Misery colored her words. "I'd planned to, the night Brody died, I swear."

And before then he'd been angry, given her little reason to reveal it. "I believe you, love," came softly and she sighed, relieved.

"I left the chest ajar so I would not forget. Honestly, I did not think it so important, since 'twas only Connal and I who knew of it and it was hard to open without noise."

"Tigheran did not construct it alone, love."

Her brows rose. "I hadn't thought of that." She probed and removed his stitches, tisking at his poor job of it. " 'Tis fresh enough that mayhaps your fouled stitches will not show." Her gaze did a quick dip down his body and it felt like a hot stoke to his skin. "Another trophy to add to the collection?"

"You are the only scar that lays upon my skin, love." He pulled her closer, running his hands up and down her spine, shaping her hips, then sweeping around to enfold her breasts. His lips closed over her nipple, sucking it through the thin fabric.

She sighed, a breathy sound, her fingers plowing into his hair. "I cannot stitch you up if you keep playing."

"I like to play with you." He shifted to her other rosy peak.

Oh, she'd missed this, his touch, his teasing. "I will reward you handsomely, sir knight, if you'd be still and let me finish."

Gazes met and he grinned like an eager boy, easing back into the chair. "Hurry then."

Smiling, she moved to the table, pouring hot water into the herbs, stirred and mashed, not saying anything, watching her movements. "I did not see the face of Meghan's killer, Gaelan. But there is something about him I cannot remember." She lifted her gaze, confusion lying there.

"What *did* you see?"

She came to him and as if to torture him, straddled his thigh and stitched the wound. "Shadows, blood, a hooded figure and—" She inhaled, her eyes wide with panic. "Culhainn!"

"He lives." He ran his palms up and down her arms, feeling the leap of tension evaporate.

"Meghan was a sweet, gentle woman. And took her fallen status as a chieftain's sister with great dignity." Her eyes burned and she sniffled, blinking as she reached for the poultice, spreading it over his stitches. "I want to see this killer drawn and quartered, husband."

That was an order, he thought, smothered anger behind her tone. " 'Tis not your fault."

Her gaze snapped to his. "Aye, it is. That beast wanted me. He hates me enough to carve a face from bone. And it should have been mine!" She choked, and Gaelan wrapped his arms around her, hushing her, and she laid her head to his uninjured shoulder and sobbed.

After a moment he said, "I regret Meghan died, love, but I cannot say I am not pleased it was not you." He rubbed her back in gentle circles. "I love you, Siobhàn, and in it, I've become selfish. I would slay an army to keep you alive and with me."

She hugged him tightly. "I would stay here and hide, if that were possible."

"I have to return. Connal will be going mad with worry."

Her heart clenched for her son and the loneliness he must be feeling. "Aye, they need you more, but not yet. A day mayhaps?"

He tipped her face and brushed his mouth over hers. "I'm not going anywhere, love, especially when I'm due such a valuable reward."

"There will be no rewards given this night," a voice said from somewhere nearby.

Gaelan stood, nearly dumping Siobhàn on the floor.

"Who the hell are you and what—?"

"Gaelan." Siobhàn laid a hand to his arm. "This is Fionna."

He eyed the figure hovering in the darkened corner of the cottage. "I know what is best for my wife."

"I know what I know, PenDragon, and I did not work so hard to keep her alive to have you destroy it simply because you are horny."

Gaelan scowled.

Siobhàn snickered to herself.

"If you know so much, woman, tell me who attacked my wife."

Fionna shrugged, her shawl slipping and revealing pale flawless shoulders. "Rhiannon sees the past and the future. I work the present."

"Then protect her," he blurted without thinking.

Her hands on her hips, Fionna seemed to glow with sudden anger. "She was safe and well when you found her, wasn't she?"

Gaelan was instantly contrite, though fascinated with the bluish haze shimmering around her. "My thanks for saving her, mistress. I am forever grateful."

Fionna tipped her head, studying him. "I know you are, English."

He heard the bitterness in her voice and sighed, seeing another war coming with this woman. He stepped, motioning her closer, and where he expected an older woman, he found one of youth and stunning beauty, the same age as Siobhàn, if he hazarded a guess.

Gaelan frowned. "You're really a witch." Half question, half statement.

She smiled, catlike.

"Splendid." Gaelan raked his fingers through his hair. "Another one."

"There are many of us, m'lord. Do we scare you?"

"Of course not."

"Good." She smiled, looking vibrant and cherry cheeked in the golden light. "For I am not the only one in your family."

"*My* family?"

"Your Irish one, my love," Siobhàn said, and Gaelan looked at her, his scowl softening as he swept his arm about her waist and kissed her lightly.

"I will give you a moment alone, then you, sir knight, must leave her to her rest."

Only his eyes shifted. "I will not."

"My love," Siobhàn warned. " 'Tis not wise to anger her."

"Aye, you could find yourself wearing fur instead of skin."

Gaelan snapped a look at Fionna, but the mysterious woman turned and faded before his eyes, a dash of vapor left in her wake. He blinked, spinning about and searching the darkness, yet she was gone.

"She is rather dramatic sometimes."

He looked down at his wife and sighed, pressing his lips to her forehead. "Get you to bed, woman. For I like my skin just as it is."

Siobhàn smiled, running her hands over his sculptured chest. "So do I."

Gaelan groaned, then ushered her quickly beneath the furs. He glanced about, as if he expected Fionna to appear, then bent and kissed his wife, a wild play of wet lips and tongue that left her shuddering and hungry as she sank into the bedding. Grabbing his tunic, he left her when he wanted to hold her in his arms till the next dawn.

The instant he closed the door, Siobhàn felt a presence in her cottage and smiled to herself. " 'Twas rude, peeking in on us like that, Fionna."

"Had I not, you'd have been wiggling beneath the furs and weakened yourself into sickness."

" 'Twould have been good weakness, though. Gaelan's prowess extends beyond the battlefield."

Fionna arched a brow, a black wing against translucently pale skin.

Siobhàn's cheeks pinkened around a secret smile.

"How is your head?" Fionna pushed curls from her forehead.

"Still there."

Smiling, Fionna lifted a small sack from the intricate silver belt wrapping her slim waist, spilling the contents into a wood cup left on the commode. She closed her eyes, her lips moving in silent prayer over the potion, her hand passing the rim and bringing a sputter of sparks. She held out the cup. "Drink."

Siobhàn pulled a childish puss. " 'Tis vile. Are you not talented enough to make it at least sweet?"

"Spoils the mixture." She shoved the cup into her face.

"You mother me." Grudgingly, Siobhàn accepted, holding her nose and draining it swiftly.

"Because you are as stubborn as a child." Fionna set the cup aside.

For a moment the two women sat silent, Siobhàn staring at her ring, Fionna watching her. "He loves you so much, cousin."

"I love him." She lifted her gaze. "I would rather be dead than live without him."

Fionna sighed, envious. Siobhàn never felt that way about Ian, she realized, and Fionna cursed the day she'd unwisely helped the Maguire kidnap her away from Tigheran before they were wed. Happening upon Siobhàn in the forest had been the first time she'd seen a relation in five years. It made her miss them all the more and feel her isolation with a deep, wrenching loneliness. But prison was of her own making, she thought, her crimes hers alone to bear.

"I cannot undue the past, Fionna, but you saved my life. I am forever thankful for your kindness and as I did before"— her gaze swept up to meet her cousin's—"I will always cherish you."

Fionna nodded, tears glossing her eyes as she rose and kissed Siobhàn's forehead, whispering, "Thank you," before she stepped back. They exchanged a smile, then, in a wisp of vapor, she was gone. Siobhàn exhaled, amused by Fionna's drama, and snuggled into the furs.

Not even a sorceress could keep him from his wife's side, Gaelan thought, quietly propping his feet on a rough-hewed table in the center of the room. The little thatched cottage was sparsely furnished, yet not without Siobhàn's warmth permeating the edge. Two cupboards, one with crockery, the other, lined with bottles and jars of herbs, a pestle and mortar and little leather sacks, covered the wall adjacent to the hearth. The rope and stick bed thickened with furs lay in the far corner, and Gaelan's gaze lingered over it, over his wife sleeping peacefully there.

Fionna was right, she needed her rest, but that did not ease the constant aching he had for her. Just to look at her made him want to claim her, to wash away the horror with tender loving and gentle kisses. His gaze swept her face and anger slithered through him as he focused on the bruises and cuts. She was alive by the kindness of this village and Fionna and he was indebted to them.

Yet their finding her in the forest barely alive told him one thing: Although the bastard had gruesomely murdered Meghan, when he realized his mistake, he did not have the stomach to kill Siobhàn. And Gaelan did not want to think on the reason why. But he knew.

This monster, in his own twisted way, loved her.

Chapter Twenty-eight

Gaelan dragged the brush over Grayfalk's gleaming black coat, thinking of Siobhàn inside the cottage, alone and possibly in pain. That Fionna popped back inside, shooing him out, did not sit well, for he hated being apart from Siobhàn. Yet he'd conceded to Fionna's advice, for after seeing Siobhàn's battered body, 'twas a wonder his wife had survived at all. He owed Fionna O'Donnel a debt he could never repay.

Fionna, the sorceress of Donegal, he thought, with a half smile. He'd never believed in magic and spirits, but after everything he'd experienced since his arrival in Ireland, he would not deny their existence any longer.

Cautiously, Gaelan slid his sword from its scabbard. "Come forth and be known," he ordered softly, then turned.

"Fine greeting that," Raymond scoffed, ducking beneath a branch before stepping into the tiny clearing.

Gaelan sheathed his sword. "Bloody braggart," he muttered, folding his arms over his chest. "You have disobeyed me."

"Aye." Raymond leaned back against the tree, unrepentant.

"And you think naught of it?"

"Not when you want to fight the world alone."

Damn the stubborn puppy, he thought, smiling.

Raymond straightened. "You found her!"

"Aye."

Relief swept through him, sinking his shoulders a bit. "Thank God, for Connal is nigh going mad."

Gaelan's heart burned for the little boy. "That cannot be helped, yet. She was beaten. Nearly to death." Anguish laced his tone.

Raymond's expression mirrored his shock and sympathy. "Well, you cannot take her back in that condition."

"I had no intention of doing so. She is safer here. No one, save her cousin Fionna knows who she is, and the murderer does not know she survived." He explained what he knew, her discovery by the villagers, that she remembered the murder, the hooded man.

"She thinks she is missing something." Gaelan shrugged. " 'Tis a detail she cannot put to words. When she does, I think she will know who did this to her."

"I have seen the like afore, Gaelan."

PenDragon's brows rose and slowly he unfolded his arms.

" 'Tis a memory so horrible the mind refuses to see it."

"I realize that."

" 'Tis like a squire seeing his first battle; you know some deny the horror of it. Even Reese could not believe the man who'd been more of a father to him could sever a man in half."

Gaelan did not need the reminder of his past atrocities, not now. "Make your point."

"The shock might not have been the crime, but the criminal."

Gaelan fanned his fingers beneath his chin, the stubble rasping in the silence. "Who would she least suspect of such a crime?"

"Ian Maguire, O'Niell, that retainer you let into the castle."

Clearly DeClare thought the latter an unwise move and the list grew.

Gaelan was not so easily convinced. " 'Twas a crime of rage, not of simple elimination. 'Twas brutal.'' Gaelan's brows drew tight as he recalled the gruesome sight. "And Maguire would have to be aware of the tunnel.''

"Would Siobhàn have told him?''

"She would not have to, secret sworn or not. O'Rourke did not dig it himself, not without notice at least.''

"Mayhaps with help from his brother?''

"O'Niell would not dare risk his lands to be behind this. He would lose everything, including his life.'' Gaelan tapped his lips. 'Twas rumored that he and his half brother had never been on congenial terms, yet Gaelan did not rule him out. "Rhiannon could be lying about this too. She protects someone with her silence, and 'tis not her sister.''

"And what one of your knights would lie or die for you, Gaelan?''

Gaelan's scowl deepened. There was no justice in that, yet he knew there were few who would take loyalty to extreme. For an instant, he thought of Sir Owen and his unexplained absences, yet was inclined to honor the man's past loyalty with the benefit of the doubt.

"Meghan was Nall O'Donnel's sister, and he lost his *tuath* to O'Rourke. Mayhaps Siobhàn was a witness and not the target.''

"Bridgett said no one knew Meghan slept there except Siobhàn.'' Gaelan shook his head. "Nay, Meghan's murder was a mistake. And this bastard, twisted as he is, could not bring himself to kill my wife. He was hoping she'd bleed to death or be food for the wolves.''

Gaelan told him of the attack on the moors.

"You let him live?'' Raymond was stunned.

"I wanted to find my wife,'' he defended. "And he is not

the root of this madness. The man did not know Siobhàn was missing, I'm certain of it.''

''Was he one of these mysterious Fenians, mayhaps?'' Raymond's distaste for the fabled warriors showed in his tone.

''Do not discount them, my friend. Those men on the moors want the English gone. Enough to send five after me and leave this land without a lord. Whoever is attacking in the guise of English soldiers does it to brew distrust and revolt.'' Gaelan stared out over the village, wondering if it was the next target. ''Clans retaliate and the culprits wait for the war to begin. When I do not slaughter in vengeance, they bid the Fenian to do it in Maguire's plaid.''

''So it looks like the chieftain is attacking you?''

'' 'Tis possible.'' Gaelan shoved his fingers through his hair.

''But why wear a plaid that would mark them, when they hide their faces?''

''Because they could be among us.'' Gaelan recalled the familiarity of the man's eyes, yet like Siobhàn and her detail, he still could not pinpoint the reasons why. ''We can trust so few, and we need evidence. More prisoners who will talk. 'Tis why I must return.''

Raymond's eyes rounded and he glanced at the village. ''You want me to remain here?''

Gaelan nodded, the thought of leaving her for an instant killing him. But he had to return, to Connal and as a presence in the castle. His absence would offer a perfect opportunity to assault Donegal in ways other than a siege. His people were stricken with grief and worry and would see hope in anyone offering the return of their princess. He stared at the village, wondering how he would find the will to leave her here.

''I do not want to scare these people. Nor alert the Fenians, if any are about. Stay close to her and''—his lips curved— ''be aware of the witch, Fionna.''

Raymond scoffed rudely. ''There is no such thing.''

Gaelan eyed him, recognizing heated bitterness in his friend just then. "Superstitions abound in this land, DeClare, in my people. Respect them or you offend the entire race."

Raymond's lips quirked. "Your people?"

"Aye," he replied in Gaelic. "And get rid of that armor. I heard you coming for a mile."

She slept most of the day and well into the night, and Gaelan realized just how badly she'd been hurt. At least she was eating well, he thought, watching her devour the trencher full of meat. His anger rose every time he thought of this bastard striking her repeatedly. Her face wore the imprint of knuckles on her temple. Her voice bore a raspiness left by the kick to her throat. His fist clenched around the wood goblet and he tossed back a large swallow of wine.

"What troubles you, husband?" she asked from across the table.

His smile was faint with self-reproach. "I cannot hide a thing from you, can I?"

She popped a piece of meat into her mouth. "Would you want to?"

"To spare you the hateful urge I have to kill."

"This killer deserves to die, and you will find him."

"And if it is Ian?"

She looked up. "So be it," she said, without a shift in her expression. "Hold no sympathy, Gaelan, as I'm sure this killer holds none for the lives lost, for Meghan."

"He is crafty."

"You are smarter."

He smiled, leaving his chair and coming to her. He went down on one knee. "How could I fail with you by my side?"

She cupped his jaw, kissing his mouth with slow deliberation. "I love you, warrior." Her mouth whispered back and forth across him. "I love you for the gentle heart you did not know you possessed, and for giving its care to me."

Gaelan sank into the heat of her kiss, rising to sweep her into his arms and bear her to the bed of furs. He laid her there and slid into the bed beside her, cradling her in his arms.

"Afraid Fionna will appear?"

The corner of his mouth quirked. "Nay, but that is irritating, never knowing when she will invade."

Siobhàn snuggled into the protection of his body and he sighed, running his hand up and down her arm. "I have to return to Donegal, even for a brief time."

"I know." Her grip tightened a bit. "When?"

"Now."

Her indrawn breath filled the little cottage and she rolled to her side and looked at him. "I will miss you."

Tears filled her eyes as she touched the lines of his face.

"Raymond is here to protect you, Siobhàn. Trust no one but him."

She nodded, kissing him, sniffling, then kissing him again.

Suddenly he rolled to his back, taking her mouth with a ferocious desperation, all devouring, all greed and hunger and unspent passion, before he released her and left the bed. Moving to the door, he grabbed his sword and paused, twisting for a last look, his expression so tormented she felt unhinged and afraid and lonely.

He pushed open the door, stepping across the threshold. She called to him and when he turned, her body impacted with his, arms clinging as she sprinkled hot kisses over his jaw, his throat, then whispered, "Come back, husband."

His throat worked furiously as he held her, cradling her head to his shoulder. God, he did not want to do this, did not want to trust her life to another. "I will, I promise."

Pushing out of his arms, she turned her face away, choking on a sob as she reentered the cottage. The door slammed behind her, rattling the walls. Gaelan stared for a moment, aching for her, wanting desperately to remain, but if he did not return, the threat surrounding his people would be fulfilled. He continued, pausing when Fionna appeared on the edge of the street, her arms folded, sympathy in her features.

"My man is here to protect her," he said, and she unfolded her arms, frowning. "He's my champion, and I trust him as I do no other." He took a step away, then looked back. "And 'tis impolite to eavesdrop, woman."

"You would trust me?"

"Siobhàn does, and that is well enough for me, sorceress. Use your magic if you must."

Fionna nodded and Gaelan walked, twice more pausing on the hillside in indecision before continuing onto where Raymond camped in the woods.

Connal sat on the edge of the parapet, his legs swinging as he shot at the ground below. His throat burned and he blinked, trying not to cry. Gaelan would not like to find him blubbering like a baby. Soldiers did not cry. Then he remembered the tears in his eyes when his lord thought his mother lay bloodied in the bed. Aye, sometimes they cried.

A man without a heart is an empty body, he'd told him. They shared many secrets. Like that Gaelan loved his mama, and that she saved him with her love, whatever that meant. Connal couldn't wait until he was older to discover all these hidden meanings grown-ups spoke of. He notched another pebble and squinted, aiming for a tuft of grass. Around him soldiers walked the guard, everyone in the castle tending to duty. He shot another pebble, then sighed, twirling the slingshot. He missed Mama. Aunt Rhiannon fussed over him, followed him around like Dermott, and he was sorry he told her to leave him alone. It hurt her feelings. But he wanted his mother. He wanted Gaelan to come home and tell him she was alive. Connal brushed at the tear working down his cheek, then glanced left and right to see if anyone noticed. He climbed to his feet, rubbing his bum, then turned to the battlements. He pushed a wood box to the wall and stepped atop it to see over the edge.

Then he saw him, the black horse tearing across the land.

"PenDragon!" he shouted, and guards looked, soldiers scrambling to open the gates. He rode through the opening, skidding to a halt, kicking up dust and stones. Reese and Jace rushed forward with the knights and soldiers as he flung from the saddle. He shook his head and Connal knew then, he had not found her.

"Connal!" His gaze scanned the crowd. "Someone find my son."

Connal called his name, pushing between the adults, and Gaelan looked down, smiling and scooping him up in his arms.

Connal sighed and hugged him and thought how lucky he was that he was still loved.

"Ahh, lad, don't cry."

"I'm not!"

His lips twitching, Gaelan rubbed his back, aching to tell him his mother lived but not trusting the tongue of a child. "Come, I am starved."

"You carry me; how much choice have I?"

Impudent whelp, he thought, swinging him to the ground as he entered the hall, noticing first that his crest, their crest, hung over the hearth, then recognized the silence. He glanced at his people, still as they awaited word. He shook his head; some sobbed and fled, others, their shoulders drooping a fraction more as they turned to their duties. The deception turned like soured milk in his stomach.

Driscoll approached, yet Gaelan waved him off, too tired to answer questions when he'd no solutions to offer. Abovestairs and secluded in his chamber, he bathed, Connal always near and quizzing him over his wound. Culhainn recovered near the fire, his gaze constantly on the bed. They dined in private, and though he knew Rhiannon paced beyond the doors, he let her wait, focusing on Connal.

"You have not ridden since I left?"

Connal shook his head, his mouth full of food.

"We shall in the morn then."

He swallowed hurriedly. "Nay. You must search again!"

Gaelan's brows rose at his vehemence. "But I just returned."

"Go again," he pleaded. "She is not dead."

Gaelan leaned over his meal. "I believe that, too."

Russet curls spilled over his forehead as Connal stared at his trencher, playing with his food, and Gaelan instantly sensed his apprehension. "You can tell me aught, Connal, and 'twill remain atween us."

He looked up. "Mama told me to keep it secret, but . . ."

Gaelan didn't think he could handle another revelation. "Go on."

"I can feel her."

Gaelan's features stretched tight. Good God, not him too. "How?"

He shrugged his small shoulders. " 'Tis like I can feel her breathing."

Gaelan marveled at the boy's intuition. "I will leave to search soon, but I returned because I thought mayhaps you were lonely."

He rolled his eyes, the notion telling him privacy was scarce. "Aunt Rhiannon wants to always play with me, eat with me—"

"Smother you," Gaelan finished.

"Aye." He yawned hugely. "She took away my slingshot."

And he'd obviously nipped it back since it was sticking out of his waistband. "Who did you hit?"

"Nova. 'Twas an accident, I swear," he insisted.

Smiling, Gaelan swiped his mouth with a scrap of cloth and leaned back in the chair. "Want me to speak to your aunt?"

"Nay." Connal left the oversized chair—Siobhàn's chair—and came to him. "She is too sad already."

Gaelan's heart did a strange flip in his chest when the lad

crawled onto his lap and promptly fell asleep. The trust nearly unraveled his soul. The boy felt warm and solid against him and he inhaled deeply, the scent of wax and lye still permeating the room.

His gaze drifted to the bed, all traces of the murder gone except for the cracked mirror. Scrubbed clean, he thought, but until Siobhàn was home, the ugliness would never leave.

Chapter Twenty-nine

'Twas good to have a moment alone, Rhiannon thought, without a guard tripping on her skirts. Squatting, Rhiannon fished for another egg and carefully laid it in the basket, then reached for another, her hand stilling.

She rose slowly, slipping her knife free from its slim scabbard as she turned. "I could alarm the entire castle with one scream," she warned.

"You won't."

She scoffed rudely. "My sister is missing and you know where she is! How think you Gaelan will treat you?"

Fear flickered in his features. "I don't know where she is. Touch me once and find the truth." He held out his hand.

She ignored it. " 'Tis all you have to say, to tell me?"

"Mayhaps that I am tired and without will? That I watched PenDragon slay four of my friends in seconds and knew I was defeated?"

"Yet you still fight, still you do not see you cannot stop him."

"I have no choice."

"And neither will he. He will show you no mercy." She choked on a sob yet held the knife poised to strike.

His gaze darted to the weapon. "You do not trust me." He took a step.

She raised the blade. "I never did."

"I love you."

Agony sprinted across her face. "You know naught of love!" she hissed, her beauty contorted with rage and heartbreak. "Or you would cease this madness!"

"He will only gather more." His voice was dead, empty of hope.

Her stance softened. "Go to PenDragon, I beg you. Tell him—"

"I cannot! I am sworn!" She was a fool to even ask.

"And what of the oath to me?"

His features twisted with remorse and pain. "And what of your *lies,* seer?"

Her posture sank, her beautiful face a portrait of regret. "They die with me."

She turned the knife to herself and two-handed, she prepared to plunge it into her breast. His eyes flew wide and he lurched, grasping it, grappling with her before tearing it from her hands and flinging it to the dirt.

He crushed her against him, tightening his hold to near punishing when she struggled to escape. Her breath was hot and angry, heating the skin of his collarbone.

Around them geese squawked.

He pushed his fingers into her hair, tilting her head, forcing her to look him in the eye.

"I hate you!" Tears fell, unheeded.

"I love you."

She gasped, choking on her own breath, her hands wedged between them and pushing at him with each word. "You have lost, Patrick. You have done too much, waited too long. This cannot be undone.''

"This can be.''

He captured her mouth, crushing the breath from her lungs, drinking it in a kiss so furious with his emotions, she could not fight it. No woman could. Rhiannon opened for him, laying her body to his with the heat of a fire, layer to layer, her small hands cupping his face and taking back the years lost in duty and self-preservation.

He groaned, a sound of dark suffering and ruination, with her first touch. It had destroyed her years before, and had haunted him since. Yet Patrick could not cease wanting her, could not crush the hunger wailing for release inside him. Both knew their hearts ached to surrender, longed to be joined and beating as one when every force around them ripped them apart. They would never agree, never compromise their beliefs or duty, not even to each other, not even for their love. Yet in the darkness of the dovecote, the stench fading to the sweetness of possession, his hands roughly mapped her body, dragging her blood red gown upward until he cupped the bare skin of her buttocks. Her breathing increased with her movements, nimble fingers tearing at his braies and he leaned back against the wall, uncaring of the people only yards beyond. Uncaring that if discovered, he would be hung in minutes, and when she freed him into her palm, stroking him, he lifted her, spreading her legs around his hips and shoving to her wet haven. Rhiannon moaned, throwing her head back, and he twisted, pushing her to the wall, withdrawing and plunging into her yielding body, taking her like a man with nothing left to lose.

Siobhàn stepped into the center of the forest. "Raymond?''

DeClare strode forward, smiling sheepishly. "My lady,'' he said with a bow.

"I hope you were not trying to hide. You trounce like a boar," she tisked, shaking her head and smothering a smile.

Suddenly he stepped closer, his eyes wide as he examined her face. "Good Lord above."

Siobhàn reddened. "Hideous, aren't I?" She was too aware that the bruises had a horrible greenish yellow cast, some still purple and scraped.

"Oh, nay, my lady. 'Tis just that Gaelan mentioned . . . I did not think . . ."

"You didn't think I would turn so ugly?"

"There is always beauty in your strength, princess. And 'tis a miracle you survived."

"I owe Fionna that credit, sir." She turned toward the village, and though he offered his arm for support, she refused it. As Raymond met her stride, the strangest feeling permeated his skin. He glanced about, swearing they were being watched, yet he could find no one in the morning light.

" 'Tis Fionna." Siobhàn paused, glancing into the thicket of trees. "Likely a bird or a squirrel this time."

Raymond made a disbelieving sound. "Great Scots."

She met his gaze, smiling. "Fionna," she called. "He does not believe in you."

"He's English," came from above. "And therefore a fool."

Scowling, Raymond looked up to see a silver gray cat laying on the fork of a branch, tail curling up and down.

"Shame on you, Fionna." Siobhàn kept walking, giggling softly.

"*That* is not a human," Raymond insisted, catching up with her and still looking back over his shoulder. He hoped the cat or any other creature didn't dig up his armor and extra provisions.

Siobhàn introduced him as they walked through the village, the people smiling and friendly, and Raymond took up a position as a wood cutter and kept a close eye on anyone approaching her.

Later that afternoon, Raymond folded the leather straps around the bundle of wood and hoisted it to his back, carting it to the next home. He traded the service for food and wine, and the townsfolk were more than generous, considering there was no hiding the fact that he was English and the folk mentioned soldiers attacking the village.

Raymond saw no benefit. It was too far from Donegal, nor was it very prosperous. It was clear someone wanted a war and for Gaelan to start it. But without an enemy, their hands were tied tight. He stopped at Siobhàn's cottage and found her sitting in a chair outside the door. It was odd to see her simply sitting, for the woman he knew moved like a whirlwind through the castle. Then he noticed her fidgeting.

"Nay, do not get up, my lady."

"Are you hungry? Please say so, Raymond. I am nigh going mad with all this *rest*," she said with disgust.

He grinned. "I will be hungry, if it pleases my lady."

She made a sour face. "Patronizing does not become you. Deliver your wood, then." She waved him off.

"After that I must check on my weapons and armor."

"Need you grain for your mount?"

"She will survive."

He walked away, delivering the wood, saluting her as he passed, and Siobhàn could not help but throw, "Beware of the witches. 'Tis dusk, you know."

Raymond scoffed, walking briskly out of the village. "Superstitious rot," he muttered, yet glanced about, seeing more in the forest than he knew was there.

Carrying a tray, Rhiannon stepped into the solar and was more than a little irritated by the sight of Connal sitting on the old desk, his feet swinging as he took aim with his slingshot. Gaelan spoke softly to him, encouragingly, and her heart clenched at the relationship the unlikely pair shared.

Connal took the shot. The pebble pinged against the wood cup sitting on a keg in the corner. Gaelan praised him, ruffling his hair.

She cleared her throat.

The pair looked up and Gaelan whispered to Connal. He immediately jammed the slingshot into his braies and hopped off the desk, moving past with only a mumbled, "Good day." *He has taken him from me,* she thought, then called herself selfish. The boy needed a father, a man to guide him. "I took that away."

His look said he was aware of the lad's behavior. "He will scrub out the kettles for the next sennight in penance to Nova."

She nodded, wishing she'd thought of that.

An uncomfortable silence stretched. "Driscoll said you were wounded?"

"Aye." Gaelan scratched at his shoulder.

She nodded to the stitches. "How long have they been in?"

He shrugged. "Four days mayhaps."

"Then they need to come out." She moved closer, setting the tray laden with a bowl of water and cloths on the desk. He pulled off his tunic and shirt in one move, then sat as Rhiannon came to his side, soaking a cloth and laying it over the healing wound to soften the dried blood. She sharpened her knife, then without a word lifted the cloth and plucked at the stitches.

She inhaled, her hand on his shoulder. "She lives."

Gaelan's gaze snapped to hers and he cursed his lack of forethought. "Aye, and keep it to yourself." Her hand lingered on him and he shoved it off.

"Why do you keep this from them?" She inclined her head to the castle folk beyond the walls.

"And have her killer find her?" he sneered. "Finish and be gone, woman."

She pulled the last stitch and padded the wound, wrapping and tying it off.

Gaelan turned to his clothes, donning them quickly, refusing to speak a word as he tucked his tunic inside the wide belt. When he was wont to leave, she grabbed his arm.

"She is my sister; I would not hurt her. I love her."

Her unguarded expression gave him pause, and he considered whether his assumptions might be wrong. "Your silence will have a price. Who do you hide, Rhiannon?"

Indecision warred in her and finally she burst with, "The raiders, they are—" She clasped her hands, staring at the floor, before sighing and lifting her gaze to his. "Without choice."

" 'Tis an easy excuse, and there is always a choice, woman."

He was right, of course. And when the wrong ones were made, one must live with the price.

"And theirs is to murder," he growled, looming over her. "I saw infants slaughtered, old women dragged till there was naught left on their bones, Rhiannon. There is naught in this world that would justify slaying innocents!"

"You did in the name of coin."

"I fought warriors, soldiers, those capable of killing me, and never *once* have I slain a child!"

He thrust her aside, yet before he reached the door she said softly, "But your men have."

He jerked a look at her.

"Did not Sir Owen, in the heat of battle, try to kill Siobhàn?"

Gaelan's expression turned black as tar pitch, for both knew that in battles innocents did die.

On his knees Raymond dug in the dirt, checking on his armor and weapons. When his fingers touched the cold metal, he quickly recovered it and stood, heading toward the spot where he'd left his horse. He walked briskly, his intentions clear, until he noticed footprints in the dirt, hoof prints he knew his mount did not make. Raymond followed the path, squatting once or twice to examine the depressions. The sun was setting, the glow offering little light, and he had naught to form a serviceable torch. He was about to turn back to his mount when he stumbled, falling to his knees and catching himself before he hit the ground. Something hard bruised his palm and he dug, fingering a thick metal ring attached to a rope. Raymond stood, pulling, and in the fading light the earth opened, a great misshapen door swinging out of the ground, like the door of a cellar.

He let it drop to the ground, sending leaves and dust into the air, then leaned over the cavern, peering.

"Great Scots."

The impact was swift and deadly, smacking his shoulder, driving blistering pain through his body and bringing him to his knees. A javelin, he thought, twisting, trying to unsheathe his sword, but it only served to drive the spear deeper. His assailant kicked him and he tumbled headfirst into the grotto. And into unconsciousness.

Chapter Thirty

Siobhàn rushed into Fionna's cottage. "Help me, please."

Twisting, Fionna frowned, noticing first the fear in her cousin's eyes, and the mammoth sword clutched in her hands. Then the blood. Quickly laying aside her spoon and covering the cook pot, she followed her outside.

Instantly, she bent to Raymond. "Oh lady be praised," Fionna muttered when she found a pulse. The javelin shaft protruded from his shoulder, snapped off inches beyond his skin, and fortunately, halting the bleeding. Fionna called for Paddy and several others to help carry the Englishman into her cottage as Siobhàn told her how she'd found him crawling on the ground.

"I dragged him till I found his horse—"

Fionna cursed the stars under her breath.

"And fear I've made his wounds worse," Siobhàn finished, waiting until Raymond was on the bed before setting the weapon aside to pull off his boots. "He had his sword in his hand still, bless his Norman hide."

Fionna spared her a concerned look, her gaze sweeping Siob-hàn's body. "You should have left him," she scolded, then glanced to be certain they were alone before adding, "You did not pierce him. This is not your fault."

"Then who's is it? He promises Gaelan to watch over me and look what happens!" She cut the tunic off him whilst Fionna poured tinctures down his throat.

"Do not speak of it now. This one will die if we do not work quickly."

She tugged at the spear tip and Raymond stirred on the bed, thrashing in pain. Fionna closed her eyes and chanted softly, laying her hand over his brow. He settled and she hiked her skirts and climbed atop him, bracing her knees on his arms and pinning him to the bed. With two hands, she grasped the javelin and yanked. He howled, arching sharply and throwing her off, dumping her on the floor, his chest oozing fresh blood. Siobhàn reached for Fionna, but she waved her off, ordering her to cover the wound.

She did. "Sweet Mary mother, how does he still live?"

"He is a stubborn, stupid English is how," Fionna muttered, climbing to her feet and corking the wound with cloth. Siobhàn sopped the blood pooling beneath him as Fionna tried treating the wound, but he shoved her hands off, clawing at them when she tried again, refusing to succumb to the painless oblivion beckoning him. "Curse the man." Fionna stepped back, dragging the back of her hand across her damp brow. "Great spirits, I cannot help him if he tears at me like this."

"Then knock him out."

Fionna spared her a glance, then straightened. With a sharp whip of her hand, as if she'd struck his face, Raymond was out cold—and still. Both women sighed, then went to work.

"I do not like doing that." It was abusing her powers, she thought.

"It did not look that way."

Fionna ignored the jibe and plucked the splinters from his

wound. *He will have the luck of the Irish in him if he survives,* she thought, flicking aside a chunk of wood. Silently Fionna chanted a prayer, not for the knight but for Siobhàn and the child she could unwittingly lose for her valiant attempt to save this man. As she worked, beyond the walls of the modest cottage the villagers armed themselves, fearing punishment for the injuries of the English knight.

He watched her from a great distance as she stood over a small pot. Stirring her herbs into a potion, likely. His shock over finding her alive served to strengthen his determination to end this masquerade quickly and take what was his. She should be a rotting corpse, he thought, and cursed his weakness for not ending her life with a swift cut to her supple throat. He stepped, hiding behind trees, his body cloaked like the forest. He withdrew his dagger. She was alone more often then not, and he could kill her and none would be the wiser. They did not know who she was anyway, he deduced, or they would have alerted PenDragon by now. He moved closer and closer still, lurching behind trees, when a dark-haired woman rushed to her side. Fionna O'Donnel, he recognized. The witch. The whore. With an arm about her shoulder, she ushered her inside the cottage, casting a look back over her shoulder at the forest. And he swore she looked right at him.

Raymond stirred on the fur pallet, his skin blistering with sweat. Soft hands bathed him and whispered words filled his mind. He tried opening his eyes, knowing he should be gone from here. His lady was his to champion, to protect, and Gaelan depended on him to stand his duty. Someone pushed a cup to his lips, briskly ordering him to drink. He tried, the liquid dripping down his chin. He would be humiliated if he had the strength to bother, he thought groggily, and sank into the furs.

His skin burned, pain radiating out from his shoulder to his fingertips, and when he could bear it no more, heard himself cry out like a child, it cooled, a soothing cloth smothering the fire growing in his body. Sounds faded in and out, voices, feminine and worried, whispered around him. He prayed one of them was Siobhàn.

Ahh, my friend, forgive me for failing you.

Hours later he stirred again and forced his eyes open. *I've risen to heaven,* he thought, blinking. For surely she was an angel. Black haired, she was naked, her back to him where she stood in a small tub, bathing, pouring water over her head. His bleary gaze watched the liquid slick over her skin, down her buttocks, her shapely thighs to the calves.

"Rest," he heard. "Your desires will do you little good and greater harm," the voice, lilting and soft, said. She twisted and met his gaze. Ice blue eyes stared back at him. His drugged gaze slipped over her body in blatant admiration.

Fionna ignored the heat sifting through her body as he mumbled, "Angel."

"Nay, English. Witch," she whispered, and he frowned.

". . . do not . . . exist."

"Of course not," she said, waving her hand.

Raymond closed his eyes, his head lolling on the pillow, yet he still thrashed.

"Why does he not rest?" Siobhàn asked. "He seems to fight the healing."

Fionna stepped from the bath, patting herself dry. "He wants to be up and about, I'm thinkin'." Siobhàn moved behind her, draping the robes over her shoulders. "To protect you."

Siobhàn nodded and leaned close to whisper, "Raymond, I am here and well. Please rest."

He struggled blindly, but Fionna pushed him down into the pallet. "You cannot protect her if you are dead, aye? Behave and do as you are ordered!" Without opening his eyes, he obeyed. The women looked at each other, then sighed tiredly.

Fionna gathered a basket full of herbs and cups, a tiny kettle and her wand. "Come, there's little time to waste."

"He is that close to death?"

Fionna refused to look at the Englishman. "Infection will take him if I do not call on the elements."

Siobhàn nodded, taking the basket and following Fionna out to the stone circle.

Halfway through the ritual of Wicca, watching the elements come into her command in flashes of light and fire, wind and water, Siobhàn wondered if Fionna hated the English so well, why was she calling on the power of their ancestors to help save this one?

Ian charged ahead, his stead overtaking the slight hill. He called out to his men and they widened their attack, chasing down the riders. Armor glinted in the afternoon light, and his anger raged. With his sword, he struck blow after blow, the ring of metal to metal bleak and damning. He whirled the steed about, bending low to catch the collar of a brigand and drag him with him. The man howled, and Ian rode, dragging him.

He strained to keep his grip, shouting for his men to give chase, and yet he refused to release his prisoner. Vassals surrounded him as he slid from the saddle, his sword poised at the brigand's throat.

"Your name?" Receiving no response, he repeated in English, yet the man stared back with blank eyes. *"Your lord!"* Ian drew back to strike.

The man did not flinch, his eyes barren, and Ian cursed, lowering his arm, sheathing his sword and calling for bindings. He lashed the man about the throat, then tied the end of the lead to his saddle. Two more attackers were caught, brought to him and refusing to speak. He would take the evidence to PenDragon and, before all, demand he secede his power for this treachery.

* * *

Raymond drifted in and out of consciousness, feeling his strength build as the pain receded. He did not know how many days had passed since he was attacked, but his first thought was of Siobhàn.

"She rests and you must," a voice called in the darkness.

"I am . . . fine."

"Then get up, go to her, wield your sword for her."

Raymond tried to do just that, but his strength vanished after a feeble attempt to slip his legs over the side of the bed.

He sagged into the bedding, licking his dry lips. "Who are you?"

"Fionna."

"The cat or the squirrel?"

"Sometimes." Amusement pricked her voice.

He squinted into the dark. "Siobhàn? Please tell me she is unharmed."

The faint shadow of a hand swept to the right and Raymond inched up to see over the foot of the bed. Seeing her asleep and curled on her side near the fire, he sank into the furs, for a moment, thoughtful, then flung the covers back.

"You haven't the strength for that."

He arched a brow. "Is that worry I hear, lass?"

"I could give a fig if you died, English, but she does, and for that I will see you healed."

Her venom made his lips curl in self-reproach. He could not expect all to accept them as the dairy maids had. "My thanks, then." A pause and then, "Come into the light."

"I am content here."

"Stubborn female."

"Bloodthirsty Englishman."

His brows shot up and he watched as her figure shifted in the shadows, a hand appearing in the dark, offering a cup.

"Drink."

He accepted without question, draining the bitter liquid and making a sour face before handing it back. "Well, at least I know you cannot cook."

She laughed, a soft burst of color in his mind.

"My sword."

"Beside you." Raymond saw the blade, the tip in the dirt floor, the hilt within his reach. It made him smile. He looked to the shadows. "Why do you not show yourself?"

"I want no memory of me in your English mind."

"Too late. I saw you naked."

She gasped and he could feel her outrage, as if the room suddenly heated. He could not resist baiting her. " 'Twas a delicious sight, lass. You've the sweetest behind I've—"

"Hush, rogue," she snapped. "Your charm will not work on me."

He tisked softly, the sound slurred, and in the far corner of the cottage beyond the light Fionna smiled, counting the minutes till the draught pulled him back to sleep. 'Twas unnerving enough with the man here, let alone awake and trying to seduce her.

Satisfied his slumber was deep and harmless, she left the sleeping pair to gather fresh herbs and wood.

Sensing he was finally alone with Siobhàn, Raymond slid his legs over the edge of the bed and sat up. His head spun dizzily and he waited for it to pass, then reached for his clothes, mended, washed and folded on a nearby chair. He was glad he still wore his braies, for dressing was painful and difficult, pulling on his boots a test of willpower against the stabbing pain. Suitably clothed, he stood slowly, using his sword like a cane and moving to Siobhàn. Kneeling, he nudged her gently and she stirred, her lashes sweeping up. When she opened her mouth to speak, he hushed her.

"Dress warmly and quickly. We must leave."

She scrambled upright, scooting back a bit. "I promised Gaelan to remain."

''I know, my lady, but I must speak with my lord and I cannot leave you here unprotected.''

Siobhàn gazed up at him, frowning. ''You are not well enough to ride, sir knight.''

Raymond knew that. Bloody hell, kneeling beside her took most of his strength. ''Come. Now.'' He stood, his eyesight blurry, and he blinked to clear it.

''I must tell Fionna—''

''Nay!'' he hissed through clenched teeth, his face crimped in pain.

Siobhàn climbed to her feet. ''I trust her.''

''I do not. Please, do not argue, my lady. Or I will use force.'' Gaelan would never forgive him if he left her behind, yet his lord needed to know what he'd discovered.

She grabbed her cloak, sweeping it over her shoulders. ''You could not force a fly. And Fionna was right. You are stupid to attempt this.''

He only smiled. ''Then have pity and help me.''

Her lips curved and she grabbed a small knife from the table, slipping it into the pouch tied at her waist. ''You are half drugged, Raymond. And 'tis I who will likely end up defending you.''

''I feel better already.'' He grinned, realizing some things had not changed a'tall.

''We return to Donegal?'' The anticipation of seeing Connal brightened her face.

''Aye. You will be safe there.''

''Gaelan said I was safer here.''

''Nay, lass, you are not.'' He inclined his head to his wound, the deep gash bespeaking the threat.

He was right, of course, for there was no reason to wound the Norman, and she feared whoever attempted his murder was trying to get closer to her. ''Come along then.'' She lent her shoulder for support.

Using his sword as a cane, he gazed down at her, her soft

body tucked to his side as they walked unsteadily to his horse. "You above all did not warrant such cruelty. I seek only to bring you safely home."

She nodded, helping him into the saddle, and when he made to pull her up before him, she shook her head. "I can walk. The ride will be harmful enough without me banging against your wound."

A lady, his lord's woman, walking whilst a knight rode was unthinkable. "Behind me," he ordered, handing her a length of rope. "Lash my ankles to the stirrups, and one hand to the saddle."

"Do not be absurd!"

"My lady," he sighed wearily, "I know my own strengths, and the potion is working well. You alone could not keep me in the saddle should I want to fall on my face."

She did not see the humor in this. "Does that not tell you to wait a sennight, at least?"

His information was vital, and Raymond did not want to think of the lives that could be lost in that time. "I cannot."

Making a disgusted face, she did as bade, securing his ankles and one wrist, then using a stump to climb up behind him. He laid the sword across his lap, ready to fight to protect her, and it touched her that so many cared for her safety. Carefully they rode, Siobhàn glancing back at the little hamlet and hoping Fionna did not worry, hoping she understood she was in his valiant care.

For miles, they clung to the woods, fitting through the thick trees like a thread to a needle. Siobhàn was exhausted with her effort to remain awake and keep him upright and decided Fionna was correct. English courage was wasted in the wrong places and DeClare would be better off if he remained in the Wiccan's care and healed. But his insistence could not be ignored.

He was willing to die to speak with Gaelan.

She tugged on the reins, guiding the horse beneath a tree and resting there. She dozed off and on, startled by an eerie feeling spilling over her skin. Frowning at the nocturnal noises, she strained to see in the dark, yet could see little in the shadows. Creatures moved; a squirrel skipped up a tree, startling her. Raymond, his head lolling forward, his shoulders hunched, swayed, his fists wrapped in the animal's mane. They will have to cut him free, she thought. Huddling inside her cloak, Siobhàn closed her eyes, yawning. Her stomach grumbled for food, a constant racket of late.

Wind speared between the clusters of trees, a sudden biting shriek.

Raymond stirred. The horse sidestepped.

A rope dropped from the tree above and before Siobhàn could alert him, the noose snapped around her neck and yanked her from the saddle.

The horse bolted, stealing her support.

Siobhàn dangled, choking, clawing at the rope, and the last thing she saw was steed and rider vanishing into the darkness.

Chapter Thirty-one

Fionna stepped into her cottage, yet knew before she did that they were gone. She moaned in despair, dropping the kindling to the floor and bracing her hands on the table. Her eyes tightly shut, she tried to sense Siobhàn, or the knight, but naught came to her. At least he has his mammoth sword, she noticed, yet doubted he could wield it if necessary, nor survive the journey to Donegal. Straightening, she stepped out into the night and called for Paddy. The older man appeared, knuckling his eyes, scowling at the late hour.

"Siobhàn and the knight are gone, and if we do not discover their path, then PenDragon will slaughter us all for our neglect."

"PenDragon?" Paddy blinked, stunned.

"Did not know you kept such noble company, eh? Siobhàn is our princess." His eyes grew even wider. "You really must travel more, Paddy," she said with disgust and headed off to her stone circle. She'd no time to waste. By morning, the English would descend.

* * *

Gaelan paced with impatience, his mind sifting through details and his heart begging him to return to Siobhàn. As before, he sensed that something was not right. Gaelan called for Reese to ready his mount.

"Nall O'Donnel is dead, my lord," Driscoll said just as the hall doors opened. "His son and clansmen come to collect his sister's body."

Flanked by two men wrapped in threadbare tartans, a slim young fellow walked forward, his gaze on the floor. Gaelan frowned at the poorly clothed lad and motioned Sir Andrew close, ordering a purse of gold offered for his aunt's life, though Gaelan thought Meghan had given more than her life for Siobhàn. She'd given him back his own in her ultimate sacrifice. It was obvious by the young son and the pair with him that O'Donnel's defeat had a higher price than his chieftainship. It cost them their dignity.

He gestured for Driscoll and the Irishman leaned close. "How has this starvation and poverty struck them harder than most?"

Driscoll shrugged. "They are under O'Niell's rule."

Gaelan's brows rose. "Pride keeps them from coming to him?"

"Likely anger, sir, O'Rourke took their land, and O'Niell being his half brother . . ." He let that hang, and Gaelan walked toward the visitors, about to greet them when Sir Owen entered the hall, removing his gauntlets as he strode toward his lord.

"Maguire and several retainers are on the ride. And the O'Niell's turned back to the river."

Men assembled behind him, the O'Donnels watching the Irish and English follow, and Gaelan had taken no more than two dozen steps beyond the keep when his enemy's name filled the air.

"Maguires! Maguires!"

Gaelan ran to the gates, his sword slapping his thigh. He skidded to a halt, swinging up the scaffolding to the parapet and staring down at the encroaching band. His camped soldier rushed forward, then stopped to await his signal, and around him bowmen lined the wall and outer curtain, torches flaring to light. He strode to the edge of the battlement and raised his arm, archers sighting as the army rode down the hill. Less than a dozen riders trotted onto the freshly milled drawbridge.

"No further, chieftain, for you have chosen the wrong day for mercy."

Ian craned his neck, meeting his gaze. "Even for one of your own?" Ian motioned and a man led a horse forward.

Gaelan swore. The sight of Raymond slumped over his horse's neck drove a bolt of fear down to his boot heels and he instantly ordered arms down as he left the parapet, helping the wide doors open. Flanked by his knights, he rushed to Raymond's side. Lashed to the saddle like a fresh kill, Raymond was unconscious, his shoulder bleeding profusely. Gaelan's gaze shot to Maguire's, the accusation clear.

Ian's lips twisted in a sneer. "We found him wandering. Alone."

Untying him, Gaelan dragged the big man down, handing him over to able hands waiting to carry him into the castle. Knights and soldiers kept the Irishmen back and Gaelan rounded on Maguire. His gaze swept the army, recognizing the recent battle in splattered blood and overworked animals, and he thought only of the village and Siobhàn. Tightly capped rage nearly exploded through him. "Raiding on my people will cost you your lands, chieftain!"

Ian's gaze narrowed with bitterness, for he knew PenDragon could do exactly as he predicted and mayhaps had, little by little. "Here is your raider, English." With his booted foot, he shoved the culprit forward. The man tripped, banging into the steed. The glint of armor flickered in the night.

Gaelan latched onto him by the gorget, scowling at the

English armor before meeting Ian's gaze. "Metal is forged with only a hammer and fire." Gaelan released him, two soldiers on guard.

Maguire yanked his remaining prisoners forward, and the men stumbled to the ground, the sound hollow on the wood planks.

Gaelan stepped closer, grabbing one man by the molded helm and tipping his head back, trying to see beneath the dirt and blood. "Driscoll," he barked, and the high sheriff rushed forward, sword drawn. "Know you him?"

Driscoll eyed the man for an instant. "Nay, my lord."

At "my lord," Maguire scoffed, delivering a nasty glare at his countryman, and Driscoll returned the stare, looking at Ian as if he were a fool.

Ian shifted his mount closer. "Why do you taunt and maim, PenDragon, when you could easily kill us all?"

"If that were true, you'd have been dead a sennight ago." Gaelan eyed the prisoners. "These are not my men." He released his hold on the one.

"How would you know? You have legions."

"I know the faces of my men," Gaelan said with deadly finality. Names oftimes escaped him, but the look of fear in the men he'd fought beside for years did not. "They are your prisoners. Do as you will, chieftain."

Ian's features stretched tight. Was he ruthless enough to give his men up so easily?

"However," Gaelan added, "it has been my experience that they will not talk."

He's taken others, Ian thought. "Mayhaps you are not asking the right questions."

"You misunderstand. They do not speak a'tall."

Maguire frowned, looking at the guilty. 'Twas true, the men had not uttered a word.

"Mayhaps"—Gaelan's tone was thoughtful and Ian's gaze flashed to his—"because if they did, 'twould mark them."

The accent. "You think they are Irish?"

Gaelan folded his arms over his chest. "Either way, we would know."

A page rushed forward, calling for him, skipping to a halt and staring dumbly at the Irish warriors illuminated by the torchlight. Gaelan nudged the lad and bent to his whispers.

He straightened. "Choose three of your vassals and come with me, Maguire. Leave your weapons at the gate. Markus, take the prisoners to the dungeon," he ordered, turning into the keep.

"And if I choose not to?"

Gaelan looked back over his shoulder. "I will kill you where you stand, Irish. Until DeClare speaks, you are now my prisoner." With a wave of his hand, the Irishmen were surrounded, their weapons stripped. Sir Andrew waited beside Ian's mount, a courtesy to his rank.

Calmly, Ian tugged off his gauntlets. "It appears we've been invited for supper."

Gaelan ran, his heart pounding furiously, and he found Raymond lying on the bed in the privacy of the solar. Rhiannon was already shouting orders for her supplies and cutting Raymond's clothes from his torso.

She stilled at the stitches in his garments, then frowned at the ones in his chest.

"He's been treated," she said, and Gaelan scowled. He doubted the Maguire would do such a thing. Which left Fionna or Siobhàn the task, and he wondered why they'd allowed him to leave in such a state. He hovered, and Rhiannon bumped into him twice.

"Go, you can do naught," she said, elbowing him back. "Not for a few hours."

He refused to move. "He knows what's happened!"

She rounded on him. "Do you not think I know that?" It was then he saw her tears. He'd no sympathy for them.

"Then touch him. Discover it. Your sister's life is at stake!"

"I've tried! He gives me naught in this weakened state and . . ." Her gaze shifted to Driscoll, framed in the entrance.

Gaelan turned, guilt crimping his face.

"The princess lives?"

"Aye."

Driscoll's features bore a multitude of anger and hurt. "Damn thee, PenDragon."

Gaelan crossed to him, grasping the man's shoulders when he was wont to leave or rail. "Be angry if you wish, but she was near dead." His voice lowered. "And safer in the village."

Driscoll's expression bespoke his understanding, the peril to her life. "Aye, my lord. But if none knew she lived, then what of DeClare?"

"He was guarding her and his presence here speaks of discovery. We must keep it that way." Driscoll nodded, trusting his judgment, and Gaelan looked to Rhiannon. "The instant he stirs, I must speak with him." He moved past with Driscoll, stopping short when he found Connal framed in the doorway, his stricken face tipped to Gaelan. Gaelan reached and the boy backed away.

"You lied!"

Gaelan grabbed the child, lifting him when he tried to tear free, held him when he squirmed, hushed him when he sobbed, then ducked into the privacy of the buttery. "Shh, shhh," he hushed. "You always knew, didn't you? But I could not tell a soul, my lad, and you must swear to not speak of it. The person who killed Meghan wanted to kill your mother, and until we catch him, she is in grave danger." He prayed to God she was not involved in this, for if a trained knight was wounded so severely, what defense would Siobhàn have?

His insides twisted at the thought.

Then, like a good prince of Erin, the child nodded and swore his silence.

Gaelan pressed a kiss to his forehead, patted his back, then set him to his feet, stepping back into the solar and staring at Raymond on the bed, his breathing shallow, his body so still. It frightened him, that he might lose his dearest friend, that with him he would take the knowledge of Siobhàn's safety. He hoped Fionna had intervened and kept her hidden. He barked orders for a patrol to assemble, sending them to protect the village.

"Nay, Owen," he said when the knight made to join them. "You remain here."

Owen's features tightened at the command, but Gaelan did not care. His absences and his prejudice for the Irish was only meanly tempered of late, and until this mystery was no longer, Gaelan trusted only a select few. He twisted around as Maguire and his chosen men were led inside.

Gaelan caught Bridgett's attention, nodding, and the woman seated them, quickly serving food and wine. The haggard O'Donnels stood back, proud and no doubt hungry. Gaelan waved and the servants ushered them to a table, quickly laying trenchers before them so they could not refuse his hospitality. He leaned his head back against the wall, his son tucked close to his side. Unconsciously his fingers sang through the boy's hair and at the tug on his tunic, he looked down into sad green eyes.

"We are surrounded by the enemy, aye?"

Gaelan scoffed a short laugh. "Aye, my lad."

"Then how will we leave to find my mama?"

Gaelan tilted his head and looked at the crowded hall, felt the nervousness of his people. One offense, one cross word, and his hall would be awash in blood. "Good question."

* * *

Ian watched him, taking in details he never thought to see in the mercenary. PenDragon was on the brink of exploding, his every gesture laced with impatience and worry. The big man paced in short steps before the raging hearth as he waited for DeClare to regain consciousness. For a moment he sat in a grand chair, the one beside it painfully empty, his elbows on his knees, his head in his hand. Maguire would swear the man was near tears. Or prepared to rip into the next person who crossed him. Then Connal moved to his side, tapping him, and his head jerked up, his hands falling away. PenDragon's smile was gentle with commiseration and he patted his knee. The boy scrambled onto his lap, burrowing into his side. PenDragon pressed his lips to the top of the boy's head. 'Twas a tenderness he'd never expected to witness, and he assumed Siobhàn had tempered the legendary knight.

Yet resentment bled through Ian. PenDragon had what should be his: this keep, the princess of it, her son. Ian frowned at Connal as the lad stared wide-eyed up at the English lord with undisguised affection and the confidence a child gave only to a hero. There was something achingly familiar about the boy. And he continued to stare, trying to find the source.

Across the hall, Gaelan's gaze shifted, meeting the Maguire's and recognizing his scrutiny of the boy. He cuddled Connal tighter, shielding him. If Siobhàn wanted Maguire to know he'd a son, she would have told him. He cared less if she chose to keep the truth from him for the remainder of her days, as long as she was returned to him. The little boy was Gaelan's only anchor, his single link to maintaining his sanity when he wanted to tear through the country to find out if she was with DeClare when he was attacked. Connal needed him, to be strong and resourceful, to be the father he never had . . . to be patient when he'd so little left. Waiting for Raymond to waken was his only choice. Running off searching would serve to tear Siobhàn farther and farther from him.

Maguire's stare narrowed.

He is my son now, Gaelan thought righteously. *Even if you have sired him, he is mine.*

In the solar, Rhiannon had stopped the bleeding, praising the healer who'd helped Raymond. The wound was mortal and would have laid a weaker man down, she thought, sitting at his bedside. He bore no fever, only exhaustion, and she mopped his brow, frowning when an odd sensation passed over her skin, a pricking awareness too keen to ignore. She twisted, staring at the entrance, then left her chair, pausing, her hand on the door frame as her gaze searched the hall, then beyond to the inner bailey. PenDragon's troops were stripping armor off three men and when a troop pulled the helm off the tallest, Rhiannon inhaled a sharp breath, taking a step.

Patrick.

Several feet to the right Gaelan watched her skin go pale as milk, her eyes filling with despair and fear. His gaze shot to the prisoner, and across the distance the man met Rhiannon's gaze, then instantly looked away. Gaelan experienced a recurrence of the past, his features tightening when he recognized a vague familiarity.

He looked to the Maguire and realized the chieftain made the same connection. Ian arched a baiting brow, as if to accuse Gaelan of being in league with the prisoners. His fists clenched, he avoided a useless confrontation when Raymond called out. Rhiannon immediately spun into the room, hurriedly felt his brow, then checked his bandage.

He was already beside her, kneeling. "Easy, my friend."

Raymond licked dry lips. "Where is she? Bring her to me, I beg you."

Gaelan's features tightened with new misery. "Maguire found you, Raymond, alone."

Raymond groaned, his head lolling on the pillow. "I did not leave her, I swear. She was behind me, on the mount." He cursed over and over, attempting to leave the bed.

"Good God man, you cannot survive this." Gaelan pushed him down and held him.

Raymond lifted his gaze, defeat in his eyes. "I failed you. I'm sorry."

Gaelan could no more be angry with Raymond than he could with Siobhàn, but at the moment, horrible images filled his brain, toying with his composure. Siobhàn was unprotected, facing a killer filled with enough hatred that he could carve the skin from her bones. "I will find her." He stood, but Raymond snagged the hem of his tunic.

"I would speak to you in private." His gaze drifted to Rhiannon and flushing, she left. Gaelan knelt as Raymond settled into the bed, swallowing repeatedly. "I found a door in the earth." Scowling, Gaelan's eyes flared as he reached for a cup, holding it to Raymond's lips, supporting him as he drank. He sank gratefully into the pillows, his eyes closed in pain. "The ground was slanted so all they had to do was ride into the cavern and drop the door of earth over it." His lashes swept up, his gray eyes bleak. "We have been fools, Gaelan."

Gaelan thought of the armored prisoners in his dungeon now, and the ones he'd captured before, covered in the Maguire tartan. "Would we not have trod on at least one of these caves?"

Raymond shook his head ever so slightly. " 'Twas heavily disguised with grasses and leaves and near trees. They attacked at night and the darkness covered their escape. You were right. They have warred wearing armor with the PenDragon crest, and they war with the garments of the Irish." He clenched his fist and smothered a moan as pain needled through his arm. "They are one in the same, Gaelan, one in the same."

Gaelan murmured for him to rest, but Raymond would not have it, grasping Gaelan's sleeve and pulling him close. His eyes were glazed with worry and pain as he said, "I swear to you, Gaelan, I did not leave her behind!"

"I know, my friend, I believe you," Gaelan soothed, but inside he was tormented with fear, raw and blistering.

"Whoever did this"—his gaze darted to his shoulder—"knows I discovered the caves."

Gaelan nodded and stood, abruptly leaving the solar. He stopped short when he found the Maguire in the doorway. Sir Andrew and Niles rushed up behind him, grabbing his arms.

"You dare much, Irish."

Ian jerked on the hold and Gaelan waved the men off. "It seems we have been made fools, the pair of us." Ian's gaze shifted once to DeClare, then to PenDragon. "She lives?"

He'd overheard too much to deny it. "Aye."

Ian's shoulders fell and he rubbed his hands over his face, praising God.

His relief was too real for Gaelan to ignore.

"Then where is she?"

"You kidnapped her once, Maguire . . ." The implication hung like a bleeding limb between them.

Ian's features pulled tight with guilt and shame. "I was a young, love-struck fool, newly jilted and trying to soothe my wounds."

"And now?"

Sadness ghosted through his dark eyes. "I admit that I would have liked to bring you to your knees, PenDragon, but not with Siobhàn's life."

Gaelan stared, desperate to sort through his own confusion for the truth. Could he have invited a killer into his home? Had he found Raymond because he was there when Siobhàn was stolen from him? Was this all a well-laid trap?

"I believe him."

Gaelan twisted to meet Raymond's stare. "You are drugged."

His lips quirked, pain glimmering beneath the half smile.

"Rhiannon is the key, Gaelan. And where is the O'Niell in all this?"

"Rhiannon? You cannot be serious?"

Gaelan merely arched a brow, and the implication struck Ian like a blow to his middle.

"But O'Niell is in the north, fighting the same band as we have."

Gaelan bid Raymond sleep and brushed past, motioning for his men to follow.

"PenDragon," Maguire shouted, and Gaelan paused, twisting, his expression speaking his impatience to be on his way. His gaze swept him, the single look thorough and disturbing. The man trusted no one, Ian thought.

"Come, question these prisoners yourself, Maguire, for Siobhàn is in the south, and O'Niell was last seen heading onto your lands."

Maguire cursed, and flanked by PenDragon's men, they headed to the dungeon.

Chapter Thirty-two

Siobhàn jolted awake with a groan, swallowing thickly, tasting dirt and the cloth stuffed in her mouth. And the foul residue of bitters. She coughed against the rag, her throat burning, the skin raw and rubbing against the thongs of her cloak as she tried sitting up. She failed, her hands bound tightly behind her and stealing her leverage.

Icy air whipped around her feet, driving the chill up her skirts, and she shivered, squinting in the dark, scenting the odor of moss and the sea, hearing the crash of waves. The dampness of wet stone seeped into her clothes. Her head pounded, as if preparing for a great explosion, and her eyes felt gritty. She blinked, praying for a glimmer of light, and wondered why she was here.

Then she remembered.

Hung like a beast for the slaughter.

She recalled dangling, swinging her legs to gain footing on the tree, then suddenly she fell to the ground, choking for air as Raymond, the poor man, rode away.

She prayed someone found him before he died in the saddle. *They carted me away in a blanket,* she thought, *and did not speak.*

Her shoulders tight and sore, she curled on her side, then shifted upright. Wind slipped around her, enveloping her in a tunnel of ice. Without the moon, she could not see an inch in front of her face, and resolutely braced her back against the stone wall, dipping her foot out to feel around her. To her right, she found the floor, and a sweep of her leg brought a strange sound, like the clatter of sticks, hollow and eerie. She extended her leg to the left. For a few inches there was stone, then nothing, pebbles falling, seconds passing before she heard them ping against rock.

Surrounded by darkness Siobhàn did not know if there was a roof above her, but there were walls, for the wind howled through cracks like the high-pitched wail of a banshee. If she called out, who would hear over the sound of the sea?

She tried, once, the effort stinging like broken glass in her throat. Closing her eyes against fatigue, she drew up her knees, working her booted toes under her skirt. *Where is the warmth of my blood when I need it?* she thought.

Suddenly she sat forward, grasping her kirtle, twisting it around her waist until the front was at her back, and felt for the dagger in the pouch. It was gone, as well as the sack.

Jager me, she cursed, and felt the wall for a sharp spot in the rock to cut her bonds. The stone was smooth from weather and age and she fell back against it. The slosh of the sea surrounded her, waves buffeting the shore with the rush of the incoming tide.

Siobhàn knew where she was. The Druid ruins. And in hours the sea would engulf her prison.

Rhiannon tossed the club aside as she stepped over the unconscious guard, then searched his body for keys. Finding none, she cursed the lost option and hurried down the narrow corridor. Dampness seeped into the cracks between stone and mortar, the freshly dug moat worsening the cold and moisture. A day in here and they will surely die, she thought, stopping before the cells.

Three men, but her attention was on the solitary figure imprisoned alone. He did not look up, refusing to acknowledge her beyond a stiffening of his body where he sat in the corner, his knees drawn up, his elbows resting atop.

"Tell him." No response, and she clutched the flat wide bars. "He will behead you afore sunrise. Confess and he will show you mercy." Her whispered words rang hollow with futility.

He scoffed. "There is no mercy for us, woman. Not anymore. Even God cannot forgive me."

She choked on a sob, rattling the bars. "You would throw your life away without a fight?"

He tipped his head back, meeting her gaze, yet he remained silent, unmoved by her pleas, her tears.

"We are damned for our lies, Patrick. For eternity we will pay for the gift we cast aside."

Dark pain skipped across his features like a ripple of water before he masked it.

They stared, defeat and hopelessness shifting between them, and yet Rhiannon still pleaded. "Beg for mercy, please."

Slowly he shook his head and she choked back a sob.

Footsteps came to her, and she reached, her fingertips grazing his cheek briefly, and he closed his eyes, savoring the sweet brush of skin to skin. Then she was gone, running.

Rhiannon darted to the right, farther down the corridor, and slipped around a corner. Something caught on her gown, jerking her back, and she wrenched around to find Gaelan glowering down at her.

He grabbed her arms, hoisting her up to his face. "Woman," he growled in a lethal voice, "I will beat you for your betrayal."

Rhiannon stiffened, refusing to fight as the corner beyond the cells filled with men.

"PenDragon, you cannot think she—"

"Trust not a word from her lips, Maguire." Gaelan hauled her toward the cells, but Ian blocked his path, looking down at Siobhàn's sister.

"Why would he think you had aught to do with this war?"

She glared at him, bright green eyes filled with venom and defeat. "You're the cause of this, Ian."

Ian scowled, yet his tone was deceptively mild. "Clarify your accusation, please, Rhi, for us all."

"You are a selfish man, Ian Maguire. If you had taken her marriage to Tigheran like a chieftain instead of a jealous boy, instead of turning your back on her, she would have had a friend whilst she suffered his abuse for us all." Her gaze raked him in disgust. "You could not be her husband, so you could not be her friend." Ian's features tightened with shame. "Then you thought to come back and take her when our lives were in the balance, call her betrayer and force her to choose between you and her people. *Again*. If you'd sworn to PenDragon, there would be no chance for a war to feed upon."

At her last, Ian's frown deepened with confusion, and Gaelan realized he was either excellent at disguising his emotions or innocent. "She speaks in riddles," he muttered, pushing past and dragging her toward the cells.

Ian followed. Beyond the cells Sir Andrew and Niles helped the groggy guard to his feet, Niles turning him back toward the stairs.

His anger raging out of control, Gaelan released her roughly. One of the prisoners shot forward.

Gaelan turned his head, a sick feeling working through his blood, and in a heartbeat, he reached through the bars and in one jerk, pulled the man close.

"I know you." They stared and Gaelan searched his memory. The eyes, the familiar eyes, he thought. "*Fenian!*"

"Nay," Ian said suddenly from his side. "They would not be party to this."

"I tell you what I know, Maguire." Gaelan spared him a brittle glance, then released the man with a shove. "I killed four of his men on the moors—on your land, less than a sennight ago. And they wore your plaid."

"It seems a popular style of late. As is armor."

Gaelan eyed him, seeing his reasoning.

"They cannot be Fenian, my lord," Driscoll said at once. "He is not big enough. Neither was I." Gaelan scowled for an explanation, for he didn't know an Irishman bigger than his sheriff. "When I was younger, I tried gaining entry into the warrior clan." His skin flushed. "And failed."

"Who is to say they do not gather more?"

Both Driscoll and Ian scoffed. "One of the tests is to run nearly halfway across Ireland," Ian said. "One stumble and you are eliminated."

Gaelan did not believe such a ritual could be endured.

"And most are gifted." Ian's head turned, his gaze pinning Rhiannon. "Like her and Siobhàn . . . and . . . others."

Like Fionna O'Donnel, Gaelan thought. *And my son.*

"Maguire is the one who wants your lands, PenDragon," Rhiannon hissed. "Your title, your wife!"

"I may have a few disreputable traits, Rhiannon, but murder is not among them, and you know how I feel about Siobhàn." Gaelan stiffened. "I would never harm her."

"You betrayed her with your negligence."

"My God, woman, what would you have me do?" Ian said. "I do not have the numbers to fight the English king!"

"But you can cause a war!"

"She is right."

All jerked around to stare at the prisoner.

Rhiannon rushed to the cell door, clutching the bars. "Patrick."

"Hush, Rhiannon." He touched her jaw, his thumb brushing over her cheek, his eyes so bleak Gaelan's chest clenched.

Gaelan stared between the two, pieces falling into place. This was the man Raymond mentioned seeing with Rhiannon. The monk. And the man Siobhàn saw in the forest with her sister. The man she sheltered with her silence. "You masquerade as English and Irish, slaughtering innocents, *your own people,* and hiding behind a legend! To what end but to bring the king's army to your door?"

The man called Patrick stared at PenDragon, his throat working. Finally he sighed, the weight of his deeds pressing down on his shoulders. "To gain your title and lands. And rid Ireland of the English."

"Can you not see 'tis impossible? How could you do this to your own?"

Patrick's chin lifted in challenge. "What would you do, PenDragon, if your family was hostage to your crimes?"

Gaelan's features yanked taut and his gaze jerked to Rhiannon's. Without choice, she'd said. Blackmail.

"We raided and were caught. Instead of the guilty imprisoned or punished, he took the innocent. Our families. And he threatened to kill them if we did not comply."

Gaelan gripped Patrick's tunic, pulling him to the bars, his lips curled in a viscous snarl as he said, "Name the bastard."

"Lochlann O'Niell," Patrick said.

Gaelan didn't take his eyes off Patrick. "O'Niell is sworn. Maguire is not. He would not dare break his oath by attacking me."

"Lochlann's loyalty goes with the highest price," Ian said.

"So did mine, for years," Gaelan remarked with a sliding glance.

"He's not above killing his own to point a finger, PenDragon, and he would not have to break his oath."

Gaelan's scowl darkened with understanding. "A war atween us would put him in a position of power."

"If we killed each other, who would be rewarded?" Ian plied and Gaelan released Patrick.

"An English lord," he said with absolute certainty.

"Not if the king thought an Irish overlord, a loyal man, would suffice," Patrick said, and they looked at him. "He had with Dermott." He glanced between the two. "And O'Niell has been in the king's court, gaining his favor, bringing him gifts. If Maguire and you were dead, once again the princess would be the only thing standing in his way to take all of Donegal. The princess and her son."

Gaelan closed his eyes, the new knowledge crushing through him. "The cart, the scaffolding. 'Tis the boy they tried to kill, and failing that, he went after Siobhàn." Tigheran's half brother would know of the tunnels, he reasoned, and could have used them to put men inside the keep. His gaze jerked to Rhiannon, accusing. What had she done for her love of this traitor? Had she ignored the enemy in the castle, let him get close enough to learn his plans, close enough to murder Meghan?

He turned to the prisoner. "Where is my wife?"

"I do not know."

Gaelan unlocked the cell, throwing the door wide, vengeance twisting his features.

"Patrick, tell him!"

Unmoved by the threat, he said, "I have naught left, Rhi. I would not lie."

Gaelan drew back his arm and drove his fist into his face. Rhiannon screamed as Patrick fell. Gaelan reached for him and Ian latched onto his arm. PenDragon shoved, sending Maguire back against the wall as knights pushed their way into the cell, restraining him.

Gaelan struggled against the human bonds, glaring down at the traitor. "I swear by all that is holy," he snarled. *"I will rip you limb from limb!"*

"We still have to catch O'Niell," Ian said, rubbing his shoulder. "If you kill him, we cannot use him."

"Release me!" They did, and Gaelan plowed his fingers through his hair, trying to see through the facts for a solution, yet he could only envision Siobhàn, vulnerable to a killer she did not recognize. *Ah, love, please be alive.*

"He gathers men to make a final strike," Patrick said, and heads came up, gazes fixed. "He leads this one himself, on *Cloch Baintreach.*"

Ian cursed.

Gaelan tipped his head back, his blood hot with impotent rage. "Andrew, bind him and bring him above."

"The others?"

"They are your captives and countrymen, Maguire." He straightened, staring at the prisoners impassively. "Do as you feel you must." Gaelan grabbed Rhiannon by the arm, pulling her from the dungeon.

Ian stared at the men clad in English tunics and thought of the children, the women and clansmen he'd buried, then spoke the fatal words. "Execute them."

The doors and windows of the keep and surrounding buildings were locked and sealed, only the PenDragon army, the Maguire clansmen and the O'Donnels allowed in the outer ward. She was the only woman. Gaelan stood behind her, forcing her to watch.

"See what your silence has wrought, woman," he said, and she tried not to flinch when Maguire warriors swung the battleax, taking vengeance for the crimes on his clan and beheading the prisoners. Her stomach revolted and she turned her face away. Her gaze landed on Patrick. And her heart broke again.

He stood in the center of the field, his hands bound, his gaze following the bodies as they were carried off the field. Then his focus swung to her. She choked, covering her mouth.

Without expression, Gaelan walked away, leaving her standing alone, abandoned as she deserved. He barked orders for the keep to be opened again, and for his men to assemble in all haste, yet whilst knights donned armor, Gaelan dismissed it, dressing in padded tunic and mail under the warmth of furs. He jerked on Grayfalk's girth, then swung up onto the saddle.

Ian caught the bridle, staring up at him. "Am I under lock and key?"

"I do not trust you."

"I've given you no reason."

Gaelan stared out over the field, the preparations for war. "I admit I need your assistance, Maguire—"

"Language barrier still a wee bit of a problem, is it?"

"Driscoll remains behind—and aye—"

"I will give it, PenDragon."

He met his gaze, a challenge in his eyes. "How much do you offer to heal this land?"

"My word, my honor."

Gaelan searched his eyes for the lie and didn't find it. He nodded, then held out his hand. They clasped, fist over wrist in a warrior's bond. " 'Twill do—for now."

With a quirk of his lips, Ian stepped back, then headed to his horse, and Gaelan wheeled Grayfalk toward the gates.

Rhiannon raced to his side. "What will you do with him?"

Gaelan's face was an unforgiving mask as he stared down at her. "I would sever his hide from his body, but we need him to end this."

"He forfeits the lives of his family, they all do"—she gestured to the bloodstain in the dirt without looking—"to help you."

Gaelan refused to be baited by her tears. Had she spoken up, this would have been solved faster. Had Patrick come to him, he could have stopped this feud before so many were slaughtered like livestock. He leaned down and said, "I have no more mercy."

She staggered in horror.

The young O'Donnel stepped forward. "My lord. O'Niell

keeps the families in Coleraine.'' Gaelan's brows shot up.
'' 'Tis why there is so little to share, I'm thinkin'. There are
too many new families without men to hunt and protect.''

Gaelan nodded, then called for his soldiers. ''Markus.
Assemble three squads, take two wagons of provisions to Coleraine with young O'Donnel here, and bring back any who wish
to live in Donegal.''

''Or south,'' Ian said, his mount sidestepping.

Gaelan eyed him for a moment, then called for Driscoll.
''You are in command.'' Driscoll frowned, clearly wanting to
join the search, yet did not gainsay the order. ''I want a guard
on her every second.'' He pointed to Rhiannon, then met her
gaze. ''Your sister will have no say in your fate, Rhiannon,
understand this. Tend to DeClare and my son.''

Driscoll, grasped her arm, ushering her toward the keep.
Gaelan ordered the weapons and mounts restored to Maguire's
men, the prisoner under Ian's supervision. Ian crossed to Patrick. Before he reached him, Rhiannon tore from Driscoll's
grasp, her body slamming against Patrick's, arms clutching
him, her sobs muffled against his chest.

''Shhh, love, shhh,'' he murmured against her hair. ''Do not
cry for me.''

''I cannot bear it.''

''You will, you must. We were never meant to be, not in
this life. Our treachery has done this and we must suffer the
price.''

His voice was resigned and she hated it, hated that she could
not have the man she loved, that he'd abandoned her only to
return and destroy them again. She tilted her head back to meet
his gaze.

''Give me my dignity in this and keep your own.'' His voice
fractured, softened. ''Do not let my last sight of you be in
tears.'' He bent and kissed her, a ferocious soul-stripping match
that stirred all who looked on. Then he stepped back and allowed

himself to be hoisted into the saddle and bound to it. Ian took the leads, riding after PenDragon.

Patrick looked back over his shoulder only once.

Rhiannon stood alone and proud, honoring him with her stiff spine, her unshed tears. They passed through the gates and she remained perfectly still until they closed behind him.

Then she sank to her knees and wept for the forever her lies had cost her.

Chapter Thirty-three

The sea raged, the crush hammering at her stone prison.

Rain splattered, and she flinched with each drop, the icy water sizzling against her body. The air was colder, the breeze swifter, brushing her hair back from her face as she lifted her head. She glanced about, suddenly aware she was not alone.

Across from her perch, a yawning hole stood where a door had once been. The storm cast shadows darker than night, silhouetting the figure framed in the crooked stone entrance.

She cursed him behind the gag.

He chuckled, thinly sinister and brittle with suppressed anger. And madness.

"I wish I could kill you now."

Her eyes spoke for her. *Do it then.*

"Not yet."

Suddenly he leapt the empty space between them, stones falling over the crumbling edge of the floor, and Siobhàn pressed against the wall till it bit into her back. He squatted and pulled the gag from her mouth.

She spat, working feeling into her jaw. "Who are you?" She could not see his face.

But he snickered as if she was a fool.

She felt the shielding warmth of his body as he moved closer, then the coldness of a blade against her unprotected cheek. "So pretty," he whispered and with a quick flick, pricked her skin.

She turned her face away, but he caught it, forcing her to meet a gaze she could not see. "Why do you do this? I know naught of you."

"I know. 'Tis the sweetest victory, my lady." He's English, she thought. "You will die and never know by whose hand."

"Then what victory is that?"

"Only mine." He dragged the blade against her jaw, down the slender column of her throat, and Siobhàn told herself if he wanted her dead, he would have done it before now. Was he a coward? Or just taunting her?

"Her face peeled away from her skull like the rind of an apple," he whispered close to her ear, and cold wracked her. "She stared into my eyes as I took her nose, her lips."

Siobhàn's stomach recoiled at the image.

"She was alive then," he hissed. "Alive." He tisked, a sound lacking in sympathy or remorse. " 'Twas you I wanted. Only you."

"Why?"

" 'Tis my right!"

"Who *are* you?"

"Your king."

Shadows moved.

Stones crunched.

Lightning cracked in rapid succession, glowing the sky a blistering white and gleaming off the silver blade in his hand.

She inhaled, wrenching back as the tip neared her throat. A swipe, and she felt the sting rip across her skin.

He leapt the crevasse, his figure a winged beast in the dark.

"Know that whilst you sit here in your lavish castle, bleeding your precious regal blood, the bastard will breathe his last."

Her breath shrank in her lungs. Oh dear God!

His knowing laugh slithered between the raindrops. Ugly. Poisonous. "Suffer, lady of Donegal. For all you cherish will be dead by morn."

Siobhàn cursed him, aware she was alone again.

My family dies this night, she thought, tugging wildly at her bonds.

Blood dripped faster down her throat, a warm rivulet splattered by the rain.

Thunder shook the land, threatening to tear it apart.

But it was the beat of hooves that brought the villagers out and to the edge of the street as the PenDragon rode into the tiny hamlet.

He skidded to a halt as Fionna raced forward.

"Where is she?" he demanded, and when her expression fell, Gaelan lost the last vestiges of hope. He bowed his head, raking his hand over his face and releasing a long, shuddering breath. *"Oh God."*

Ian observed him, the agony in his features he thought no one saw, the way his hand shook slightly as he brought it to the pommel. The way his fingers tightened, and the wood beneath the leather cracked.

Fionna stared up at PenDragon and hated to add another burden to the pile weighing his broad shoulders. "Forgive me, PenDragon."

Gaelan frowned, sliding from the saddle. She was terrified. "I will not take this out on you, woman. My God —"

"Then why do you bring him?" She inclined her head to the Maguire.

Gaelan sent a speculating glance his way. "Not as well loved as you think, eh, Irish?"

Ian left his saddle with a jolt. "She holds a grudge."

Fionna advanced on Ian like a hawk to a mouse, and the man stood his ground, his expression masked. "Because of my deed for you, I was banished, Maguire. I have lost my home, my family. Only for this one sennight in years have I known my cousin again." Tears glossed her eyes and Gaelan stepped protectively closer. "And when she is found, they will all turn their backs on me again!" With two hands, she shoved his chest and whirled away.

Gaelan ordered Ian to stay put and followed Fionna, catching her arm and forcing her around. The proud Irish Wiccan stared at her bare feet.

"Forgive my behavior, PenDragon. 'Twas foolish to waste energy on that man. I should simply turn him into a toad and cage him."

Gaelan gazed down at her bowed head, thinking her much like her cousin and wondering what crime she'd committed to get herself banished.

She sniffled, composed, and lifted her gaze. "I found the hole in the earth."

"Show me."

Returning to the mounts, Gaelan swung up onto the saddle, hoisting her before him.

He leaned close to whisper, "He lives, lass."

Her posture withered with relief and Gaelan wondered how long she'd have waited to ask.

"Stupid English fool. I warned him not to go."

Gaelan heard the affection in her voice. "DeClare is stubborn to his duty."

"DeClare?" She twisted to meet his gaze, clearly shocked. "Pembroke's—?"

"Nephew, aye," he finished. "He's rather proud of the association. I am surprised he did not mention it."

"He was not in the mood for talking."

Gaelan's lips flattened into a thin line. "He does not recall you any more than a dream, I fear."

"Good. He does not believe my kind exist."

"Neither did I, but then, he will survive a killing wound only because of your help."

She twisted to meet his gaze. " 'Twas magic that saved him, PenDragon, not me."

"Then for both, I am in your debt."

She looked skeptical.

"You have my word; ask, and if I can provide, I will."

Her gaze sketched him again, as if testing the truth in her mind before she faced forward, silent as they rode into the forest, the trees thick with bramble and low, dying branches. She called him to halt, then she slipped to the ground, going down on her knees and feeling the earth. Gaelan followed.

" 'Twas here, I swear!"

Gaelan knelt, touching her shoulder. "I know it is, lass. Be patient."

"How can you be when she is gone, English?"

"I have no other choice."

Under a flash of lightning, Fionna saw it. He was in agony, tormented with the unknown. Fear clawed at his will and she admired him for his restraint, for the heart so strong he would keep his composure when he was wont to rage.

"Here, PenDragon." Ian pulled the ring, the rope, then heaved. " 'Tis empty."

Gaelan spun away and paced, grinding a rut in the earth. No one spoke, no one moved. The rain came, quick and drenching, and still none uttered a word. Even as his boots splashed. Even as lightning severed the blackened sky. Then he stilled, and in a burst of paralyzed rage he threw his head back and roared like the dragon he was named.

"Feel better?"

He tipped his head to glare at Maguire, then past him to the prisoner. "Where would he take her?"

"His castle, mayhaps. Or a farm near the edge of his lands." His look said he didn't think she was alive and Gaelan ignored it. He had to.

"The Fenians are in the middle of this."

"They have not been in Donegal for years," Fionna defended. "I would know." He jerked a look at her and she backstepped at the savagery borne there. "My brother is one of the clan."

"He's forbidden to speak to you," Ian reminded.

"Shut thy mouth, chieftain," she gritted. "Or you will be croaking instead of sitting there smug in the saddle." Only then did she look at him, her haunting blue eyes filled with bitterness and stabbing through Ian with a force that left a trail.

He opened his mouth to speak when Gaelan pointed at him. "Not a word or I gag you." He turned to Patrick, pulling him from the saddle and slamming him against the horse. "Tell me something that will appease me, traitor, for your life hangs on a slim thread."

Patrick stared, rain pelting his face. "I can show you a dozen caverns, but they will be empty as well. He awaits me in five days. He gathers at the end of the Finn river, in armor." His gaze shifted past to meet the Maguires. "Then onto *Cloch Baintreach.*"

"Nay," Fionna gasped, her gaze tripping to Ian's. Her family was there.

"Then we know where he will be in five days," Gaelan said, as if he did not notice the horror on her lovely face. He stepped back, pulling on his leather gauntlet as he moved to his mount. "Andrew, remain here with your men and comb the forest for a trail. Fallon," he said to the Irishman. "Count our best and pair them to scrap over every inch of this land to the shore. Disguise your trappings." He gestured to the clothing that marked them soldiers. "Trade them, mix them, I do not care, but I do not want to frighten the people O'Niell has already harmed. We do this peacefully."

The Irishman nodded, and Ian watched the man assemble his squads with the efficiency he'd seen in PenDragon's ranks. But it was the fairness and trust bestowed that stunned him more.

"Sir Pierce, take yours to the river's end and remain out of sight. We watch only. O'Niell is mine," he said with crisp command, and Pierce nodded. "Maguire—" Ian's head came around, his jaw bearing an undignified slack. "I suggest you send word to your holdings to prepare, should this not be a lie." Gaelan's look said he would cut Patrick slice by slice if it was. "But for God's sake, be certain they are discreet. This may be our only chance."

"Where will you be?"

"Searching."

"Alone?"

Gaelan held his hand out for Fionna and she climbed to the saddle.

"Not quite," Fionna said with a cryptic look at Ian. His features went tight with understanding, and if she did not know better, she would swear he was afraid for PenDragon.

Gaelan didn't notice the exchange as he wheeled the beast about and tossed, "Keep that bastard alive"—he gestured to Patrick—"until we need him," before riding into the dark.

"She is not dead."

"Sweet Jesu, I pray not."

Fionna tilted her head to look at him. "In your heart, Gaelan. You know."

His features worked into misery. "I want to believe." He halted before her cottage and she slid from the mount, her back to him for a moment before she turned to face him.

The storm whipped at her long hair, dragging it across her throat.

Rain pearled on her upturned face.

"Trust what you hear and see this day, PenDragon." She laid her hand over his. " 'Tis the magic of ancients. Of *your* family." She pressed something into his hand, closing his fist around it. "Your love for her will not fail you." She turned into the cottage and Gaelan opened his hand, staring at the small smooth stone, the color of his wife's eyes.

Clutching it tightly, he kissed his fist and turned into the woods.

In the downpour, Fionna stood in a circle of white stones, naked to nature's wrath, pointing the wand and marking the ground. The ground burst with a ring of blue fire and she laid the branch on a block of stone. She spilled water into a bowl, a sprinkle of herbs, then straightened and raised her hand, palms out, her head dropped back.

She chanted. Over and over.

A heavy blue vapor surrounded her, swept like tendrils to envelop her until she was scarcely recognizable. She faced north, south, then east and west, chanting softly in Gaelic.

"Erinn Fenain. Son of Finn MacCoul. Warrior creed. Come to me. Defend your right, your honor pure."

She repeated the words, and slowly figures joined her in the circle, the shape of tall men surrounding her like towers. Each bore a javelin like a staff, a short sword at their waists and gleaming in the blue light. Then abruptly the blue vapor dissipated, the fires smoking to naught.

The men turned, facing her, the tallest scowling like the thunder clouds clapping above them. "Damn you, witch." He looked around, shrugging into the fur mantle draping his shoulders, trying to recognize the land. "Donegal."

"Welcome home, brother." Fionna despised the eagerness in her voice, but she missed him.

He met her gaze impassively. "All are prohibited to speak—"

"I need your help."

"Your requests betray your honor."

"I was doing what I thought she wanted. What harm was in that?"

" 'Twas a spell without the asking and you were forbidden!" He stepped out of the circle.

"I am still your sister!" She grabbed his arm. "Listen to me now, Quinn, or I will curse you with breasts, then see how you survive."

His lips trembled with a smile.

"Men masquerading as Fenian and English are slaughtering our people."

His smile fell.

"And Siobhàn is missing."

"You could not call me with good news?" he raged.

Fionna gripped his thick bare arms. "Help PenDragon."

Siobhàn whimpered and hated the sound. But images came to her, flashing and receding in her mind with slaps of pain. The back of her skull throbbed mercilessly, the explosion she'd abated for days now threatening to take her life. Her blood still poured.

Her skin warmed, mist rising. She stretched her arms, fighting the bonds, fighting the waves of pain lapping at her head with the beat of the sea. She forced her hands beneath her, beneath her buttocks, her knuckles scraping the stone floor as she tugged and tugged. Her shoulders felt as if they'd tear from the sockets. She rocked from side to side, uncaring of the mash of fragile bones. Her hands jerked forward, tucked beneath her knees, and she worked them under her calves, huddling, stretching her arms to get them over her booted feet. The jerk of freedom drove her back into the wall, her head smacking hard, and pain exploded. She screamed, the agony ripping into the barren night, only the spray of the sea answering her.

For a moment she was still, the horrible night coming in a rush like water from a fall, hard and cold, the sweet with the ugly.

A breeze against bed drapes. A thick trembling hand. And blood. So much blood.

The blade. Oh God.

Tigheran's dagger.

He knows. He knows my lies.

Oh, Gaelan. My husband. My love.

Forgive me.

The terrain was too heavy for Grayfalk and Gaelan towed the creature through the forest. His mantle caught on a curled branch of blackthorn and he wrenched it free, readjusting the fur and feeling as if he'd come full circle. He was decidedly lost, and Gaelan knew there would be no sweet Irish lass running through the thicket to enchant him again.

Sadness bludgeoned his heart, fear for her life already numbing his emotions.

He leaned back against a tree and slumped to the ground. For the first time since before DeClare returned, he closed his eyes. The grit stung, and with thumb and forefinger he rubbed his eyes. The hours waiting for Raymond to waken and dealing with Maguire, the prisoners, was precious time lost to finding her. He'd no notion if he was even headed in the right direction. Bloody hell, he didn't know where he was.

He was a fool to do this alone and should have taken Maguire or Paddy with him.

Horrifying images he'd kept at bay plagued him. Of her

buried alive in one of the caves, of walking past her or over her without a clue. Of O'Niell taking her life when he hadn't the rocks to do it before. *He will kill her once he knows I've discovered his treachery.*

With frantic moves, he removed the stone from his pouch, clutching it tightly in his fist, praying she was alive. For all his brawn and wit, he was helpless. For the soldiers who followed without question, for the riches he'd collected, they held little benefit without Siobhàn.

His eyes burned.

I have no heart.

I am without substance without her. I live because I love her. I am whole and truly a man because of her.

In the rain, Gaelan slid to one knee, his fist against his chest, his sword piercing the ground. He bowed his head.

I beg you. If there is magic in this land, show it to me.

Give her back to me.

Grayfalk stamped. Gaelan pressed his forehead to the hilt of his sword. His throat worked furiously to hold back his anguish, his heart ripping from his chest in pieces.

The torture was killing him, and if O'Niell thought to destroy him, he had. As surely as a blade in the heart, he was dying.

He pinched his nose, then mashed his hand over his mouth before he lumbered to his feet, reaching for the reins. He took a step, the feeling of being watched littering the air around him along with the rain. Gaelan brandished his sword, shoving his wet hair from his eyes as he searched the darkness.

Shadows moved like currents in a velvet black river, bringing a surge of warmth.

The rain lessened.

A mist rose softly, delicately.

Then he saw it, a flicker of light, a glint on silver.

A man stood in the woods, his shoulders mantled with silver gray pelts, his thighs wrapped in leather, his knees bare to fur-lined boots. His hair was long and braided, his beard thick, yet trimmed. Charms hung around his neck and as he stepped closer, he threw the cloak of skins back over his shoulder. His chest was bare and as wide as Grayfalk's.

Gaelan knew who he was without asking, without a word uttered. Gaelan bowed. The respect was returned.

He sheathed his sword. The Fenian turned, glancing back once and nodding ever so slightly, regally. Gaelan followed, then frowned as the man faded in a twist of vapor.

He continued, clutching the stone in his fist.

Siobhàn woke to dawn, the gray-blue sky thick with clouds and dropping rain like stones. She tipped her face to it, lipped water in a feeble attempt to appease her thirst. Her stomach rumbled and coiled, threatening to spill when there was naught to vomit.

The gag lay beside her, large footprints in the dirt.

Then she saw the bones, stacks of them, and a human skull.

She looked away and studied her surroundings. She could see little beyond but stone, crooked and wasting. The ruins in the sea. And when the tide rose farther, she would be washed beneath the waves.

She brought her bound hands to her mouth, using her teeth to tug at the ropes, but the knots were soaked and tight. She sighed, tired, pressing the back of her hand to her throat. She bled without pain, yet could feel it pump with the beat of her heart, and tried to stem it. Her vision foggy, she tried to stand, her skirts heavy with water, her balance wobbly with the loss of blood.

Connal. She needed to get to Connal. He was unprotected. Not even Rhiannon knew he was in danger.

Braced against the wall, she closed her eyes, aching to sleep. But she could not. She had to find a way out. For the child in the keep and the one in her belly.

Suddenly across the crevasse, the crooked entrance crumbled, water fountaining through cracks and gaps as thick stones fell, piling to block her only path out. Rocks spilled, knocking away a portion of the ancient floor, and she scrambled to safer ground, yet more gave, falling to the abyss below.

Chapter Thirty-four

Gaelan trudged on, deeper into Maguire territory, toward the sea. The true Fenian led him here, and he cursed the wind, the rain and the ancient sect that would not offer more to save their princess. Still, battling exhaustion, he walked, rode, then walked some more, overturning loose bushes, seeking clues in the abandoned cottages burned by O'Niell's game. He called her name, then cried it out like a lonely child. No one answered.

He hacked through trees and rode over stone piles, searching.

And found naught but decaying branches and a hovel of rabbits.

On the crest of a hill, he stopped, sheathing his sword in the scabbard lashed to the saddle, then suddenly pressed his forehead to the burnished leather. He slammed his eyes shut and silently chanted her name. Over and over.

And over still.

Speak to me, love. Show me how to help you.

Show me the mist.

His skin prickled and he glanced around at the ground ending ahead, the crash of waves. Swinging up to Grayfalk's back, he rode to the edge, the horse prancing at the loose ground and the scent of the sea. Gulls skipped around a pile of stones several yards beyond the ocean's shore.

The only shape visible was a broken tower, a fine spray shooting up from the center like a spitting dragon. Then Gaelan recognized the thick curl of mist.

Siobhàn held on to the fragments of the wall, gazing down at the rocks and rushing water below. Her weight and the constant rain threatened the ruins. Her head back, she tipped her face to the sky and concentrated.

Gaelan. Hear me.
Feel me.

Gaelan found a way down, following the cliff edge for half a league before racing across the battered shore toward the ruins. Water fountained behind horse and rider, hooves ripping the sand. Mist cloaked the water's surface, tendrils seeking to grip the shore. He slid from the saddle, stripping off his tunic and mail, discarding all but his braies, then diving into the water. He did not think she could possibly be alive beneath the pile, yet when loose stones rolled into the sea he doubled his effort, strong arms knifing through the water. He grasped the edge of a boulder and, hoisting up, he climbed.

Siobhàn!

In his mind the words came, like a whisper, warm and filling him with relief.

I live, my love.

Gaelan choked on his joy and climbed, reaching the summit.

"Siobhàn!"

"Hurry, Gaelan, hurry. The ground falls."

Waves crashed, funneling up to the roofless tower.

Gaelan reached the top, clawing at the mounds of rock and mortar walling her inside. His muscles flexed and strained as he heaved stone after stone into the sea. Then he saw her, clinging to the wall with naught but inches beneath her feet. She cast a look over her shoulder and smiled, relieved and weary and whole.

He smiled hugely.

A piece fell and he shouted her name, for her to be still.

"I do not have much choice, do I now?"

"Tart-mouthed female." He smiled encouragingly, positioning himself on the ledge, cramming the stones into a more secure position.

"Slow-witted Englishman," she muttered back, love in every syllable.

Waves slapped and churned below and between them.

"You will have to jump to me."

She did not argue and nodded, tried turning toward him. Pebbles broke.

"Gaelan!"

"Trust me, my love. Trust that I will not let you fall." Gaelan reached, his palm out.

Siobhàn nodded shakily, terrified of losing everything to her fear. At least her hands were free.

Water shot through the old tower, soaking them, blinding them with stinging salt, and when the gush receded, he swiped at his face.

"Wait for the beat of the sea. And when I tell you, you must jump to me."

"Aye."

"I love you, Siobhàn."

"I love you too, husband."

They counted aloud, Gaelan watching the gush, and when it sucked back, he opened his arms to catch and yelled, "Now."

Siobhàn twisted and flung herself toward him, but the remains of the floor gave just then, dropping her too soon. He lurched, catching her arm.

"Gaelan!"

She dangled over the rocks, the water, spinning, and he grabbed for her gown, hooking his knees and feet on the rocks to keep from going over with her. Her garments ripped. The next surge would tear her from his grasp. He heaved, dragging her up over the edge and into his arms.

She clung, her arms around his neck, their bodies tightly wedged.

Their lungs labored and Gaelan buried his face in the curve of her neck and sobbed like a babe. She joined him, kissing his bare shoulder, his hair, choking on her tears.

It was a long moment before he could bare putting a fraction of space between them enough to look her in the eye.

"I love you," he chanted. "I thought he'd killed you." He squeezed her. "Oh sweet Mother of God, Siobhàn, I wanted to die."

"Shhh," she soothed, stroking his head, feeling him tremble against her and loving him more for it. She tipped her head back. "Kiss me, I beg you."

He did. A tender brush of lips, frightened that she would vanish. She would not have such coddling, cupping his head and pulling him harder to her mouth. Gaelan gave and tasted the sweetness of his wife, his heartache slipping away with the retreating pull of the sea.

And on the rain-soaked land, atop a primitive Druid stronghold, Gaelan felt the magic of Ireland sing through his soul.

" 'Tis only a little cut."

On his knees on the beach, dripping with seawater, Gaelan scowled at the wound, tilting her head back to get a better look. "Little, aye, but deep." He meant for her to bleed to death, the cowardly bastard.

Siobhàn frowned at the black look and cupped his face in her hands. "It stopped bleeding. I am tired and hungry and wish for a bath."

"And where do you propose to find one?"

"Me father's house . . . his old house," she corrected, "is near."

"So is Maguire." He stood, helping her to her feet, then helping her wring the water from her dress.

She tilted her head back, blinking repeatedly. " 'Tis the one he oversees."

At her last words she folded and Gaelan caught her, laying her to the ground and stroking the wet hair from her face. He called her name and her eyes fluttered open, still slits of weary pain.

"Forgive me, Gaelan. I've—"

"Hush." Leaving her briefly to dress, he cradled her in his arms and swung into the saddle. Grayfalk tore across the land, feeling Gaelan's urgency. For his wife, he realized, had lost much more blood than he first thought.

He'd sent couriers to find Maguire and his knights, to bring back the prisoner. And Fionna. They should arrive by nightfall, but Gaelan would not be satisfied until he saw O'Niell bleeding on the ground at his feet. He cursed the bastard who'd left her to die and rage pushed through his blood, taunting him as he paced before the grand bed, soothing him only when he paused to touch her brow, her lips, with his.

Noise from belowstairs penetrated the chamber and he knew the shock of finding him on the doorstep and demanding his way inside drove the meek to seek cover. Gaelan didn't care. Siobhàn was alive and he only wanted privacy with her.

Dropping to a chair, he sighed, then mashed his hand over his face. She was so still, her usually warm skin cool, and he wanted to bark at someone to bring Fionna to him now. But that would be hours, he knew. Instead, he pulled the chair closer and rested his head on the bedding, clutching her hand to his lips.

And then he prayed.

Her arms laden with a tray and a maid at her heels, Fionna rushed into the chamber, yet Ian remained on the threshold, his gaze shooting to PenDragon, asleep at her bedside, her small hand in his callused palm. He could see the stain of tears on the big man's cheek, the weariness in his features, and something broke inside his chest.

"I do not know who looks worse," Fionna muttered, shaking Gaelan gently so she could get to Siobhàn. He stirred and lifted his head, his gaze direct on his wife, then dragging to Fionna's. His relief at seeing her was palpable and he told her how he found her, and of the blood loss.

Ian heard the desperation in his voice.

"Go fill your belly and rest elsewhere, English."

"I will not leave her!"

She gripped his arm, forcing him to meet her gaze. "Neither will I. But you've work to tend." She inclined her head to the doorway and Gaelan's gaze turned to Maguire. When he looked to protest further, she added, "Make yourself useful. Send up a tray of broth and bread. She is undernourished and needs food quickly. And get him"—she pointed to Ian—"out of here."

Gaelan nodded, pleased to have something to do, and strode to the door, grabbing Ian by the shirt and pulling him along with him. Fionna heard him say, "I would not anger her further with your presence, man. You're liable to be growing gills if you're not careful."

* * *

Gaelan paced before the hearth and around him his people gathered, each forming a plan and discarding it for its frailty. He was not paying attention, his focus on his wife and the hours Fionna worked over her. He could not bear it if she perished now. Now when he'd just found her, he thought, and fell into a chair, bending, bracing his elbows on his knees and his head in his hands. He wished for Connal and his smiles and the feel of the little boy in his arms. But they would not arrive till morning. Twice he'd gone above, only to be sent away. Maids flitted in and out of the chamber, carrying buckets of water and baskets of linen, but none would tell him a thing. He was ready to kick the door down and demand Fionna speak with him, yet he knew she would call him when she had news.

He swallowed and lifted his gaze, scanning the group. Knights and Irish hovered over precious paper and trenchers of food, slaking their hunger as they considered each avenue. Gaelan was infinitely proud of these people, their camaraderie.

The prisoner, Patrick, sat alone against the west wall, his hands bound at his back. He focused on the stone floor near his feet, his expression detached, and Gaelan wondered what a man thought of when his hours were numbered.

Tired of waiting, Gaelan pushed into the chamber, past the maids, and strode to the bed.

Siobhàn smiled. "Good day, my love."

He grinned hugely, climbing onto the bed and pulling her into his arms.

Fionna motioned the maids to leave, gathering her things and following. She stilled when she found Ian standing on the threshold. The man stared, his shoulders stiff, as Gaelan and Siobhàn renewed their love in a heated kiss.

Slapping a hand to his chest, Fionna shoved Ian back and pulled the door closed.

"You have lost again, Maguire."

His gaze snapped to hers. "You're taking a good deal of pleasure in that, aren't you?"

"Aye." She swept past him.

He caught her arm, forcing her around. "Is that what you want, Fionna, to see me brought low?"

Her gaze slid over him from head to foot, a glance of pure disgust. "You are no lower than you were when you begged me to conjure for you," she snapped, twisting free.

"What do you want from me? I cannot change the past. I am sorry you suffered, but the clan counsel ruled."

"A counsel of Maguires, aye. You tolerated a bit of embarrassment, leaving till the wounds were soothed, whilst I lost my reputation, my family. My magic came back to me threefold and left me with these." She jerked on the neck of her gown, pulling it down to show the scars across her back.

Ian could not be more shocked.

"Tell me now why I should forgive you."

She turned away, adjusting the gown as she headed belowstairs. Ian watched her go. Oh God, she'd been whipped.

On his knees on the bed, Gaelan could not stop kissing her, touching her, his mouth creating a warm, moist path down to the curve of her breast. "Oh God, I've missed you," he said against her skin and she clutched him, kissing the top of his head.

"And I you, my love."

My love. Gaelan would never grow tired of hearing that. He'd come too close to losing her too often and he never wanted her out of his sight, wanted her to lie with him, let him cherish her. And he pulled her between his thighs, aching to feel skin to skin, heart to heart.

"I want you, Gaelan." She tugged the belt at his waist, tossing it aside.

He groaned. "You are not well enough for this," he murmured, yet hooked the edge of her shift, dragging it down, bending.

"I am, I am. Oh Gaelan," she cried softly as his lips closed over her nipple, drawing it deeply into his mouth. He played there, tasting her scented flesh, but her impatience for him could not be denied. She worked her hands beneath his tunic, feeling warm male flesh as she pushed it up, bending to lick his nipple and eliciting a dark groan from her husband. She shifted restlessly, pressing harder, her mouth wide and provocative on his skin as he shoved the tunic off over his head. She could feel him, heavy and warm against her, and jerked at his laces, shoving her hand inside.

"Oh sweet merciful—" He thrust into her touch, covering her hand and meeting her gaze. "You seek to unman me?"

"I seek to have you inside me, Gaelan," she whispered, then teethed his lobe. He shuddered against her. "And I will not wait a moment longer."

She released him, pulling her shift off over her head, and Gaelan turned away to remove his boots and braies. When he turned back she was in his arms, climbing onto his lap. Naked and warm and eager.

Gaelan cupped her buttocks and ground her to him. Her eyes flared and he ducked, bending her back and taking her nipple into his mouth. He laved and suckled, teased and licked, his velvet-rough tongue slicking a narrow band over her warm flesh. Vapor hovered over her skin like a fragrance and he spread his knees, spreading her thighs wider and dipping into her softness. Moist flesh slid over his touch and she gripped his arms, gasping.

"Knock knock," he growled, circling the bead of her sex over and over, slick and ready.

"Oh Gaelan," she moaned darkly. "Do come in."

She wrapped her arms around his neck and, cupping her bottom, he lifted her. Her legs closed around his hips as he drove into her in one swift stroke. She moaned, fused with him, feeling him pulse through her to her soul. She met his gaze, her fingers sifting through his hair. "I love you," she choked on a breath.

He rubbed her sides, fingered the curve of her spine as his gaze rapidly searched her face, followed the drape of her hair and wished she wore the bells, before coming back to meet her gaze. His eyes glossed.

And her expression crumbled. "Oh, Gaelan."

"I . . . was lost . . ." His throat worked. "Without you, I am naught but a stray mongrel without a place to belong. I need you so badly. You've shown me what living is and without you, I merely exist."

"I live to love you, Gaelan." She stroked his hair from his temple. "Come, welcome me home." She laid back, taking him with her, her gaze locked with his.

Braced above her, he withdrew fully, the moment suspended, his arousal brushing, taunting. He plunged and retreated, never breaking eye contact. It was more intimate than they'd ever shared, though bodies melted, yielded, hearts sang and opened wide for the pour of new love. Gaelan made love to her soul as well as her body, exquisitely, with great care to her pleasure. His every touch spoke of how much he adored her, how he missed her smiles and the sound of her voice, that he never wanted to be apart from her like that again.

And she heard him, heard the sound of his heartbeat, felt it pulse with every smooth stroke of his body into hers. Strong and ruthless, in her arms he was gentle, in their bed he let himself be vulnerable, shedding the cape of his title and be the man she loved. The man who filled a room full of jewels to please her and left her heritage untouched in a dusty chamber. The man who let her challenge him with a javelin and so easily loved a lonely little boy.

Her eyes teared as she smiled up at him, touching his lips, the column of his throat, felt the power hidden beneath the bronzed skin layered over his wide chest. And still she wanted more, and lured him in ways only she could, in the possession in her eyes, with the heat of her passion.

She felt the motion of his hips, hers tilting to greet him, her legs wrapping him in her supple warmth. The mist rose, curling around them, cocooning them in the massive bed, her ancestors' bed, shielding them from the outside world, from the treachery and lies that could yet tear them apart. In love and fear and desperation for the spine-tingling rapture, Siobhàn clung to him, her breathy gasps spilling like spiced wine into his mouth.

He drank of her, pushing, pushing, slick and strong. Savage.

Her body clawed for him, voluptuous pleasure flexing around him.

He chanted her name, called her daughter of the mist, his gaze never leaving hers as he drove her across the sheets—as her body bowed beneath him in feminine splendor—as rapture exploded across her incredible face.

She cupped his jaw, holding his gaze, and he shoved once more, disjointed Gaelic tumbling from his lips as the exquisite thrash roared through him and into her. He held her tightly, suspended in the dance, blood and sinew and muscle quaking with raw pleasure.

His breath escaped in a long rush of pure masculine completion.

Tender mercy in her eyes, she smiled, pulling him down for a kiss, and he came to her, rolling to his back, cradling her head in his rough palms and ravishing her mouth.

"God above," he rasped. "I lose a piece of my soul every time that happens."

" 'Tis not lost, 'tis given in love."

Slipping a coverlet over them, the lord of Donegal snuggled his lady in the protective shell of his body, and together they sank into needed slumber. For a few precious hours, they ignored the world beyond and the secrets not yet uncovered.

* * *

Tucked to his side, Siobhàn watched him sleep, her heart smiling to be near him and whole again. Tears wet her eyes as she looked out over the chamber, sparse for its lack of use. 'Twas time to confess. Would he banish her here?

He stirred, sitting up as she did, then frowning. "Why do you weep?"

"I've a confession, my love."

His heart skipped a beat. "Speak of it, love. I'll have no secrets atween us now."

She looked at him then, and he knew that whatever she concealed, he would not be pleased.

"I know why O'Niell tried to kill me, of the accident with the cart . . . 'Tis because of Connal." She lifted her gaze. "He is not Tigheran's son."

"I know." Her features pulled. "I suspected as much when Driscoll said he was born in the abbey in late winter. Tigheran had only died in the spring, Siobhàn." After a few false starts, he said, "Connal is Ian's son."

Her lips quirked a fraction, almost in amusement. Therein lies the dark seeds of his jealousy, she thought. "Nay, he is not."

His brows drew tighter.

"He's Rhiannon's."

He surged to his feet. "What! This cannot be. He is not even *yours?*"

Flinching, she turned her face away, crushing the bedclothes in her fist, and instantly contrite, he sank to the mattress again, taking her hands, bringing them to his lips.

"Forgive me, love. Speak what you will."

"Rhiannon was betrothed to a laird in the north, in Antrim, but he died unexpectedly. She'd already left to meet him and did not learn of his death till her arrival there. She was escorted back by the overlord's captain of the guard. And she fell in love with him. When she reached the abbey he was summoned to return. She found herself with child and abandoned. 'Twas then she sent for me.''

His gentle smile soothed as he said, ''I thought there were no bastards in Ireland?''

''Aye, but there must be a claim, Gaelan, support and acknowledgment in the honor price, or she is shamed by the lack.''

''Did she not try to send him word?''

'' 'Tis much to trust anyone with such information when 'twas secret still. But aye, she sent word without response and assumed he did not want her or the child. He denied it, insisting he'd gone to the abbey, but the sisters would not speak to him. Because they had already given their faith and secrecy to me.''

''He told her? Then they have corresponded.'' A horrible sensation slithered through him.

''He is here, Gaelan, wanting to claim Connal as his son and Rhiannon as his woman.''

''Connal is my son!'' Gaelan stood abruptly, turning away from the bed and jamming his legs into his braies. ''And I will be damned if I let that traitorous bastard get near him!''

''Gaelan, remain calm, please.'' He turned back to her then, sweeping her off the bed and into his arms. For an instant he simply held her, seeking peace in the sudden turmoil of his mind. ''You know of him, how?'' she said, cupping his face and holding his gaze.

'' 'Twas the eyes that were familiar, so like my lad's.''

My lad's. He loves him so, and she did not know how to break his heart over this. ''He was the man in the glen, my love. The Fenians, the false ones you thought were Maguires.''

His features tightened and slowly he released her. ''Aye, and I suspect we owe him a debt with a runaway cart.'' He pushed his fingers into his hair, then rubbed the back of his neck. ''But he is also a traitor.''

Siobhàn's eyes widened. "Nay," she whispered, falling back on her calves.

"Patrick sides with O'Niell, Siobhàn. O'Niell threatened to kill his kin if he did not war for him."

Her eyes glossed. "Oh Gaelan, all those people, slaughtered like animals. Oh, if only they'd come to us."

"Why would he think we would help? We had his son. Two caught have been dealt with." She winced at the finality of that. "And Patrick arrived with Ian." He waved, as if to dismiss the matter for the moment, and sat beside her. "Tell me, love, why did you do this? Why would Rhiannon give her son to you to raise?"

She sighed, fidgeting with the edge of the sheet. "Word of Tigheran's death reached the abbey first. Donegal's leader, their king, was dead, and I was scarcely keeping the people from feuding amongst themselves when he first left for England. Tigheran made no secret of his love for Devorgilla and his distaste for me." Her lips twisted sourly. "They followed his lead and would turn on the MacMurroughs again if I did not do something." She gripped the sheet so hard it tore. "Then all I'd suffered would have been for naught. Tigheran was dead and Donegal needed a leader. They needed an heir." She lifted her gaze to his. "Rhiannon was in a precarious position. She birthed the child and handed him over to me."

"You returned with the heir and ruled in his stead."

"Aye."

His shoulders drooped and he stared at his hand clasped around hers. " 'Tis why you begged me to accept him, to care for him if aught happened to you. You were afraid Patrick would try to take him back and reveal your secret."

She nodded, sniffling.

"He won't, Siobhàn. He has no rights after his crimes. And Rhiannon must be punished for her secrets. Though I do not believe she understood 'twas O'Niell behind it, she was aware of the treachery and her silence cost lives.'' A pause and then, ''Will Rhiannon admit to being his mother?''

''Never. If only to protect me from the lie born those years past.'' Siobhàn shifted off her knees to sit beside him, the sheet scarcely concealing her lush body. ''What will you do to her?''

Gaelan tipped his head. ''She is your sister and Connal's birth mother, but I cannot be lenient.''

She nodded, understanding the depth of her sister's hand in this. ''I think O'Niell knows Connal is not Tigheran's son.''

Gaelan cursed.

''Forgive me, but 'tis what he said.''

His eyes flared with fresh rage. ''He visited you in that place? Damn the man for his arrogance!'' He started to leave the bed and she grabbed his hand.

''His accent was English, yet it must have been him.''

''Owen?''

''Nay, I'd recognize his voice.''

''What did he say to you?''

''All I loved will perish. The bastard will die.''

Gaelan was already at the doors, bellowing for his knights and giving orders to bring Connal to him at once.

Chapter Thirty-five

As usual when Gaelan was upset, he wore a rut in the floor. And though she had every confidence in Driscoll to keep her son safe, apparently her husband trusted only himself and wanted Connal with them. Quickly.

Siobhàn watched, then called to him. He did not respond, rubbing the back of his neck and making another turn about the chamber.

"Gaelan!"

"What!" He jerked around, then sighed. "Forgive me, love."

"Am I forgiven?"

He lowered his hand. She looked so forlorn, sitting at the edge of the bed, her hands folded on her lap, a borrowed dressing gown wrapping her body. He came to her, going down on one knee.

"There is naught to forgive, my love. You'd little choice and found a solution to a delicate problem." A little relieved moan escaped her and her eyes teared.

"Oh, do not weep, love, shhh," he hushed. He felt helpless and tortured when she cried. "Your people had their heir to keep them together, your sister kept her reputation and Connal is well-loved, a fine lad. Would that I had a parent like you when I was a boy."

She ran her fingers over his dark hair, touched his features. "You will have the chance yourself, Gaelan."

His brows furrowed. He looked completely confused, so very male.

"I carry your babe."

The color drained from his face and he looked her over as if searching for signs before bringing his wide gaze to hers. He swallowed deeply. "We—we've made a child?"

Her lips twitched a bit. " 'Tis the usual result of so much loving, husband."

"Oh merciful God." His voice fractured, broke, his hand trembling as he brought it to her belly, smoothing the tiny life shrouded inside, then very quietly, he laid his head there, his arms slipping around her waist. "Ahh, my princess."

Her fingers sifted through his hair and Gaelan sighed, squeezing his eyes shut and thanking God for the day King Henry sent him here.

The meal was subdued, for all waited for the hours to pass and bring them to the moment of conflict. Yet Siobhàn and Gaelan had only eyes for each other, Ian thought, watching them. He fed her, poured her honeyed wine, and although his own experience proved PenDragon a fierce man, Siobhàn tempered his mercenary soul. A knight called to PenDragon, and he turned away to address him. Ian leaned close to Siobhàn.

"You love him, don't you?" He knew the answer, had known it from the moment he'd first seen them together, yet chose to ignore it for an old love cheated away from him by war. A love he'd abused.

"Aye." She glanced at Gaelan's back. "More than my life."

Ian sighed, resolute. "Can you forgive me for the wrongs I've done you?"

Her lips curved. "I forgave you years ago, Ian. 'Tis Fionna's forgiveness you must seek. You ruined her."

Ian's expression darkened with shame, his posture stiff as he glanced at the dark-haired woman. As if sensing his gaze, she looked up, venom in her blue eyes.

He deserved it, regretting his foolishness those years past and the price she paid. He would beg her forgiveness and prayed she'd accept. He turned his attention to Gaelan, his chair appearing small for his grand size, and Ian remembered his tenderness with a small motherless boy, the slow agony in his face when he was forced to wait for DeClare to wake and, when he'd discovered his wife was unprotected, the supreme control he exhausted. He could have killed the traitors on sheer suspicion, yet gave the matter over to a countryman. One he did not trust.

"He is a worthy man."

Tapered brows shot up.

"He offered only fairness and trust these past days, Siobhàn, when I know he wanted to slaughter and rage to find you."

She scoffed a short laugh. "Then I am thankful I was no there. Trust him to keep this land together, Ian. I do."

Gaelan turned back, glancing between the two, then smiling at his wife.

"I commend you, Maguire; you've kept this keep well stocked and prepared."

Ian glanced around at Siobhàn and PenDragon's holding. "I chose a good steward."

"Inform him that he remains as long as he wishes."

Ian nodded and Gaelan focused on Siobhàn, but when the man did not move, he frowned. "Have you a problem Maguire?"

"I'm afraid so."

Gaelan arched a brow.

"I'm wondering how delicious crow tastes these days."

Gaelan sputtered with sudden laughter. "I fear I've eaten my share, Irish. My wife insisted you were innocent."

Ian flashed Siobhàn a tight smile and a regal nod. "But I did not help end this treachery. I tried my best to see you fail."

Gaelan leaned back in his chair. "I did my best to see you hung."

"I would say you are well even, then," Siobhàn added, and Gaelan looked at her, aghast.

"Nay, we are not. And will never be."

Gaelan's gaze flew to his.

Ian stared at him for a long moment, admiration for the man swimming to the surface. PenDragon ruled without his personal bias, and with regard to Ian's part in this foul treachery, he'd every right to misjudge. Ian had given him no other choice and made it abundantly clear he'd desired his woman. But that was in the past, Ian thought, and a freedom suddenly swept through his soul at the admittance.

Ian withdrew his sword, and around them servants jerked back, sharp breaths and whispers filling the hall. He did not kneel, but placed the sword on the table before Gaelan, laying his hand over the hilt. "I swear my oath to you, Lord Donegal."

Gaelan stared, solemn, thinking of the pride that cost this fine man, then stood and held out his hand. Wrist to wrist, they clasped.

A lump formed in Siobhàn's throat, her gaze darting between the two. And so the healing begins, she thought.

Connal raced into the keep pell-mell and into Gaelan's arms. "You did it! I knew you would."

Gaelan hugged him, loving his little arms tight around his neck, the way he kicked with excitement. "And how did you know that?" He swung him down to cradle him like a babe, then with a false gasp, he sharply released his torso, letting him drop a fraction before holding him out by only his ankles. Connal giggled wildly before Gaelan heaved him into his arms again.

"Because you are big and strong and mighty. And because you are me father."

Gaelan's heart broke open just then and he clutched him to his chest. "And you are my son," he whispered. Over the lad's shoulder he met Patrick's gaze and felt a sting of regret for the man, but if he survived their plan, he would be brought before the king for trial. Patrick's gaze scraped over Connal with a longing that was bitter and poignant, before his eyes clashed with Gaelan's.

They stared for a moment, then Patrick nodded ever so slightly. Nodded his acquiescence. With a sigh, Gaelan returned it in kind, then left the hall, carrying the child abovestairs to his mother as Driscoll hoisted Patrick from the floor. He led him outside where the army prepared to ride.

Gaelan strode quickly to the small stables, seeking Reese the broken bridle in his fist. He stopped short when he heard the disguised murmur of voices. Cautious and hating that there were still betrayers yet to uncover—the one who set the car in motion and Owen's strange absences—he slowed his steps moving to the rear.

He caught sight of Sir Owen slipping beyond and into the small cookhouse. Gaelan followed and found the man with his arms locked around a slender girl, his mouth devouring hers. And she was responding. Vigorously.

Gaelan cleared his throat. The pair separated and Gaelan recognized Driscoll's daughter.

"Is this why you would not speak of where you were?"

"Aye, my lord. Driscoll forbade her to associate with th

English. I feared for her and her father's anger''—Owen flushed a little—"and I would not shame her.''

"You suspected Owen and we knew, until you did not, Father would not give his blessing.''

If Gaelan did not understand what the man was feeling, he would have fined him for going against Driscoll's wishes. But he did and was more than a bit relieved 'twas a woman who'd stolen Owen's time. His gaze moved between the pair, the familiar way Owen laid his hand at her waist, and knew he'd best be quick about repairing this situation.

His gaze fell on the girl. "Are you still pure?''

She turned bright red and Owen pushed her protectively behind him. "My lord!''

Gaelan had his answer, fighting a smile. "I will speak to Driscoll.'' Peeking around Owen, the girl beamed, yet Gaelan put his hand up, staying her joy. "I cannot order him to give his only daughter to you, Owen. You may have some work involved.'' Just because Driscoll and Gaelan were friends did not mean the Irishman was willing to accept an English knight into his family. "The men assemble.'' Owen straightened and nodded, kissing her once before heading outside.

Gaelan eyed the lovely young girl. She flushed and looked at the floor.

"Behave yourself, lass. And get you to your lady's side.''

"Aye, my lord.'' She bobbed a curtsey. Gaelan watched her flee and did not miss the smile wreathing her innocent face.

Now, he thought, who put the cart in motion?

Siobhàn gazed out the window, toward the sea so close she could feel the mist. Connal rested in the great bed, a tiny speck curled in the soft center. Her lips curved with recent memory. When Gaelan told him he was to have a sibling and entrusted him with the secret, Connal had raced into the room, leaping to the bed and jumping enough to shake the posted frame, then plopped on the cushion and giggled.

Then he proceeded to offer his suggestions for names. For his sister, he declared.

Resting her head against the casement, she sighed, wishing Gaelan were here, safe. His plan of attack, to beat O'Niell to Cloch Baintreach, was risky, and she feared for his success. Even with so many men willing to die for the chance to capture O'Niell. Regardless, a small contingent was left behind at the modest keep, yet without an outer curtain for protection—for the stone building was not meant as a powerful fortress, but a true home and safe retreat for the small amount of fishermen living near the shore, they were vulnerable. And the hall was crowded with people.

She felt secure with so many about, for not in a century had anyone tried to scale the cliffs hemming the province.

"He will be hours, Siobhàn. You should rest and be prepared when he returns."

Siobhàn smiled, then turned her gaze to Fionna. "I've slept enough, but why do you not join Connal and nap, cousin?"

Fionna blinked rapidly, then looked away. "You would trust me with your son?"

"Of course."

Only her gaze shifted, ridicule and years of isolation laying there.

"I was not part of the counsel who banished you, Fionna. But I ask your forgiveness for my lack of conviction. My one excuse is that I felt you were a willing conspirator to drug and kidnap me when you knew well that I *had* to wed Tigheran."

"I'd thought you wanted to be with Ian."

"Not at the cost of lives."

Fionna rubbed two fingers over the skin between her eyes. "I know, I swear I knew this then, but he convinced—"

"He does have that charm about him."

Fionna's look went sour as week-old milk. "Aye, like the maggots beneath a dead log."

Siobhàn smiled, crossing to her and taking her hands in hers. "Forgive yourself, cousin, then forgive him."

Fionna's gaze faltered. "Ofttimes I've only my anger to keep me company, Siobhàn." No man would want her the way she was now, scarred and bitter. "And I choose not to forgive him."

" 'Tis your decision, cousin, but you needn't be alone." Siobhàn tried looking under her bent head. "You've a family to join, if you chose."

She tipped her head, eyes wide. The same eyes, crystal blue and so light only the black line around the irises gave them substance, teared.

"Welcome home, my cousin," Siobhàn said, pulling her into a warm hug.

Over her shoulder Fionna squeezed her eyes shut, ignoring Ian standing just beyond the threshold, and the dejected droop of his shoulders.

Siobhàn stirred from a nap she hadn't meant to take, frowning into the dark. The door burst open and she lunged for the sword Gaelan had left her.

"He's coming!"

She recognized Fionna's voice and relaxed. "Gaelan?"

"Nay," she gasped, out of breath. "O'Niell and his army!"

Siobhàn staggered, then darted to the window. "Sweet lady," she whispered, awed by the sight of the hundreds riding toward the small keep, torches lighting the ground like hellish spires. Banners, false banners of her husband's crest, snapped in the breeze.

"But . . . Gaelan is riding to the west!"

And they would be slaughtered. Whilst the lord of Donegal rode to save a castle that did not need saving.

* * *

"I knew I should have gone along," Ian muttered, arming himself and every able man about. He even pulled the ancient weapons hanging on the wall.

"You can't think to fight them alone, with a handful."

"What would you have me do, Siobhàn, open the gates and offer him scones?"

"It worked once."

He looked at her, handing over the long bow and murmuring to the young servant to hunt down arrows and take position in the turret before he came to her. " 'Twill not work this time, princess. He does not want this place, only to slaughter us all but a few who will give account to PenDragon's wrath." His handsome face mirrored her fears. They had no chance. "We can only seek to delay and pray Gaelan realizes his mistake and returns."

That would take hours, they both knew, and Siobhàn swallowed back the frustrated scream rising in her throat.

"Take the women and children to the towers," he told her and she nodded, holding her hand out for Connal, then crowding the folk up the staircase.

Ian strode to the arrow loop, watching the army advance.

A voice from below spoke to him, a whisper meant for his ears alone. "Ask me and I will weave a spell to protect us, Maguire. But you must ask." Only then could she work magic for others. And none, ever, for herself. To disobey the rules of her banishment, the elders of her coven, was not without grave result. But for her family, she would break them regardless, to keep them safe.

Ian kept his gaze out the arrow loop as he said, "Never again will I make a request of you, Fionna."

"Not even to save lives?"

"Not even to save my own."

"Then you give me little choice."

Ian jerked a look at her, but all he saw was a pale blue bird hovering in the air. It swooped, forcing Ian back before slipping through the narrow arrow loop.

Flanked by the strongest and largest, he rode the line of troops, feeling the power in their numbers, the blue banner with the bar sinister tight against the wind.

"Sir," his second called, riding up beside him. "We veer; *Cloch Baintreach* is—"

"I know exactly where the castle is!" he shouted over the rumble of hooves. "Let the king deal with Maguire." Stone Widow, *Cloch Baintreach*, was of little consequence now. Especially when PenDragon was occupied with his search for Siobhàn and whilst most of his army were scattered over the land, he would seize the weakness. A pair of strategic keeps, this one, then onto the next, banking the shore near Sligo. The stronghold in sight, he slowed, better than a hundred warriors reining behind and forming a semicircle around the stone keep.

Victory surged through Lochlann's veins, pounded like molten steel through his heart.

PenDragon warring on the Maguire was a just move, for Ian refused to swear his oath. He was the outsider. And paying tribute to an English bastard had gone on long enough. After this he would kill the bastard she passed as his brother's son.

He pulled the helm down over his features, the iron molded in a duplicate of PenDragon's.

"Yield or perish," he shouted with the accent of the English he'd mastered.

None showed.

He motioned, and men tipped torches to the ground, setting it aflame. Fire crept closer. Horses stomped, the scent of smoke dancing over them and spinning fear.

'Twas a manner of PenDragon, burning them out.

Suddenly the flames softened, the air warm and graying with

mist. Lochlann glanced around, then ordered the battering ram positioned.

A figure moved on the parapet, climbing to the battlements.

He tipped his head back and as the figure straightened, behind the helm, his features went slack. *Siobhàn.*

He blinked. Nay. She was dead. She had to be. The tide was high and he'd made certain the floor was weakened enough for her to fall. She could not have lasted—yet vapor spun in ever-deepening swirls around the base of the keep, cloaking one turret and reaching for the next level. Lochlann would not be deterred by a little fog.

"Ram the gates."

Soldiers rushed to position the massive wheeled log before the doors.

Suddenly they opened, a single figure sauntering forward as if to meet a caller coming to visit.

Lochlann's eyes widened.

"You think to slaughter us all, PenDragon?" Ian said. "We are defenseless."

"Then lay down your weapons and yield."

"I cannot."

His horse lurched, and O'Niell brought his sword down to tuck under his throat. "Yield and give me my wife!"

Maguire's brows drew down. How did he know Siobhàn was here? "Why would she be here? Have a fight, did you?"

"Give me the little bitch!"

"I take exception to that, chieftain," another voice said.

Lochlann jerked a look to his right.

His sword a'ready, the soldier pulled the helm from his head, tossing it aside.

Lochlann stared into the ice-cold eyes of Gaelan PenDragon, immediately raising his own weapon in defense. The ramifications of his presence hit him square in the chest. "You are outnumbered. Shall I kill you both now?"

The crash of hooves blistered the cold air, soldiers riding

toward the keep. Panic erupted. Men, his men, tore the false tabard from their chests, helmets from their heads, and Lochlann glanced, recognizing Driscoll and Niles, Owen and Fallon.

Lochlann met Gaelan's gaze.

Weapons trained on each other, they slid from their mounts, shoving the horses aside. "Come, traitor," Gaelan said. "Appease your soul on the end of my blade. Quickly."

Lochlann unhooked the helm, removing it. Then he smiled. All was not lost, he thought. He could kill the Cornish bastard and be done with this matter entirely. There wasn't a man amongst his flock who would risk the lives of his kin.

English and Irish warriors rode in all directions, too numerous to avoid, and half of O'Niell's army threw down their weapons and tried to flee. At Sir Owen's command, they were surrounded, soldiers binding them. But more than half chose to battle, and the sudden clash of sword, the thunk of javelins into soft flesh seared the midnight air.

In the center of the field, Gaelan and O'Niell circled each other.

"Come. Die as swiftly as your brother did."

"Tigheran was a fool," O'Niell said, and Gaelan realized he'd known all along that he'd killed the Irish overlord. "He knew naught of taking what he wanted. Naught of construction of a fortress, naught of who's favor to cull." His gaze flickered to Siobhàn on the turret. "Nor of the right woman to keep."

Gaelan heard the hunger, the twisted love in his voice. "Neither of you deserved her."

They sidestepped, neither advancing nor retreating. Around them a battle waged, O'Niell loyalists defending their clansmen as Lochlann shrugged carelessly. "Mayhaps, but I've the right. And when you lay bleeding on his land, PenDragon, I will have her."

Gaelan's expression turned molten, black with vengeance.

"And when she and her sister are dead, I will have her lands."

Gaelan scoffed, tired of this game. He swung, battering O'Niell back with decisive lashes. "Every MacMurrough, O'Donnel and Maguire for leagues will have your hide."

They lurched apart. "Not if the king grants them."

"Henry is not a fool."

Lochlann struck, but Gaelan caught the blade, letting it slide to the hilt and bring him face to face with his enemy. "Your captives in Coleraine have been freed," he taunted, and with a shove drove him back, and the contest continued.

Lochlann thrust, his strikes hard and ringing down Gaelan's arm. Gaelan retaliated, blow after blow, forcing Lochlann to step back. Still the chieftain swung, a second blade in his free hand. His sword clutched in both hands, Gaelan advanced, a wide arch nicking him on the shoulder, yet having little effect. He tried for more.

Surrounding them, the PenDragon army subdued the raiders and there was silence as the lord of Donegal defended his people.

He fought without mercy.

He fought to kill.

He fought for the love of a land he called his own.

Lochlann saw his months of work falling about him, his men dying and pleading for mercy.

PenDragon refused to give it. He lashed and lashed, each strike ringing with bitter anger at the lives lost.

Lochlann was no match, and winded, his aim faltered.

Gaelan raised his sword for a final blow.

From out of the darkness a man shouted a harsh war cry, running toward Gaelan's back.

Siobhàn gripped the stone ledge, helpless as the man raised a sword to cleave her husband. Suddenly a figure darted into the path, taking the downward swing and the impact meant for Gaelan. Yet as he did, he thrust his sword upward and into the man's heart and as they fell, Siobhàn recognized the attacker as Tigheran's retainer.

And Gaelan's savior was Patrick.

Her gaze flashed to her husband just as he brought the blade down, severing Lochlann's arm. O'Niell dropped to his knees, blood fountaining from his stump.

"For those you have murdered," Gaelan roared. "You die without honor!" Gaelan swung, separating his head from his shoulders. The head rolled. The body fell with a decisive pound to the cold earth.

He stared, breathing hard, then stabbed the sword in the ground. He lifted his gaze and met Ian's across the carnage. Ian staggered, clutching his bleeding shoulder and bowed.

A cheer rose.

Gaelan acknowledged it, swiping the back of his hand across his sweaty face.

A voice called his name, sweet and feminine. He jerked a look at the gate, then strode across the bloody field as Siobhàn ran toward him. The impact of her body drove him back a step as he wrapped her in his embrace. For a long moment they simply stood, locked, letting the sound of their heartbeats envelop them.

"Oh dear lord, I thought I would see you die!"

"You doubt my skills," he said with mock insult.

"Nay, oh nay." She kissed him quick and hard. "But Tigheran's retainer attacked your back . . ." She pointed and Gaelan saw the pair slumped across each other, a sword impaling the retainer. "Patrick saved your life."

Gaelan walked to the bodies, pulling O'Rourke's man off, then going down on one knee. He stared at the face of Connal's father, whispering a prayer, then closing his vacant eyes. "Rest peacefully, Irishman. Your son is safe and loved."

Siobhàn moved up behind him, laying her hand on his shoulder, and he covered it, releasing a deep sigh. "Come, my husband, 'tis time to go home."

* * *

Beyond the walls of the solar, the revelry permeated the air with laughter, the clink of tankards raised in toasts, yet in the privacy of stone and stained-glass windows, Rhiannon stood silent, keeping her tears at bay as Gaelan spoke.

"He died valiantly, sister. He gave his life for mine."

She nodded, mute, and Gaelan could see her throat working to hold back great, wrenching sobs. "I am truly glad that you prevailed. Though I knew you would." She lifted her gaze, sliding once to Siobhàn standing beside him. "If my lord would permit, I wish to enter the abbey."

Siobhàn inhaled, her hand clasping Gaelan's, yet she remained silent.

"You will not change your mind?" Gaelan ventured. "Remain here?"

She shook her head vigorously. "My heart died with him, my lord. He was not the best man to love, nor the wisest. I tried to convince him to come to you—" She stopped, swallowing hard. There was no point in matching wits over what they should have done. "In death he will pay for his crimes. And in life, I must pay for mine."

"Nay!" Siobhàn said, rushing to her.

"Shhh," Rhiannon hushed in a gentle voice, tenderly pushing a stray curl from her forehead, feeling as if each cut and bruise on her beautiful face were struck by her own hand. "I must go. I need to find peace with what I have done, sister." She tipped her head, her lower lips trembling, her eyes glossed with unshed tears. "You were a far better mother than I could ever be, Siobhàn. He's a fine boy"—her voice fractured with her torment—"and under Gaelan's tutelage, he will be a fine man. What you choose to tell him is your decision. I release you of our pact and I relinquish any claim to him."

Siobhàn looked up at Gaelan, then to her sister. Briefly, they hugged, and Rhiannon turned to Gaelan, awaiting his decision.

"To the convent, then."

Rhiannon's shoulders sagged with relief and Gaelan bent, pressing a kiss to her forehead. Her tears fell, his forgiveness in the simple touch. She turned and left them alone.

Gaelan held his wife, feeling her sorrow, and would have stayed there, except Connal raced in, happily screaming, "Father, come see!"

Gaelan leaned close to his wife, brushing his mouth over her temple as if to soothe away the marks left on her beauty. That she held his child in her body after all she'd suffered was a miracle neither of them could ignore. God shined upon them, he thought as she patted his hand with understanding, smiling down at Connal on his lap. Gaelan ruffled the boy's hair and he beamed up at him, his cheeks stuffed with sweet cake. Gaelan whispered for him to slow down, that this night he could have all he desired.

Around them the celebration in the hall was in high abandon, Irish and English joined as one. Fiddlers played, jugglers tossed sticks of fire and dancers twirled, a few women trying to teach the English to dance.

Siobhàn laughed at the knights' attempts, then gasped. "Oh Connal, go get Dermott afore he's trampled." The tiny lamb was trying to move between the dancers.

Connal scrambled off Gaelan's lap, all knees and poking elbows, and crawled under the table to pop up on the other side and dash after his pet. Jace joined him and the pair raced off through the crowd. To get into mischief, she thought.

Gaelan nudged her, then nodded. Her gaze shifted and she smiled. Raymond DeClare was frowning at Fionna as she moved past, and for some reason was staring rather intently at her behind.

"Think he will know where he saw her?"

"Not unless she chooses."

Gaelan grinned. " 'Twould serve him well to be sniffing after a skirt and not know if it's the right one."

Siobhàn smiled. "Has Driscoll given his permission?" She nodded to Owen and Driscoll's daughter Margaret, talking privately off to the side, constantly glancing at the sheriff. "They want to be married by Christmas."

She looked at him. "And?"

"I advised Driscoll to wait afore consenting."

"For the love of Mary, why?"

"He went behind his back, Siobhàn. I cannot tolerate such behavior and neither should Driscoll in a son-in-law."

"Oh, and you are such an authority on marriage," she huffed with a playful shove.

He wrapped his arm around her and growled, "I was wise enough to marry you, was I not?"

Her smile was radiant. "Aye."

"Did I not give my permission for Andrew and Bridgett to wed?"

Siobhàn glanced at the couple kissing in a darkened corner. "Aye."

"Is not Ian pleased with his lands and holding, his new vassals?"

She leaned closer and whispered, "Have I thanked you for being so generous?"

"Aye, but you may again, later." He wiggled his brows and she blushed. "So now, my love," he said, with a touch beneath her chin and a kiss to her lips, "are there any more chieftains prepared to defy the king to save you from my wretched soul?"

Siobhàn brushed a lock of sable brown hair from his forehead. "And if there was?" she said with a challenging spark.

He grinned. "Then I am glad I have a bigger army."

"We have a big army."

His brow shot up. "We?"

She tried to frown, but it just would not stay put. "Do not start with me, husband."

He nipped the finger in his face. "Oh-ho my Irish princess—" He pulled her from her chair and onto his lap. "There are plenty of things I wish to start with you."

"What might they be?"

"Loving the defiance out of you."

" 'Twill take a century," Ian muttered as he passed behind them.

Laughing, Gaelan stared into the eyes of the woman who'd breathed life into his decaying soul and said with an Irish lilt, "Jager me, that soon? 'Twas an eternity, I was hopin' for."

She cupped his head, drawing him to her mouth to whisper, "Ahh my love, we will make you an Irishman yet." She kissed him, deeply, lovingly, her heart soaring for the courageous man he'd become, for the life they would build and the love she knew would last beyond the stone keeps and proud castles . . . and for the wild magic of Erin growing in his heart.

Epilogue

London, twelve years past.

Galean flinched when the king struck Connal across the face. It was part of the ritual, the prayer and fasting, the pledge and the presentation in purest white. Irish linen, of course, but the slap delivered was the symbol of the pain he would suffer to uphold the king's laws.

Connal was now a knight of the realm.

Pride swelled in Gaelan and his gaze slid discreetly to Siobhàn. He nudged her, and she looked up, unshed tears glassing her eyes.

"Barbaric," she muttered, and he knew she wished Rhiannon could see this, but the woman had not left the convent in years.

Gaelan grinned, bending to kiss the top of her head.

"If you can pull yourself away from your wife, Pen-Dragon . . ." the king said, and Gaelan faced his sovereign.

Henry Plantagenant eyed him, pleased the man had grown accustomed to the life of a lord. He'd wanted this man in his court, for his armies, his skill, and had done everything in his power to bring the lady princess and PenDragon together. A well-made match, he thought smugly. But then his sources a dozen years ago had told him Siobhàn O'Rourke was a woman destined to be a legend. What better than to bring two legends together? He glanced at the young man Connal, his looks sending half the ladies into a swoon, his size as great as PenDragon's, though he knew they were not related in blood. He was a fine addition to his legions, he thought, watching him secure his spurs.

Henry inclined his head and Gaelan gestured to Connal's squire. The slender lad led a horse from the stables as Gaelan stepped off the dais. He took the reins, gave the mount a pat, then handed them to Connal.

"May he serve you well, my so—Connal."

" 'Tis all right, my lord. I feel more English than Irish right now." Connal tried to remain solemn, but the pride in his father's face made him grin.

Gaelan glanced about, at the people gathered, to his wife, her belly round with their fourth child and the line of girls stretched out beside her. Where was Aslyn? he wondered, the little troublemaker.

"PenDragon!" the king bellowed, and they turned. Henry gestured regally and a man stepped forward, kneeling before his king. Henry waved impatiently and Connal rushed forward. "My gift to you." The attendant presented Connal with the sword.

Connal tried not to gape at the massive thing, wondering if he'd embarrass himself if he couldn't lift it off the pillow.

"It looks like DeClare's, my liege."

"A duplicate."

Connal's gaze jerked up as he handled the balance of the sword. Exceptionally long, the top third was serrated, yet where DeClare's hilt had been studded with gems, Connal's bore the Celtic marks of his heritage.

"I am humbled."

"Good. A knight should be humble."

Connal slid a glance at Gaelan and smirked. Henry chuckled with understanding, and Gaelan eyed them both, a warning in his eyes when his gaze landed on Connal.

"I can still thrash your hide, puppy," he muttered under his breath, then called for the remaining gifts, his armor and shield, the symbol of his house emblazoned on the shield. The hooded squire stumbled and Gaelan darted forward to catch the lad, bringing him upright.

The scent of spice filled his nostrils.

"Aslyn!" he hissed, his eyes flaring with quick anger.

Henry peered. "Isn't that your oldest girl, PenDragon?"

Gaelan shoved the girl behind him. "Aye, your majesty."

"Bring her here."

Gaelan groaned, pulling his daughter forward and praying the king could not understand the string of Gaelic curses spilling from her lips.

Connal stood nearby, the swordpoint in the ground, his hands folded over the top as she passed him. "You've done it now, piglet," he murmured, and she shot him a murderous glance.

Gaelan pushed his daughter before the king and was thanking God when she dipped a proper curtsey. He glanced at Siobhàn. She shrugged, a half smile curving her beautiful mouth. The king left his chair and stopped before her.

"Arise, child."

She popped straight up, defiance hinting there, and Gaelan tensed. *Please keep your wild tongue in your mouth,* he prayed.

Henry pushed the hood back. "You are lovely."

"So everyone keeps telling me."

Henry's brows rose and he glanced at her father. Gaelan looked ready to beat the child, he thought. "You do not like being beautiful."

"Not when everyone treats me as if I've no brain behind this face, your majesty."

"And what would you use this brain for?"

"Aught more than stitching samplers, my liege."

Henry grinned, tugging on the long red braid. "Mayhaps we can find something better for you to do." Her eyes lit up like green fire. "When you have grown up a bit." She wanted to rebel, he could see, yet knew her place. Henry admired her for it. The girl was utterly fearless. Like her father.

Henry looked up and smiled. "I pity you, PenDragon."

" 'Tis well placed, my liege," he said, grabbing Aslyn by the arm and directing her toward her mother.

"Let us celebrate!" As the king and his entourage headed into the castle, Gaelan turned to Aslyn. And found her missing.

He looked at Connal.

"Who knows?" he said, sheathing his sword. " 'Tis your fault."

"Mine! You instigate it with allowing her to page for you. Her defiance is her own difficulty."

"She doesn't see it as defiance. She is being Aslyn." Connal moved closer, lowering his voice. "If you'd not allowed her to make you so weak, my lord, she would be stitching samplers and liking it."

"Hah. No daughter of Siobhàn's would be so complacent."

"No daughter of yours, either. And just think, you have three more to contend with. Mayhaps four, Father."

Gaelan stopped in his tracks, turning to Connal. He had not called him that since he'd come of age. And though he was not his blood sire, Gaelan could not love the young man any more than if he was his own.

"Go to your friends, and show them your prizes. Tomorrow you earn the right to be called knight."

Connal frowned. "A tourney?"

Gaelan nodded. And Connal smiled hugely, handsome in his excitement. "If Siobhàn doesn't interfere," he muttered, watching as Connal led his new stallion toward the group of young men.

* * *

Halfway through the feasting, Siobhàn quietly left the hall and headed to her chamber. Gaelan frowned, glancing at Fionna, and she nodded. The goblet slipped from his hand and crashed to the floor. He started for the staircase and the king caught his arm.

"You can do naught but wait."

Gaelan did wait, refusing wine and too often staring at the staircase.

"Did you do this when we were being born, Father?"

Gaelan looked at his daughter, smiling. "Aye."

"And with me, Father?"

"Aye."

"And me?"

"Aye!" The girls didn't flinch at his bellow, staring sweetly up at him, and Gaelan sighed, apologized, excusing himself from the king's side, and moved toward the wide hearth. He sat on a bench, firmly padded and luxurious, and the girls scrambled up into his lap. They burrowed around his big body like bunnies in a hollow, and Henry envied the lord of Donegal.

How he wished he could have known his sons like that, able to touch and kiss them freely, he thought. He settled to a chair, waving off the offer of wine as he listened to the girls question him. He didn't tell them of each birth, but a story of a lonely, savage man seeking peace and finding it in the green isle of Erin. The girls were rapt with awe, and though Henry knew they'd heard the story before, he was well pleased with the telling. He glanced at Connal, the youth gone still in his revelry with the other young lads knighted this day.

His expression was tender and loving toward Gaelan, and Henry understood the young man's private plea to be named PenDragon. To honor the man who'd raised him.

A tiny cry filtered from above and Gaelan gently placed his daughters aside and, ignoring all, raced toward the stairs. Gaelan pushed the door open, finding Fionna stowing soiled sheets. She nodded slightly and left the room as Gaelan crossed to the bed. Siobhàn lay still, their child at her breast, and Gaelan lowered himself to the bed gently.

Her lashes swept up and she smiled, patting the space beside her. He shifted, gathering the pair in his arms.

She tipped her face up. "We have a son, my love."

Gaelan's breath caught.

"Now you will have to work at being a father."

Gaelan tried to look affronted and failed.

"Your daughters think you are a God."

"And you do not."

"They are innocent. I am not."

"Praise be," he muttered, kissing her deeply. "Poor boy, with all those sisters babying him . . ."

"I'm sure with the blood of the dragon in his veins, he will do his own share of roaring and bellowing—"

"I do not bellow."

"Hah."

Smiling, Gaelan sighed and held his wife and son in his arms, feeling small and inconsequential in a world brimming with power and battle. He was at peace, had been for years now, and was eager to return home. Ireland, he thought, was a part of one's soul, calling you back when you were away, and if you lived long enough, you understood there was no other place in the world where magic and love abounded.

No other place, he thought, looking down at his wife and son. Except in the arms of his Irish princess.

ABOUT THE AUTHOR

Amy J. Fetzer lives with her family in Beaufort, South Carolina, and is the author of over ten time-travel, historical and contemporary romances. Amy loves to hear from readers, and you may write to her at P.O. Box 9241, Beaufort, SC 29904-9241 or fetzer@hargray.com or visit her Web site:

http://www.apayne.com/amyfetzer

Please include a self-addressed stamped envelope if you wish a response.

BOOK YOUR PLACE ON OUR WEBSITE AND MAKE THE READING CONNECTION!

We've created a customized website just for our very special readers, where you can get the inside scoop on everything that's going on with Zebra, Pinnacle and Kensington books.

When you come online, you'll have the exciting opportunity to:

- View covers of upcoming books
- Read sample chapters
- Learn about our future publishing schedule (listed by publication month *and author*)
- Find out when your favorite authors will be visiting a city near you
- Search for and order backlist books from our online catalog
- Check out author bios and background information
- Send e-mail to your favorite authors
- Meet the Kensington staff online
- Join us in weekly chats with authors, readers and other guests
- Get writing guidelines
- AND MUCH MORE!

Visit our website at
http://www.zebrabooks.com